3-11

D1430776

Rue Morgue No. 1

Rue Morgue No. 1

EDITED BY
REX STOUT
AND LOUIS
GREENFIELD

NEW YORK

CREATIVE AGE PRESS, INC.

Designed by Jerome Mulcahy

Printed in the United States of America
American Book–Stratford Press, Inc., New York

55

10255

ACKNOWLEDGMENTS

THE EDITORS hereby make grateful acknowledgment to the following authors' representatives, publishers, and authors for giving permission to reprint the material in this volume:

Popular Publications, Inc. for *Cold Figures!* by William Hellman.

Trojan Publishing Corporation for *Gun from Gotham* (which first appeared as *Sleep for a Dreamer*) by Robert Leslie Bellem; and for *Death in the Tank* by Hugh Speer.

Street & Smith Publications, Inc. for *Death Lies Waiting* by Roland Phillips; for *Need a Body Cry* by H. Wolff Salz; and *It Had to Be—* by Dorothy Dunn.

Woman's Home Companion and Paul Hoffman for *The Listening House* by Paul Hoffman.

Columbia Publications, Inc. for *Suicide* by Frank Kane.

Sydney A. Sanders for *Dead As in Blonde* by D. L. Champion.

Harry Altschuler for *Slay-Mates* by Charles Larson.

Marguerite E. Harper for *Midnight Rendezvous* by Margaret Manners.

Monica McCall for *The Cat's Eye* by John van Druten.

Kerry O'Neil for *Murder Is Stupid.*

H. Bedford-Jones for *What More Can Fortune Do?*

Jack Snow for *Second Childhood.*

Julius Schwartz for *The Watchers* by Ray Bradbury.

Seabury Quinn for *The Green God's Ring.*

Matt Taylor for *Manhattan Manhunt.*

Bruno Fischer for *I'll Slay You in My Dreams.*

TABLE OF CONTENTS

INTRODUCTION

IN THESE NINETEEN STORIES A LOT OF PEOPLE ARE MUR-
dered. That of itself does not make them either better or
worse than any other bunch of stories of similar length. The
important thing about a story is not whom or what it deals
with, but whether it is a good story or not.

It is more difficult to write a good story—or anyhow an exciting story—about a child catching a butterfly than one about
a man catching a murderer. Some judges of the art of writing,
both professional and amateur, seem, therefore, to think that
it is more commendable for a storyteller to tell about catching butterflies than about catching murderers. That line of
reasoning is over my head. The greatest commendation does
not necessarily go to the greatest overcomer of difficulties. It
is harder to eat soup with a fork than with a spoon, but not
ergo more praiseworthy.

A good deal of the current irritation in certain quarters
with writers of mysteries (or detective stories or murder tales)
appears to be based on a resentment of the fact that they do
not instead try their hands at another *Hamlet* or *Divine Com-
edy* or a novel by Henry James. Surely that is asking for trouble. It would be just as sensible to interrupt a man digging a
ditch with the angry demand, "Why the devil aren't you re-
pairing watches or painting murals?" Should he, incredibly,
accept the criticism as valid and start to do a mural or fix a
watch, the result would be painful. It would be similarly
painful should a murder story writer attempt a Henry James;
and more painful still should a Henry James undertake to
write a detective story. He wouldn't have what it takes.

What it takes is more than the simple faculty of getting excited about a corpse and a man hunt, though that is essential. A poet or a philosopher can write about life and death, but only a storyteller can write about *this* life and *this* death. Not only is there no occasion for comparison; there is no basis for one. The poet or philosopher stirs your soul; the storyteller makes you sit on the edge of your chair. It all depends, not on some transcendental scheme of ultimate values, nor on the slow pronouncement of the tribunal of time, but on what you are after at the moment.

Since you are now more or less committed to reading this book, having bought, borrowed or stolen it, I hope that what you are after is the crime, the chase, and the awful triumph of justice, for that is what you'll get. There are tales of many kinds and flavors in this collection, and it is therefore not to be expected that all of them will be exactly to any one reader's taste. No man, no matter how catholic his appetite, could find the same measure of delight in the penumbral hocus-pocus of *The Green God's Ring* as in the sentimental ruthlessness of *It Had to Be* or the devastating argotmania of *Gun from Gotham.*

Then there is the horrid and fantastic improbability of *Death in the Tank;* the goofy but inevitable doom of *The Watchers;* the deadly satisfying irony of *Manhattan Manhunt;* the patient intrepidity of McGuire in *Death Lies Waiting;* the simple subtle vengeance of Lester Rungate in *Midnight Rendezvous;* and the inexorable vise of the trap in *I'll Slay You in My Dreams.* Indeed, a searcher for support of the doctrine that all murder stories are alike will have poor hunting here. He will find instead fresh and ample proof of the opposite—of how different they can be.

He will also find as wide a variance in excellence of execution as in flavor, but he will find a minimum of bathos, baloney and blah. Those abominable qualities abound in tales about catching butterflies, but are seldom present in murder stories. The complaint has been made that a murder is a terribly obvious thing to make up a story about. No doubt it is. It is in fact so obvious that if a writer once gets a murder in his mind it is next to impossible *not* to make up a story about it. The quality of the story will depend on many factors—inventiveness or imagination, ability to construct and organize, craftsmanship, and so forth—but in any case it is practically certain there will be a story. Whereas let a writer get a butterfly in his mind, and God knows what will happen. Many and many an expectant reader has coughed up his two bucks or three-fifty and gone home to his easy chair under the lamp and discovered to his sorrow and exasperation what did happen.

That should be enough to give you a fairly strong hint as to what is between these covers, and no more can reasonably be expected of me, except to give you my friendly wish that your favorite flavor is here in the strength and proportion that you like best.

REX STOUT

Brewster
New York

THE LISTENING HOUSE

PAUL HOFFMAN

S HE HELD THE HEAVY DOOR DISCREETLY OPEN AND WAVED
twice as the little cavalcade set out—the limousine with
Madame followed by Mr. Jared in the station wagon with
Cook and Giblin and Marcie. No one saw her wave but it
didn't matter.

After they had disappeared down the drive she backed inside and turned around. The dim lofty hall loomed above
her. A long shaft of sun streamed past the suit of armor on
the landing down over the thick red rug. She felt the empty
rooms beyond it, heard the silence of them. At last she was
alone. And not just alone here in this great house but alone
in all this street. For Madame had been the last to leave and
only she preferred not quite to close up for the summer. In
other years Marcie had stayed but Marcie was tired and
needed a holiday.

The tall clock on the balcony struck nine. Nine until four
—that gave her exactly seven hours in which to get ready.
She walked quickly to the door leading below. She must
begin at once for when the time came, what she intended to
do must be done unhurriedly. There must be no overlapping
of functions; no thought, as she would be then, of the self
she was now.

By foregoing lunch she managed everything admirably and

on the stroke of four she set the great silver tray down in the library. Then she went to her room on the third floor and changed out of her uniform into the silk wrapper she had never worn. It trailed along the stairs behind her, which delighted her—she couldn't remember having that happen ever before. When she reached the second floor she went directly to the north guest room, the one with the toile curtains. It was, she thought, the coolest and pleasantest room in the house in summer.

Closing the door softly behind her she walked to the chaise, unfolded the light satin puff, stretched out under it and closed her eyes. She hoped she could nap. For sleep, even only a little, would accomplish better than anything else what she wanted.

It was not easy—she was too excited this first time—but finally she dozed. She was gratified when she waked up that she knew at once where she was, and that she was not surprised to be there.

She got up and slipping out of the wrapper she picked up the white dress laid out neatly on the bed. It was simply but elegantly cut like all of Madame's daytime dresses. It became her very well, she felt, as she went to the dressing table to arrange her hair.

At a quarter to five she entered the library. Before she sat down behind the tea table she casually lifted the bells over the sandwiches and wafers. After she had lighted the flame under the kettle she began to nibble a rolled sandwich of cream cheese and cress. Then she leaned back and looked at the rows and rows of books.

Books made her think of her father. He had been "a great reader"—a term not always complimentary, sometimes even a little scornful, as used among the people they had known. He had been especially partial to Dickens.

She was afraid she had been a disappointment to her father. Reading to herself invariably put her to sleep and when he had once tried to read aloud to her she had burst into tears several times—as much over the happy and dull parts as over the sad ones. Perhaps it had been her father's voice which affected her, but even now the mere mention of Dickens' name made her feel distinctly ill.

The kettle began to spout small blasts of steam. Like someone talking out of doors in cold weather, she thought. The analogy pleased her—it was an unaccustomed one for her—and she promptly forgot all about her father. She readied herself for the ceremony of brewing tea as Madame did.

When she had finished the careful ritual and sat sipping, she felt almost as if she were swallowing some soothing medicine. Which indeed she was, for by the time she had taken a second cup of tea that sharp division of her day she had so insisted upon was a perfectly accomplished thing.

The sensation of being her mistress never left her as she slipped back upstairs to dress for dinner or as she served herself to the dinner she had herself arranged in the dining-room three hours before. That meal had offered problems at first but she had solved them by planning a simple chafing-dish meal, as Madame occasionally did on Cook's night out.

The evening she spent quietly in the little upstairs sitting-room listening to the radio and working on a bit of needle-work. Nearly before she knew it, it was bedtime.

Having to open the bed in the north guest room put her out for a moment. She must anticipate that tomorrow. But her perturbation was softly smothered as she reached out from under the cool smooth cover to pull out the light.

The next day passed without flaw. But by the following day the hours before four in the afternoon began to move too slowly for her; there were too few chores to fill it. So she made her preparations earlier by two hours and, like Madame, took long naps.

After two weeks she felt as if she had never lived in any other manner. But she began to resent waking in the morning to the prospect of having to resume even the lessened labors of what she now regarded as her former self. Soon after that she began to oversleep.

It was on one of these mornings that the first of the strange happenings occurred.

She wakened slowly—which had always been unlike her—and as fuller consciousness came she was sure someone had knocked on the door. She turned her head and although thoroughly startled, heard herself call her own name. Though there was no answer she felt certain she heard discreet footsteps hurry away and down the stairs. It took courage for her to follow them and even when her search revealed nothing she was uneasy.

She hurried to the third floor and donned her uniform. But the uneasiness lingered and as she worked to make up for lost time she could not shake the feeling that she was no longer alone. Her fear became increasingly acute. In an attempt to reassure herself she decided to go to market herself rather than order by telephone. Yet no sooner had she locked the service door behind her than she was seized by apprehension about returning—apprehension that grew until on her return the hand that held the key trembled so she had to set her packages down and guide it with the other.

Once inside, however, she lost her fear almost instantly in the familiar look and feel of all her senses encountered. The house was obviously empty of any presence except her own. She went about her work as if she were doing a curious penance but one for which she was nonetheless grateful.

That afternoon she was so late getting to her prepa-

tions she decided for this one day to forego the formal tea
and dinner and to spend the rest of the day quietly in the
room on the third floor. But at dusk a new uneasiness attacked her—a feeling akin to guilt. It was almost as if Madame were belowstairs without anyone to do for her. The
feeling became so strong that for the second time she determined to leave the house, if only for a walk. But again apprehension about returning seized her. With a kind of desperate
courage she made herself go back. And once there she was
again reassured. She even went to sleep promptly.

In the morning over her breakfast she tried to take quiet
stock of the day before. As she did, however, its outlines began to blur. Except as a mood, a dreaminess, she could
scarcely remember anything which had happened. And finally it became only something that stood in her mind as life-
less—but as dynamic too—as the suit of armor in the hall.
She did remember calling her own name through the door—
that had been so unaccountable as still to trouble her. She
began to feel it would be well for her to forget the whole
queer matter, including her experiment with a double life.

And so for the next week she lived like an automaton. To
fill the days she wrote labored letters to people she customar-
ily remembered with no more than a card at Christmas. She
made engagements to see the few acquaintances she had—
her close attachment to Madame and her household for so
many years had made her quite independent of other people
and affairs outside. And she even made herself sit through
two films.

But it was no good. That other life had taken hold of her
and she must return to it—without question or thought of
how she could relinquish it when the summer was ended and
Madame and Mr. Jared and the others would return. They
might, to be sure, return sooner—for a day or two to shop or

to see the dentist—but there was little risk that they would surprise her since they had assured her they would let her know beforehand if they came. So she returned to her ritual of a divided day.

For more than a week all went better than well. So exquisitely now had she pared down her schedule it had become a habit. But she had modified it too in certain of its details. Recalling the delusion—she was convinced now it had been that—of someone knocking on the guest-room door, she forced herself to wake before dawn and return to the third floor to finish her sleep. It seemed more appropriate that when she was to be the servant she should wake in the setting proper to that role. And she no longer anticipated her metamorphosis either in her thoughts or by any transition other than the short nap she had devised in the beginning to transfer her from one state to another.

She grew increasingly secure too, since during this well-ordered period she had cards from all of them—Marcie, Cook, Giblin and even Mr. Jared and Madame. To be sure, the cards carried only the customary news about fine weather, rest, good times. But in essence they meant that nothing short of disaster would bring any of them back before the summer ended.

And then the delusion came again—only this time in reverse.

She wakened in the third-floor room and dressed in her uniform for the hours before four. As she often did now, to save time—she came down by the front stairs to make up the guest room even before she should have her breakfast. When she reached the door she found with a curious belated start that it was closed. She felt certain she had left it open—she always left it open. Perhaps a gust of wind—

But with her hand already on the knob she was amazed at a presentiment that she must not enter. After only a moment's hesitation she knocked discreetly—as one would if Madame had asked to be waked up earlier than usual. She acted without any volition, as if she had all along known she would knock.

It was then that she heard her name. Softly, but indubitably, it came through the heavy panels—in a voice that was her own and yet not her own.

She wanted to cry out, to flee down the shallow thickly carpeted stairs, past the suit of armor and out the front door she had not opened since that morning she had watched them all off. But even with her heart beating in her throat and full of terror, she found herself walking quietly belowstairs as if what she had heard were expected and as it should be.

As she crossed the lower hall she heard the footsteps following her. Panic seized her then and she fled to the kitchen and beyond into the garden. Here was all peace and sun and as she sped down one path and up another—looking always downward at the trim borders and the perfect flagging—she was a little restored. But she vowed she would never return to the house, not even to lock the service door. Yet she must. She must cover up her uniform, at least not look like a madwoman hurrying along.

She looked up then and saw the garage, a handsome miniature replica of the house behind her. Over it, she remembered, were the chauffeur's rooms. She would take temporary refuge there. She fumbled for the key ring she carried always in the deep pocket of her petticoat and found the proper key. Safely inside, she groped her way up the narrow stairs to a small dim room doubtless intended for a living-room. It was untidy and had the unlived-in look rooms sometimes have where men live alone. A heavy scent of stale tobacco lingered in the room. She walked quickly to a window and threw it wide.

She could see far up and down over the narrow perfect gardens to shuttered house upon shuttered house. Looking at their blank walls she felt as if she were hemmed in by blind faces, all of them staring, all unseeing—save one. It seemed to crowd closer and she turned her back on it swiftly.

Her movement was dimly repeated across the room and for an instant she fancied she was not alone even here.

Then she saw the mirror.

She would go to it and find what solace she could in her own reflection. A movement of the hand, a turn of the head —surely these would disenchant her. But as she started toward it, fear again assailed her and she sank into a chair half turned from the window. She was too unsure of what she would see. A trick of light, an unexpected shadow, and she just might find herself facing that other who had once been herself but now stood, as it were, outside and a little away from her.

She remembered the voice that had spoken her name through the door not five minutes ago—and the time she had unwittingly spoken it herself from the other side of that door. In her mind she heard again the retreating footsteps and then retraced her own that had led her out here. They became like a sound and that sound's echo and as they did, time was dissolved for her. That morning and this—could they have been one and the same? The sense that they were grew upon her, imprisoned her. She was living but not at any measurable speed.

She tried hard to remember simple things, like what day it was. But now all was dream-like in her awareness and the near and far were only repetitions one of another.

The house began to draw her back.

Neither willingly nor protesting but only urged on by a compulsion she could not deny, she returned. And for the third time she felt no fear as she moved through the house. Even when she placed her hand on the north guest-room door she felt no qualm about entering.

But there was a difference too about this time. *She* was not the same. Though she was not apprehensive, she was not reassured either. And what she did she felt she had no part in —as she had felt no part in knocking on the guest-room door. It was as if she were in a trance with all the days of her life rolled into this one.

Thus the day drew on.

She was in the kitchen when the clock chimed four. All the way down from the balcony she heard it. A light sound, it spoke too with authority—very much like Madame. She knew then she must fight. Not against any impulse in herself but against what would be taking shape now abovestairs. For it was taking shape, she knew it.

She wanted frantically to busy herself but she could think of nothing to do. The tea tray—she could remember only that. But she would not give in. Even if she must sit with clenched hands to control herself.

The quarter hour struck. It would be coming down from the third floor now, trailing the silk wrapper behind it.

The half hour. It must be drowsing now for she felt easier, freer. And she began to remember a little—how she had not been always alone through these weeks. Matthew, the gardener, had been there—two days a week, was it? And the postman had left the postcards.

By a quarter to five she felt better than she had felt for a long time.

Then it came. From the library as she had known it would,

and on the stroke of five. She had known so well that she was even watching the signal board at the time.

She could feel the cold beads of perspiration come out on her forehead and the palms of her hands grow clammy. She hoped she was going to faint but she knew she would not. Her first impulse was to bolt out at the service door and as far as possible from this horror. And at the same moment she knew that she dared not. Instead, she scrabbled to get the tea tray.

Then the bell rang again, a little insistently. That angered her. No one had ever had to ring twice for her. She determined to settle affairs up there no matter what the cost or outcome. Putting the tea tray back, she removed her apron —without it she felt more equal to the ordeal.

She had needed courage rarely in her life—and never courage of such proportions. That she had courage now delighted her. And as she began to mount the curving stairs she seemed to herself as much different from her usual self as that foolish demanding other self which she must now face. It was curious, she reflected, to be one person and yet so many.

At the head of the stairs she paused to compose herself, to gather this new strength more securely about her. And then the bell purred a third time—not insistently but with the quiet confidence that knows it will be rewarded.

Her courage ebbed and left her in abject fear. Now she could not even run away.

She slipped through the door in the dark paneling into the hall. That room, always the noblest in the house for her, frightened her now with its dimness and height. In the little light of late afternoon it looked at once sad and cruel. And in that light the suit of armor seemed to move just perceptibly. She forced her eyes to focus on the door to the library.

The wide expanse of red carpet deadened her steps until

she felt like a ghost as she walked. And then, half a dozen paces from the door, she faltered. Through the slightly open draperies of the doorway she saw the fire burning in the fireplace. That was going too far—never when she had played out her bit of nonsense had she presumed to such lengths. It was outrageous and somehow the most frightening thing of all.

She plunged through the thin slit of light into the room itself.

It was a long room and, like the rest of the house, heavily carpeted, heavily hung with drapery of one kind or another to minimize sound. Madame loved things quiet. So her precipitate entrance made no stir, was only a little movement with no overtones. The thick hangings let her in and fell back behind her silent and motionless. With the firelight in her eyes she saw nothing.

And then as she forced her eyes slowly *there* where she had always sat, she saw the hand. White and perfectly cared for.

She covered her face with both her own hands and began to sob in utter terror. This—this, was this her other self?

She felt it coming forward then, swiftly, and heard the cool voice.

Kind and stirring, it purred closer and she felt herself led toward the light.

Madame—it was Madame!

"*There there,*" the voice was saying, "*we have startled you. We should have let you know but we came away so unexpectedly this morning. . . . You have been too long alone too. But Marcie is here now—when you didn't answer the bell, she went to the third floor looking for you. She is going to stay in your place and you will go back with me for your holiday.*"

She felt herself forced gently onto the deep sofa—but still

she could not uncover her eyes, whimper her thanks and relief. For she wept now from something more than these. From the deep shame she must henceforth endure in her own eyes. She had been so poor a dreamer and would never dream again.

WHAT MORE CAN FORTUNE DO?

GORDON KEYNE

———————

IT WAS AFTER THE WAR'S END, AND IN THE LONG INTERREGNUM while the peace treaties and the World Court were being formed, that Quest got its start. Under the title of "Quest, Incorporated," it quickly gained prominence, and in the succeeding years became a strong and worldwide organization.

In its earlier period, when the world was still shaken by the great war, when the systematic massacres perpetrated by the Nazis had wiped out millions of persons, when men and women and entire families had disappeared on all sides without leaving a trace, Quest of necessity kept its files strictly secret. Many of its most remarkable cases, such as that of the Liberian millionaire, or the one involving the Austrian Chancellor, could not then be given to the world.

The lapse of time, however, has permitted certain of these early achievements to become known—for while Quest, Incorporated, built its fame upon the finding of lost persons, its activities sometimes extended further; and it was only two years following the peace in Europe that Sir Eric Hascourt, then British ambassador in Washington, walked into the New York office of Quest and for an hour was closeted with Steve Luring, the president. When the visitor departed, Luring sent for Bert Greene.

Greene was one of the first operatives or field agents, as

Luring called them, to work for the company. He had been in France for the two last years of the war, in a tank unit. He was a rather small man, quick of eye, pleasant of manner.

It was three years now since Bert Greene had even thought about war, and he wanted never to think about it again. Of course, it bobbed up at times, and then he got it over with in a hurry. He had a wife and two kids over in Brooklyn, was doing well with Quest, and only regretted the times he had to be out acting as field agent on some job.

He came into Luring's office now and took the chair Luring indicated.

"I understand you were with the Seventh Army in France," said Luring.

"Yes, some of the time."

"I suppose you'd like to go over the ground you went then? Or have you been?"

"No, sir," Greene replied slowly. "I never want to see it again, on my own. Maybe when the kids grow up, I'll take 'em there and show them where their old daddy came ashore with an LCT and ran his tanks over that damned gravelly section and on to Toulon, and then on to Grenoble and so forth. No hurry about it, though."

"That's too bad," said Luring. "I had picked you to go now, on a job."

"Oh!" said Greene. "That's different, sir. Let's have it."

Steve Luring smiled. He knew his man.

"Okay, then. The client is Sir Eric Hascourt. His younger son, Lance Hascourt, was a captain in the British Intelligence, attached to the headquarters staff of the Seventh Army. He knew the south of France like a book, had spent years there, knew the people, and so forth. Somewhere between Toulon and Grenoble he disappeared; supposedly he was killed by some mistake, by the F.F.I. or the Maquis.

Nothing was sure then; nothing's sure now. The British have investigated and learned nothing."

"The old man thinks he's alive?" Greene asked shrewdly.

"In a way, yes; just a hunch. No clues. It seems that before the expedition started, Lance made a remark to his father—they both knew the objective, you see—that has stuck in Hascourt's mind. There was some mention of Crange, a town en route to Grenoble and Lance said that if he ever got that far, he meant to double back. Why? Not known. No reason, nothing. Just a remark. Now we're engaged to find the guy or get some proof of his death. After three years, it's no hot trail."

"No," said Greene. "Anything behind it?"

Luring gave him a look. "Probing devil, aren't you? Yes. He was last seen in a staff jeep with a driver and a Captain Anderson of our own forces, a staff officer. Hascourt was going to a meeting with some officer of the Maquis, somewhere, to get promised maps of the Nazi position ahead. They were with the advance of General Butler's force, a fast motorized unit."

"So was I," said Greene thoughtlessly. "Excuse me. Go ahead."

"Apparently the jeep ran into a field of tank and personnel mines set by the Maquis for the Huns. Nobody can be certain. Anderson and the driver were reported dead at the time. When Hascourt was remembered later, no one knew anything about him; he was posted as missing, and has been ever since. So have the papers he carried, documents valuable to British headquarters. That's all I know. I have all reports, and a photograph of him."

"Was this Hascourt married?"

"Yes. Left a wife and a kid. Pictures enclosed." He shoved a large envelope across the desk. He seldom questioned or

directed his field agents, but turned them loose to achieve
their ends in their own way.

Greene picked up the envelope and rose.

"Very well, Chief. I'll catch the Paris Stratoliner tomorrow, if I can get a seat."

"Good luck, then. And, Bert—"

"Yes, sir?"

"The client is the British Ambassador. The sky's the
limit."

Greene departed. Luring, probably to save time, had not
mentioned just where Hascourt's jeep had been blown up.

That evening Greene went carefully through the papers,
looking for some clue overlooked by prior investigators. There
was none. Hascourt was not young; he was twenty-eight. He
had spent several pre-war years as a loiterer on the Riviera, a
spendthrift playboy. His early career touched a couple of
minor scandals over cards and women; nothing of note. He
had married, during the war, a young woman of good family
who bore him a posthumous son.

"A rather useless member of society, decidedly not a devil,
but neither a fool," thought Greene. "Just a drifter with too
much coin for his own good."

Hascourt had vanished a hundred miles south of Grenoble,
where Butler's fast motorized units were kiting up the back
hill roads and while the main expeditionary forces were mop-
ping up along the lower Rhone. The precise spot was outside the town of Sisteron, at the conjunction of the Durance
and the Bueche rivers. That stretch of country, verging toward the Alpine, was a bleak and rocky sector known to few
tourists; there were some queer highways and byways there
along the tumbling gravelly Durance River.

Getting a place aboard the Paris skyliner, Greene was off in
the morning. It was only three years after the war's end, re-

member; air travel was still in course of development, and even the nonstop stratosphere express was far from what it is today. It required full fifteen hours for the Paris flight.

During this time, Greene carefully canvassed the campaign ahead. Several courses were open to him; he finally decided to go straight on to Marseille and work north from there. He would need to rent a car, which he could do more easily at Marseille than elsewhere. Automobiles were still very hard to come by in France, and autogiro travel, now so prevalent, was yet in its infancy. He sent a radio ahead and secured a place in the connecting flight for Marseille; and, upon reaching the magnificently rebuilt Le Bourget airfield of Paris, he transferred and was off anew.

It was morning when he landed at the Marseille airport and motored in to the city. He had witnessed some of the eight-day battling here, when the Cannebière, street of hotels and shops, had become a no-man's land; and later on he had been back there. Now the famous street was built up anew, paint and plaster covering the vestiges of war. He was taken to the Hotel des Allies, a new luxury hostelry replacing the old Splendide. Yet the little second-story Italian restaurant he had once frequented, just up the street, was still going, and bouillabaisse still beckoned the alleged palates of witless tourists.

Quest, Incorporated, reckoned no cost. That same day Greene rented a small Citroën car, bought what supplies he needed, and was ready. Next morning he got away.

He planned to pick up the same route to the northeast his light tank unit had taken in those war days—up along the Durance toward Sisteron and Grenoble. Before leaving Marseille, he fitted the portrait of Hascourt into a leather-and-glassine frame. It showed the man bareheaded; he had curly yellow hair fitting closely to his head, a big beak of a nose, and bony features. His mouth and chin were rather badly disfigured by a wound he had received earlier in the war. It was not an easy face to forget.

Upon this face, Greene pinned all his hopes of fulfilling his mission—and upon the odd little chance remark about doubling back. He had a hunch that the remark might mean something.

First he headed for Aix, to pick up the route of Butler's greyhound tanks—less than an hour's drive. Greene fancied he would shrink from the old memories. Instead, he began to revive them. Here was the vast stony gravel plain, the Crau. He touched upon the edge of it; here was a spot exactly like the one he had seen, when getting into Aix that other time—the burning German tank with the three naked, blackened bodies of its crew in the road. He had shivered then. Now, in recalling that scene, he smiled slightly.

Aix—how they had rolled through it that day! He chugged into town, passed the Gare and came to the Place de la Rotonde with the big fountain. No crowds yelling at him now or waving flags. He remembered how they had shoved on then, trying to make the bridge over the Durance, on to the north, before the Germans could blow it up, and reach the back-country road for Grenoble.

He kept on now, the little Citroën chugging away for dear life, and a long half-hour later was through Meyargues and on across the tumbling river, turning east now for Mirabeau. How it all came back to him! There was the Mount of Victory, where Marius had massacred the Teutons a hundred years before Christ; there were the long arches of the Canal du Verdon—there was Manosque ahead, and he stopped here for lunch at the little Hotel Pascal.

At the sidewalk table, he looked up the street as he had looked that day. They had stopped here in this very spot, grabbing wine and whatever could be had to eat from the eagerly reaching arms of the crowd. Three dead men lying here that day—collaborationists, shot that morning by the Maquis. And four women, stripped to the buff, marched along by yelling townfolk, taken and released by the Maqui riflemen, their hair clipped close—and turned off with no further harm.

"By God, we saw things those days, and no mistake! Hard to imagine it now," he muttered at the placid street. Then he checked himself, checked everything, stopped recalling old times. That had been three, four years ago—now he had a job to do. He must get on to Sisteron that night, to start his campaign.

To do this was no great task for the little Citroën; farther on, into the mountains, might have been another story. Late in the afternoon, with all the little towns of Provence behind him, he sighted the towering citadel and the Eleventh Century towers of the ramparts. He did not remember Sisteron from the old days; his tank outfit had passed through at night, hell-bent for Grenoble, with Maquis for guides. Hascourt must have been in the van of that very advance—here and there the night road had smelled of decaying bodies, and several cars had been ambushed and were burning. Some German outfit had them up around here, to be potted by Maqui sharpshooters and gunned by the motorized units in the fore of the northward rush. Yes, Hascourt must have disappeared then, thought Greene.

The town amazed him; it was like some ghost town of dream. Under the high rock of the citadel, the houses shot up in the air, tall and narrow and crowded, almost meeting far overhead, the streets rising from level to level, some of them tunneled steeply down beneath the houses. Across the river rose a second weird and grotesque crag, with a few houses clustered about its foot. This marked the end of fair Provence; on to the north ran the Route Nationale, and the naked crags and rocks that ended with the Alps.

Finding a room at the Touring Hotel, Greene went to work immediately. Here was not the end of his road, but the beginning. By the one main street of the town, crooked and dark and narrow, he came to the Hotel de Ville and there interviewed the prefect of police. When he showed the picture of Hascourt, the official laughed.

"Oh! The lost Englishman!"

"You know of him, then?" Greene asked in surprise.

"Yes. An Englishman was here last year, asking questions —lost during the war, eh? They gave me one of those pictures, too. Later on, Simon Lézan, who lives down the river at Arnoux, was here one day on a law case—he is an *avocat,* you understand. He saw the picture and remembered the man."

"Oh!" said Greene. "And what about him?"

The other shrugged. "How can I remember? It was something about the war. Simon was in the Maquis."

Green swallowed hard. "Did you write the Englishman who had left the picture?"

"Write? Why should I write him? When he came again would be time enough. And here you are, so I tell you."

Greene spurred his memories with a banknote but could get only the address of Simon Lézan, with which he had to be content. He went back to the unkempt little hotel and ordered a drink and sat pondering the ways of destiny.

He had expected to print handbills with Hascourt's picture on them and scatter them far and wide in hopes of jogging some memory—and lo! He was on the track already! That English investigator had come here first, naturally, had learned nothing; but the search had borne fruit, the picture had been recognized.

"Neither luck nor coincidence; just plain cause and effect," reflected Greene happily. "Tomorrow I must turn around and go back to Arnoux, and locate this *avocat*. And all thanks to a town official who was too lazy to write! I tell the guy practically the story of my life, and he coughs up all he knows. Probably that English investigator was stiff and formal and got disliked on the spot."

That night he climbed flight after flight of stairs to his bedroom, and thanked his stars he was getting out of Sisteron. . . .

It was only a matter of ten miles down the burly Durance to Arnoux—a mere hop for the Citroën, but a grave distance for countryfolk, in this naked land of rocks and hills. Arnoux was a bare little village, with the larger town of Valeron perched across the river, beside its ruined castle and the high suspension bridge. The *avocat* Simon Lézan was the big shot of the place, and very luckily Greene found him at home and at liberty—a polite, wary, resolute man of thirty-odd.

Here, as with the Sisteron official, Greene exerted the requisite tact—not going bull-headed at the subject, but introducing himself and Quest, Incorporated, then speaking of his search and what it meant to him, telling how he picked up the trail at Sisteron, and finally plumping the whole thing into the lap of Lézan. Greene had long ago learned that this was the only method of breaking down the suspicious Gallic mind.

In this case it worked perfectly. Lézan relaxed, gazed at Hascourt's photograph, and nodded.

"Yes, I remember the man quite well; a pleasant fellow, who spoke both French and Provençal—quite a rare thing, I assure you, for an Englishman! He was in the advance. I had been coming to meet him, with certain information. I was, you comprehend, of the Maquis."

"So I understand," said Greene.

"The road had been mined for German armored cars, then expected; this jeep struck one of the mines, unfortunately. It was an appalling catastrophe, monsieur. Germans were in flight before your troops, all was in confusion, no one could be certain of anything. All in the jeep were reported killed. Later, we found this Englishman, who had been carried off by a peasant. I visited him; he was wounded, hurt. Meantime, your armored column had gone on north."

"I was with it," said Greene, smiling. A bond between them was instantly established, and Lézan thawed perceptibly.

"He told me that he had friends at St. Remy," he went on. "But at that time, your main army had not ascended the Rhone. However, he insisted, and we had just captured a German staff car with plenty of *essence* in the tank. So, in this, we sent him. I remember he insisted on paying us well for the use of the car—not that we required it, but he had money and desired to recompense the cause."

"The name of his friends at St. Remy?" Greene asked eagerly.

Lézan shrugged.

"No. He did not say. We never heard from the car or driver again—no doubt it was snapped up as an enemy vehicle by our own people or yours." Lézan chuckled. "Ha! I have in my own garage the car of a German officer; I use it still."

Greene looked blank; surely the trail could not end here!

"And you don't know whether Hascourt lived or died?" he asked.

"Oh, yes! He reached St. Remy. Some weeks later I had a postal card of thanks from him. Just a word, recalling himself to my memory."

"Have you the card now?"

"No, monsieur. My house, all that I owned, burned down that next spring. Everything was destroyed. It was a sad loss."

With this information, Greene shook hands and departed. He drove on to the town of St. Auban, where the railroad crossed the Durance, and lunched. How odd, that remark of Hascourt's to his father, about doubling back—as though the man had prescience of the future! For this was precisely what he had done, St. Remy being far down the wide curve of the Durance, almost to Tarascon and the Rhone.

"There was a reason in his mind, therefore," reflected Greene. "Even before the expedition started from England, he had a reason. He had lived all over this part of the country and knew it like a book. What could this reason have been? A woman? But he left a wife, and their expected child, in England."

He consulted his maps. By pressing the Citroën to the limit and driving late, he might reach St. Remy that night. No particular sense to this. He drove unhurriedly that afternoon and enjoyed himself on the way; more than once he passed great rusting masses, stripped German Mark IV tanks, guns yawning to the sky, set up as memorials to the ultimate victory of liberty. He stopped for the night at Pertuis, where the Hotel de Provence afforded good food, wine and lodging, not to mention a moonlight view of the racy old fountain and the church square that was worth the whole trip.

Next morning, on down the roads of Provence to St. Remy —an uninteresting town in the midst of uninteresting, though historic, country. Greene had never been in the place, or even heard of it, before now. It was a sleepy little place, the streets shaded by trees, with a few Roman ruins in the outskirts but nothing to attract the tourist, except the house of Nostradamus and other remains of the Renaissance. No more quiet, out-of-the-way place than this could have been found.

Greene brought himself and the Citroën to rest at the little
Hotel de Provence, lunched well, and inquired for the local
antiquary. In all the towns of southern Europe there is always a local antiquary, a student of ancient times. In this
case it proved to be Dr. Benezet, a physician who lived in a
side street behind the big modern church. Greene went to
call upon him, in mid-afternoon.

Here, he knew, finesse must be exercised. Hascourt had
certainly come here, might still be here—anything was possible, and there could be no direct investigation. In conformity
with the usual European custom, the office of the physician
was a room in his own house, a dingy place without and still
dingier within. The rooms were crowded with fragments of
Roman carvings and statuary, the walls were hung with tap-
estries; a drab, cluttered air pervaded every room.

The good doctor himself proved to be a scrabbly old man
with thick spectacles and stubby white whiskers. Greene
spoke of his antiquarian theories—picked up at the hotel—
and Benezet showed himself pleasant enough. Learning that
Greene had been here with the Seventh Army, he insisted on
producing wine and cakes, and became garrulous. They
talked of those war days, now fast receding into the distance.
The visit lengthened. It was past five o'clock when Greene
ventured a direct question.

"You were practicing here all through the war, then? I
suppose you don't recall a couple of our men, wounded, who
were brought here and left, when we advanced?"

Benezet shook his head, as well he might, at this wholly
mythical mention.

"No, no, we had no wounded here at all; you must be
mistaken," he said. "There was only Jean Gavot's friend—"
He checked himself abruptly.

"Yes? Then you did have wounded men here?" Greene queried with bland insistence.

"No," snapped Dr. Benezet. "One or two of the Maquis, of the F.F.I.—but one does not mention them today. It is not liked. Of the armies, none at all."

Having pried loose one slight clue, at least, Greene came back to antique lore and presently took his leave. It was quite obvious that Dr. Benezet knew something and meant to reveal nothing—whether or not about Hascourt, was only a guess. But if Hascourt had been brought here, then Dr. Benezet had certainly treated his wounds, for there had been no other physician here or anywhere near.

"So!" reflected Greene contentedly, as he dined by himself. "Willing or not, Dr. Benezet has served his turn, thanks to a momentary indiscretion. Hascourt had friends here. Jean Gavot had a friend, wounded. Who, then, was Jean Gavot? At all events, we're advancing and not drawing blank."

Next day he started on the new trail. Already he found himself known all over town as the American who had been here with the Seventh Army—which was not so. The little place garbled every item of news, apparently; he must be careful. However, he could mention a Frenchman whom he had met during the war, and who was said to have come from St. Remy—Gavot or some such name.

His mentions brought no response. He drank in all the wineshops, made purchases in most of the shops, and the name of Gavot drew only a shrug. Quietly, unhurriedly, he persisted. Certainly Dr. Benezet had mentioned the name, so it must exist. The day passed without yielding any result.

Next morning he visited the Mairie, where a few antiquities found in the vicinity stood on view. A wrinkled caretaker who looked as old as his charges, popped up out of nowhere to tell the tourist about them, and Greene listened.

At the close, he fed the old man liberally, and once more rehearsed his little story.

"Gavot? Gavot? Why, certainly! Monsieur must mean my wife's third cousin, Jean Gavot!" he chirped. "He lived on the Duthier farm, four miles east of the Cavaillon road."

"Lived, you say? Doesn't he live there now?" queried Greene, with a thrill.

"But no, m'sieu. He died the second winter after the war —the hard winter. His daughter married a man from beyond the mountains, a Frenchman named Verdier, who bought the farm."

Greene went back to the hotel and got lunch.

"Not so bad—so we've run Jean Gavot to earth, quite literally!" he reflected. "Now to visit the farm and get Madame Verdier to talk, and we may yet learn what became of Lance Hascourt."

Out came the Citroën, and Greene headed back on the road by which he had gained St. Remy.

The four miles—expressed, naturally, in kilometers—ambled past and brought to light a farmhouse at which Greene made inquiries. The Duthier farm? But yes; turn to the right at the next road and follow it two kilometers. This was all very well, but the next road was little better than a cowpath. However, it proved passable; the grayish green of olives appeared ahead, and beyond these almond-trees, which almost concealed a low, rambling house of stone, obviously very old. There had been no Duthier here for a hundred years and more, but it was still called the Duthier farm.

A dog came barking when Greene halted the car—a large, nondescript sort of dog, with savage bristly snout and large brown eyes. Greene spoke to him as to a friend, and smiled into the brown eyes, so the dog stopped barking and sniffed. An intelligent dog reads a man's face; he may be largely color blind, being a dog, but he can sense the eye-vibrations and the tonal quality of the voice—a sense too often lost to man.

Greene saw nobody around until he had mounted the rude stone steps leading to the house, and was almost at the door. Then, to the left, he glanced down a shaded arbor that ran along the front of the place, a trellis almost completely enclosed by grapevines, and was startled to see a man sitting there, apparently watching him.

"Who is it?" growled a harsh, angry voice. "Speak up! Who is it?"

There was more to the demand, but Greene did not understand it.

"Good day," he replied, turning. "I don't speak Provençal."

"Then speak French. Who are you? What d'you want?" The voice was rude, inhospitable, unfriendly. The speaker was a man in a wheel-chair. He had a bushy black beard, wore a beret cocked over his head, and heavy dark glasses hid his eyes.

Greene gave his name. "I would like a few words with Madame Verdier, if she's about—"

"What's your business with her?" snapped the other abruptly. "I'm Verdier. What have you to do with my wife? You're American, by the voice, or English. I'm very nearsighted, can't see you even now, but you're here for no good. Asking for my wife, eh, not for me? Explain yourself!"

An invalid, obviously; the dark glasses were not sun-goggles but were thick of lens. Verdier was wrapped in a shawl; his hands lay idle in his lap.

"Pardon my abruptness," said Greene amiably, stopping to fondle the dog's head.

"Don't touch the dog! He's savage," broke in the other quickly.

"Well? Go on."

If he could not see, how could he have known?

"The dog has intuition and politeness, monsieur," said Greene. "I understand that Madame Verdier was the daughter of one Jean Gavot. I have come here to trace a man who disappeared during the war; his name was Hascourt. He was a friend of Jean Gavot, and madame might be able to tell me what became of him."

"I can tell you that myself," snapped Verdier. "Why do you want to know?"

"I was engaged by M. Hascourt's father, who has tried vainly to learn whether his son was alive or dead."

The dog licked Greene's hand in apology, then went to Verdier and nuzzled him.

"Down, Bidot. So the fellow is an honest man, is he? So, Mr. Verdant Greene or whatever your name is—sit down. I have neither intuition nor politeness, as you infer; I leave those things to dogs. I speak a little English: 'Goddam! Go to hell!' It is enough for me. A savage tongue.—Alix! I am ready for my table!"

A woman's voice made response from inside the house. Then she herself appeared, a slender, brown, smiling young woman with a child following her. She carried a wide shelf-like board which she put across the arms of the wheel-chair, giving Greene a glance of surprise and a nod.

"My wife," said Verdier. "Alix, this man is a M. Greene, who has come to speak privately with me. Bring the things and put them within reach, then leave us. And bring the little green box from the shelf."

Madame Verdier bobbed her head, caught up the child, and went inside. Fastened to the board or table was an enormous magnifying-glass on an adjustable mount. From a receptacle at one end, Verdier produced brushes, paints, little vials of liquid.

"You behold the life-work of a useless crippled fool," he

said, his voice dry acid and venom. "A man who paints miniatures—ha! Yet it is something. It keeps me alive. And it is wonderful how men hang on to the thread of life. Eh, Bidot? Men are fools, my good dog, are they not?"

Bidot wagged his tail and looked at Greene for assent.

Madame Verdier returned, without the child. She brought a large box containing more paints, bits of porcelain, varied objects, and laid it within her husband's reach. Under his hand she placed a small green case.

"Thank you, my dear," said Verdier. He spoke in Provençal, and his voice became gentle, soft, tender. She stooped, kissed his forehead, and with a quick smile at Greene, reëntered the house. Somewhere a door slammed.

"Now we can talk in peace," said Verdier. "You understand, monsieur, I have no feet, thanks to the damned Germans and one of their personnel mines. You were in the war?"

"I was with the American Seventh Army, in these parts," said Greene quietly.

"Oh! The devil! Then I apologize for my gruffness. I was in the Maquis; I knew many of your fine men. I was born in Touraine, and during the war I came to Provence, fighting in the brush. It is odd—the thorny Corsican brush that sheltered so many outlaws and was named *maquis,* came to be the word for French patriots! Well, you want to know about Hascourt."

Verdier softened, thawed, lost his rough manner.

"Then you knew him," said Greene.

"Oh, very well! I was here when they brought him, wounded; I was affianced to Alix Gavot, you see, only in those days I had my feet, I was not a cripple. It was not a nice story, that of Hasçourt. Poor fellow, he paid for his folly."

Greene produced cigarettes. Verdier refused, and stuffed a

pipe with vile French *regie* tobacco. He needed no more prodding. He was talking away now at full speed.

"Hascourt had been injured in some sort of explosion. He had known Jean Gavot in years before the war. There was a girl in St. Remy; he had been in love with her and they had a child. When he was wounded, he thought of her and was brought here."

"He had a wife in England," said Greene.

The other nodded and puffed thoughtfully at his pipe.

"When one is wounded, one thinks only of realities, not of shadows," he observed. "This Hascourt had his fun in Provence, you understand. The war came; he went back to England and to the life he detested—a life of rigid formality, a father who was what you call a stuffed shirt, inhuman and precise, a politician of the ruling caste. There was not even a pretense of affection between father and son. Hascourt was caught in the machine and he conformed; he went into the Army, he married a girl in order to provide an heir, and so forth. There was no affection, either, between him and his wife; it was purely a marriage of convenience. Then Hascourt got a bit of shell-splinter and was invalided home. It was a nasty little wound, making his lower face a caricature. I suppose you've seen a photograph."

Greene nodded. The voice, quieter now, went on smoothly.

"This woman he had married, a hard, self-seeking woman of the world, was horrified by the sight of him. She recoiled in bitter disgust; this provoked frightful scenes between them. Like all Englishmen—most people everywhere indeed —he took the attitude that any war wound was an honorable scar. He left her for good and told her as much, moving his things into rooms in London. Almost at once, he was given orders and joined the invasion expedition for the south of France."

Verdier sucked at his pipe, got it going anew, and went on.

"Here in France, he hoped to be killed; he was merely wounded again. And at this moment his thoughts, his entire being, turned to the girl he really loved, here in Provence. She had really loved him also, you see. They brought him here and sent for the girl. She came, bringing the child at her breast. And Hascourt told her the whole truth. Did you meet Dr. Benezet in St. Remy, by the way? Did he put you on the trail of Hascourt?"

Greene, who had been absorbed in the story, was startled by the abrupt query.

"No, I met him, but he was careful to say nothing. He had incautiously mentioned a friend of Jean Gavot, wounded in the war. I jumped at this clue and looked up Jean Gavot, and arrived here."

"I see. A fine old chap, that Benezet!" Verdier cackled a laugh. "Hascourt's wounds were bad, but Benezet saved his life and made him well again."

"Tell me about the girl," Greene begged. "Not for the record, but for my own interest. How did she receive him?"

"Monsieur, like the Queen of Heaven! She truly loved him. Disfigurement, family and all—these made no difference. She would take care of him all his life, she said. And what happened? Hascourt married her in a civil ceremony."

Greene started. "But he couldn't do that! It would have been bigamy!"

"So?" Verdier's voice was sarcastic. "Bigamy—and what is that? A word invented by the law, a legal term, nominally a crime. Very well, he became a criminal, in the eyes of the law. Who cares about the law, these days? They went to a little near-by town and were married at the Mairie; thus, the child was made legitimate. Hascourt abandoned all his other life, his English existence and heritage, to the family in England; he cut it out of his memory and amputated it like an unclean thing."

"He had loyalties," said Greene. "He did wrong."

"So? His prior loyalty was to this girl here, whom he had loved all the while. His spiritual existence was here, not there. So he decided to send word home that he was dead. And to them he was indeed dead."

"He didn't send any such word."

"No. He talked with me about it. When it came to sending the message, I think he hesitated, fearing it might be traced to him and his secret uncovered. And in the following winter, a bitter hard one, he came down with pneumonia and died suddenly. I might have sent the news to his family in England, but I did not. So that is all."

"All!" Greene met the man's eyes, with a sense of shock. "But his wife and child here—"

"It is not for you to ask about them." Verdier spoke almost sternly. "The secret is theirs, not yours. It shall not be opened up; this would serve no good purpose. Nor would the respectable English family want the story known."

"Yes, you're right," Greene assented thoughtfully. "That's no part of my job. I don't want to know. Where's Hascourt's grave?"

"None of your business. He was buried under another name, as he asked. I have some of his effects here; you may take them, as proofs of his death. Certain documents he was carrying, and personal belongings—"

He opened the little green case. From it he took and passed over several medals, a watch, a ring, and a batch of papers. He held up a folded document.

"Death certificate; Hascourt had it carefully forged. It will afford them no information, you may be sure! The story is yours, so tell what you like. By the time you report, I shall not be here. The farm has been sold, and we are leaving."

Greene left it at that, asking no questions. He was not interested in this man's comings and goings; he had performed his own mission. As Verdier said, rather bitterly, the Hascourt family would be satisfied to know that Lance Hascourt was dead; they would not be too particular about details, if the law could be set at rest.

"The law! The *law!* The bane of humanity!" Verdier growled. "But before you go, my friend, we must have a glass of wine. It is good wine."

He called to his wife, who brought wine with a smile, and drank with them.

"Are your miniatures done for sale?" Greene asked, looking at the kit.

"Oh, they sell at times!" Verdier shrugged and champed at his pipe-stem. "Look you, it is the law of compensation—rather, justice. I do not like that accursed word 'law'! My feet were damaged by a personnel mine, in the war. Now I work with my hands and brain, and it makes me happy; therefore we are all happy people—eh, *chérie?*"

The woman smiled brightly.

"That is fame, my friend," Verdier said impressively, earnestly. "To be happy in one's work, to have the faith of those who love you, to see smiles upon the lips you love—by God, what more can fame and fortune do for a man?"

Greene looked hard at him. "Do you know, Verdier, you've said something memorable there. I'm glad to take it with me. Good-by, and good luck."

He drove back to St. Remy with some tiny thing buzzing in his brain; he could not place it for the moment. So, before dinner, he sat down and cabled Quest, Incorporated, that he had confirmed the death of Lance Hascourt and was following the cable at once with full proofs. He got the cable off, and relaxed; his job was done, he was free.

Dinner was over, and he was enjoying a *café fine* and a cigarette when something kicked in his brain. "The Adventures of Verdant Green," of course—that old early Victorian Oxford story of alleged English humor! Verdier had called him *Mr. Verdant Green;* how would a Frenchman know of that book?

Other things jerked at him. That child at the farm; Verdier's possession of Lance Hascourt's effects—

"I wonder!" he mused reflectively. "How much of that yarn was his own story? A bigamist wouldn't stick at a few lies to cover up his past. Was there a disfiguring scar beneath that big beard of his—could his black hair and whiskers have been yellow in the beginning? And the undisclosed grave of Hascourt—yes, by gad! It's possible!"

Greene nodded to himself as the possibility came into clear focus, but it did not worry him in the least. For one thing, his cable had gone; he was committed. For another, he thought back to the strange and beautiful and true thing Verdier had uttered, a thing, he reflected, worth being writ in letters of gold:

"To be happy in one's work, to have the faith of those who love you, to see smiles upon the lips you love—what more can fame and fortune do for a man?"

Bert Greene's lips twitched slightly.

"Just one thing he might have added," came his thought. "And yet, he did say as much, or imply as much, come to think of it. I might put it into words for him."

So he did, and it ran like this: Higher than all man-made law, is Justice.

IT HAD TO BE—

DOROTHY DUNN

———

"DID YOU KILL HIM, PAUL?"

Considering the corpse of Quiller Darst on the floor and the gun in Paul's hand, that must have sounded like a stupid question. But I felt stupid when I opened the door and saw a young man I liked standing over the body of an older man I hated. Just standing there with the gun in his hand, looking down as though he were fascinated by the vacuous eyes that stared up. I touched his arm.

"You didn't kill him, Paul!" It was a statement this time.

"Who else? Go away, Anton."

The tone of his admission was sulky, moody. No bravado; no fear of being caught; no regrets. Hate seemed to well from inside him to the surface of his dark eyes as he gazed at the crimson stain spread across the flabby face of the well-known producer.

"Paul, snap out of it! You're like a man under hypnosis. For God's sake, stop staring—"

He looked directly at me then, and smiled. A born actor. The timing would have been just right on the stage. The chin level was good and I couldn't help noticing that he struck a pose as he pointed to Quiller's face.

"Look at it, Pop! Isn't it a great satisfaction to see him blush? He never had the grace to be ashamed of any of his lousy tricks. He was a tin god. He could make or break any of us and he knew it. His filthy dough—"

"Take it easy, Paul. We've got to think."

Paul went right on acting. I was surprised, because I'd never seen him pull any hammy stuff offstage.

"I like that permanent blush," he said. "It belongs there, congealed on his thick skin!"

Melodramatic. If I hadn't quit writing plays years ago, I might have got a germinal idea from that line. But right now I needed a full-fledged idea. And quick. A soft knock on the door, however, surprised everything else out of my mind.

"Police so soon?" breathed Paul. "The rest of the cast cleared out, didn't they, Pop?"

"All except—"

Leah Travis came in. She didn't react the way women are supposed to react. But Leah wouldn't. She was the best leading lady I had ever seen. Potentially. Right now she didn't have enough depth, but you could feel the capacity for greatness. Her stage presence was perfection. Just a little warmth for humanity in her nature and she could be a name to remember for all time. Loving Paul Cornelius was helping, but sympathy and feeling for underlings would help more. She was too imperious. Being just a stage doorman, I knew. She brushed me aside.

"Paul darling, no! You idiot, I know you didn't kill him. Wipe off that gun handle."

"Butt," corrected Paul, striking the pose of sophisticate.

"No buts about it. Now, don't argue. We both saw Quiller alive before we went into my dressing room. I came out ten minutes ago, leaving you there. The door to Quiller's office was open and I saw his body lying there. So you couldn't have killed him. I went on down the hall and called the police from the booth phone. So stop looking like a murderer before they get here."

"I'm sorry, Lee. There's no use trying to alibi me. Pop came in and caught me red-handed. And as my wife, you can't testify. We got married last night. Remember?"

I drew in a sharp breath. Married! Quiller wouldn't have liked that even a little bit. Leah began talking desperately. She grew careless of her words in her eagerness to straighten things out before the police came.

"Don't be a fool, Paul. This . . . this man here— We'll pay him. He can say that—"

I broke in. The suggestion came from that hard spot in her that kept her from appreciating the human race as a whole. It was like her to take it for granted that I was just another heel who would do anything for money.

"Lady," I said, "I wouldn't keep my mouth shut for all the dough you'll inherit from Quiller Darst. And that's quite a pile!"

She turned toward me, pivoting. Her emotion was magnificent. What a play could be written for a woman like that! I wrote one once. But now I've slumped too far down ever again to ride the crest of my brief wave of creative genius. When it's gone, it's gone.

"Can I help it if my guardian hasn't anyone else to inherit his money? I didn't ask for it!"

"But you hated your guardian. Always have. I've been around since you were teen age. You never noticed me much, but I've kept an eye on you."

"Of all the insolent—"

"It's true. You never could stand Quiller."

"Well, what of it? You couldn't name very many people who didn't hate Quiller Darst. Everybody knows I've kept myself in check. I had to. My only support through child-

hood. And lately— He was old enough to be my father—
Revolting old—"

A slow drawl drifted over to us from the door that Leah
had left ajar.

"Very interesting little scene, folks. I'm Tyler Martin.
Homicide squad. You'll pardon me for just standing there
and listening to your conversation. Come in, boys."

Of all the unlucky breaks! I'd been wasting valuable time
exploring Leah's motive when I should have been getting
that gun out of Paul's hand.

Martin pulled out his handkerchief and took the gun
away from the young actor.

"This registered to you?"

"No. Quiller kept it in his desk drawer. I got it from
there."

I took big, quick steps and got around the desk.

"The gun was kept in this drawer, lieutenant." I pulled
it open, running my hand across the wood, fingering the
handle.

Martin glared.

"Don't touch another thing in this room. Prints, you
idiot!"

"Sorry," I murmured. "I just wanted to help. Paul didn't
kill Mr. Darst no matter what he says. I can prove it."

"If you can prove it, I can do the same thing. So stop
meddling. Go over there and sit down."

They examined the corpse. The fat man in the baggy
clothes who had been kneeling beside Quiller seemed surprised.

"Strange," he muttered in a low tone. "There was a heavy
blow on the side of the skull. This man must have been
knocked out, maybe dead, before he was shot. Crushed in
here. I doubt if the bullet was necessary."

Martin didn't seem to attach much importance to the words of the fat man. At least it didn't show as he turned his lazy, dangerously cold eyes toward us. But the announcement of the crushed skull started Leah trembling. I called Martin's attention to her.

"I used to write plays, lieutenant. Get to understand human emotion that way. Take a look at this young lady's face."

Martin studied her. She was shivering. "She can't act off-stage," I thought. "That's a good sign."

She turned a look of pure malice my way, but she didn't seem to recognize me as a human being. I could have been a brick that she had stubbed against in her open-toed shoes.

"You take a lot on yourself, you— Oh!"

Her shudder was more eloquent than a completed line. Her portrayal of majestic hate for someone who was putting her in a spot was wonderful.

"Yes, I think you are," agreed Paul with some confusion. We had always liked each other. I hated to hurt him by what I was doing to Leah. But I had to do it.

"You seem to have it all figured out," said Martin. There was a trace of sarcasm in his voice now.

"Yes," I said, weighing my words carefully. "You're wasting your time having your squad round up the scrub women and the stage hands still around. Your killer is right here in this room. Leah Travis has always hated her guardian, and it's common knowledge that he was going to leave his money to her. I happen to know that Quiller threatened to change his will if she married Paul Cornelius. Quiller had a loud mouth. A few dozen other people can tell you the same thing. Well, they were married last night.

"It's obvious, lieutenant. Leah came in and told Quiller. Then she shot him. For two reasons: She didn't want him to have time to change his will, and she had also had enough of his revolting possessiveness."

If Martin's face showed anything, it was amusement.

"And the crushed skull?" he asked.

"She had to do that to get the gun. Quiller wouldn't just let her take it out of the drawer and shoot him. She had to take him by surprise. Maybe he leaned over. She could pick up a heavy object from the desk and strike him. Then she could get the gun and finish the job."

Paul jumped up, his face white. He wasn't acting now.

"You're mad, Anton! You were a playwright once. You're just weaving a fantastic—"

"Nothing fantastic in it. I'm sorry, Paul. But I was standing at the edge of the wings. I saw Leah come out of her dressing room. She didn't pass the open door as she said. She went inside and later I saw her come out. A silenced gun has a sound of its own. You must have heard something and come out a little later. I watched Leah go into the phone booth and by the time I got back here, you were holding the gun. But you're just trying to shield your bride."

I felt successful. There was an impressive silence when I had finished speaking. Leah was staring at me and this time her look was less haughty. It was as though the brick had become large enough to trip over. Paul put a protective arm around her and looked at Martin piteously.

"Sure, Leah hated Quiller, lieutenant. But no more than I did. Not as much. Pop here is a good guy, but look at him. Seventy-five if he's a day, and he can't even see well enough to get a number out of the phone book! He just thought he saw Leah come out of this office. It's an open-and-shut case. Why make a mystery out of it? I killed him!"

One of the men who had been working with a fingerprint kit came over to Martin.

"Only one set of prints, chief. This guy's, I guess, since he was holding the gun when we came in."

I was exultant.

"That's proof of Paul's innocence! That gun belonged to Quiller. It would have been handled many times by Quiller. His prints ought to be there along with the murderer's. They *would* be if Paul hadn't wiped it off to get rid of Leah's prints! He wouldn't have removed the prints before the killing, and if he was just going to stand here and confess, why should he wipe them off *after* the murder?"

Martin just glared at me with eyes that were growing colder and harder.

"That's enough," he said. "I know a guilty man when I see one."

That was the statement that broke Leah. She did what I'd been hoping she would do. If Martin was going to consider Paul, she had to tell how it really happened.

"I was foolish to think there might be a way out," she began in a calm, deliberate voice. "This old man is right, lieutenant. It happened just the way he said. I shot Quiller and he was dead when I left him. I wiped my own prints off the gun and then went out to the booth and called the police. So many people have felt like murdering Quiller that I thought it might be impossible to prove who did it. But if you're going to believe Paul, I have to tell you the truth. I didn't intend to kill him, but he was so . . . so—"

She shuddered at the memory of whatever Quiller had been like during their interview. It was thrilling to watch her. For me, anyway. The theater has been my whole life. That's why I was contented to be a hanger-on for Quiller after I lost my grip. That's why I couldn't take my eyes off Leah Travis. Even with the spot of hardness in her, she was good. If that callous streak that Quiller had kicked into her character could be melted, she would achieve greatness. Real, vibrant, warm splendor would animate her performances.

"There's just one thing," she added, "I didn't hit Quiller with anything. That place on his head—I didn't do that."

"I know you didn't," said Martin softly.

He began staring at me. Not at my face. His eyes were fixed on the pocket of my black alpaca coat. I looked down. There was a wettish spot that showed, dull against the shiny black!

He didn't even turn his head as he called to one of his men. "See if you find a small, heavy object in that desk drawer, Casey. A square corner, I'd say."

I took a step backward, keeping my eyes on Martin's face. He leveled a gun at me.

"Don't try anything. Just stand still and keep your hands out of your pockets."

Then Casey came over with the bloody paper-weight that I had slipped into the drawer.

Martin just glanced at it out of the corner of his eye.

"I knew it would be there," he said, turning to me. "I saw your sleight-of-hand, you know. Just let you talk to see what you were planning. It wasn't a good plan. We never pay much attention to the confessions of people in love, but it's a good idea to listen to a suspect who is anxious as hell to blame somebody else. Messy job, this. Why did you bash in his head? With just the gun as evidence, you might not have been suspected."

That was right. Leah and Paul had the most obvious motives. I wouldn't have been taken seriously as a suspect if there had been just the bullet. But—

"I guess it was brute anger," I said. "I shot him and he

died so quickly— It seemed too easy for him— I hit him then."

Leah gasped. "Oh!" she said throatily.

Her eyes met mine briefly, then I held her gaze with what I believed to be a God-bless-you smile.

Martin clamped a handcuff on my wrist, and as he did so, I staged the scene I had been rehearsing in my mind. I was acting my own lines for the first time.

"Take your filthy hands off me! Do you know who I am, you young upstart? George Anton, do you near? George Anton! Ask your father about that name and he'll tell you who I am. I was a genius in the last generation. People have been crushed in crowds trying to get close enough to touch my garments. I have lived for the theater, you fool. I would die for the theater!"

"Sorry, but it's murder you'll die for," said Martin, not unkindly. I know he thought I was a crazy, pitiful old man. "Come along."

"Wait," said Leah.

She came up to me, looking deep into my eyes. I was not a brick now. I was a human being to her.

"I didn't know you were George Anton," she said. "I tried to get Quiller to let me do your 'Crossroads' not long ago. He refused."

"I know he refused. But now that he's dead you can produce what you like," I said, giving Lieutenant Martin a satisfactory motive for the crime.

Then a strange thing happened. Leah Travis raised up on her toes and kissed my cheek. Warmth. Splendid warmth that she was beginning to feel for humanity showed in her movement.

"I promise to do it," she whispered. "Would I make a good Sylvina?"

"You would now. Superb!"

Martin pulled me away impatiently and I caught a glint of the tears that were coming into Leah's eyes as I turned. And Paul, looking bewildered.

In the car going uptown, Martin was mulling it over.

"So you killed a man just to get an old play revived! Genius must be a hair-trigger substance."

I leaned back against the cushion, contented. I hadn't known about the play at all, but I liked to think about it now. Leah Travis would make it a triumph.

Martin tried to get me talking.

"What did you bash in his head for?" Plainly, that puzzled him.

I closed my eyes to show Martin that I had no intention of answering. I suppose it was possible for me to hit Quiller so hard because I was doing some hack work for him in the anteroom of his office and heard some of the insults that provoked Leah's anger. I had no idea she would shoot him, or I would have butted in on their quarrel. When I heard the *ping* of the silenced shot, I gave her a few minutes to get away. Then I went out, smashed Quiller's head with the weight and put it in my pocket on purpose so the blood would soak through. Maybe he wasn't dead when I hit him. I didn't look.

I didn't see that it mattered much. Someone was bound to kill the rat someday. He kept a gun in his desk because he knew that. But I couldn't let it be Leah Travis. I've watched her acting deepen ever since her kid parts and it was something to watch!

I went out then to check on Leah. When I saw her phoning, I dashed back to the office. Paul was there, stealing my stuff.

He looked so silly in his eagerness to be blamed that I

decided it would be more convincing to try to make the police suspect Leah. It worked. And something else will work, I'm hoping.

I struck Quiller so hard that his death might have been caused by either the blow or the bullet. Leah will never be sure.

But there will be just enough doubt in her mind that she won't ever forget that someone did something for her. Quiller made her fight for what she got. Now somebody had given her something without anything in return. She needed that experience to soften her up.

My mad genius scene was to let her know that I wanted her to glorify the stage with true greatness.

She'll do that. You'll be going to see Leah Travis someday.

I can feel the moment already. The hush falling over the audience, the gradual darkening of the house, the split second of time suspended in silence and expectation as the curtain goes up.

The car stopped and Martin jerked on my arm that was cuffed to his. "We're getting out," he said.

"Ah, the theater!" I breathed rapturously, thinking of Leah Travis playing in "Crossroads."

"No," corrected Martin. "Police headquarters."

SLAY-MATES

CHARLES LARSON

———

SHE LAY QUIETLY WHERE I HAD PLACED HER, HER VOICE whispering across the room to me as though she was dreaming sounds, and not speaking them at all.

". . . everyone had left me. They said it would be all right because I was ten. At first I didn't mind it. I pretended I was a queen, and the empty house was my castle. I found a deck of cards, and I made believe all the face cards were courtiers. . . ."

I thought, listening to her: Psychology isn't new. People say, "You *know,* that cute idea about mind-sickness," when they've forgotten the name for it. But this is the oldest science ever practiced. This is a little boy crying and telling his mother he'd been smoking when she looked frightened over his stomach-ache. This is a young man in a dim cabinet murmuring to a priest in the cabinet next to him. Except that they call it "confession."

Her voice, steady until now, broke only enough for me to notice it.

". . . but then the darkness came. There was no moon. I was sitting in the center of the room with my cards spread around me, and I couldn't see them. I tried to get up, and the darkness wouldn't let me move. When they came home, I was alone, pushing and screaming at the night. . . ."

I said, "It's all right," gently, and her voice lowered. Her face relaxed. She hadn't realized she was crying, and I could tell by the turn of her head that she was ashamed.

It was a very pretty head. If I were a writer, instead of a psychologist, I might put the proper words together and let you see her there, but I'm not, and I can't. Think of nobility. New and strong and regal. Small, fine hands. Clear eyes. Dress the young body in clothes by Irene, dip the fingernails in scarlet, and over everything place the wise, careful sheen of twenty.

She had come to me forty minutes before, a little confused, laughing because she was shy, to tell me that she couldn't sleep nights, and was there anything to be done about that?

Perhaps. Yes, very likely something could be done about that. I had taken her and the young man with her into my office, and while she sat on the sofa answering my questions like a prim little girl-child, I had marked the high points of her life on the questionnaire before me.

Her name, it seemed, was Marcy King. Still *Miss* King—an awkward clearing of the young man's throat at this point, and a charming blush from *Miss* King—but not, she hoped, for long. Her parents were both dead—she lived with an uncle.

And her uncle was called?

Roger Brighton.

I'm afraid my hand shook when I formed the words. A spot of blue ink hung glistening over the "i" and dried there because I couldn't find a blotter.

Roger Brighton. You muttered the name with reverence or with loathing, depending entirely on whether or not you believed in money. In the financial hierarchy, Kaiser spoke only to Ford, and Ford spoke only to Brighton. Brighton didn't speak.

I asked a few more questions, rather unimportant ones. Then I put down my pen, and folded my hands in front of me.

"Now, Miss King—"

"Yes."

She crossed her knees, and drew her skirt over them with one slim, gloved hand.

"Your trouble, as I understand it, is that you have difficulty in sleeping."

"That's quite right."

"I see." I moved a crystal figurine over my desk. "You're lying. I wish you'd stop."

I watched her mouth form a startled O, and then slowly straighten.

"What?" she exclaimed.

"You're lying." The figurine caught the light from the window, and fantastic colors sprayed from it.

"Miss King," I said, "my fee is stiff. It isn't that way by accident. People buy pills when they can't sleep, they don't consult me. I wish you'd be honest. It saves so much time and money."

Her face had reddened. I could see the unconscious tightening of her muscles while she tried to decide whether to kick me or to leave simply, without fuss.

Her companion saved the situation nicely. He was a young man made for saving situations. I could imagine him going through life putting in the right word at the right moment, averting disaster, thrusting out his shoulder to be cried upon. He was tall and husky and curly-haired. A faint trace of England shone through his speech.

"I think the man's right," he said, grinning at me. "Marcy, I suggest you tell him the truth."

Voila. Fait accompli, and all that. The girl was smoothing the hem of her blue skirt. Obviously she was going to kick me.

"Well—I—" she faltered.

"I've found that it's easiest to begin at the beginning, Miss King," I observed. "You came here because you wanted help. Help for what?"

"All right."

Abruptly she raised her head. I couldn't help noticing the way the sunlight caught at her hair. It gave one the faintest impression of a halo.

"Would you laugh," she asked, "if I told you I was afraid of darkness? Desperately, terribly afraid?"

"No," I said. "I wouldn't."

She looked startled, as though she'd turned the cold-water handle in a shower, and a warm, soft spray had come out.

"There's more," she added. "Sometimes, in the darkness, I want to—to hurt people."

"Sadistically? I mean by that—"

"I know what it means. No. Not that way at all." She bit her lip. "I want to kill someone."

"Who, Miss King?"

The answer was very soft.

"My uncle."

I kept my eyes on my own desk. My right hand was becoming stained again. I should have to go a bit easier on the smoking.

"I've told her it was nonsense," the boy broke in.

His mouth was calm, but his gray eyes appeared worried. His name, I believe, was Jerry Freen. Frankly, I hadn't quite got it when she introduced us. He took pictures for one of our local papers.

"It isn't nonsense in the least," the girl said quickly. She stared at the floor.

"When did this wish to kill your uncle first appear?" I asked.

"I don't know. Two years ago. Three. Does it matter?"

It didn't, very much. Recently I'd come across a case like this one in Stekel, and I felt the same elation I'd known when I was five, and my father had given me an electric train. I'd pored over dozens of pictures of that train, but when I held the real thing in my hands, I was terrified to discover that I knew absolutely nothing about the way it should be run.

I hoped I wouldn't make the same mistake here.

The diagnosis of the case was simplicity itself, but the cure? Evidently Miss King was suffering from one of the most common neuroses known to psychology. Noctiphobia. An unreasonable fear of the darkness. Her tendency to want to murder her uncle must stem from the fact that he had been instrumental in leaving her alone at night during her childhood. Subconsciously, she resented his neglect when he had been most needed. With the coming of night, or darkness, resentment returned to her, and childlike, she wished to kill.

"I'd really like to get started on this as soon as I can," I said. "Have you an hour free?"

"Yes, of course."

I turned to Freen. "You don't mind?"

"No, no." He rose and shook my hand as though he were the patient. "Luck, Doctor," he said.

I stifled an impulse to mutter, "Stout fella!" and watched him leave the office.

"And now—" I said, when I came back.

I caught myself and stopped grinning.

But it was too late. The girl had seen it, and she began to look vaguely ashamed of herself, as though she wished to apologize for being pretty, and making dignified young psychologists grin at her.

Embarrassed, I found myself a chair, drew it to the sofa.

"Have you any relatives?" I began. "Other than your uncle, of course."

"I have. A brother."

"Older than yourself?"

"A few years. His name is Glen."

Her eyes were on her shoes, inspecting them critically.

"You played together quite a lot when you were young?" I asked.

She glanced up.

"What?"

I repeated my question.

"Obviously you're an only child, Dr. Conover," she said, laughing. "Brothers don't have anything to do with their little sisters. The only time Glen bothered with me was when he thought he could irritate me or frighten me. He used to tell me the goriest stories about Bluebeard and Captain Kidd."

"What does Glen do now?" I wanted to know.

"Almost nothing. He's of age. When he became twenty-one, he got quite a tidy sum from Dad's estate. It's in trust until Uncle Rog dies, but he gets trickles now and then." She pursed her lips thoughtfully. "Oh. He's an air-raid warden," she added.

I laughed a little.

"I must have phrased my question badly. I meant, of course, what is his relation to you? Does he continue these stories? Or has he forgotten them?"

"He hasn't done that sort of thing since he went to high school. Sometimes he mentions one or two little episodes when we're reminiscing, but he certainly doesn't dwell on them."

"I see."

I rose then, and walked to the venetian blinds on the long windows behind the girl, who was watching me as though she suspected I were going to attack her. The scrape of the wooden bars sounded loud in the room when I pulled them shut.

"Just lie back," I murmured.

"Why?"

"Oh, lady, please—" I said.

But then I caught the shine of her eyes on me, and I could see how tightly her hands were clasped over the sofa's cushions. I knew enough about unconscious actions to realize that she was very, very frightened.

I'd been terribly stupid. But she had seemed so normal.

"Is it the darkness?" I asked softly.

She didn't answer, and in a moment I opened the blinds again. The thick comfort of gray light came in. The day was gloomy, it had rained in the morning, but I hadn't thought that the pulling of the shades could have darkened the room so.

Slowly the girl twisted her head to glance at the sky outside.

"Thanks," she whispered. "I'm sorry."

For a moment I considered her. I wondered how long this had been going on. Evidently, it wouldn't be at all the easy job I'd imagined.

Slowly I took my chair again.

"It's quite all right," I said soothingly. "Just lie back, and talk to me, and we won't do that again."

She swung her legs onto the sofa, and rested her head gently on the pillow.

"What shall I talk about?" she asked.

She seemed perfectly sensible now, except that her voice was much lower than it had been, and that she turned her eyes constantly to the window.

"Anything. Memories. Childhood escapades. Tell me whatever comes into your mind. Tell me what came into your mind when I closed the shades."

There in the brightly-lighted room she began to speak. Hesitantly at first, and then freely. A day when she'd gone to the cellar, and her uncle had accidentally locked the door behind her. Another evening when her brother and four friends had let her in on a contest of ghost story-telling. Night after night of hearing unnatural sounds in her darkened room.

Some of the stories were unusual, and some were so much extra-weight. But by the time we were through, I had convinced myself that I was on the right track, and I imagine that I had convinced her of that, too. Psychology is like a flashlight in many respects. Turn it on darkness, and darkness is no longer there.

I took her home that afternoon, and all the way I was conscious of her beside me. Before I left her, I managed to press her hand and to tell her that things would be fine. A few more consultations, a few more beams of light on her peculiar past, and we would have it.

I think she believed me. I know darned well I believed myself. She was laughing when I drove away.

At eleven-thirty that evening, our city had its first blackout.

The next morning, the newspapers, including the one Freen worked for, were going wild over a shiny new crime.

Roger Brighton had been killed at midnight.

When I stopped my car in front of Roger Brighton's home,

and got out, I was struck foolishly with the basic sadness of living. There were so many little people in front of the immense white house, so many cars in the street, so much hush everywhere. Everyone was looking at the grounds, pretending not to look, and in their eyes was this terrible trite relief that dying hadn't happened to them yet.

At the same time I was embarrassed for them, and sympathetic toward them. Because I was relieved, too.

I was met at the door by Jerry Freen, his handsome face worried into a caricature. He was wearing the same suit he'd worn in my office, heavy green-brown tweeds, with baggy knees and bulging pockets.

"Hello, Freen."

"Come in." He stood back, and half-turned like a puppy expecting a ball to be thrown. "Marcy will want to see you. I'm glad you dropped by."

"Thanks. I got here as soon as I could."

While we climbed the stairs to Brighton's second-floor room, Freen told me as well as he could what had happened.

At seven-thirty that morning, Lorraine, one of the maids, had knocked on Mr. Brighton's door. This was a daily duty required of her by Brighton, who was an early riser, although he detested alarm clocks. There was no answer from the old man, and the girl had tried the door, only to find it locked on the inside.

At this point she had called Parsons, the butler, who had also failed to get an answer.

By this time both of them were frantic. The old man was weak. For months his heart had been bothering him. Perhaps, during the night—

While they were debating the next course of action, Miss King had come along. She had seemed upset and nervous, and her first words had been strangely prophetic.

"Is he dead?" she had asked.

At this, Lorraine had broken down completely, crying spasmodically into her handkerchief, and Miss King had said, "Call my brother and phone Mr. Freen as soon as you can."

I broke into Freen's story then to inquire, "Did Miss King have an alibi for last night?"

"Marcy? Good heavens, you can't think—"

"What was the alibi?"

"She was with me. We went to a nightclub, and we were caught there when the blackout started. Fifty people must have spoken to us. It's air-tight, Doctor. We didn't get home until three this morning."

"And do they know how and when Brighton was killed?" I asked.

We reached the top of the stairs, turned down a large, many-windowed corridor.

"That's the funniest part of the whole business," Freen answered. "When I got here, there wasn't a mark on him. He was lying just inside the room, face down, and everything in the place was in perfect order.

"I don't know what I expected. Blood. Confusion. Chaos of some sort. I'd brought a few things along in my briefcase— ammonia, for instance—but I might as well have left the blasted thing at home. He was cold. The M.E. said this morning that he'd been dead about eight hours."

We stopped in front of a bedroom door, hanging raggedly by its hinges where Freen had crashed against it.

"From what you've told me," I put it slowly, "there seems to be no reason at all for the publicity the papers gave it. The room was locked on the inside. I suppose I'm right in assuming it was a heart attack?"

"Yes," Freen said. But his voice was too quick. "Yes, of course. Only—"

"Only what?"

"Only—" Freen looked at the floor. "There was something in his face—when I turned him over. I wouldn't let them see. I made all of them get out of the room and stay out until the police came."

He glanced up at me.

"Fright," he said. "Insane, unbelievable fright." When he continued, his voice was almost a whisper. "The M.E. said he hadn't come across anything like it since the last war, when he treated a man who'd watched his brother hit by a tank."

The bedroom itself had taken on, as bedrooms seem to do, many of the characteristics of its owner. The individual traits and stiffness of Brighton were everywhere. In the precise order of the bureau. In the smell of tobacco from the curtains. Even in the Andrew Carnegie biography on his bedstand.

There were two people with us: Detective Tad Stevens, whom I recognized from a photo which had appeared in the morning extras, and a good-looking, weak-mouthed youngster who could have been no one but Glen King, Marcy's brother.

They looked up when we came in, and Glen's head moved back a little as he tried to focus his eyes. He was very drunk.

"Yeah?" from the detective.

"I'm sorry," Freen said. "We were looking for Miss King."

Slowly Detective Stevens came toward us, his long hands held straight and stiff at his sides, like those of a Japanese wrestler. Between the fingers of his left hand he held a richly-worked leather diary. He was tall and stooped from too many years of being ashamed of it. He watched me closely.

"You a friend of Miss King's?"

"In a way, yes."

"Then you knew Brighton, too."

"No. I'm Miss King's doctor. I thought she might be taking this a little—roughly."

"Doctor, rats," Glen King said abruptly.

All of us turned toward him. He still had on his air-raid warden's arm-band, and I wondered what his alibi might be.

"I know the family doctor," he said. "This guy ain't him."

I felt myself beginning to grow red.

"Don't be an utter fool," I said. "I'm a doctor of psychology. I was treating Miss King for a nervous disorder. And may I ask the reason for all the comic-strip innuendoes? Are you trying to hint that Brighton didn't die of a heart attack?"

"Brighton was murdered," Stevens said. "His heart was bad, but it had to have a reason for stopping. He was frightened to death. We want to know how, why, and who by. And *I* want to know where you were at twelve o'clock last night."

"I was home. In bed."

"Married, are you?"

"No."

"Ah."

The detective turned away.

"Now, look here—" I started to say.

I stopped then, because it had suddenly occurred to me how very neatly I had been trapped. I felt a little foolish. Psychologists didn't get mixed up. They didn't fall for every tiny trick pulled on them like some fifth-rate vaudeville stooge. And if they did, they got out of it. They were a cunning lot, those psychologists.

So I became cunning—and I almost sealed my own death warrant.

"Has it ever entered your pealike mind," I asked, "that a

blackout is a singularly unlikely time for the average man to commit a murder?"

Stevens looked at me.

"It has, but go on."

"If I were in charge of this case, I think I should forget all this nonsense about strangers groping through the dark. I'd begin thinking about the one man who could possibly have had an opportunity to kill. *If* Brighton was killed at all."

I didn't look at Glen King, but I could feel the tension in the room, the small stretching of the rubber band, the microscopic focusing of emotions.

Detective Stevens let his eyes flicker toward Marcy's brother and back to me.

Understand this. I had been forced into a corner. I had nothing against Glen. I was certainly not trying to convict the man of his uncle's murder, but my words—

"All right," Glen said. "I've had about enough of this." He came close to me. "I don't know who you are, or what the blazes Marcy is to you, but when a two-bit quack comes in here, and shouts to the world I've killed someone, it's about time he was shut up."

"Hold it, son."

Freen started across the room.

I'd turned to tell him to stay where he was, when the first blow landed, and in a detached, professional sort of way, I admired it. It was high and sharp and cutting, and the boy's follow-through brought me face to face with his shoulder. Off-balance, I spun backward against the wall.

I heard the crash of a lamp when I reached too far for something to grab hold of. I fell heavily onto one knee, feeling the ache and dull push of pain roll like a wave up my leg to my hip. The globe in the lamp had broken, and everywhere around me tiny slivers of glass caught the sun and became diamonds for a moment.

Then Freen had twisted Glen around, holding him so tightly by his vest that the youngster appeared to be straining back on his toes as though he were about to hurl himself into a particularly tough ballet exercise.

I watched the curl of Freen's hand jump through the air, slap against Glen's face.

"Sober up," Freen ordered.

Detective Stevens hadn't moved. He was smiling.

"Now, boys," he said.

Startled, Glen stared at Freen, and let his eyes drop to me. With the blood returning to his white, slapped face, tears came.

"Curse you," he said softly. "Oh, curse you."

Slowly Freen let his arms drop to his sides.

"Hold onto yourself," he snapped. "Nobody's accused anybody of anything. It was an accident."

"It wasn't an accident," Glen murmured. He raised one of his hands to his eyes, shook his head. "I—"

"You what?"

Stevens walked toward him.

"Why in heaven should I trust you? You think I killed him. You think I came up here last night and did something to him. Why should I tell you anything? I don't know who did it. I only know how it was done. I saw it."

He turned toward the door, and walked away from us.

"You *saw* it!"

Detective Stevens swore long and beautifully, and Glen looked at him carefully before he went out of the room.

Quickly Stevens motioned to Freen.

"Get him. Stay with him. And be careful until he comes out of the drunk."

Freen nodded, and slipped through the door.

When I moved, it was as though my hip was made of dough, but I couldn't stay on the floor forever. I got to my feet, stared at the palm of my hand where a bit of glass had lodged.

"Nice boy," I said.

"Yeah." Stevens looked at me narrowly. "I almost hate to hang this rap on him."

I brought up my head.

"Are you serious?"

"I'm serious. We're waiting for him to make a break. Just one. He almost made it when he said he'd seen the crime committed. In a blackout? He's got himself into the most peculiar net I ever saw. Everything points toward him, and he knows it. But he also knows that we can't possibly tell how he did it. Everybody's waiting for a misstep. He'll make it before long."

"What of the maid? Or the butler?"

"Opportunity, of course. No motive."

"And me?"

"Opportunity, maybe."

"And—Miss King?"

The detective hesitated.

"Miss King," he repeated. "Motive enough, but no opportunity. We checked on her story of night-clubbing with Freen. It's foolproof. Freen is an amateur drummer, and a dozen people swear that he was on the bandstand from eight-thirty until twelve, with Miss King always accounted for. From midnight until three they were caught in the club while the blackout was in effect. Incidentally, the club is ten miles out, near the beach."

I nodded.

"I suppose you have a fine motive for Glen King?"

Without a word he opened the diary, showed it to me.

"A peach of a fine motive," he retorted.

I followed his finger down the page, and read Glen King's ruin in the sprawling, thick handwriting of Roger Brighton.

"Sept. 10, 1943. . . . I know now what G. has been doing. Marcia told me of her fear of darkness, and of course his suggestion-power over her is tremendous. The boy is trying to drive her insane. I've tried to tell her, but she refuses to believe me. Obviously he's planning for the future—for when I'm gone. My money, added to Marcia's, will amount to a compelling motive. I shall tell him today, that, if he goes any further with this thing, I will change my will completely. . . ."

I pursed my lips.

"And that seems to be that."

Stevens nodded, and bent down to pick up the lamp I'd knocked over. He turned it around in his hands.

"It would be, *if* we knew how. Everything fits. Opportunity. Motive. Everything—except that blasted locked door." He threw the lamp down suddenly. "How in the devil can we explain that? How can we face a jury and say: 'This man went into a room locked on the inside, made a face at his uncle which promptly frightened the old man to death, and then left the room, locking it behind him, *on the inside,* on his way out.'" He snorted. "They'd laugh us out of court."

Gently rolling, the lampshade had come to rest at my feet and slowly I leaned down, picked it up. Very curious thing about that lampshade. It was new, it was modern, and yet there were tiny brown pockmarks on the inside, as if something had accidentally spattered on the surface.

"You find something?" Stevens asked.

He walked over to me.

"You see anything odd in this?"

He took the shade, turned it in his hands.

"So it's been burned," he agreed. "So what?"

He looked at me.

"Rather senseless thing to do, wouldn't you think? Burn a lampshade. Why?"

"Maybe the light was out. Maybe the maid lit a match to see what she was doing when she put a new one in."

"Oh, come now."

"Yeah—"

He took the shade again, staring at it.

I stepped across the room, lifted another shade off its base. Under this one was no bulb. And yet the shade was also pitted.

"Is there any poison—" I began.

"Brighton's heart stopped," the detective interrupted. "He wasn't poisoned."

"You're sure?"

His "of course" was slower than it should have been.

By the time I'd left the room, Detective Stevens was dialing the coroner.

I can't tell you why I did what I did then. I'd like to pretend that I knew everything about the case from the very beginning and that its solution was as plain as brandy laced through tea.

But I didn't, and it wasn't—until I got into the hall.

Even then I didn't understand everything.

At the head of the stairs, a police photographer was systematically taking shots of the hallway. Inquisitively he glanced at me when I stopped, waiting for me to get out of his way.

But oddly I couldn't. Suddenly I was watching his hands, and the equipment behind him. And it was there, the way a murderer could kill a man in a locked room, all of it, like thunder on a clear day.

"Photographs," I said stupidly, and the photographer's eyes widened.

"Photographs," he confirmed. "Yes," as though he thought I might be preparing to accuse him of carrying bombs.

"I'm sorry," I said. "Do you know the layout of this place? Where can I find Glen King?"

"The old guy's nephew?"

"Yes. Where can I find him?"

"Down the hall. Third door."

He must have thought I was completely insane, but he didn't try to stop me or ask questions. I left him staring at his camera while I hurried to catch a murderer.

In Hollywood, when they wish to create horror or suspense or gloom, they accent shadows. They hold on tiny sounds, and twist the camera into odd angles. But this wasn't Hollywood. This was a well-lighted bedroom, and the horror in it was cheap, and the bright sunlight made the whole rotten business frivolous.

I thought at first I was too late. A man was lying on the disordered bed and another man was standing over him, the sunlight picking out a glass vial in his hands. A common bottle of iodine.

I closed the door behind me, stood with my back placed against it.

"Hold it, Freen," I said.

He must have heard me. He must have heard me come in. But he didn't turn. Only his shoulders twitched, as though something spidery were clinging to them.

I began to move across the room, smelling the sharp odor of good Scotch on the air. A half-empty bottle stood on the stand beside Glen King's bed.

"I think you and I ought to have a talk with the police," I said.

"Yes. Glen killed Brighton. I left him for a moment, and when I came back he had the iodine in his hands. I had to knock him out to get it away from him."

Freen's voice was almost normal, but he hadn't turned.

"It won't work," I remarked. "We know how the murder was committed, and we know what Glen saw that night."

"Doc, have you lost your mind?"

"I've just found it. You took one devil of a chance, Freen, but you were lucky. Or maybe it wasn't such a chance after all. You knew Brighton's heart was bad. You knew no one would dare enter the room while he was away. You *didn't* know we were going to have a blackout, and that Glen would be out front watching."

"I don't know what you're talking about."

"Your alibi fooled me at first," I went on. "But you didn't have to be here in the house when you killed the old man, did you? You could have been a million miles away—after you put the lights in."

"Lights?"

"Lights. Yes. That's what Glen saw. Flash bulbs. Flash bulbs from your photographic equipment in every light socket in that enormous room. No wonder Brighton had a look of terror on his face. A dozen flash bulbs exploding when he pushed a simple light-switch would darned near kill a man with a good heart.

"It must have made a fine sight in a blackout. And they were easy to change and replace, weren't they? You were the first one to enter the room, and you made everyone get out and stay out because of the sight of the old man. I believe you told me you carried a large briefcase with you. I'd like to see that briefcase, Freen."

I saw the tightening of his muscles when he began to swing toward me. I tried to step back, but unaccountably there was a chair behind me, and I fell awkwardly into it, scrambling like a crippled duck.

Sometimes I wonder whether this business about guardian angels is as silly as it sounds. From now on I'm taking no sides. For that fall, that one slip, saved my eyes—and perhaps my life with them.

Over my head, I could see the spray of iodine Freen had hurled, flash like blood from a fighter's crushed mouth. Then he was on me, fighting, clawing, trying to get behind me to the door.

I am not a fighter. When you practice psychology, there seems to be no time for fighting, but they tell me I held my own. I don't remember.

I remember only pushing and slugging on the floor until I was blind with wanting to kill this man. I remember fingers on my neck, and the good feeling of bone crushing beneath my own hands.

There seemed to be two of him after a while, and then three and four. It was long afterward before I discovered that Detective Stevens and the police photographer were in the fight with me. I rolled out of the way then, and the carpet was suddenly soft under my cheek. I heard them fighting behind me, but I didn't care. I just wanted to rest.

Later, when it was all over, when Glen had been pronounced safe, though drunk, by the M.E., and Freen was on his way to the station, Stevens came into the bedroom, where Marcy was clucking and painting my forehead with some of the unspilled iodine.

He put his hands on his hips and shook his head.

"My friend," he said, "you deserved that beating. Why the blazes didn't you tell me what you were going to do?"

I winced even when I spoke.

"I didn't know what I was going to do."

"Tell me one thing."

I looked up at him.

"The diary," he said. "Explain the 'G' in Brighton's diary, and I'll be happy."

"Freen's first name is Jerry," I said.

"So?"

"So the 'G' stood for Gerald Freen. Not Glen King."

"Of course," Marcy put in dutifully.

She replaced the iodine stopper, and leaned back to smile at me.

I knew then the one sure way to cure this girl of her darkness-fear. I was surprised that I hadn't seen it sooner. She stayed late at night-clubs—because she was afraid to be alone. She was frightened of darkness, because she had been so alone in darkness.

Now, if she had a husband—

I sighed, and stretched out on the bed. This was going to be a marvelous cure.

THE GREEN GOD'S RING

SEABURY QUINN

S T. DUNSTAN'S WAS PACKED TO OVERFLOWING. EXPECTANTLY
smiling ladies in cool crêpe and frilly chiffon crowded
against perspiring gentlemen in formal afternoon dress while
they craned necks and strained ears. Aisles, chancel, sanctu-
ary, were embowered in July roses and long trailing garlands of southern smilax, the air was heavy with the humid
warmth of summer noon, the scent of flowers and the perfume from the women's hair and clothes.

The dean of the Cathedral Chapter, the red of his Cam-
bridge hood in pleasing contrast to the spotless white of linen
surplice and sleek black cassock, pronounced the fateful
words, his calm clear voice a steady mentor for the bridegroom's faltering echo:

"I, Wade, take thee Melanie to be my wedded wife, to
have and to hold from this day forward—"

"From this day forward," Dean Quincy repeated, smiling
with gentle tolerance. In forty years of priesthood he had
seen more than one bridegroom go suddenly dumb. "From
this day forward, for better, for worse—"

His smile lost something of its amusement, his florid,
smooth-shaven face assumed an expression of mingled surprise and consternation which in other circumstances would
have seemed comic. Swaying back and forth from toes to

heels, from heels to toes, the bridegroom balanced uncertainly a moment, then with a single short, hard, retching cough fell forward like an overturned image, the gilded hilt of his dress sword jangling harshly on the pavement of the chancel.

For what seemed half a minute the bride looked down at the fallen groom with wide, horrified eyes, then, flowing lace veil billowing about her like wind-driven foam, she dropped to her knees, thrust a lace-sheathed arm beneath his neck and raised his head to pillow it against the satin and seed pearls of her bodice. "Wade," she whispered in a passionless, cold little voice that carried to the farthest corner of the death-still church. "Oh, Wade, my belovèd!"

Quickly, with the quiet efficiency bred of their training, the young Naval officers attending the fallen bridegroom wheeled in their places and strode down the aisle to shepherd panic-stricken guests from their pews.

"Nothin' serious; nothin' at all," a lad who would not see his twenty-fifth birthday for another two years whispered soothingly through trembling lips as he motioned Jules de Grandin and me from our places. "Lieutenant Hardison is subject to these spells. Quite all right, I assure you. Ceremony will be finished in private—in the vestry room when he's come out of it. See you at the reception in a little while. Everything's all right. Quite—"

The pupils of de Grandin's little round blue eyes seemed to have expanded like those of an alert tom cat, and his delicate, slim nostrils twitched as though they sought to capture an elusive scent. *"Mais oui, mon brave,"* he nodded approval of the young one-striper's tact. "We understand. *Certainement.* But me, I am a physician, and this is my good friend Dr. Trowbridge—"

"Oh, are you, sir?" the lad broke in almost beseechingly

"Then for God's sake go take a look at him; we can't imagine—"

"But of course not, *mon enfant*. Diagnosis is not your trade," the small Frenchman whispered. "Do you prevail upon the congregation to depart while we—*attendez-moi*, Friend Trowbridge," he ordered in a low voice as he tiptoed toward the chancel where the stricken bride still knelt and nursed the stricken bridegroom's head against her bosom.

"*Sacré nom!*" he almost barked the exclamation as he came to a halt by the tragic tableau formed by the kneeling bride and supine man. "*C'est cela même.*"

There was no doubting his terse comment. In the glassy-eyed, hang-jawed expression of the bridegroom's face we read the trade mark of the King of Terrors. Doctors, soldiers and morticians recognize death at a glance.

"Come, Melanie," Mrs. Thurmond put a trembling hand upon her daughter's shoulder. "We must get Wade to a doctor, and—"

"A doctor?" the girl's voice was small and still as a night breeze among the branches. "What can a doctor do for my poor murdered darling? Oh, Wade, my dear, my dear," she bent until her lips were at his ear, "I loved you so, and I'm your murderess."

"*Non, Mademoiselle,*" de Grandin denied softly. "You must not say so. It may be we can help you—"

"Help? *Ha!*" she almost spit the exclamation at him. "What help can there be for him—or me? Go away—get out —all of you!" she swept the ring of pitying faces with hard bright eyes almost void of all expression. "Get out, I tell you, and leave me with my dead!"

De Grandin drew the slim black brows that were in such sharp contrast to his wheat-blond hair down in a sudden frown. "*Mademoiselle,*" his voice was cold as icy spray against her face, "you ask if any one can help you, and I reply they can. I, Jules de Grandin, can help you, despite the evil plans of pisacha, bhirta and preta, shahini and rakshasa, I can help—"

The girl cringed from his words as from a whip. "Pisacha, bhirta and preta," she repeated in a trembling, terrified whisper. "You *know*—"

"Not altogether, *Mademoiselle*," he answered, "but I shall find out, you may be assured."

"What is it you would have me do?"

"Go hence and leave us to do that which must needs be done. Anon I shall call on you, and if what I have the intuition to suspect is true, *tenez*, who knows?"

She drew a kneeling cushion from the step before the altar rail and eased the dead boy's head down to it. "Be kind, be gentle with him, won't you?" she begged. "Good-by, my darling, for a little while," she laid a light kiss on the pale face pillowed on the crimson cushion. "Good-by—" Tears came at last to her relief and, weeping piteously, she stumbled to her mother's waiting arms and tottered to the vestry room.

"Heart?" I hazarded as the bridal party left us alone with the dead man.

"I should think not," he denied with a shake of his head. "He was on the Navy's active list, that one, and those with cardiac affections do not rate that."

"Perhaps it was the heat—"

"Not if Jules de Grandin knows his heat prostration symptoms, and he has spent much time near the Equator. The fires of hell would have been cold beside the temperature in here when all those curious ones were assembled to see this poor one and his belovèd plight their troth, but did he not seem well enough when he came forth to meet her at the chancel steps? Men who will fall prone on their faces in heat collapse show symptoms of distress beforehand. Yes, of course. Did you see his color? Excellent, was it not? But certainly. Bronzed from the sea and sun, *au teint vermeil de bon santé*. We were not thirty feet away, and could see perfectly. He had none of that pallor that betokens heat stroke. No."

"Well, then"—I was a little nettled at the cavalier way he dismissed my diagnoses—"what d'ye think it was?"

He lifted narrow shoulders in a shrug that was a masterpiece of disavowal of responsibility. *"Le bon Dieu* knows, and He keeps His own counsel. Perhaps we shall be wiser when the autopsy is done."

We left the relatively cool shadow of the church and stepped out to the sun-baked noonday street. "If you will be so kind, I think that I should like to call on the good Sergeant Costello," he told me as we reached my parked car.

"Why Costello?" I asked. "It's a case of sudden unexplained death, and as such one for the coroner, but as for any criminal element—"

"Perhaps," he agreed, seeming only half aware of what we talked of. "Perhaps not. At any rate, I think there are some things about this case in which the Sergeant will be interested."

We drove a few blocks in silence, then: "What was that gibberish you talked to Melanie?" I asked, my curiosity bettering my pique. "That stuff about your being able to help her despite the evil plans of the thingabobs and whatchamaycallems? It sounded like pure double talk to me, but she seemed to understand it."

He chuckled softly. "The pisacha, bhirta and preta? The shahini and rakshash?"

"That sounds like it."

"That, my friend, was what you call the random shot, the

drawing of the bow at venture. I had what you would call the hunch."

"How d'ye mean?"

"Did you observe the ring upon the index finger of her right hand?"

"You mean the big red gold band set with a green cartouche?"

"*Précisément.*"

"Not particularly. It struck me as an odd sort of ornament to wear to her wedding, more like a piece of costume jewelry than an appropriate bridal decoration, still these modern youngsters—"

"That modern youngster, my friend, did not wear that ring because she wanted to."

"No? Why, then?"

"Because she had to."

"Oh, come, now. You can't mean—"

"I can and do, my friend. Did not you notice the device cut into its setting?"

"Why, no. What was it?"

"It represented a four-faced, eight-armed monstrosity holding a straining woman in unbreakable embrace. The great God Siva—"

"Siva? You mean the Hindu deity?"

"Perfectly. He is a veritable chameleon, that one, and can change his form and color at a whim. Sometimes he is as mild and gentle as a lamb, but mostly he is fierce and passionate as a tiger. Indeed, his lamb-like attributes are generally a disguise, for underneath the softness is the cruelty of his base nature. *Tiens,* I think that he is best described as Bhirta, the Terrible."

"And those others with outlandish names?"

"The pisacha and preta are a race of most unlovely de-

mons, and like them are the rakshash and shahini. They
attend Siva in his attribute of Bhirta the Terrible as imps
attend on Satan, doing his foul bidding and, if such a thing
be possible, bettering his instructions."

"Well?"

"By no means, my friend, not at all. It is not well, but very
bad indeed. A Christian maiden has no business wearing
such a talisman, and when I saw it on her finger I assumed
that she might know something of its significance. Accordingly I spoke to her of the Four-Faced One, Bhirta and his
attendant implings, the shahini, rakshasa and pisacha. *Par-
bleu*, she understood me well enough. Altogether too well, I
damn think."

"She seemed to, but—"

"There are no buts, my friend. She understood me. Anon
I shall understand her. Now let us interview the good Costello."

Detective-sergeant Jeremiah Costello was in the act of putting down the telephone as we walked into his office. "Good
afternoon, sors," he greeted as he fastened a wilted collar and
began knotting a moist necktie. " 'Tis glad I'd be to welcome ye at any other time, but jist now I'm in a terin' hurry.
Some swell has bumped himself off at a fashionable wedding,
or if he didn't exactly do it, he died in most suspicious circumstances, an'—"

"It would not be Lieutenant Wade Hardison you have
reference to?"

"Bedad, sor, it ain't Mickey Mouse!"

"Perhaps, then, we can be of some assistance. We were
present when it happened."

"Were ye, indeed, sor? What kilt 'im?"

"I should like to know that very much indeed, my friend.
That is why I am here. It does not make the sense. One mo-

ment he is hale and hearty, the next he falls down dead before our eyes. I have seen men shot through the brain fall in the same way. Death must have been instantaneous—"

"An' ye've no hunch wot caused it?"

"I have, indeed, *mon vieux,* but it is no more than the *avis indirect*—what you would call the hunch."

"Okay, sor, let's git goin'. Where to first?"

"Will you accompany me to the bride's house? I should like to interview her, but without official sanction it might be difficult."

"Howly Mackerel! Ye're not tellin' me *she* done it—"

"We have not yet arrived at the telling point, *mon ami.* Just now we ask the questions and collect the answers; later we shall assemble them like the pieces of a jigsaw puzzle. Perhaps when we have completed the mosaic we shall know some things that we do not suspect now."

"I getcha," Costello nodded. "Let's be on our way, sors."

The Thurmond place in Chattahoochee Avenue seemed cloaked in brooding grief as we drove up the wide driveway to the low, pillared front porch. A cemetery quiet filled the air, the hushed, tiptoe silence of the sickroom or the funeral chapel. The festive decorations of the house and grounds were as incongruous in that atmosphere of tragedy as rouge and paint upon the cheeks and lips of a corpse.

"Miss Melanie is too ill to be seen," the butler informed us in answer to Costello's inquiry. "The doctor has just left, and—"

"Present our compliments to her, if you please," de Grandin interrupted suavely. "She will see us, I make no doubt. Tell her it is the gentleman with whom she talked at the church—the one who promised her protection from Bhirta. Do you understand?"

"Bhirta?" the servant repeated wonderingly.

"Your accent leaves something to be desired, but it will serve. Do not delay, if you please, for I am not a patient person. By no means."

Draped in a sheer convent-made nightrobe that had been part of her trousseau, Melanie Thurmond lay rigid as death upon the big colonial sleigh bed of her chamber, a madeira sheet covering her to the bosom, her long auburn hair spread about her corpse-pale face like a rose gold nimbus framing an ivory ikon. Straight before her, with set, unseeing eyes she gazed, only the faint dilation of her delicate nostrils and the rhythmic rise and fall of her bosom testifying she had not already joined her stricken lover in the place he had gone a short hour before.

The little Frenchman approached the bed silently, bent and took her flaccid hand in his and raised it to his lips, "Ma pauvre," he murmured. "It is truly I. I have come to help you, as I promised."

The ghost of a tired little smile touched her pale lips as she turned her head slowly on the pillow and looked at him with wide-set, tearless sepia eyes. "I knew that it would come," she told him in a hopeless little voice. Her words were slow and mechanical, her voice almost expressionless, as though she were rehearsing a half-learned lesson: "It had to be. I should have known it. I'm really Wade's murderess."

"Howly Mither!" Costello ejaculated softly, and de Grandin turned a sudden fierce frown on him.

"Comment?" he asked softly. "How do you mean that, ma petite roitelette?"

She shook her head wearily from side to side and a small frown gathered between her brows. "Somehow, I can't seem to think clearly. My brain seems seething—boiling like a caldron—"

"*Précisément, exactement, au juste,*" de Grandin agreed with a vigorous nod. "You have right, my little poor one. The brain, she is astew with all this trouble, and when she stews the recrement comes to the surface. Come, let us skim it off together, thou and I"—he made a gesture as if spooning something up and tossing it away. "Thus we shall rid our minds of dross and come at last to the sweet, unadulterated truth. How did it all start, if you please? What made you know it had to happen, and why do you accuse yourself all falsely of the murder of your *amoureux?*"

A little shudder shook the girl's slim frame, but a hint of color in her pallid cheeks told of a returning interest in life. "It all began with The Light of Asia."

"*Quoi?*" de Grandin's slim brows rose in Saracenic arches. "You have reference to the poem by Sir Edward Arnold?"

"Oh, no. This Light of Asia was an Oriental bazar on East Fifty-sixth Street. The girls from Briarly were in the habit of dropping in there for little curios—quaint little gifts for people who already seemed to have everything, you know.

"It was a lovely place. No daylight ever penetrated there. Two great vases stood on ebony stands in the shop windows, and behind them heavy curtains of brocaded cloth of gold shut off the light from outside as effectively as solid doors. The shop—if you could call it that—was illuminated by lamps that burned scented oil and were encased in frames of carved and pierced teakwood. These, and two great green candles as tall as a man, gave all the light there was. The floors were covered with thick, shining Indian rugs, and lustrous embroideries hung against the walls. The stock was not on shelves, but displayed in cabinets of buhl and teak and Indian cedar—all sorts of lovely things: carved ivories and molded silver, hand-worked gold and tortoise-shell, amethyst and topaz, jade and brass and lovely blue and green enamel, and over everything there hung the scent of incense, curiously and pungently sweet; it lacked the usual cloying, heavy fragrance of the ordinary incense, yet it was wonderfully penetrating, almost hypnotic."

De Grandin nodded. "An interesting place, one gathers. And then—"

"I'd been to The Light of Asia half a dozen times before I saw The Green One."

"The Green One? *Qui diable?*"

"At the back of the shop there was a pair of double doors of bright vermilion lacquer framed by exquisitely embroidered panels. I'd often wondered what lay behind them. Then one day I found out! It was a rainy afternoon and I'd dropped into The Light as much to escape getting wet as to shop. There was no other customer in the place, and no one seemed in attendance, so I just wandered about, admiring the little bits of *virtu* in the cabinets and noting new additions to the stock, and suddenly I found myself at the rear of the shop, before the doors that had intrigued me so. There was no one around, as I told you, and after a hasty glance to make sure I was not observed, I put my hand out to the nearer door. It opened to my touch, as if it needed only a slight pressure to release its catch, and there in a gilded niche sat the ugliest idol I had ever seen.

"It seemed to be carved of some green stone, not like anything I'd ever seen before—almost waxen in its texture—and it had four faces and eight arms."

"*Qu'est-ce-donc?*"

"I said four faces. One looking each way from its head. Two of the faces seemed as calm as death masks, but the one behind the head had a dreadful sneering laugh, and that which faced the front had the most horrible expression—

not angry, nor menacing, exactly, but—would you understand me if I said it looked inexorable?"

"I should and do, *ma chèrie*. And the eight arms?"

"Every hand held something different. Swords, and sprays
of leafy branches, and daggers—all but two. They were empty
and outstretched, not so much seeming to beg as to demand
an offering.

"There was something terrible—and terrifying—about that
image. It seemed to be demanding something, and suddenly
I realized what it was. It wanted me! I seemed to feel a sort
of secret, dark thrill emanating from it, like the electric
tingle in the air before a thunderstorm. There was some
power in this thing, immense and terrifying power that gave
the impression of dammed-up forces waiting for release. Not
physical power I could understand and combat or run from,
but something far more subtle; something uncanny and indescribable, and it was all the more frightening because I
was aware of it, but could not explain nor understand it.

"It seemed as if I were hypnotized. I could feel the room
begin to whirl about me slowly, like a carrousel when it's just
starting, and my legs began to tremble and weaken. In another instant I should have been on my knees before the
green idol when the spell was broken by a pleasant voice:
'You are admiring our latest acquisition?'

"It was a very handsome young man who stood beside me,
not more than twenty-two or -three, I judged, with a pale
olive complexion, long brown eyes under slightly drooping
lids with haughty brows, and hair so sleek and black and
glossy it seemed to fit his head like a skullcap of patent
leather. He wore a well-cut morning coat and striped trousers, and there was a good pearl in his black poplin ascot tie.

"He must have seen the relief in my face, for he laughed
before he spoke again, a friendly, soft laugh that reassured

me. 'I am Kabanta Sikra Roy,' he told me. 'My dad owns this place and I help him out occasionally. When I'm not working here I study medicine at N. Y. U.'

" 'Is this image—or idol, or whatever you call it—for sale?' I asked him, more to steady my nerves by conversation than anything else.

"The look he gave me was an odd one. I couldn't make out if he were angry or amused, but in a moment he laughed again, and when he smiled his whole face lighted up. 'Of course, everything in the shop's for sale, including the proprietors—at a price,' he answered, 'but I don't think you'd be interested in buying it.'

" 'I should say not. But I just wondered. Isn't it some sort of god, or something?'

" 'Quite so. It is the Great Mahadeva, third, but by far the most important member of the Hindu Triad, sometimes known as Siva the Destroyer.'

"I looked at the thing again and it seemed even more repulsive than before. 'I shouldn't think you'd find a quick sale for it,' I suggested.

" 'We don't expect to. Perhaps we'll not sell it at all. In case we never find a buyer for it, we can put in our spare time worshiping at its shrine.'

"The utter cynicism of his reply grated on me, then I remembered having heard that many high caste Hindus have no more real faith in their gods than the educated Greeks and Romans had in theirs. But before I could be rude enough to ask if he really believed such nonsense, he had gently shepherded me away from the niche and was showing me some exquisitely carved amethysts. Before I left we found we had a dozen friends in common and he'd extended and I'd accepted an invitation to see *Life With Father* and go dancing at the Cotillion Room afterward.

"That began the acquaintance that ripened almost over-night into intimacy. Kabanta was a delightful playfellow. His father must have been enormously rich, for everything that had come to him by inheritance had been given every chance to develop. The final result was this tall, slender, olive-complexioned man with the sleek hair, handsome features and confident though slightly deferential manner. Before we knew it we were desperately in love.

"No"—her listless manner gathered animation with the recital—"it wasn't what you could call love; it was more like bewitchment. When we met I felt the thrill of it; it seemed almost to lift the hair on my head and make me dizzy, and when we were together it seemed as if we were the only people in the world, as if we were cut off from everyone and everything. He had the softest, most musical voice I had ever heard, and the things he said were like poetry by Laurence Hope. Besides that, every normal woman has a masochistic streak buried somewhere deep in her nature, and the thought of the mysterious, glamorous East and the guarded, prisoned life of the zenana has an almost irresistible appeal to us when we're in certain moods. So one night when we were driving home from New York in his sports roadster and he asked me if I cared for him I told him that I loved him with my heart and soul and spirit. I did, too—then. There was a full moon that night, and I was fairly breathless with the sweet delirium of love when he took me in his arms and kissed me. It was like being hypnotized and conscious at the same time. Then, just before we said good night, he asked me to come to The Light of Asia next evening after closing time and plight our troth in Eastern fashion.

"I had no idea what was coming, but I was fairly palpitant with anticipation when I knocked softly on the door of the closed shop shortly after sunset the next evening.

"Kabanta himself let me in, and I almost swooned at sight of him. Every shred of his Americanism seemed to have fallen away, for he was in full Oriental dress, a long tight-waisted frock coat of purple satin with a high neck and long, tight sleeves, tight trousers of white satin and bright red leather shoes turned up at the toes and heavily embroidered with gold, and on his head was the most gorgeous piece of silk brocade I'd ever seen wrapped into a turban and decorated with a diamond aigrette. About his neck were looped not one nor two but three long strands of pearls—pink-white, green-white and pure-white—and I gasped with amazement at sight of them. There couldn't have been one in the three strands that was worth less than a hundred dollars, and each of the three strands had at least a hundred gems in it. The man wore twenty or thirty thousand dollars' worth of pearls as nonchalantly as a shop girl might have worn a string of dime store beads.

"'Come in, White Moghra Blossom,' he told me. 'All is prepared.'

"The shop was in total darkness except for the glow of two silver lamps that burned perfumed oil before the niche in which the Green God crouched. 'You'll find the garments of betrothal in there,' Kabanta whispered as he led me to a door at the rear, 'and there's a picture of a Hindu woman wearing clothes like those laid out for you to serve as a model. Do not be long, O Star of My Delight, O Sweetly Scented Bower of Jasmine. I swoon for the sight of you arrayed to vow love undying.'

"In the little anteroom was a long, three-paneled mirror in which I could see myself from all sides, a dressing-table set with toilet articles and cosmetics, and my costume draped across a chair. On the dressing-table was an exquisite small picture of a Hindu girl in full regalia, and I slipped my

Western clothes off and dressed myself in the Eastern garments, copying the pictured bride as closely as I could. There were only three garments—a little sleeveless bodice like a zouave jacket of green silk dotted with bright yellow discs and fastened at the front with a gold clasp, a pair of long tight plum-colored silk trousers embroidered with pink rosebuds, and a shawl of thin, almost transparent purple silk tissue fringed with gold tassels and worked with intricate designs of lotus buds and flowers in pink and green sequins. When I'd slipped the bodice and trousers on I draped the veil around me, letting it hang down behind like an apron and tying it in front in a bow knot with the ends tucked inside the tight waistband of the trousers. It was astonishing how modest such a scanty costume could be. There was less of me exposed than if I'd been wearing a halter and shorts, and not much more than if I'd worn one of the bare-midriff evening dresses just then becoming fashionable. For my feet there was a pair of bell toe rings, little clusters of silver bells set close together like grapes in a bunch that tinkled with a whirring chime almost like a whistle each time I took a step after I'd slipped them on my little toes, and a pair of heavy silver anklets with a fringe of silver tassels that flowed down from the ankle to the floor and almost hid my feet and jingled every time I moved. On my right wrist I hung a gold slave bracelet with silver chains, each ending in a ball of somber-gleaming garnet, and over my left hand I slipped a heavy sand-molded bracelet of silver that must have weighed a full half pound. I combed my hair straight back from my forehead, drawing it so tightly that there was not a trace of wave left in it, and then I braided it into a queue, lacing strands of imitation emeralds and garlands of white jasmine in the plait. When this was done I darkened my eyebrows with a cosmetic pencil, raising them and accenting their arch to the 'flying gull' curve so much admired in the East, and rubbed green eye-shadow upon my lids. Over my head I draped a long blue veil sewn thickly with silver sequins and crowned it with a chaplet of yellow rosebuds. Last of all there was a heavy gold circlet like a clip-earring to go into my left nostril, and a single opal screw-earring to fasten in the right, giving the impression that my nose had been pierced for the jewels, and a tiny, star-shaped patch of red court plaster to fix between my brows like a caste mark.

"There is a saying clothes don't make the man, but it's just the opposite with a woman. When I'd put those Oriental garments on I *felt* myself an Eastern woman who had never known and never wished for any other life except that behind the purdah, and all I wished to do was cast myself prostrate before Kabanta, tell him he was my lord, my master and my god, and press my lips against the gold-embroidered tips of his red slippers till he gave me leave to rise. I was shaking as if with chill when I stepped from the little ante-room accompanied by the silvery chiming of my anklets and toe rings.

"Kabanta had set a fire glowing in a silver bowl before the Green God, and when I joined him he put seven sticks of sandalwood into my hands, telling me to walk around the brazier seven times, dropping a stick of the scented wood on the fire each time I made a circuit and repeating Hindu invocations after him. When this was done he poured a little scented water from a silver pitcher into my cupped hands, and this I sprinkled on the flames, then knelt across the fire from him with outstretched hands palm-upward over the blaze while I swore to love him, and him only, throughout this life and the seven cycles to come. I remember part of the oath I took: 'To be one in body and soul with him as gold and the bracelet or water and the wave are one.'

"When I had sworn this oath he slipped a heavy gold ring —this!—on my finger, and told me I was pledged to him for all time and eternity, that Siva the Destroyer was witness to my pledge and would avenge my falseness if I broke my vow. It was then for the first time I heard of the pisacha, bhirta and preta, shahini and rakshasa. It all seemed horrible and fantastic as he told it, but I believed it implicitly—then." A little rueful smile touched her pale lips. "I'm afraid that I believe it now, too, sir; but for a little while I didn't, and so—so my poor lover is dead."

"*Pauvre enfant,*" de Grandin murmured. "*Ma pauvre belle créature.* And then?"

"Then came the war. You know how little pretense of neutrality there was. Americans were crossing into Canada by droves to join up, and everywhere the question was not 'Will we get into it?' but 'When?' I could fairly see my lover in the gorgeous uniform of a risaldar lieutenant or captain in the Indian Army, leading his troop of wild Pathans into battle, but Kabanta made no move. When our own boys were drafted he was deferred as a medical student. At last I couldn't stand it any longer. One evening at the shore I found courage to speak. 'Master and Lord,' I asked him—we used such language to each other in private—'is it not time that you were belting on your sword to fight for freedom?'

" 'Freedom, White Blossom of the Moghra Tree?' he answered with a laugh. 'Who is free? Art thou?'

" 'Thou art my lord and I thy slave,' I answered as he had taught me.

" 'And are the people of my father's country free? You know that they are not. For generations they have groaned beneath the Western tyrant's lash. Now these European dogs are at each other's throats. Should I take sides in their curs' fight? What difference does it make to me which of them destroys the others?'

" 'But you're American,' I protested. 'The Japanese have attacked us. The Germans and Italians have declared war on us—'

" 'Be silent!' he commanded, and his voice was no longer the soft voice that I loved. 'Women were made to serve, not to advise their masters of their duty.'

" 'But, Kabanta—'

" 'I told you to be still!' he nearly shouted. 'Does the slave dare disobey her master's command? Down, creature, down upon your knees and beg my pardon for your insolence—'

" 'You can't be serious!' I gasped as he grasped me by the hair and began forcing my head down. We'd been playing at this game of slave and master—dancing girl and maharajah —and I'd found it amusing, even thrilling, after a fashion. But it had only been pretense—like a 'dress-up party' or the ritual of a sorority where you addressed someone you'd known since childhood as Queen or Empress, or by some other high-sounding title, knowing all the while that she was just your next door neighbor or a girl with whom you'd gone to grammar school. Now, suddenly, it dawned on me that it had not been play with him. As thoroughly Americanized as he appeared, he was still an Oriental underneath, with all the Oriental's cynicism about women and all an Eastern man's exalted opinion of his own importance. Besides, he was hurting me terribly as he wound his fingers in my hair. 'Let me go!' I demanded angrily. 'How dare you?'

" 'How dare I? Gracious Mahadeva, hear the brazen Western hussy speak!' he almost choked. He drew my face close to his and asked in a fierce whisper, 'Do you know what you vowed that night at The Light of Asia?'

" 'I vowed I'd always love you, but—'

" 'You'd always love me!' he mocked. 'You vowed far more than that, my Scented Bower of Delight. You vowed that from that minute you would be my thing and chattel—vowed yourself to Siva as a voluntary offering, and accepted me as the gods' representative. As gods are to humanity, so am I to you, O creature lower than the dust. You're mine to do with as I please, and right now it pleases me to chastise you for your insolence.' Deliberately, while he held my head back with one hand in my hair, he drew one of his moccasins off and struck me across the mouth with its heel. I could feel a thin trickle of blood between my lips and the scream I was about to utter died in my throat.

" 'Down!' he commanded. 'Down on your face and beg for mercy. If you are truly penitent perhaps I shall forgive your insolence.'

"I might have yielded finally, for flesh and blood can stand only so much, and suddenly I was terribly afraid of him, but when I was almost beyond resistance we heard voices in the distance, and saw a light coming toward us on the beach. 'Don't think that I've forgiven you,' he told me as he pushed me from him. 'Before I take you back you'll have to walk barefoot across hot coals and abase yourself lower than the dust—'

"Despite the pain of my bruised lips I laughed. 'If you think I'll ever see you again, or let you come within speaking distance—' I began, but his laugh was louder than mine.

" 'If you think you can get away, or ever be free from your servitude to me, you'll find that you're mistaken,' he jeered. 'You are Siva's, and mine, for all eternity. My shadow is upon you and my ring is on your finger. Try to escape the one or take the other off.'

"I wrenched at the ring he'd put on my hand. It wouldn't budge. Again and again I tried to get it off. No use. It seemed to have grown fast to the flesh; the more I tried to force it off the tighter it seemed to cling, and all the time Kabanta stood there smiling at me with a look of devilish, goading derision on his dark handsome features. At last I gave up trying and almost fainting with humiliation and the pain from my bruised mouth, I turned and ran away. I found my car in the parking lot and drove home at breakneck speed. I suppose Kabanta managed to get a taxi. I don't know. I never saw him again."

"*Très bon*," de Grandin nodded approval as she completed her story. "That is good. That is very good, indeed, *ma oisillone*."

"Is it?" the irony of her reply was razor-thin.

"Is it not?"

"It is not."

"*Pourquoi? Nom d'un chameau enfumé!* For why?"

"Because he kept his word, sir. His shadow *is* upon me and his ring immovably upon my finger. Last year I met Wade Hardison, and it was love at first sight. Not fascination nor physical attraction, but love, real love; the good, clean, wholesome love a man and woman ought to have for each other if they expect to spend their lives together. Our engagement was announced at Christmas, and—"

"*Et puis?*" he prompted as her voice broke on a soundless sob.

"Then I heard from Kabanta. It was a post card—just a common penny post card, unsigned and undated, and it carried just eleven words of message: 'When you remove the ring you are absolved from your oath.' He hadn't signed it, as I said, but I knew instantly it was from him.

"I tried desperately to get the ring off, wound my fingers with silk, used soap and olive oil, held my hand in ice cold water—no use. It wouldn't budge. I couldn't even turn it on my finger. It is as if the metal had grown to my flesh and become part of me. I didn't dare tell anyone about it, they wouldn't have believed me, and somehow I didn't have the courage to go to a jeweler's and have it filed off, so . . ."

The silence that ensued lasted so long one might have thought the girl had fainted, but the short, irregular, spasmodic swelling of her throat told us she was fighting hard to master her emotion. At last:

"Two days ago," she whispered so low we had to bend to catch her words, "I had another note. 'He shall never call you his,' was all it said. There was no signature, but I knew only too well who the sender was.

"Then I told Wade about it, but he just laughed. Oh, if only I had had the courage to postpone our wedding. Wade might be alive now. There's no use fighting against Fate," her voice rose to a thin thread of hysteria. "I might as well confess myself defeated, go back to Kabanta and take whatever punishment he cares to inflict. I'm hopelessly enmeshed, entrapped—ensnared! I am Siva's toy and plaything, and Kabanta is the Green God's representative!" She roused to a sitting posture, then fell back, burying her face in the pillow and shaking with heart-breaking sobs.

"Kabanta is a species of a cockroach, and Siva but an ape-faced piece of green stone," de Grandin answered in a hard, sharp voice. "I, Jules de Grandin, tell you so, *Mademoiselle;* anon I shall say the same thing to them, but much more forcefully. Yes, certainly, of course."

"That dame's as nutty as a fruit cake," Costello confided as we left the Thurmond house. "She goes an' gits herself involved with one o' these here fancy Hindu fellies, an' he goes an' tells her a pack o' nonsense, an' she falls fer it like a ton o' brick. As if they wuz anny such things as Shivas an' shahinnies an' raytors an' th' rest o' it! Begob, I'd sooner belave in—"

"You and I do not believe, my friend," de Grandin interrupted seriously, "but there are millions who do, and the power of their believing makes a great force—"

"Oh, come!" I scoffed. "You never mean to tell us that mere cumulative power of belief can create hobgoblins and bugaboos?"

"*Vraiment,*" he nodded soberly. "It is indeed unfortunately so, my friend. Thoughts are things, and sometimes most unpleasant things. Yes, certainly."

"Nonsense!" I rejoined sharply. "I'm willing to agree that Melanie could have been imposed on. The world is full of otherwise quite sane people who are willing to believe the moon is made of green cheese if they're told so impressively enough. I'll even go so far as to concede she thinks she can't get the ring off. We've all seen the cases of strange inhibitions, people who were convinced they couldn't go past a certain spot—can't go off the block in which they live, for instance. She's probably unconsciously crooked her finger when she tried to pull it off. The very fact she found excuses to put off going to a jeweler's to have it filed off shows she's laboring under a delusion. Besides, we all know those Hindus are adepts at hypnotism—"

"*Ah, bah!*" he broke in. "You are even more mistaken than usual, Friend Trowbridge. Have you by any chance read *Darkness Out of the East* by our good friend John Thunstone?"

"No," I confessed, "but—"

"But be damned and stewed in boiling oil for Satan's supper. In his book Friend Thunstone points out that the rite of walking barefoot seven times around a living fire and throwing fuel and water on it while sacred *mantras* are recited is the most solemn manner of pronouncing an irrevocable oath. It is thus the neophyte is oath-bound to the service of the temple where she is to wait upon the gods, it is so when the wife binds herself forever to the service and subjection of her lord and husband. When that poor one performed that ceremony she undertook an oath-bound obligation which every Hindu firmly believes the gods themselves cannot break. She is pledged by fire and water for all time and eternity to the man who put the ring of Siva on her finger. While I talked to her I observed the amulet. It bears the device of a woman held in unbreakable embrace by Four-Faced Siva, and under it is written in Hindustani, 'As the gods are to mankind so is the one to whom I vow myself to me. I have said it.'

"As for her having the ring filed off—she was wiser than she knew when she refrained from that."

"How d'ye mean?" Costello and I chorused.

"I saw an instance of it once in Goa, Portuguese India. A wealthy Portuguese planter's *femme de la main gauche* had an *affaire* with a Hindu while her protector was away on business. She was inveigled into taking such a vow as Mademoiselle Thurmond too, and into having such a ring slipped on her finger. When she would have broken with her Hindu lover and returned to her *pourvoyer* she too found the ring immovable, and hastened to a jeweler's to have it filed off. *Tiens,* the life went out of her as the gold band was sawn asunder."

"You mean she dropped dead of a stroke?" I asked.

"I mean she died, my friend. I was present at the autopsy, and every symptom pointed to snake bite—except the stubborn fact that there had been no snake. We had the testimony of the jeweler and his two assistants; we had the testimony of a woman friend who went with her to the shop. All were agreed there had been no snake near her. She was not bitten; she merely fell down dead as the gold band came off."

"O.K., sor; if ye say it, I'll belave it, even if I know 'taint so," Costello agreed. "What's next?"

"I think we should go to the morgue. The autopsy should be complete by this time, and I am interested in the outcome."

Dr. Jason Parnell, the coroner's physician, fanned himself with a sheaf of death certificates, and mopped his streaming brow with a silk handkerchief. "I'm damned if I can make it out," he confessed irritably. "I've checked and rechecked everything, and the answer's the same each time. Only it doesn't make sense."

"*Qu'est-ce donc?*" de Grandin demanded. "How do you say?"

"That youngster has no more business being dead than you or I. There wasn't a God's-earthly thing the matter with him from a pathological standpoint. He was perfect. Healthiest specimen I ever worked on. If he'd been shot, stabbed or run down by a motor car I could have understood it; but here he is, as physiologically perfect as an athlete, with positively no signs of trauma of any sort—except that he's as dead as a herring."

"You mean you couldn't find a symptom—" I began, and he caught me up before I had a chance to finish.

"Just that, Trowbridge. You said it. Not a single, solitary one. There is no sign of syncope, asphyxia or coma, no trace of any functional or organic weakness. Dammit man, the fellow didn't die, he just stopped living—and for no apparent reason. What'n hell am I goin' to tell the jury at the inquest?"

"*Tiens, mon ami,* that is your problem, I damn think," de

Grandin answered. "We have one of our own to struggle with. There is that to do which needs immediate doing, and how we are to do it only *le bon Dieu* knows. Name of a little blue man, but it is the enigma, I tell you."

Sergeant Costello looked unhappily from Parnell to de Grandin. "Sure, sors, 'tis th' screwiest business I've ever seen entirely," he declared. "First th' pore young felley topples over dead as mutton, then his pore forsaken bride tells us a story as would make th' hair creep on yer neck, an' now you tell us that th' pore lad died o' nothin' a-tall. Mother o' Moses, 'tis Jerry Costello as don't know if he's comin' or goin' or where from an' where to. Can I use yer 'phone, Doc?" he asked Parnell. "Belike th' bhoys at Headquarters would like to know what I'm about."

We waited while he dialed Headquarters, heard him bark a question, and saw a look of utter unbelief spread on his broad perspiring face as some one at the other end answered. " 'Tain't so!" he denied. "It couldn't be.

"We wuz just up to see her, an' she's as limp as a wet wash—"

"What is it, *mon Sergent?*" de Grandin asked. "Is it that—"

"Ye can bet yer bottom dollar it is, sor," the Sergeant cut in almost savagely. "It sure is, or I'm a monkey's uncle. Miss Thurmond, her we just seen layin' in th' bed so weak she couldn't hold up her head, has taken it on th' lam!"

"*Diable!*" de Grandin shot back. "It cannot be."

"That's what I told 'em at Headquarters, sor, but they insist they know what they're a-talkin' about; an' so does her old man. 'Twas him as put the call in to be on th' look-out fer her. It seems she lay in a half stupor when we left her, an' they'd left her alone, thinkin' she might git a bit o' rest, when zingo! up she bounces, runs to th' garage where her car wuz parked, an' rushes down th' street like th' divil wuz on her trail."

"*Ha!*" de Grandin's hard, dry, barking laugh had nothing whatever to do with amusement. "*Ah-ha-ha!* I am the greatest stupid-head outside of a *maison de fous, mes amis.* I might have damn anticipated it! You say she ran as if the devil were behind her? *Mais non,* it is not so. He was before her. He called her and she answered his summons!"

"Whatever—" I began, but Costello caught the little Frenchman's meaning.

"Then what th' divil are we waitin' fer, sor?" he demanded. "We know where he hangs out. Let's go an' peel th' livin' hide off 'im—"

"*Ma moi, cher Sergent,* you take the words out of my mouth," the small Frenchman shot back. "Come, Friend Trowbridge, let us be upon our way."

"Where to?" I asked.

"Where to? Where in the foul name of Satan but to that so vile shop called The Light of Asia, where unless I am more greatly mistaken than I think, the dove goes to a rendezvous with the serpent. Quickly. Let us hasten, let us rush; let us fly, *mes amis!*"

The rain that had been threatening since early afternoon came down in bucketsful as we crept slowly through East Fifty-sixth Street. It poured in miniature Niagaras from cornices and rolled-up awnings, the gutters were awash, the sidewalks almost ankle-deep with water.

"*Halte la!*" ordered de Grandin, and I edged the car close to the curb. "My friends, we are arrived. Be quiet, if you please, make no move unless I request it, and—" he broke off with a muttered "*nom d'un coq!*" as a wind-whipped awning sluiced a sudden flood of icy water over him, shook himself like a spaniel emerging from a pond, and laid his hand upon the brass knob of the highly varnished door.

Amazingly the door swung open at his touch and we stepped into the dim interior of The Light of Asia.

The place was like a church whose worshipers had gone. The air was redolent of incense, the darkness was relieved by only a dim, ruddy light, and all was silent—no, not quite! At the far end of the long room a voice was singing softly, a woman's voice raised in a trembling, tear-heavy contralto:

"Since I, O Lord, am nothing unto thee,
See here thy sword, I make it keen and bright . . ."

"Alons, mes enfants, follow!" whispered Jules de Grandin as he tiptoed toward the rear of the shop.

Now the tableau came in view, clear-cut as a scene upon a stage. In an elevated niche like an altar place crouched a green stone image slightly larger than man-size, the sightless eyes of its four faces staring out in cold, malevolent oblivious-ness. Below it, cross-legged on a scarlet cushion, his hands folded palm-upward in his lap, was a remarkably handsome young man dressed in an ornate Oriental costume, but these we passed by at a glance, for in the foreground, kneeling with her forehead pressed against the floor, was Melanie Thur-mond dressed as she had been when she took her fateful vow and had the ring of Siva put upon her hand. Her hands were raised above her bowed head, and in them rested a long, curved scimitar, the ruddy lamplight gleaming on its jeweled hilt and bright blade with ominous redness.

"Forgive, forgive!" we heard her sob, and saw her beat her forehead on the floor in utter self-abasement. "Have pity on the worm that creeps upon the dust before thy feet—"

"Forgiveness shall be thine," the man responded slowly,

"when dead kine crop the grass, when the naked rend their clothes and when a shining radiance becomes a void of blackness."

"Have mercy on the insect crawling at thy feet," the prostrate woman sobbed. "Have pity on the lowly thing—"

"Have done!" he ordered sharply. "Give me the sword."

She roused until she crouched upon her knees before him, raised the scimitar and pressed its blade against her lips and brow in turn, then, head bent low, held it out to him. He took it, balancing it between his hands for a moment, then drew a silk handkerchief from his sleeve and slowly began polishing the blade with it. The woman bent forward again to lay her brow against the floor between her outstretched hands, then straightened till she sat upon her crossed feet and bent her head back till her slender flowerlike throat was exposed. "I wait the stroke of mercy, Master and Lord," she whispered as she closed her eyes. " 'Twere better far to die at thy hands than to live cut off from the sunshine of thy favor. . . ."

There was something wrong with the green god. I could not tell quite what it was; it might have been a trick of light and shadow, or the whorls of incense spiraling around it, but I could have sworn its arms were moving and its fixed, immobile features changing expression.

There was something wrong with me, too. A feeling of complete inadequacy seemed to spread through me. My self-esteem seemed oozing out of every pore, my legs felt weak, I had an almost irresistible desire to drop upon my knees before the great green idol.

"*Oom, mani padme hong!*" de Grandin cried, his voice a little high and thin with excitement. "*Oom, mani padme hong!*"

Why I did I had no idea, but suddenly I echoed his invocation, at the top of my voice, *"Oom, mani padme hong!"*

Costello's rumbling bass took up the chant, and crying the unfamiliar syllables in chorus we advanced toward the seated man and kneeling woman and the great, green gloating idol. *"Oom, mani padme hong!"*

The man half turned and raised his hands in supplication to the image, but even as he did so something seemed to happen in the niche. The great green statue trembled on its base, swayed backward, forward—rocked as if it had been shaken by a sudden blast of wind, then without warning toppled from its embrasure, crushing the man seated at its feet as a dropped tile might crush a beetle.

For a long moment we stood staring at the havoc, the fallen idol lying athwart the crushed, broken body of the man, the blood that spread in a wide, ever-broadening pool about them, and the girl who wept through lowered lids and beat her little fists against her breast, unmindful of the tragedy.

"Quickly, my friends," bade de Grandin. "Go to the dressing room and find her clothes, then join me here.

"Oom, mani padme hong! the gods are dead, there is no power or potency in them, my little flower," he told the girl. *"Oom, mani padme hong!"* he bent and took her right hand in his, seizing the great ring that glowed upon her forefinger and drawing it away. *"Oom, mani padme hong!* The olden gods are powerless—they have gone back to that far hell from whence they hailed—" The ring came off as if it had been several sizes too large and he lifted her in his arms gently.

"Make haste, my friends," he urged. "None saw us enter; none shall see us leave. Tomorrow's papers will record a mystery, but there will be no mention of this poor one's name in it. Oh, be quick, I do beseech you!"

"Now," I demanded as I refilled the glasses, "are you going to explain, or must the Sergeant and I choke it out of you?"

The little laughter wrinkles at the outer corners of his eyes deepened momentarily. *"Non, mes amis,"* he replied, "violence will not be required, I assure you. First of all, I assume you would be interested to know how it was we overcame that green monstrosity and his attendant by our chant?"

"Nothin' less, sor," Costello answered. "Bedad, I hadn't anny idea what it meant, or why we sang it, but I'm here to say it sounded good to me—I got a kick out o' repeating it wid ye, but why it wuz I dunno."

"You know the history of Gautama Buddha, one assumes?"

"I niver heard o' him before, sor."

"Suel dammage! However"—he paused to take a long sip from his glass, then—"here are the facts: Siddhartha Gautama Buddha was born in India some five hundred years before the opening of our era. He grew up in a land priest-ridden and god-ridden. There was no hope—no pride of ancestry nor anticipation of immortality—for the great mass of the people, who were forever fixed in miserable existence by the rule of caste and the divine commands of gods whom we should call devils. Buddha saw the wickedness of this, and after years of meditation preached a new and hopeful gospel. He first denied the power of the gods by whose authority the priests held sway, and later denied their very existence. His followers increased by thousands and by tens of thousands; they washed the cursed caste marks from their foreheads, proclaimed themselves emancipated, denied the priests' authority and the existence of the gods by whom they had been terrorized and down-trodden for generations. Gautama Buddha, their leader, they hailed and honored with this chant: *'Oom, mani padme hong!*—Hail, thou Gem of

the Lotus!' From the Bay of Bengal to the Himalayas the
thunder of their greeting to their master rolled like a mighty
river of emancipation, and the power of it emptied the rock
temples of the olden deities, left the priests without offerings
on which to fatten. Sometimes it even overthrew the very
evil gods themselves. I mean that literally. There are recorded instances where bands of Buddhists entering into
heathen temples have by the very repetition of 'Oom, mani
padme hong!' caused rock-hewn effigies of those evil forces
men called Vishnu and Siva to topple from their altars. Yes,
it is so.

"En conséquence, tonight when I saw the poor misguided
mademoiselle about to make a sacrifice of herself to that
four-faced caricature of Satan I called to mind the greeting
to the Lord Gautama which in olden days had rocked him
and his kind from their high thrones, and raised the ancient
battle cry of freedom once more. Tiens, he knew his master,
that one. The Lord Gautama Buddha had driven him back
to whatever hell-pool he and his kind came from in the olden
days; his strength and power to drive him back was still
potent. Did not you see it with your own four eyes, my
friends?"

"U'm," I admitted somewhat grudgingly. "You think it
was the power of the Green God that called Melanie back to
The Light of Asia tonight?"

"Partly, beyond question. She wore his ring, and material
things have great power on things spiritual, just as spiritual
things have much influence on the material. Also it might
well have been a case of utter frustration. She might have
said in effect, 'What is the use?' Her lover had been killed,
her hopes of happiness blasted, her whole world knocked to
pieces. She might well have reasoned: 'I am powerless to
fight against my fate. The strength of the Green God is too

great. I am doomed; why not admit it; why struggle hope-lessly and helplessly? Why not go to Kabanta and admit my utter defeat, the extinction of my personality, and take what-ever punishment awaits me, even though it be death? Sooner or later I must yield. Why not sooner than later? To struggle futilely is only to prolong the agony and make his final tri-umph all the greater.' These things she may have said to her-self. Indeed, did she not intimate as much to us when we in-terviewed her?

"Yes," he nodded like a china mandarin on a mantelpiece, "it is unquestionably so, my friends, and but for Jules de Grandin—and the Lord Gautama Buddha assisted by my good friends Trowbridge and Costello—it might have been that way. *Eh bien,* I and the Buddha, with your kind as-sistance, put an end to their fine schemes, did we not?"

"You seriously think it was the force of the Green God that killed Wade Hardison?" I asked.

"I seriously do, my friend. That and naught else. The Green One was a burning glass that focused rays of hatred as a lens does sunlight, and through his power the never-to-be-sufficiently-anathematized Kabanta was enabled to destroy the poor young Hardison completely."

He stabbed a small, impressive forefinger at me. "Consider, if you please: What was the situation tonight? Siva had tri-umphed. He had received a blood-sacrifice in the person of the poor young Hardison; he was about to have another in the so unfortunate Mademoiselle Melanie, then *pouf* comes Jules de Grandin and Friend Trowbridge and Friend Cos-tello to repeat the chant which in the olden days had driven him from power. Before the potency of our chant to the Buddha the Green One felt his power ebbing slowly from him as he retreated to that far place where he had been driven aforetime by the Lord Gautama. And what did he do as he fell back? *Tenez,* he took revenge for his defeat on Kabanta. He cast the statue of himself—a very flattering likeness, no doubt—down from its altar place and utterly crushed the man who had almost but not quite enabled him to triumph. He was like a naughty child that kicks or bites the person who has promised it a sweet, then failed to make good the promise—"

"But that idol was a senseless piece of carved stone," I protested. "How could it—"

"*Ah bah,* you irritate me, my friend. Of course the idol was a senseless piece of stone, but *that for which it stood was neither stone nor senseless.* The idol was but the representation of the evil power lurking in the outer darkness as the tiger lurks in ambush. Or let us put it this way: The idol is the material and visible door through which the spiritual and invisible force of evil we call Siva is enabled to penetrate into our human world.

"Through that doorway he came into the world, through it he was forced to retreat before the power of our denial of his potency. So to speak, he slammed the door as he retreated—and caught Kabanta between door and jamb. *En tout cas,* he is dead, that miserable Kabanta. We are well rid of him, and the door is fast closed on the evil entity which he and the unwitting and unfortunate Mademoiselle Melanie let back into the world for a short time.

"Yes," he nodded solemnly again. "It is so. I say it. I also say that I should like my glass refilled, if you will be so gracious, Friend Trowbridge."

GUN FROM GOTHAM

ROBERT LESLIE BELLEM

H E WAS A NICE LOOKING GUY WITH "NEW YORK" WRITTEN all over him. Here in Hollywood we go for sport jackets and plaid coats; baggy slacks in rainbow colors. They dress differently back on the Atlantic Coast: tailored business suits, white shirts, cravats of conservative pattern. You can spot an easterner eleven times out of ten.

I spotted this one the minute he ankled into my office and asked me if I was Dan Turner, the private snoop. I said: "Yeah. What can I do you for?"

"Help me locate a missing millionaire." He turned on a big infectious smile that irradiated his youthful puss like splashed sunshine. He had sandy hair, a dozen freckles on his trumpet, and his greenish glims were steady. "My name's Lanahan; Oliver Lanahan. My friends call me Ollie. I'm an op for the Consolidated Agency in the big town."

I did a double take. He didn't look like a gumshoe; didn't have the hard-boiled air. However, maybe they were picking them that way these days in the Manhattan offices; copying the F.B.I. formula. G-men don't look tough either, but appearances can be deceptive.

I said: "Credentials, Ollie?"

He seemed to like my friendly use of his nickname. He showed me his New York card, his badge, his roscoe, and the

Sullivan law permit to carry it. "I need a private man, a local, to give me a lift," he said.

"I see. Drink?" I poured a pair from the fifth of Vat 69 in my desk. "What's this caper about a missing millionaire?"

Lanahan tossed off his snort. "Name of Harry Pencroft. Rich family on Long Island but not social register. Harry's the only son. Late twenties, tall, dark; the wolf type if a guy can be a wolf and a black sheep at the same time." He put a snapshot on my blotter.

I studied it. The party in the picture looked thirtyish instead of twentyish but that might have been from dissipation or ill health—or lousy photography. The background was out of focus on a blurry flower pattern and the bozo himself wore commonplace threads that didn't fit like a millionaire's tailoring. I took an immediate dislike to the coldly staring peepers and the grinning kisser; it was an expression that seemed more sardonic than mirthful. If he was a wolf, it was his dough the dames fell for, not his winning personality.

"You wouldn't take him for a lady killer," I remarked.

Lanahan stared. "Where did you get that idea?"

"What idea?"

"Him being a killer."

I said: "You misunderstood me. By 'lady killer' I mean a lug that cuts a swath with the fillies."

"Oh. Well, the funny part is, some folks think he *did* kill a lady. Not a lady exactly; a chorus girl. That's why I'm out here hunting for him."

"Whistle the patter," I said.

"Okay. Pencroft and this chorine were pretty chummy. After a while, though, she started needling him to marry her and he told her nothing doing. She died."

"Heartbreak?"

He said. "No, veronal. Overdose of sleeping tablets. The

law called it accidental, not knowing she'd been jilted."

"You think it was suicide?"

"I'm not paid to think; I'm giving you the facts. Pencroft's name never entered the case officially; but the dead girl had a sister who figured it was his fault. This sister didn't beef to the police, however."

"No?"

Lanahan shook his head. "She probably realized she had nothing tangible on Pencroft. Maybe he was morally responsible for the overdose of veronal; but not legally. The law doesn't electrocute a man for jilting a woman who subsequently eats poison. Get the picture?"

"Thus far," I said. "Keep singing."

"Well, so then the sister decided to take the law in her own hands. She threatened to kill Pencroft; actually took one shot at him and missed. He got scared, drew a hundred thousand bucks from the bank, and hiked out."

I said: "Traveled west, hunh?"

"Yes. Naturally his family started worrying. They hired Consolidated to locate him and I drew the assignment. I traced him all the way to Hollywood, then lost the scent."

"Have you asked the cops to help? The Missing Persons division?"

"Hell, no!" he looked indignant. "We don't want cops or newspaper headlines on this thing. Family orders. My job is to find Pencroft and drag him away from danger."

I said: "Danger? The west coast ought to be his safest hideout from the defunct doll's pistol-packing sister in New York."

"She's not in New York; she's here. I spotted her by accident this morning. She must have trailed him."

"Oh-oh!" I torched a gasper. "Gunning for him?"

"What else? So I've got to locate him before she does—and

I need local assistance; somebody who knows Hollywood. I'd read a lot about you, and—" He stripped ten fifties from a roll of greenery. "What do you say?"

I took the geetus. "You've hired a partner, Ollie. Truck on back to wherever you're staying; give me a couple of hours so I can put my wires out. I'll phone you as soon as I'm ready to begin moving."

"Thanks." He gave me his hotel address; lammed. And just as he went out the door, I picked up my phone, dialed the grog shop where I knew I'd catch Joey Brockman at this time of day.

Brockman was what you might call king of the newsboys around town, a self-appointed czar who looked after the interests of everybody that peddled papers on filmland's street corners. I had done him some favors in the past and I had a working arrangement with him that allowed me to muster his services when I needed them. This agreement came in handy at times; a private ferret frequently requires more eyes and ears than he was born with, and you can't beat a squad of newsies for picking up stray hunks of information.

"Joey?" I said when he came on the line. "Dan Turner. How's for helping me locate a guy?"

"Sure thing, Sherlock. Shoot me the dope."

I gave him a description of the missing millionaire; used the snapshot on my desk to make the verbal portrait clear, complete. I mentioned the loose-fitting threads, the sardonic grin, the staring peepers; added any other details that might do any good. Finishing up, I said: "I understand he's under cover; but a bozo on the lam usually buys newspapers. One of your lads may remember dealing with him."

"I'll see what we can do. You want him lumped up if we find him, or shall I just call you back?"

"Just call me," I said, and rang off. Then, keeping my fingers crossed, I settled down to await results. Whereupon another prospective client barged into the office.

This time it was a red-haired cupcake with big blue glims and a refrigerated voice cold enough to congeal your gravy. "I want to hire you, Mr. Turner," she said. "I want you to find a rat for me; a rat named Harry Pencroft. You see, he killed my sister."

I took one flabbergasted gander at her; realized coincidence had slapped me in the mush with a screwy load of luck. The luck could be good or bad, depending on which way I played the hand. Undoubtedly this gorgeous red-haired tomato was the one Lanahan had told me about; but I certainly didn't dare let her know I'd already been paid to hunt the Pencroft bozo and whisk him out of her reach.

With my map completely deadpan I said: "That sounds interesting, Miss—er, Miss—"

"Starr. Prudence Starr."

Her monicker was a misfit; the first part, anyhow. A Prudence ought to be meek and mild, colorless and self-effacing. This cutie didn't meet those specifications by a damned sight. Her frock was pastel green silk with big print designs on it, and it clung to her contours like a caress. The contours deserved it; spectacular was the only word to describe them. Her stems were shapely, her complexion gorgeous, and her wavy tresses were the color of a bonfire in a dark night. Moreover, she wore perfume; a fragrance that reached out and filled you full of tingles.

I said: "About your sister. How did this Harry Pencroft murder her and what are the cops doing about it?"

"Nothing, because it wasn't murder in the eyes of the law. I didn't say Pencroft murdered her. I said he killed her."

"Is there a distinction?"

"Yes. He refused to marry her and she committed suicide

with an overdose of sleeping medicine. Now he's in Hollywood and I'm after him."

"With what purpose in mind?" I said, tensing myself.

She regarded me calmly. "That part is none of your business. Your job is to find him; I'll attend to the rest of it."
She opened her big green wool handbag, dredged around in
it, produced a thin wad of cabbage. "I can afford two hundred dollars. May I have a receipt, please?"

"Yeah," I rasped. "Here it is." And I jumped her, fed her
a stinger across the chops that sent her reeling. I hated to
do it but I'm a sentimental guy and sometimes I get chivalrous inclinations. This was one of the times.

Maybe it doesn't sound chivalrous to bop a jessie when
she's not expecting it, but the paradox was valid in this case.
What would happen if she caught up with Harry Pencroft?
Obviously she intended to cream him in his tracks. And then
she'd wind up sitting in the gas chamber at San Quentin,
which would be a hell of a thing.

So I followed her as she staggered; wrapped my arms
around her and squeezed. She moaned, tried to claw herself
loose from my clinch. "You—you dirty heel—!"

"Quiet, hon," I panted, and managed to glom her handbag. It had a rod in it; a .25 auto, stubby as a toy and deadly
as a rattlesnake. I'd got a hinge at the heater when she offered
to pay me the two centuries; which was why I'd gone into
action in such a thundering yank. Now, abstracting the
miniature cannon, I felt better. I even felt good enough to
release the cookie who owned it, much as I enjoyed holding
her.

I said reprovingly: "Naughty, naughty. Little girls shouldn't
tote artillery. You might hurt somebody."

"Give m-me that g-gun!"

"Not by a damned sight, sis. I'm a private dick, but that's

something like being a cop. Cops are sworn to uphold law and order, and California has a statute against committing killery. I have to live up to the rules."

"If you th-think you can stop me from—"

"Thanks," I said.

She stared at me, her optics brimming with brine. "What do you m-mean, thanks?"

"You just gave me an idea," I said. "That's just what I *will* do. I'll stop you from, period."

"Wait," she quavered. "You've got it all wrong. I'm not going to sh-shoot Pencroft. I only w-want to frighten him; to see him grovel on his knees, beg for his life."

"You're not a very good liar, babe. The story stinks."

"Oh-h-h, please—"

I moved close to her. "Look. This may sound tough, but it's for your own good. I'm going to tie you up; handcuff you to something substantial here in the office. Then I'll go hunt the Pencroft louse and warn him to powder before you can catch up with him. Neat, eh?"

"You rotten double crosser!" she breathed unsteadily. "What good do you think that will do? I'll get him sooner or later. I won't give up until I do."

I said: "That's up to you; but at least it won't happen anywhere in my bailiwick and it won't be on my conscience. Now pardon me while I fit you with a pair of bracelets." I got out the nippers; stalked her.

She backed away. "If you're going to d-do that, let me fasten my g-garters first." She pulled up the hem of her skirt, and I thought for a minute she was trying to bribe me, but I was haywire. She had another .25 automatic in a chamois holster rigged to her thigh, and she unshipped the rod before I guessed her intentions.

"Now," she drew a bead on my tripes. "We'll see if you handcuff me."

"Ix-nay!" I caterwauled. "You can't—"

She raised the roscoe, slapped me on the side of the noggin. For a wren who didn't look hefty, she packed a terrific wallop. I staggered, felt my knees turning to jelly. She maced me another swat that put me down for the count with bells jangling in my think-tank. I passed out.

The bells were still tinkling when I snapped out of my coma. I stirred on the floor, discovered I was all in one piece. As a matter of fact, I now had an extra part: a lump on my dome the size of Grant's Tomb that throbbed like an abscessed tooth. Barring this, I seemed to be okay.

If I was okay, though, why did those bells keep on clanging? I pushed myself groggily upright, looked around to ask the red-haired cupcake if she heard what I heard. She wasn't on deck to answer. She'd scrammed.

Then I realized my phone was ringing.

I lurched over to the desk, lifted the instrument from its cradle. The bells stopped. "Yeah?" I said.

"Sherlock? This is Joey Brockman. Excuse me for pestering you, but—"

"You're not pestering me. I told you to call me."

"Well, sure, only you didn't say to call back twice. I mean I didn't know you had a secretary these days, and I sort of wondered if she slipped you the message."

I felt the short hairs prickling at the nape of my neck. "A secretary?" I yeeped. "Are you dopey?"

"Not so you could prove it," he said defensively. "All I know is I phoned you a while ago and some jane said she was your stenographer, and you was out and she would be happy to take the message, and—"

"Damned right I was out," I growled. "I was unconscious

from a clonk on the thatch delivered by this alleged steno. What was the message? Please, for Pete's sake don't say you told that damsel anything about the guy I asked you to hunt for."

He sounded disturbed, but he wasn't half as disturbed as I was. "Yeah," he said. "I gave her alla dope." Then he repeated it for my benefit, to the effect that a man answering the description of the snapshot on my desk was living in a rented bungalow on Rampart Street and had been seen as recently as this morning, buying an *Examiner*. As usual, he had acted in a furtive manner; as if scared someone might be watching him.

I screamed: "And you told this to the jane on the phone?"

"Yeah. I didn't know—"

"Okay, bub. Skip it. It wasn't your fault." Then I rang off; twisted the dial so fast it gave out smoke. I got a connection with Ollie Lanahan's hotel and presently Ollie himself answered. I said: "Lanahan? Turner this end. Hell's to pay."

"What do you mean?"

I fed him the whole ugly lump. "That dead chorine's sister, Prudence Starr, was in to see me. Coincidence? Sure, based on the fact that I'm the best private sniff in town if you want to get technical. When *you* needed help in hunting Pencroft, you came to me, didn't you? All right; so she came to me for the same reason. Yeah. She wanted me to find Pencroft for her. No, I didn't tell her you'd already hired me for that job. I played it close to my vest."

"Smart," he said.

I made a bitter mouth. "Not smart enough. She had a gat, and I took it away from her. Then she had another gat and bashed me with it. While I was senseless, one of my connections called and she answered the phone."

"Well?"

"Here's the tough part. My connection had located Pencroft's hideaway and he spilled his guts, thinking he was talking to my secretary."

"Good God—!"

"You said it, chum. She's probably on her way right now with homicidal notions. Your missing millionaire may be looking down the muzzle of her fowling piece any moment. I'll give you his address and you'd better flag your diapers over there in a hell of a dither if you crave to save him from having his giblets punctured."

Lanahan's voice pitched to a high, taut register. "I'll want you with me. Maybe it's more than I can handle alone. I—"

"Look," I said. "You slipped me five C's to find the guy. So I just gave you his number. Now it's in your lap. I wish no further dealings with Prudence; she hits too hard."

"Five hundred more, Turner. Hell, man, you can't throw me down now. I'll make it a thousand."

Well, what the hell? I'm in this racket for all the dough I can collect; I'm trying to save up enough war bonds so I can retire some day and get fat. I said: "Be outside your hotel, pronto. I'm on my way." Then I dashed down to my parked jalopy, put the spurs to it.

Lanahan was waiting for me as I drew up at the curb in front of the Hollywood Roosevelt. He bounced in alongside me and I fed another charge of ethyl to my cylinders; lit a shuck for Rampart Street. Dusk was falling and traffic was pretty thin; the dinner hour generally clears the boulevard. I made knots.

Presently we found the stash we wanted; the little bungalow where Harry Pencroft was allegedly holed up. I blipped to the shabby porch, thumbed the bell-push. Nothing happened. I rapped a blister on the portal; again no dice. Bye and bye I tried the knob.

It turned.

Lanahan said: "Let's go in." Then he raised his voice. "Pencroft!" All he got for an answer was echoes.

Standing at the threshold, I tried the same thing myself. I yelled: "Hey, Pencroft!" But Pencroft didn't respond.

There was another cottage next door, and now an elderly hag came out of it to stand on her own porch and take a hinge at us. She had gray hair, bleary optics, and a shape like a bundle of soiled laundry. She also had a serious case of hiccups. "If you men *heek* are looking for the *heek* gent who lives there, I *heek* ain't saw him since *heek* morning."

I said: "Has a girl been here recently?"

"Girl? I *heek* wouldn't know. What *heek* kind of girl?"

"One with red hair and curves."

"Nope. Not in the past *heek* hour. I been at my window that long." She patted herself on the stomach and leered. "Indi-*heek*-gestion."

"Try a little gin," I said.

She looked indignant. "How the hell do you *heek* suppose I got the hic-*heek*-hiccups in the first place? Ignorant, that's what you are. You *heek* don't know a lady when she's *heek* drunk when you see one." She went inside, muttering.

Lanahan turned to me. "Well, at least we know the Starr baby wasn't here. That's something. But she may be on her way. I still say we ought to go in."

"Okay. Lead the way." We ankled into a short entrance hall. "See if you can find a light switch."

He fumbled, located one, clicked it. No lights came on. An uneasy premonition nipped me. I didn't like the joint's gloom, the silence, the pungent stink of gas or cleaning solvent that seemed to saturate the dead air. I wondered why the electricity was off. I wondered why Pencroft didn't answer when we called to him. Was he hiding? Or was he—?

I snicked on my pencil flashlight. "What the hell!"

"Huh?" Lanahan whispered.

"Look."

And I aimed my torch at a figure sprawled on the faded front room carpet, supine and motionless against the dim flower design. It was the citizen we were searching for, and there were two or three bullet holes in his ellybay. These had rendered him deader than Confederate money.

"Pencroft!" Ollie Lanahan gulped. "That girl got here ahead of us after all! She—she—" He got a grip on himself. "It's a police job now." He scurried across the room, picked up a phone. "What number do I call?"

I took it away from him. "I'll handle it. I've dialed Headquarters so often I can do it in the dark." I twirled the dingus, got an answer; asked for my friend Dave Donaldson of the homicide squad.

Presently Dave's voice rumbled in the receiver. "Yeah, what's wanted and who wants it?"

"Dan Turner squalling. I'm with a Consolidated Agency op from New York and we've just stumbled over a cadaver, a missing millionaire with a gut full of slugs. The address is—Oh, hell!"

"Hunh? What's that? What did you say?"

I yelled: "Hell's boiling over!" and hurled the phone away from me. I wasn't kidding. There was a roar, a crackle, a spurt of flame from one corner of the room; whereupon all of a sudden the whole damned tepee was afire.

I knew, abruptly, what had caused the smell I'd noticed as I first ankled into the stash. It was kerosene or gasoline spilled around by some incendiary maniac. "A trap!" I screeched at Ollie Lanahan. "Let's get out of here before we're both converted into slabs of roast pork!"

He pelted toward me and we made for the door where a

licking sheet of flame blocked us. The wikiup was like tinder and there was just enough draft to spread the blaze to furnace dimensions. "We're caught!" Lanahan gasped.

"Duck your noggin. Cover your mush with your arms. We'll go through!" I yeeped back at him. Then we surged through the barricade of fire, Ollie first. He moved faster than lubricated lightning but I overtook and passed him before we gained the outside porch. Even so, my haircut got a singe that a professional barber would have envied. We hit the sidewalk; stopped.

Ollie panted: "How in the name of—?"

"It was a touch-off," I grunted. "Maybe a wire or a length of string hooked to the phone and running to a gadget in the corner. Lifting the phone pulled the trigger. Blooie."

"But—but wh-why—"

"To cover the kill," I said. "Use your gray matter. Prudence Starr bumped the guy and rigged a dead-fall for me."

"For you?"

I nodded grimly. "She knew I was hunting him. She found that out by intercepting a telephone message from one of my helpers. That same message gave her the location of Pencroft's hideaway. She came here, bumped him, and fixed her incendiary contraption. She realized I'd be showing up pretty soon, and that I'd discover Pencroft's remnants. In which case I'd be in a position to put the finger on her as the killer."

"I get it. She wanted you to die so you couldn't sic the law on her. That way she'd keep her own skirts clear."

"Yeah," I said. "Here comes the fire engines. Somebody turned in an alarm. Let's go contact Donaldson and give him the sinister score."

"But—Pencroft's body—still inside that house—"

I said: "He'll never feel the heat. Come on." And we

piled into my jalopy; headed downtown. Fifteen minutes later we were in Dave Donaldson's sanctum at headquarters, spilling the works and explaining the details.

Dave's beefy features wore a thoughtful expression when we'd finished beating our gums. "It's open and shut," he said. "This red-haired Starr dame croaked Pencroft; motive, vengeance. Burning his corpse won't help her, because no matter what condition it's in when the firemen snag it out of the embers we can establish the fact of murder from the bullet wounds."

"You can establish the body's identity, too," Ollie Lanahan put in. "Turner and I both saw it before the place started blazing." He looked glum. "Which just about washes it up, as far as I'm concerned. I'll wire a report to New York that I found Pencroft but he's dead. Meantime you'll be arresting Prudence Starr for the kill—and I hope you get a conviction."

I said: "So do I. I'm not forgetting how she bopped me over the steeple. As a matter of fact I think I'll go snooping for her right now, lone wolf."

Donaldson glowered at me. "That's a police job. I'll attend to the dragnet stuff." He stood up. "No interference from you, understand?"

"Sure." I made for the door, cocked a snook at him. "Write me a letter." And I powdered with my hair in a braid. Any time I take orders from a numskull flatfoot, elephants will be nesting in hydrangea bushes.

Besides, I had a clue.

Earlier in this screwball clambake, at the time I'd taken a roscoe from the Starr cupcake's handbag, I'd noticed something else in that big green wool reticule: a receipted hotel statement. The printed letterhead hadn't registered on me very hard then, but I remembered it now—both the name and the address. If Donaldson hadn't been so supercilious about not needing my assistance, I might have given him the information and a chance to cover himself with dubious glory. The way things now stood, though, I decided to make my own play and crow over him later.

Besides, I was sore, I'd been taken for a sucker and I dislike to be thought stupid. A private dick can't afford that sort of shenanigans. Rumors might start floating around that I was a bit deficient in the brains department, and my business would be shot to hell. I aimed my bucket for Sunset and Western; the hotel where I figured Prudence Starr was holed up. I hoped to Whozit she was still there.

She was.

Five bucks to the desk clerk bought me her room number and a go-ahead signal. I stalked upstairs, loosened my .32 in the armpit rig where I always tote it; slapped my knuckles on the door. "Telegram, ma'am," I said.

The portal opened and the red-haired dish blinked at me. She'd exchanged her pastel green frock for a negligee that flowed around her delishful shape like poured mist, and when she tabbed me, she turned eleventeen shades of pallid. "You said—I—I thought it was—"

"Sorry to disillusion you, hon," I snarled truculently, and drew my heater; shoved it ferninst her brisket. "I lied. There's no telegram. There's only a .32 caliber token for your delicate tripes in case you try anything fancy. Back up."

She cringed away from me. "You can't—can't sh-shoot me in c-cold b-blood! You w-wouldn't d-do a thing like that j-just because I hit you over the head!"

"Quiet," I said, crossing the threshold and kicking the door shut behind me. "Put some clothes on in a hurry. We're about to go places."

"Go wh-where?"

I growled: "You'll know when you get there and meet the minions of the law. Do you get dressed or do I take you out the way you are? Decide quick."

"But—but I don't—"

I stepped toward her; shoved my ferocious scowl close to her piquant puss. "I whapped you across the map once, remember? I'l! do it again if you don't obey. This time it'll be harder."

"All r-right. Close y-your eyes."

"And let you bash me? Ix-nay."

"Well, th-then, turn your b-back."

I grinned. "You play too rough, babe. Nothing stirring."

Her lilting shoulder slumped despondently. "You might tell me wh-what it's all about."

"Don't you know? It's croakery."

"Cr—I don't understand."

"Homicide," I said. "Garb yourself."

She turned away from me, let the negligee drip off. Under it she was wearing a slip, so there was really no reason for her jittery modesty; you couldn't see anything through heavy white satin. While she was investing herself in a dress, I moved to the room's wall phone, got myself hooked up with police headquarters, asked for Dave Donaldson.

"Well?" he barked.

"Turner calling. Meet me in front of the Hollywood Roosevelt as fast as you can roll. I've got Prudence Starr and we can use Ollie Lanahan in the identification."

Dave exploded like a boiler with a defective flue. "Huh? You got Prudence Starr? Well, I'll be go to hell! How did—?"

"The Hollywood Roosevelt. Fast," I said, and hung up to save my eardrum from unnecessary questions. By that time the red-haired cookie was embellished in street attire. She blinked woefully at me. "Won't you p-please explain?"

"Deceased guys need no explanation, Tutz." I prodded her toward the corridor. "Especially deceased millionaires named Harry Pencroft. Forward march."

"Pencroft? He's d-dead?"

I leered at her. "You tell me." Then we went down to my vee-eight coupe and zoomed away from there in a cloud of peanut butter. Seven minutes subsequently and we parked in front of Ollie Lanahan's hotel. Donaldson was just squealing to an anchorage in his official sedan.

He bounced out, raced across the pavement, yanked my door open. "So this is the Starr wren!"

"So I believe. Lanahan can confirm it. I imagine he left you as soon as I pulled my freight?"

"Yeah. He said he was coming here to the hotel to prepare a report for his home office."

I set fire to a gasper. "Let's go up and get this doll identi-fied." We trooped indoors, crossed the lobby, rode an ele-vator to the New York bozo's floor and made for his portal. I thumped it. "Ollie."

Then I gathered my hundred and ninety pounds of heft, backed off, hurled myself at the woodwork and smashed it inward with a hell of a crunch. The Consolidated dick was standing in the middle of the room with two packed grips in his mitts and a flabbergasted expression on his pan. "Tur-ner—!" he said.

"Yeah. You going somewhere, friend?"

"Why, er, ah, I, that is, I mean—"

I said: "Prudence. Take a gander at this ginzo."

The red-haired twist entered with Donaldson; stared and let her peepers bulge like oysters being squeezed. "Why, that's—that's—but you said he was dead!"

"Ollie Lanahan is the one that's defunct," I grunted. "The genuine Ollie Lanahan, private op for Consolidated of New

York. This guy's an impostor. He's the millionaire we're hunting. I mean this is Harry Pencroft." Then I added: "Pencroft, murderer. Get it?"

"See here!" the dapper character yipped. "If this is a rib, I don't like the smell of it."

I gave him a sour sneer. "It's no rib, bub. Your name's Pencroft. Miss Starr will back me up."

"You'd take the word of a killer? A girl who—"

"She's not the killer. You are. I said that once. How many times must I repeat it?" Then I dished him the business. "Look. You're Pencroft. You caused the death of a chorus girl back east. Maybe she committed suicide because you jilted her; or maybe you shoved an overdose of veronal down her throat by brute force, or gave it to her in a drink she didn't suspect. The point is, she kicked the bucket and you were responsible.

"Her sister, Prudence here, started gunning for you. So you drew a load of shekels from your bank account and lammed to California. This part of the story I'm sure of, because you told me yourself. The rest I'll fill in with guesswork."

"Your guesswork stinks," he said sullenly.

I stared him down. "When you sit in the gas chamber, it'll stink worse. Your family engaged the Consolidated Agency to put a tracer on you. They assigned a snoop named Ollie Lanahan. He found you here in Hollywood. You were scared he'd been hired by Prudence Starr, so you bumped him off."

"Nuts!"

"Then you glommed his papers, badge, and roscoe. You exchanged identities with him. Now comes what you thought was the clever part. Posing as a detective named Lanahan, you called me into the mess. You wanted me to discover the real Lanahan's remainders and identify them as your own.

Then you rigged an incendiary gadget which would destroy the corpse so that nobody could later learn about the mistaken identification. You, still using Lanahan's name, would scram out of town and disappear. The news would go out that Harry Pencroft was dead. This would cause Miss Starr to quit gunning for you."

"A likely story!"

I said: "An ugly story, chum. It might have worked, though, except for the fact that you made one bad error. You showed me a snapshot, allegedly of Pencroft, but actually of Lanahan, the detective you croaked. It had certain peculiarities; the background was out of focus on a blurry flower pattern, the glims had an odd stare, the clothes were mussed and there was a sardonic grin on the subject's kisser.

"Okay. The instant I lamped the corpse I saw the same faded flower background, which was the carpet; the same staring glims and sardonic smile and mussed duds. In other words, the picture had been snapped by aiming a camera straight down and photographing the corpse.

"Since you were the one who had the snapshot, you knew the bozo was defunct when you first came to me and asked me to help find him. Moreover, while we were still in the bungalow, you'd crossed the room and found a phone *in the dark*. So you'd been there before. That made you a prime murder suspect. It indicated that you must have rigged the sudden fire."

He laughed unpleasantly. "Determined to shield this woman here, aren't you?"

"Sure, because she was plain coincidence. Your plot had nothing to do with her except to throw her off your scent; but when you learned she was in town and had visited me, asked me to find Pencroft, you naturally hoped to throw suspicion on her. She was a natural fall guy. If she went up for cooling the false Harry Pencroft—or rather, the real Ollie Lanahan—then you, Pencroft, would never need to worry about her again. But that snapshot tripped you. As soon as the bungalow fire started, I realized you were guilty."

"Then why didn't you arrest me?"

I said: "I had no proof at the time. I had to find Prudence Starr first, so she could identify you."

"Which I do," the red-haired doll grated.

It was too much for him. "All right, I surrender." Then he pulled an unexpected fast one. He had these two grips in his dukes, and now he hurled them—one at Donaldson, one at me. I got smacked in the bellows; reeled off-balance. So did Dave. As we righted ourselves the dapper slug grabbed Prudence from behind; clamped his arms around her and held her, squirming, in front of him as a shield.

And he ducked out.

There was a scuffling noise in the corridor; a faint feminine whimper. Donaldson tugged at his service .38 and snarled: "I'll plug that scum if it's the last thing I do! Come on, bright-eyes. You started this shindig. Now I'll finish it!"

He was wrong though. From the hallway a small-caliber roscoe sneezed: *Ka-Chow! Chow!* and I heard the sound of something slumping, hitting the floor. I catapulted outside with Dave breathing fire and brimstone down my neck. Then we froze.

Pencroft, alias Lanahan, was stretched out deader than slapstick comedies. The Starr chick stood over him with a .25 auto in her dainty clutch. Smoke was coming out of the miniature cannon, and words were coming out of the jessie's firm crimson kisser. "I asked him to let me fix my garter."

I said: "And you had your rod in a thigh holster. I know. I had the same experience."

She nodded; looked at Donaldson. "You can take me to j-jail now. I've done what was necessary."

"Jail?" I said. "It was self-defense, wasn't it?"

"Y-yes."

I grinned. Then I laid hold of the lassie's arm and took her the hell out of there.

SECOND CHILDHOOD

JACK SNOW

"HE HAS COME BACK, JOHN," MISS LUCY STATED SIMPLY with a faint smile. "All the way back over all those years—what a bridge of memory he has crossed!"

The old lady sighed, her voice sounding thinly in the dying garden like the memory itself of a voice, just as the ruined blossoms and splotched leaves were silent mementoes of a once lovely garden.

"Is that what you wished to tell me, Miss Lucy?" I asked. The fragile body, withered as a leaf, leaned to me for support as we walked slowly down the garden path. "Merely that memories of your childhood are growing stronger? That is not uncommon, you know, with people of your age. As you approach the end of your long journey," I added, "memory becomes brilliantly clear and vivid and you recall many childhood scenes that have lain buried for long years in the depths of memory."

"Yes, yes, I know," answered Miss Lucy. "But this is something more—something more, John, than just memory. Willie has come back. He is just as he was when I was a little girl and we played in this very garden through the long summer days. I see him, John; I talked with him."

"Just who is this Willie?" I asked patiently, knowing that it was far better for Miss Lucy to discuss these fancies with me, her doctor and friend of long standing, than to close them away morbidly in her aging mind.

"Willie was my childhood playmate—my only playmate. I was a very lonely child and lived a solitary life here in this huge old house. There were only Father, my governess and the servants for companions, and they were poor enough companions for an imaginative child." Miss Lucy paused, fumbling among her memories. "Of my mother I recall nothing. I know her only as she appears in the painting which hangs in the library: a forceful-featured, stern-faced woman. "Strange," Miss Lucy went on musingly, "that with all her strength she yielded so easily to death and died so young."

I could not help adding silently in my own thoughts, "And equally strange that this fragile wisp of humanity beside me should endure and persevere against death for so long a time."

"Was Willie the son of one of the servants?" I prompted. Miss Lucy glanced at me in surprise.

"No, no!" she exclaimed with a bird-like little chirp. "I do not know really who he was. I know only that my earliest memories are of Willie. He was always with me. It is as though he had been born or had entered this world at the same time I did—accompanied me. Father and the others were at first amused when I told them about Willie. I was scarcely able to talk then. But as I grew older their amusement changed to impatience and then anger. They said I must stop all my foolishness about Willie. They never understood."

"You mean they never saw Willie?" I aske

"Oh, no! He was much too clever to a' him. He revealed himself only to me."

I sighed and faced the old lady. "Miss

you mean to tell me that this Willie of yours was nothing more than one of those dream children that lonely boys and girls sometimes invent when they are deprived of human playmates?"

Miss Lucy's faded old eyes opened wide with indignation as she replied stubbornly, "Now you are talking just like the others. I tell you Willie was very real—as real as I am. And," she concluded with triumph, "he has kept his word. He has done as he said he would—he has come back!"

"He told you he would come back?" I asked curiously.

"Threatened, rather," the old lady replied, staring into the shadows. "I can remember the scene as clearly as though it were only yesterday instead of seventy years ago. I was seventeen at the time. I had just met David and fallen in love with him. It seemed that within the space of an hour I had grown up, had stopped being a child and had become a woman.

"It was right here in this garden in the twilight of a faraway June night that I sent Willie away forever—or so I thought. I was to go to a ball with David that evening, and I was eager to begin dressing, so perhaps I was a little hasty and rude with Willie. I told him he must go away, that I was no longer a child. Oh, he was furious! He accused me of forsaking him for David. And really he was almost pathetic—so small and so angry as he turned from me and ran down the garden shouting to me that he would go, but that he would come back. There were actually tears in his black eyes —tears of rage," she added absently.

"Then Willie did not grow as you did; he remained a small child?"

"No," Miss Lucy replied, "Willie never changed. He was then and he is now just as I first remember him—a boy about seven years of age. He is dressed in the children's fashions of seventy years ago. Why," the old lady went on, the flicker of a smile haunting her face, "he still carries that ugly stone hatchet that he loves so well. He calls it his tomahawk. It is the only toy he ever had. He used to play Indian with it here in this garden when I was a child. Poor little Willie, it was so long ago. At least *he* has been faithful. Ten years meant nothing to him." The old lady's voice drifted vacantly and forlornly into the thickening shadows of the garden.

For a brief time we were both silent, lost in meditation. Then, feeling the chill and dampness of the garden as evening drew on, I escorted Miss Lucy to the house where I left a mild sleeping potion for her and cautioned Hannah, Miss Lucy's housekeeper and companion, not to leave her charge too much alone—melancholia and hallucinations grow out of solitude and loneliness. With that I departed for my house where I was long overdue for dinner.

As I walked the short distance to my own comfortable house, I reflected on Miss Lucy's unhappy life. As family physician and friend, I had known Miss Lucy as long as I had known anyone. Always everyone had referred to her as "Miss Lucy," and as "Miss Lucy" I, first as a child and then as a man, had known her. My earliest memories of her were of a beautiful but sad-faced woman in her early thirties. The death of her sweetheart in a tragic hunting accident a few days before the day set for their wedding had blighted her entire life. She had shut herself up in the gloomy house and lived out her days as a lonely recluse. And now this was the end. She was turning back to her childhood, seeking the companionship of that first friend—an imaginary child playmate.

"Truly," I ruminated, as I walked swiftly through the damp of that darkening October evening to the beckoning cheer of a hearty dinner and a warm fireside, "this was a splendid example of the evolution of the life span, moving from childhood to adulthood and back to childhood again—the completed circle." As I stepped over my threshold, and was greeted with the aroma of dinner waiting to be served, I forgot for the time all about Miss Lucy wandering in her dead garden with her pathetic imaginings.

From that time on I made it a point to look in on Miss Lucy at least once a week. Not that she needed medical care. But I knew that I was her only visitor, and someone from outside her own small world was necessary to keep her from sinking too deeply into her dreams. To all outward appearances my aged patient remained unchanged. And yet, I found myself disturbed by something in her manner—a furtive restlessness, an unexpressed apprehension that lurked in her tired old eyes.

At last one day I asked Miss Lucy the question, the answer to which, I felt sure, would explain the old lady's uneasiness. "Have you seen Willie lately?"

Miss Lucy started, then folding her thin hands, she regarded me quietly from pale gray eyes set in a lace filigree of tiny wrinkles.

"Yes, John," she murmured, "I see him quite often now. He comes to me almost every day. And, John, he—he is so very angry with me!"

"Angry?" I asked. "Why should you imagine he is angry with you?"

"Because I will not go away with him," Miss Lucy stated simply. "Willie says that he can make me a little girl again and that we shall be able to play in the shadows in the garden just as we used to so many long years ago—if—if I will go away with him."

"But this is nonsense, Miss Lucy," I said firmly. "You are letting your imagination run away with you."

"You do not know Willie," replied Miss Lucy stubbornly.

"He wants a playmate. I have kept him alone for a long time —all those years when I sent him away from me. He will not stay alone any longer."

"But you really don't believe," I began, and then broke off with a smile. "Come, Miss Lucy," I said, adopting the condescending tone one uses with unreasonable children, "this imaginary child of yours is claiming altogether too much of your attention. You must think of other things."

Miss Lucy stared at me with empty eyes like a ghost.

"Imaginary? Other things? There are no other things in my life," she said hopelessly. "Willie is the only reality left."

And then she went on as though I hadn't spoken. "You don't know Willie," she repeated persistently. "Willie is not like other children. He is not *good*. There is something strange about him—something I never could quite understand, although he has tried to whisper to me about himself, and then his manner and tone frightened me so that I would not listen. The first time he tried to tell me I was only a little girl and could not have understood. Nevertheless, something of the evil of his words I must have sensed, for I clapped my hands to my ears and burst into tears. No, Willie is not like other children. I believe him. I believe he can do what he says. He can take me away with him and make me like himself if he wants to—only, I am afraid." Miss Lucy's voice had subsided to a whisper as she finished this strange speech.

I realized the uselessness of arguing with the old lady in her present state of mind. I recognized symptoms of cumulative hallucination indicating extreme aging, and—I believed—dissolution of her mind. I concluded this visit by instructing Hannah to keep a close watch on her mistress.

The occasion of my last visit to Miss Lucy found me making my way hastily to the old Victorian mansion in answer to a phone call from Hannah, saying that Miss Lucy had not risen that morning as was her custom, but had remained in bed all day. I had been absent from my office making calls and had not received this message until nearly evening. Hannah said Miss Lucy was in no pain. She was only very weak and tired. From these symptoms I knew that my patient was suffering from no other malady than old age. I knew, too, that the end was near.

Hannah met me at the door, asking me to go directly up to Miss Lucy's room. Hannah had left her only a minute before and now hurried away to the kitchen to prepare some warm broth for her patient.

It was late afternoon of a damp, gray day in early February. As I softly opened the door to Miss Lucy's room, a ray of winter sunlight fell chillily across the faded carpet.

Instantly I stopped, frozen in the doorway with shock and amazement. What I saw was no trick of the wan winter sunlight. Of that I was sure. For the merest fraction of a second there flashed before my vision the unmistakable forms of a small girl and boy. The boy's right hand clasped the left hand of the girl. Both children were dressed in the clothing of generations ago; the boy in knee breeches and velvet jacket with lace collar, while the girl wore a pinafore and had flaxen hair done in two tight little pigtails. In that split second in which I glimpsed the figures, their backs were to me, and they were running to the window through which the rays of the last cheerless sunlight of the short winter day poured. I experienced an overpowering and unforgettable sense of revulsion as the figure of the little boy flitted before me. He was short and squat, and his body in some manner conveyed a hint of deformity without actually revealing any defect. His child clothing somehow did not fit properly as it would a normal child. It was as though the garments were masking or cloaking some abnormality. His black hair hung lankly down his back, and around his head there seemed to hover a nimbus of evil. In his free hand the boy grasped an ancient stone hatchet—his plaything. It flashed through my mind that he was more of an imp or gargoyle than a human child. While my eyes blinked in amazement, the two visions winked out of existence like dancing motes in the sun's rays.

Shaken by this apparition more than I cared to confess, I turned after a moment to the bed. One glance told me that Miss Lucy was dead. She lay with her head turned to a peculiar angle, and her right arm thrown up across her forehead in a gesture curiously suggesting defense.

Reaching with one hand under her head to straighten it on the pillow, I removed her arm from her forehead with my other hand. As I did this, that happened which will haunt me until my dying day.

As I gently lifted Miss Lucy's arm from her forehead, thin trickles of blood descended like a red veil over her brow, and, as my other hand simultaneously sought the back of Miss Lucy's head, the long, fine filaments of her soft, silver hair and the delicate, parchment-thin scalp from which they grew came gently loose in my trembling hand.

COLD FIGURES!

WILLIAM HELLMAN

———————

JOE POPE WAS CERTAIN OF TWO THINGS—THAT HE HAD TO kill Jessie Diston, and that he wasn't going to be found out. It wasn't that he had elaborate plans for the execution of the perfect crime. To Joe, murder was like any other job —a little clear thinking, prompt action, and most important, the opportune moment.

That was how he had taken care of Pete Jones, the assistant cashier.

It had been absurdly simple. One of the bank's guns— available to any employee—a typewritten suicide note, with its easily forged signature, confessing the defalcation—and the opportune moment. As simple as that. Pete was gone, his wife grieved, and Joe was entirely in the clear.

Except for Jessie Diston, an old-timer and a wizard with figures; today he had let something slip that had alerted Joe instantly, and he realized that Jess's long, inquisitive nose was ferreting out the real thief—and so Jessie had to go, and the opportune time was now.

Tonight. The old man was alone in his suburban home. . . .

Silently, Joe came out of the shadows, crossed the porch, and went in the open French windows. Coolly he closed and locked the windows, drew the drapes and turned to the man at the desk, all so quickly, effortlessly, that he was beside Jessie almost before the old man was aware of his presence. Jessie looked at him without surprise.

Joe grinned. "Kind of expected me?"

"Not so soon," Jess said slowly. "I figured it had to be you, but I wasn't sure, and I wanted—" He sighed. "Must have tipped my hand today."

"You did," Joe said. "Sorry as hell, Jess, but I can't—nothing personal, you know."

The old man nodded, did not look up, but continued at his task of putting neat columns of figures on a clean sheet of white paper, totaling each column up meticulously.

Joe laughed. "Jess, I believe you have a comptometer for a brain. You're a whiz. I'll miss you, Jess."

Jessie looked at him, then. "You took the money." It was a statement.

"Yes."

"And killed Pete, after you'd forged the suicide note."

"Yep. Someone had to take the rap—Pete could do it better than I." He looked rueful. "Pete was a nice kind of guy."

"Yes," Jessie agreed. "Right proud of that boy of his in the Pacific." He sighed. "His wife's taking it pretty hard—the disgrace of the theft, and the suicide." He looked at the gun. "The same pattern for me."

"Yep. Only you're going to write your own note—makes it easier, surer for me."

"What if I refuse?"

"You might as well do me the favor, Jess," Joe said reasonably. "It'll make no difference to you. You're going, regardless. Save me a heap of work if you write the note first."

"I guess so," Jess agreed. "Look, won't it seem odd, two of us, the same—"

"No. Makes it safer. The police expect it. An unusual crime always provokes a wave of similar crimes; a widely publicized suicide always induces a rash of similar suicides. Besides, in your case, it's remorse, at poor Pete taking the whole blame."

"I guess," Jess ventured, "you wouldn't let me off, if I promised—"

"No. I can't, Jess."

Jess carefully laid aside the paper with its neat columns of figures, took a clean sheet, and wrote Joe's dictation.

The gun went off suddenly, close to Jess's temple, with a small snapping sound, and the thin, old body slumped forward, the gray head resting close to the paper.

Swiftly, Joe pressed Jess's fingers around the gun, dropped the weapon to the floor beneath the dangling hand. Swiftly, too, he searched the papers on the desk, although he was certain Jess had left no message, for he had not expected death so soon. Then he went out, the snap lock catching as the door closed.

It was two days later that he was back in that same room. Only this time Detective Inspector Flynn sat at the desk, several of his huskies stood stolidly by.

"Ever in this room before?" Flynn asked.

"No," he said promptly. "Never had occasion to. If there's anything I can help with—"

"There is. This paper here." He let Joe see it. It was that last sheet of figures Jess had totaled up while Joe had watched. "Would you say that was Diston's work?"

"It is," Joe said. "A work sheet—"

"Yeh, that's what I figured it was," Flynn said, mouthing his fat cigar. "But after I'd looked it over, I seen something kind of odd." He gave the paper to Joe. "Notice anything?"

Joe read the neat columns:

```
306    4347      306      306
 21    7432     7042     3909
732     347     3739       21
 07    3704    23406       41
70042    07    _____      07
_____ -4406   312236     332
312236 312236            _____
                         312236
```

He frowned. "No, I don't—yes," he admitted. "All the totals are identical."

"And all one hundred percent wrong! That got me. I figured it might be a code, and I sure sweated my brains out on it. Then I got it, so simple it's a laugh. Old Diston only had ten letters to work with, but he sure did a neat job—considering he had to do it with the murderer watching him!"

"Murderer? Why he—"

"No, he didn't! He left this paper to prove it. To read it, you just reverse the sheet to a strong light, or read it upside down in a mirror. Here, read it."

He held the sheet up to the bright desk light, and the neat columns stood out in stark clarity. But they were columns of letters, not figures! Hypnotized, Joe read:

```
JOE    JOE     THEN     JOE
POPE   SHOT    SENT     IS
IS     PETE    THE      SET
TO     JONES   NOTE     TO
SEE    _____  TO       SHOOT
JESSIE JESSIE  JOHN—    JESSIE
                JESSIE
```

Strong hands kept him from collapsing in a sniveling heap.

"Yes, Pope," the Inspector said grimly. "They all add up to the same total—the Chair."

THE WATCHERS

RAY BRADBURY

IN THIS ROOM THE SOUND OF THE TAPPING OF THE TYPE-
writer keys is like knuckles on wood, and my perspiration falls down upon the keys that are being punched un-
ceasingly by my trembling fingers. And over and above the
sound of my writing comes the ironical melody of a mosquito
circling over my bent head, and a number of flies buzzing
and colliding with the wire screen. And around the naked
filament-skeleton of the yellow bulb in the ceiling a bit of
torn white paper that is a moth flutters. An ant crawls up the
wall; I watch it—I laugh with a steady, unceasing bitterness.
How ironical the shining flies and the red ants and the
armored crickets. How mistaken we three were: Susan and
I and William Tinsley.

Whoever you are, wherever you are, if you do happen
upon this, do not ever again crush the ants upon the sidewalk, do not smash the bumblebee that thunders by your
window, do not annihilate the cricket upon your hearth!

That's where Tinsley made his colossal error. You remember William Tinsley, certainly? The man who threw away
a million dollars on fly-sprays and insecticides and ant-pastes?

There was never a spot for a fly or a mosquito in Tinsley's
office. Not a white wall or green desk or any immaculate surface where a fly might land before Tinsley destroyed it with

an instantaneous stroke of his magnificent flyswatter. I shall never forget that instrument of death. Tinsley, a monarch, ruled his industry with that flyswatter as a scepter.

I was Tinsley's secretary and right-hand man in his kitchen-ware industry; sometimes I advised him on his many investments.

Tinsley carried the flyswatter to work with him under his arm in July, 1944. By the week's end, if I happened to be in one of the filing alcoves out of sight when Tinsley arrived, I could always tell of his arrival when I heard the swicking, whistling passage of the flyswatter through the air as Tinsley killed his morning quota.

As the days passed, I noticed Tinsley's preoccupied alert-ness. He'd dictate to me, but his eyes would be searching the north-south-east-west walls, the rug, the bookcases, even my clothing. Once I laughed and made some comment about Tinsley and Clyde Beatty being fearless animal trainers, and Tinsley froze and turned his back on me. I shut up. People have a right, I thought, to be as damned eccentric as they please.

"Hello, Steve." Tinsley waved his flyswatter one morning as I poised my pencil over my pad. "Before we start, would you mind cleaning away the corpses."

Spread in a rumpled trail over the thick sienna rug were the fallen conquered, the flies; silent, mashed, dewinged. I threw them one by one in the waste-bin, muttering.

"To S. H. Little, Philadelphia. Dear Little: Will invest money in your insect spray. Five thousand dollars—"

"Five thousand?" I complained. I stopped writing.

Tinsley ignored me. "Five thousand dollars. Advise im-mediate production as soon as war conditions permit. Sin-cerely." Tinsley twisted his flyswatter. "You think I'm crazy," he said.

"Is that a p.s., or are you talking to me?" I asked.

The phone rang and it was the Termite Control Company, to whom Tinsley told me to write a thousand-dollar check for having termite-proofed his house. Tinsley patted his metal chair. "One thing I like about my offices—all iron, cement, solid; not a chance for termites."

He leaped from his chair, the swatter shone swiftly in the air.

"Damn it, Steve, has THAT been here all this time!"

Something buzzed in a small arc somewhere, into silence. The four walls moved in around us in that silence, it seemed, the blank ceiling stared over us and Tinsley's breath ached through his nostrils. I couldn't see the infernal insect anywhere. Tinsley exploded. "Help me find it! Damn you, help me!"

"Now, hold on—" I retorted.

Somebody rapped on the door.

"Stay out!" Tinsley's yell was high, afraid. "Get away from the door, and stay away!" He flung himself headlong, bolted the door with a frantic gesture and lay against it, wildly searching the room. "Quickly now, Steve, systematically! Don't sit there!"

Desk, chairs, chandelier, walls. Like an insane animal, Tinsley searched, found the buzzing, struck at it. A bit of insensate glitter fell to the floor where he crushed it with his foot in a queerly triumphant sort of action.

He started to dress me down but I wouldn't have it. "Look here," I came back at him. "I'm a secretary and right-hand stooge, not a spotter for high-flying insects. I haven't got eyes in the back of my head!"

"Either have They!" cried Tinsley. "So you know what They do?"

"They? Who in hell are They?"

He shut up. He went to his desk and sat down, wearily, and finally said, "Never mind. Forget it. Don't talk about this to anyone."

I softened up. "Bill, you should go see a psychiatrist about—"

Tinsley laughed bitterly. "And the psychiatrist would tell his wife, and she'd tell others, and then They'd find out. They're everywhere, They are. I don't want to be stopped with my campaign."

"If you mean the one hundred thousand bucks you've sunk in your insect-sprays and ant-pastes in the last four weeks," I said, "someone should stop you. You'll break yourself, me, and the stockholders. Honest to God, Tinsley—"

"Shut up!" he said. "You don't understand."

I guess I didn't, then. I went back to my office and all day long I heard that damned flyswatter hissing in the air.

I had supper with Susan Miller that evening. I told her about Tinsley and she lent a sympathetically professional ear. Then she tapped her cigarette and lit it and said, "Steve, I may be a psychiatrist, but I wouldn't have a tinker's chance in hell, unless Tinsley came to see me. I couldn't help him unless he wanted help." She patted my arm. "I'll look him over for you, if you insist, though, for old times' sake. But half the fight's lost if the patient won't cooperate."

"You've got to help me, Susan," I said. "He'll be stark raving in another month. I think he has delusions of persecution—"

We drove to Tinsley's house.

The first date worked out well. We laughed, we danced, we dined late at the Brown Derby, and Tinsley didn't suspect for a moment that the slender, soft-voiced woman he held in his arms to a waltz was a psychiatrist picking his reactions apart. From the table, I watched them, together, and I shielded a small laugh with my hand, and heard Susan laughing at one of his jokes.

We drove along the road in a pleasant, relaxed silence, the silence that follows on the heels of a good, happy evening. The perfume of Susan was in the car, the radio played dimly, and the car wheels whirled with a slight whisper over the highway.

I looked at Susan and she at me, her brows going up to indicate that she'd found nothing so far this evening to show that Tinsley was in any way unbalanced. I shrugged.

At that very instant, a moth flew in the window, fluttering, flickering its velvety white wings upon the imprisoning glass.

Tinsley screamed, wrenched the car involuntarily, struck out a gloved hand at the moth, gabbling, his face pale. The tires wobbled. Susan seized the steering wheel firmly and held the car on the road until we slowed to a stop.

As we pulled up, Tinsley crushed the moth between tightened fingers and watched the odorous powder of it sift down upon Susan's arm. We sat there, the three of us, breathing rapidly.

Susan looked at me, and this time there was comprehension in her eyes. I nodded.

Tinsley looked straight ahead, then. In a dream he said, "Ninety-nine percent of all life in the world is insect life—"

He rolled up the windows without another word, and drove us home.

Susan phoned me an hour later. "Steve, he's built a terrific complex for himself. I'm having lunch with him tomorrow. He likes me. I might find out what we want to know. By the way, Steve, does he own any pets?"

Tinsley had never owned a cat or dog. He detested animals.

"I might have expected that," said Susan. "Well, good-night, Steve, see you tomorrow."

The flies were breeding thick and golden and buzzing like a million intricately fine electric machines in the pouring direct light of summer noon. In vortexes they whirled and curtained and fell upon refuse to inject their eggs, to mate, to flutter, to whirl again, as I watched them, and in their whirling my mind intermixed. I wondered why Tinsley should fear them so, should dread and kill them, and as I walked the streets, all about me, cutting arcs and spaces from the sky, omnipresent flies hummed and sizzled and beat their lucid wings. I counted darning needles, mud-daubers and hornets, yellow bees and brown ants. The world was suddenly much more alive to me than ever before, because Tinsley's apprehensive awareness had set me aware.

Before I knew my actions, brushing a small red ant from my coat that had fallen from a lilac bush as I passed, I turned in at a familiar white house and knew it to be Lawyer Remington's, who had been Tinsley's family representative for forty years, even before Tinsley was born. Remington was only a business acquaintance to me, but there I was, touching his gate and ringing his bell and in a few minutes looking at him over a sparkling glass of his good sherry.

"I remember," said Remington, remembering. "Poor Tinsley. He was only seventeen when it happened."

I leaned forward intently. "It happened?" The ant raced in wild frenzies upon the golden stubble on my fingers' backs, becoming entangled in the bramble of my wrist, turning back, hopelessly clenching its mandibles. I watched the ant. "Some unfortunate accident?"

Lawyer Remington nodded grimly and the memory lay raw and naked in his old brown eyes. He spread the memory out on the table and pinned it down so I could look at it, with a few accurate words:

"Tinsley's father took him hunting up in the Lake Arrowhead region in the autumn of the young lad's seventeenth year. Beautiful country, a lovely clear cold autumn day. I remember it because I was hunting not seventy miles from there on that selfsame afternoon. Game was plentiful. You could hear the sound of guns passing over and back across the lakes through the scent of pine trees. Tinsley's father leaned his gun against a bush to lace his shoe, when a flurry of quail arose, some of them in their fright, straight at Tinsley senior and his son."

Remington looked into his glass to see what he was telling. "A quail knocked the gun down, it fired off, and the charge struck the elder Tinsley full in the face!"

"Good God!"

In my mind I saw the elder Tinsley stagger, grasp at his red mask of face, drop his hands now gloved with scarlet fabric, and fall, even as the young boy, struck numb and ashen, swayed and could not believe what he saw.

I drank my sherry hastily, and Remington continued:

"But that wasn't the least horrible of details. One might think it sufficient. But what followed later was something indescribable to the lad. He ran five miles for help, leaving his father behind, dead, but refusing to believe him dead. Screaming, panting, ripping his clothes from his body, young Tinsley made it to a road and back with a doctor and two other men in something like six hours. The sun was just going down when they hurried back through the pine forest to where the father lay." Remington paused and shook his head from side to side, eyes closed. "The entire body, the arms, the legs, and the shattered contour of what was once a strong, handsome face, was clustered over and covered with scuttling, twitching insects, bugs, ants of all descriptions, drawn by the sweet odor of blood. It was impossible to see one square inch of the elder Tinsley's body!"

Mentally, I created the pine trees, and the three men towering over the small boy who stood before a body upon which a tide of small attentively hungry creatures ebbed and flowed, subsided and returned. Somewhere, a woodpecker knocked, a squirrel scampered, and the quail beat their small wings. And the three men held onto the small boy's arms and turned him away from the sight. . . .

Some of the boy's agony and terror must have escaped my lips, for when my mind returned to the library, I found Remington staring at me, and my sherry glass broken in half, causing a bleeding cut which I did not feel.

"So that's why Tinsley has this fear of insects and animals," I breathed, several minutes later, settling back, my heart pounding. "And it's grown like a yeast over the years, to obsess him."

Remington expressed an interest in Tinsley's problem, but I allayed him and inquired, "What was his father's profession?"

"I thought you knew!" cried Remington in faint surprise. "Why, the elder Tinsley was a very famous naturalist. Very famous indeed. Ironic, in a way, isn't it, that he should be killed by the very creatures which he studied, eh?"

"Yes." I rose up and shook Remington's hand. "Thanks, Lawyer. You've helped me very much. I must get going now."

"Good-by."

I stood in the open air before Remington's house and the ant still scrambled over my hand, wildly. I began to understand and sympathize deeply with Tinsley for the first time. I went to pick up Susan in my car.

Susan pushed the veil of her hat back from her eyes and looked off into the distance and said, "What you've told me pretty well puts the finger on Tinsley, all right. He's been brooding." She waved a hand. "Look around. See how easy it would be to believe that insects are really the horrors he makes them out to be. There's a Monarch butterfly pacing us." She flicked a fingernail. "Is it listening to our every word? Tinsley the elder was a naturalist. What happened? He interfered, busybodied where he wasn't wanted, so They, They who control the animals and insects, killed him. Night and day for the last ten years that thought has been on Tinsley's mind, and everywhere he looked he saw the numerous life of the world and the suspicions began to take shape, form and substance!"

"I can't say I blame him," I said. "If my father had been killed in a like fashion—"

"He refuses to talk when there's an insect in the room, isn't that it, Steve?"

"Yes, he's afraid They'll discover that he knows about Them."

"You can see how silly that is, yourself, can't you? He couldn't possibly keep it a secret, granting that butterflies and ants and houseflies are evil, for you and I have talked about it, and others too. But he persists in his delusion that as long as he himself says no word in Their presence . . . well, he's still alive, isn't he? They haven't destroyed him, have They? And if They were evil and feared his knowledge, wouldn't They have destroyed him long since?"

"Maybe They're playing with him?" I wondered. "You know it is strange. The elder Tinsley was on the verge of some great discovery when he was killed. It sort of fits a pattern."

"I'd better get you out of this hot sun," laughed Susan, swerving the car into a shady lane.

The next Sunday morning Bill Tinsley and Susan and I attended church and sat in the middle of the soft music and the vast muteness and quiet color. During the service Bill began to laugh to himself until I shoved him in the ribs and asked him what was wrong.

"Look at the Reverend up there," replied Tinsley, fascinated. "There's a fly on his bald spot. A fly in church. They go everywhere, I tell you. Let the minister talk, it won't do a bit of good. Oh, gentle Lord."

After the service we drove for a picnic lunch in the country under a warm blue sky. A few times Susan tried to get Bill on the subject of his fear, but Bill only pointed at the train of ants swarming across the picnic linen and shook his head, angrily. Later he apologized and, with a certain tenseness, asked us to come up to his house that evening, since he couldn't go on much longer by himself, he was running low on funds, the business was liable to go on the rocks, and he needed us. Susan and I held onto his hands and understood. In a matter of forty minutes we were inside the locked study of his house, cocktails in our midst, with Tinsley pacing anxiously back and forth, dandling his familiar flyswatter, searching the room and killing two flies before he made his speech.

He tapped the wall. "Metal. No maggots, ticks, wood-beetles, termites. Metal chairs, metal everything. We're alone, aren't we?"

I looked around. "I think so."

"Good." Bill drew in a breath and exhaled. "Have you ever wondered about God and the Devil and the Universe,

Susan, Steve? Have you ever realized how cruel the world is? How we try to get ahead, but are hit over the head every time we succeed a fraction?" I nodded silently, and Tinsley went on. "You sometimes wonder where God is, or where the Forces of Evil are. You wonder how these forces get around, if they are invisible angels. Well, the solution is simple and clever and scientific. We are being watched constantly. Is there ever a minute in our lives that passes without a fly buzzing in our room with us, or an ant crossing our path, or a flea on a dog, or a cat itself, or a beetle or moth rushing through the dark, or a mosquito skirting around a netting?"

Susan said nothing, but looked at Tinsley easily and without making him self-conscious. Tinsley sipped his drink.

"Small winged things we pay no heed to, that follow us every day of our lives, that listen to our prayers and our hopes and our desires and fears, that listen to us and then tell what there is to be told to Him or Her or It, or whatever Force sends them out into the world."

"Oh, come now," I said impulsively.

To my surprise, Susan hushed me. "Let him finish," she said. Then she looked at Tinsley. "Go on."

Tinsley said, "It sounds silly, but I've gone about this in a fairly scientific manner. First, I've never been able to figure out a reason for so many insects, for their varied profusion. They seem to be nothing but irritants to us mortals, at the very least. Well, a very simple explanation is as follows: the government of Them is a small body, it may be one person alone, and It or They can't be everywhere. Flies can be. So can ants and other insects. And since we mortals cannot tell one ant from another, all identity is impossible and one fly is as good as another, their set-up is perfect. There are so many of them and there have been so many for years, that we pay no attention to them. Like Hawthorne's 'Scarlet Letter,' they are right before our eyes and familiarity has blinded us to them."

"I don't believe any of that," I said directly.

"Let me finish!" cried Tinsley, hurriedly. "Before you judge. There is a Force, and it must have a contactual system, a communicative set-up, so that life can be twisted and adjusted according to each individual. Think of it, billions of insects, checking, correlating and reporting on their special subjects, controlling humanity!"

"Look here!" I burst out. "You've grown worse ever since that accident back when you were a kid! You've let it feed on your mind! You can't go on fooling yourself!" I got up.

"Steve!" Susan rose, too, her cheeks reddening. "You won't help with talk like that! Sit down." She pressed against my chest. Then she turned rapidly to Tinsley. "Bill, if what you say should be true, if all of your plans, your insect-proofing your house, your silence in the presence of these small winged creatures, your campaign, your ant-pastes and pitifully small insect-sprays, should really mean something, why are you still alive?"

"Why?" shouted Tinsley. "Because, I've worked alone."

"But if there is a They, Bill, They have known of you for a month now, because Steve and I have told them, haven't we, Steve, and yet you live. Isn't that proof that you must be wrong?"

"You told them? You told!" Tinsley's eyes showed white and furious. "No, you didn't, I made Steve promise!"

"Listen to me." Susan's voice shook him, as she might shake a small boy by the scruff of his neck. "Listen, before you scream. Will you agree to an experiment?"

"What kind of experiment?"

"From now on, all of your plans will be aboveboard, in

the open. If nothing happens to you in the next eight weeks, then you'll have to agree that your fears are baseless."

"But they'll kill me!"

"Listen! Steve and I will stake our lives on it, Bill. If you die, Steve and I'll die with you. I value my life greatly, Bill, and Steve values his. We don't believe in your horrors, and we want to get you out of this."

Tinsley hung his head and looked at the floor. "I don't know. I don't know."

"Eight weeks, Bill. You can go on the rest of your life, if you wish, manufacturing insecticides, but for God's sake don't have a nervous breakdown over it. The very fact of your living should be some sort of proof that They bear you no ill-will, and have left you intact."

Tinsley had to admit to that. But he was reluctant to give in. He murmured almost to himself, "This is the beginning of the campaign. It might take a thousand years, but in the end we can liberate ourselves."

"You can be liberated in eight weeks, Bill, don't you see? If we can prove that insects are blameless? For the next eight weeks, carry on your campaign, advertise it in weekly magazines and papers, thrust it to the hilt, tell everyone, so that if you should die, the word will be left behind. Then, when the eight weeks are up, you'll be liberated and free, and won't that feel good to you, Bill, after all these years?"

Something happened then that startled us. Buzzing over our heads, a fly came by. It had been in the room with us all the time, and yet I had sworn that, earlier, I had seen none. Tinsley began to shiver. I didn't know what I was doing, I seemed to react mechanically to some inner drive. I grabbed at the air and caught the tight buzzing in a cupped hand. Then I crushed it hard, staring at Bill and Susan. Their faces were chalky.

"I got it," I said, crazily. "I got the damned thing, and I don't know why."

I opened my hand. The fly dropped to the floor. I stepped on it as I had seen Bill often step on them, and my body was cold for no reason. Susan stared at me as if she'd lost her last friend.

"What am I saying?" I cried. "I don't believe a damn word of all this filth!"

It was dark outside the thick-glassed window. Tinsley managed to light a cigarette and then, because all three of us were in a strange state of nerves, offered to let us have rooms in the house for the night. Susan said she would stay if: "You promise to give the eight-week trial a chance."

"You'd risk your life on it?" Bill couldn't make Susan out.

Susan nodded gravely. "We'll be joking about it next year."

Bill said, "All right. The eight-week trial it is."

My room, upstairs, had a fine view of the spreading country hills. Susan stayed in the room next to mine, and Bill slept across the hall. Lying in bed I heard the crickets chirping outside my window, and I could hardly bear the sound.

I closed the window.

Later in the night I got no sleep and I began imagining that a mosquito was soaring freely about in the dark of my room. Finally, I robed myself and fumbled down to the kitchen, not actually hungry, but wanting something to do to stop my nervousness. I found Susan bending over the refrigerator trays, selecting food.

We looked at each other. We handed plates of stuff to the table and sat stiffly down. The world was unreal to us. Somehow, being around Tinsley made the universe insecure and misty underfoot. Susan, for all her training and mind-culture, was still a woman, and deep under, women are superstitious.

To top it all, we were about to plunge our knives into the half-shattered carcass of a chicken when a fly landed upon it.

We sat looking at the fly for five minutes. The fly walked around on the chicken, flew up, circled, and came back to promenade a drumstick.

We put the chicken back in the ice-box, joking very quietly about it, talked uneasily for awhile, and returned upstairs, where we shut our doors and felt alone. I climbed into bed and began having bad dreams before I shut my eyes. My wrist-watch set up an abominable loud clicking in the blackness, and it had clicked several thousand times when I heard the scream.

I don't mind hearing a woman scream occasionally, but a man's scream is so strange, and is heard so rarely, that when it finally comes, it turns your blood into an arctic torrent. The screaming seemed to be borne all through the house and it seemed I heard some frantic words babbled that sounded like, "Now I know why They let me live!"

I pulled the door wide in time to see Tinsley running down the hall, his clothing drenched and soaked, his body wet from head to foot. He turned when he saw me, and cried out, "Stay away from me, oh God, Steve, don't touch me, or it'll happen to you, too! I was wrong! I was wrong, yes, but near the truth, too, so very near!"

Before I could prevent him, he had descended the stairs and slammed the door below. Susan suddenly stood beside me. "He's gone mad for certain this time. Steve, we've got to stop him."

A noise from the bathroom drew my attention. Peering in, I turned off the shower which was steaming hot, drumming insistently, scaldingly, on the yellow tiles.

Bill's car thundered into life, a jerking of gears, and the car careened down the road at an insane speed.

"We've got to follow him," insisted Susan. "He'll kill himself! He's trying to run away from something. Where's your car?"

We ran to my car through a cold wind, under very cold stars, climbed in, warmed the motor, and were off, bewildered and breathless. "Which way?" I shouted.

"He went east, I'm certain."

"East it is, then." I poked up the speed and muttered, "Oh, Bill, you idiot, you fool. Slow down. Come back. Wait for me, you nut." I felt Susan's arm creep through my elbow and hold tight. She whispered, "Faster!" and I said, "We're going sixty now, and there are some bad turns coming!"

The night had gotten into us; the talk of insects, the wind, the roaring of the tires over hard concrete, the beating of our frightened hearts. "There!" Susan pointed. I saw a gash of light cutting through the hills a mile away. "More speed, Steve!"

More speed. Aching foot pressing out the miles, motor thundering, stars wheeling crazily overhead, lights cutting the dark away into dismembered sections. And in my mind I saw Tinsley again, in the hall, drenched to the skin. He had been standing under the hot, scalding shower! Why? Why?

"Bill, stop, you idiot! Stop driving! Where are you going, what are you running away from, Bill?"

We were catching up with him now. We drew closer, yard by yard, bit by bit, around curves where gravity yanked at us and tried to smash us against huge granite bulwarks of earth, over hills and down into night-filled valleys, over streams and bridges, around curves again.

"He's only about six hundred yards ahead, now," said Susan.

"We'll get him." I twisted the wheel. "So help me God, we'll get to him!"

Then, quite unexpectedly, it happened.

Tinsley's car slowed down. It slowed and crept along the road. We were on a straight length of concrete that continued for a mile in a firm line, no curves or hills. His car slowed to a crawling, puttering pace. By the time we pulled up in back of him, Tinsley's roadster was going three miles an hour, just poking along at a pace like a man walking, its lights glaring.

"Steve—" Susan's fingernails cut my wrist, tight, hard. "Something's—wrong."

I knew it. I honked the horn. Silence. I honked again and it was a lonely, blatant sound in the darkness and the emptiness. I parked the car. Tinsley's car moved on like a metal snail ahead of us, its exhaust whispering to the night. I opened the door and slid out. "Stay here," I warned Susan. In the reflected glare her face was like snow and her lips were trembling.

I ran to the car, calling, "Bill, Bill—!"

Tinsley didn't answer. He couldn't.

He just lay there behind the wheel, quietly, and the car moved ahead, slowly, so very slowly.

I got sick to my stomach. I reached in and braked the car and cut the ignition, not looking at him, my mind working in a slow kind of new and frightened horror.

I looked once more at Bill where he slumped with his head back.

It didn't do any good to kill flies, kill moths, kill termites, kill mosquitoes. The Evil Ones were too clever for that.

Kill all the insects you find, destroy the dogs and the cats and the birds, the weasels and the chipmunks, and the termites, and all animals and insects in the world, it can be done, eventually by man, killing, killing, killing, and after you are finished, after that job is done you still have—microbes.

Bacteria. Microbes. Yes. Unicellular and bicellular and multicellular microscopic life!

Millions of them, billions of them on every pore, on every inch of flesh of your body. On your lips when you speak, inside your ears when you listen, on your skin when you feel, on your tongue when you taste, in your eyes when you see! You can't wash them off, you can't destroy all of them in the world! It would be an impossible task, impossible! You discovered that, didn't you, Bill. I stared at him. We almost convinced you, didn't we, Bill, that insects were not guilty, were not Watchers. We were right about that part of it. We convinced you and you got to thinking tonight, and you hit upon the real crux of the situation. Bacteria. That's why the shower was running at home just now! But you can't kill bacteria fast enough. They multiply and multiply, instantly!

I looked at Bill, slumped there. "The flyswatter, you thought the flyswatter was enough. That's a—laugh."

Bill, is that you lying there with your body changed by leprosy and gangrene and tuberculosis and malaria and bubonic all at once? Where is the skin of your face, Bill, and the flesh of your bones, your fingers lying clenched to the steering wheel. Oh, God, Tinsley, the color and the smell of you—the rotting fetid combination of disease you are!

Microbes. Messengers. Millions of them. Billions of them.

God can't be everywhere at once. Maybe He invented flies, insects to watch His peoples.

But the Evil Ones were brilliant, too. They invented bacteria!

Bill, you look so *different*. . . .

You'll not tell your secret to the world now. I returned to
Susan, looked in at her, not able to speak. I could only point
for her to go home, without me. I had a job to do, to drive
Bill's car into the ditch and set fire to him and it. Susan drove
away, not looking back.

And now, tonight, a week later, I am typing this out for
what it is worth, here and now, in the summer evening, with
flies buzzing about my room. Now I realize why Bill Tinsley
lived so long. While his efforts were directed against insects,
ants, birds, animals, who were representatives of the Good
Forces, the Evil Forces let him go ahead. Tinsley, unaware,
was working for the Evil Ones. But when he comprehended
that bacteria were the real enemy, and were more numerous
and invisibly insidious, then the Evil Ones demolished him.

In my mind, I still remember the picture of the elder Tinsley's death when he was shot as a result of the quail flying
against his gun. On the face of it, it doesn't seem to fit into
the picture. Why would the quail, representative of Good,
kill the elder Tinsley? The answer to this comes clear now.
Quail, too, have disease, and disease disrupts their neutral
set-up, and disease, on that day long ago, caused the birds to
strike down Tinsley's weapon, killing him, and thus, subtly,
animals and insects.

And another thought in my mind is the picture of the
elder Tinsley as he lay covered with ants in a red, quivering
blanket. And I wonder if perhaps they were not giving solace
to him in his dying and decay, talking in some silent tongue
none of us can hear until we die. Or perhaps they are all.

The game of chess continues, Good against Evil, I hope.
And I am losing.

Tonight I sit here writing and waiting, and my skin itches

and softens, and Susan is on the other side of town, unaware, safe from this knowledge which I must set on paper even if it kills me. I listen to the flies, as if to detect some good message in their uneven whirring, but I hear nothing.

Even as I write, the skin of my fingers loosens and changes color and my face feels partially dry and flaking, partially wet, slippery and released from its anchorage of softening bone, my eyes water with a kind of leprosy and my skin darkens with something akin to bubonic, my stomach gripes me with sickening gastric wrenches, my tongue tastes bitter and acid, my teeth loosen in my mouth, my ears ring, and in a few minutes the structure of my fingers, the muscles, the small thin fine bones will be enmeshed, entangled, so much fallen gelatin spread over and down between the black lettered keys of this typewriter, the flesh of me will slide like a decayed, diseased cloak from my skeleton, but I must write on and on and on until . . .

MANHATTAN MANHUNT

MATT TAYLOR

T HE ACCIDENT OCCURRED IN THE LATE AFTERNOON OF A HOT
June day. The downtown street was crowded, but of
the witnesses to be questioned later no two would agree in
every detail. Some would say the fuel-oil truck rounded the
corner too far to the left; others that the Army prison van
was traveling too fast. The soldier who was driving would
claim something had snapped as he slammed his foot on the
brake pedal.

The Army truck had been the last of a group to leave the
dock, and the jeep that followed, carrying armed Military
Police as a rear guard, had avoided piling into the wreckage
by only the narrowest margin. Of the prisoners who were
spilled into the street three were killed. Six others were injured. One escaped, apparently unhurt.

It was an unavoidable accident and a most fortunate one
for Unteroffizier Kurt Strohm, late of the Afrika Korps and
previously Storm Trooper and member of the army of occu-
pation in Poland. It had seemed incredible that he should
ever escape, and now that the chance had come, he welcomed
it. At El Alamein, at the gateway to Egypt, his headlong
flight had started, and at Cape Bon, with his back to the sea,
it had ended. Now, because of this lucky smashup, it was
to start again in the heart of downtown New York.

154

In the first confusion he had run swiftly, stripping off his jacket with the telltale "P.W." stamped on its back to mark him as a prisoner of war. Now he slowed to a less conspicuous walk and moved west on a street marked "Wall Street." A police car sped past, its siren screaming, and he bent over quickly, pretending to tie his shoe. Next an ambulance passed. His lips tightened. He had seen his comrades killed in Africa with complete indifference, but for these who had been hurtled from the United States Army truck to die grotesquely on the pavement he felt some compassion. They bore no arms and they wore blue denim workclothes instead of the proud uniform of the Reich.

He alone had been thrown clear so that he could lose himself in the gathering crowd. Why? he wondered. He smiled suddenly, his teeth white against his sun-darkened skin. In this escape he saw the hand of Fate. He was marked to carry on his work from here, in the heart of the enemy's homeland. He saw himself outwitting the stupid Americans and becoming an instrument of magnificent destruction.

In his excitement he did not notice that he was once more running. He cursed himself for a fool. His only chance lay in losing himself in the late-afternoon crowd. The heat was such that there were others like himself in the streets wearing sleeveless undershirts. In his denim trousers, he might be a laborer or a seaman from one of the freighters near by.

At the corner of West Street he turned north along the water front. Across the avenue, Military Police patrolled before the docks. But he went on. There were many longshoremen dressed like himself and as deeply tanned by the sun. Even if he were questioned, he could tell a plausible story in decent English, with only a faint accent that could, if need be, pass for the accent of a Swede or a Swiss or even a despised Norwegian. In school in Freiburg, he had always made his best marks in languages, just as his brother Fred, with his amazing memory, had taken honors in history. His father had managed a tourist hotel on the edge of the Black Forest. Often, when he was a young man, he had talked with Americans, studying their idiom and tricks of speech.

He tried to form a plan. He could not stay here for long. Eventually he must go to someone for help, but first he must have suitable clothes, and for clothes he must have money. Clearly he must steal without loss of time.

He studied the women who passed him. There were no purses worth snatching here. His best chance was to the east, amid towering buildings, banks and shops. Resolutely he turned at the street marked "Cortlandt."

Two hours later a broad-shouldered, deeply-tanned man found an empty bench in Union Square, picked up a discarded newspaper and pretended to read. He wore a checked sports coat, dark gray flannel trousers, a white shirt with a striped tie, and a wide-brimmed soft straw. Beside him on the bench was a valise. Behind the screen of his paper he permitted himself a smile of satisfaction. These stupid Americans! He had snatched the purse from the woman in Maiden Lane and they had not caught him. He had lost himself among the derelicts along the Bowery, stopping at different stores and buying his wardrobe piece by piece, and no one had suspected him. Finally he had bought the valise to pack away his incriminating work-clothes.

But he must not count too much on the stupidity of the Americans. He had only twelve dollars of the stolen money left. He would be forced to look for work, and they would ask him for some identifying papers. So he must find someone to help him.

He had relatives who had settled here between the two

wars. There was his brother Fred, one year his senior; his young sister Anna, who lived in a city called Paterson that was near New York; his aunt Louisa in the suburb called Flushing; his uncle Wilhelm in Bridgeport.

He thought the problem through carefully. Bridgeport, he knew, was too far away. His aunt Louisa would not be one to help—she had been in America for twenty years and she had married a Jew. His sister Anna had no respect for the Party. There remained only his brother Fred.

It was not that there was any strong bond between himself and Fred. The opposite was true—there had been bad feeling during their last few years together. Fred had been so clearly his mother's favorite. He remembered saying good-by to Fred in 1931 in Freiburg and feeling nothing at all except relief.

And later, when the letters came from America, his indifference changed to anger. There was nothing but boasting in those letters Fred had written to his father—he had made this much money in New York. Not a word about the coming to power of the new Fuehrer, or the rebirth of the Reich and the creed of blood and iron that would make it strong again. He was to become an American citizen, Fred wrote. If he had ever joined the German-American Bund, as was his duty, he did not mention it. Until finally he, Kurt, who had joined the Party at the beginning and made it his religion and his life, felt more than anger against his brother. He began to hate him.

At the time of his last letter to his father, Fred had lived in a section of Manhattan called Yorkville. He had married an American woman who had borne him two children. This was in 1936, before their father had died. Now Kurt Strohm arose from the bench in Union Square and walked to the nearest drugstore. He found the telephone directory, and the name of Frederick A. Strohm. He lived on East Eighty-seventh Street.

It was nine o'clock when he finally stood before the middle-class apartment building. He studied the names beside the bells in the foyer. He saw "Frederick A. Strohm, Apartment 1B," and walked to the door of the ground-floor apartment and put his finger to the bell. Then the door was pulled back and his brother, whom he had not seen in twelve years, stood before him.

It was a shock, seeing Fred. There had been a time in their early boyhood when people had mistaken them for twins. That time had passed, but now again it was as though Kurt Strohm looked upon himself. His brother was not burned by the sun, and his shoulders were stooped a little. But the features were his features. The same piercing, gray eyes, straight nose and strong chin.

Fred peered into the gloomy hall. "Who is it?" he asked.

"Let me in," Kurt said. "You'll know who I am as well as you know yourself."

Fred stepped back. "Kurt!" he cried.

Their hands clasped. Fred closed the door behind them. "You took my breath away," he said. "I thought you were in the thick of the fighting in Europe."

Kurt laughed loudly. "Not me. I've been in California for six years." He paused and looked swiftly around the living room. It was an American room, just as Fred's speech and clothes and manner were American. There were American magazines on the table; a war-bond sticker on the window, a picture of the President on the wall. So this was the way it was with Fred! But Fred would be made to help him, just the same. He was not clever; he would be easy to fool. "Don't look as though you were seeing a ghost!" Kurt cried.

"It's been a shock, Kurt. I never dreamed—"

"I just got to New York," Kurt said. "I thought I would come here before going to a hotel. Am I upsetting any plans?"

"I have no plans. My family's away at the shore for the summer."

"Splendid, Fred!" Kurt watched his brother carefully. "Not many men in Germany can afford two homes. Just the Nazi bigwigs, eh? Oh, those grafters! You've done well in America."

Fred lighted his pipe deliberately. "There's a chance for everyone here," he said. "That's why I like this country." He turned abruptly. "We'll have a bottle of beer. I want to hear all about you."

Alone in the room, Kurt thought rapidly. Fred would believe anything he told him. Later, Fred would ask him to spend the night. And then . . .

Kurt Strohm's eyes began to glow. The plan that had occurred to him was clever and daring. These Americans wanted their escaped prisoner back, did they not? Very well, then, they should have him. There would be no doubt about it. The prisoner they would recapture would be of the same build and have the same features. His shoulders would be slightly stooped, and his skin not quite as brown as they remembered. But they would find ample proof of his identity on his person—his papers and serial number in the Afrika Korps; the Iron Cross he had won at Tobruk. He would also be wearing the same denim trousers in which he had made his escape.

There would be no connection between their recaptured prisoner and the fact that a man of the same surname had disappeared. This other Strohm—Frederick A. Strohm—with his draft card in his pocket, would turn up in some other city and what he did there would be his own business.

He was smiling at the thought of his cleverness, and suddenly he was aware of Fred standing in the doorway holding glasses and beer and watching him curiously. Again his mind moved swiftly. "It's funny, Fred," he said. "If I were still in Germany I would have to look at the face of the little paperhanger up there on the wall, instead of the President."

Fred placed the beer on the table. "The President's a great man," he said. "I'm glad I voted for him."

"I'll be voting myself before long." Kurt took the beer his brother handed him. "I've taken out my first papers."

Fred nodded. "Good," he said. "It's better to cut the old ties completely. The country that gives a man his home and a chance for success deserves his loyalty."

"It's a great country, Fred."

"The best on earth." Fred raised his glass. "To the United States and her victory!" They drank together, and when they had finished Fred said, "There's still a lot I don't understand. In the letters Father wrote before he died—"

Kurt's laugh interrupted him. "Oh, I know what he told you! That I had joined the Party, eh? But that was when I was young. Before I knew better. If you could only have seen the terror when they came into power!"

Fred watched him sharply. "It was as bad as they say, then?"

"It was—oh, I don't even like to talk about it! I made up my mind to get out in 1937. I could see the war coming, even then. Those stupid Nazis, they've been digging their own graves for years!"

"But you didn't look me up when you first came?"

"I sailed direct to Los Angeles to work for Herman Goetz —you remember him from school, perhaps?—at his orange grove in California."

He talked easily. He had Fred believing every word of it!

His story fitted together neatly, and his details gave it the color of truth. Once, when he was a boy, he had made friends with a tourist from California and all that he had heard he now told Fred. "I should have written you," he finished, "but first I wanted to make something of myself, I said I would become as American as you, and then walk in and surprise you."

"You surprised me, all right."

They talked for another hour, remembering old friends and the days of their boyhood. Then Kurt yawned. "I should be finding a hotel," he said. "Unless, of course, you could put me up."

Fred sucked at his pipe. "There's a bed in my son's room," he said finally.

The room opened from the hall and was closest to the living room. Fred was to sleep in a room down the hall. When they had said good night, Kurt closed the door and opened it again noiselessly a few inches. He had only to wait now until he heard Fred going back to his room. Then another half-hour, perhaps, to make sure he was asleep. It would be simpler to do what he had to do if Fred were in a deep sleep.

He took off his coat and shoes and lay on the bed for an hour, and still Fred did not go back to his room. Cautiously, then, he tiptoed to the door and peered out. Fred was still in the living room. As Kurt watched, his brother arose and went through the door to the kitchen.

Kurt frowned. He could not wait all night. Let it happen, then, when Fred was awake and on guard. He moved noiselessly into the empty living room, and passing the mantel, paused. There was a brass candlestick on top of it, and he slipped it into his trousers pocket, just in case.

There was still no sound as he crossed the living room.

The door to the kitchen was open, and he could see Fred. He had the refrigerator door swinging wide, and he was munching a slice of cheese. As Fred bent over to reach into the lowest shelf, Kurt stepped forward.

A floorboard creaked under his weight. Fred straightened and turned. He looked at his brother angrily. "You scared me," he said, "creeping in like that."

Kurt smiled apologetically. "I forgot I had my shoes off," he said. "I'm sorry."

"I thought you were asleep."

"I can't get to sleep, Fred. Perhaps it's the heat. I thought a bottle of cold beer might help me drop off."

Fred turned to the refrigerator and stooped again to the lowest shelf.

Kurt had his blow started even before Fred turned. His fist crashed into his brother's face like a ball of steel and Fred reeled back, his mouth twisted with pain and a widening red line showing from the corner of it. Again, and still a third time, the ball of steel was thrown against Fred's jaw, and before it could land the fourth time, he sank leadenly to the floor.

Kurt was breathing heavily. The brass candlestick would have done it quicker. Now came the hardest part. Grunting and cursing in whispers, he carried Fred's limp body to the bedroom. There he stripped off his coat and shirt. Next he went at the trousers and shoes. Then came the job of getting his own prisoner's workclothes on Fred. Before he was finished sweat dripped from his forehead.

He looked regretfully at his Iron Cross before he slipped it into Fred's pocket. Fred's wallet he glanced at quickly and saw what he wanted to see—draft and social-security cards. He tied Fred's feet with the cord of a bathrobe and strapped his hands behind him with a belt. And as a final precaution he tied a small towel tight across Fred's bleeding mouth. Only then, when Fred could not move or talk, did Kurt pause to light a cigarette.

He sat on the edge of the bed, smoking and catching his breath. Fred's eyes opened and there was such astonishment and fear in them that Kurt had to laugh. "It's a night of surprises, eh?" he said. "First I arrive from nowhere. And next —the biggest surprise of all—I am no longer me, and you are no longer you. We have changed places."

He felt he had said it cleverly, and he chuckled. And then, because Fred's eyes were upon him so strangely, he frowned. "Why do you look at me like that?" he said angrily. "Do you think it matters to me that you are my brother?"

He leaned forward. Fred was moving his head, shaking it protestingly. There was no longer panic in Fred's eyes, only such pleading as Kurt had never seen.

"So you want to talk, do you?" Kurt cried contemptuously. "Oh, I'm sure you do! You want to shout at the top of your lungs for the police. And then perhaps give me a lecture about loyalty to this dear America! I take no chances with you! I think of everything!"

He arose and looked at the watch on his wrist—Fred's watch that he had taken from him. "It's one o'clock," he said. "In another hour, when the streets are emptier, we will leave. I'll untie your feet and you will walk. It won't be far. Any empty doorway will do. There, we'll end it! They'll find you, and the papers in your pockets will prove you are Unteroffizier Kurt Strohm, of the Afrika Korps, an escaped prisoner of war. You will be wearing his prisoner's clothes. Later, they may find they have made a mistake. But I will be safe by then."

All the time he spoke Fred's eyes never left him. The pleading in those eyes angered him. Hate he would not have minded. He had seen hate in the eyes of the Jews and the Poles. But there had also been resignation. They had not pleaded for mercy.

His anger burst forth uncontrollably. "Take your eyes off me! Do you hear what I say? I know what you're trying to tell me! That I should remember, eh? All right—I'll remember! I'm not afraid. We were born of the same mother, and when we were little we played together. In 1917 we were hungry together. Once, when the ice on the river broke, you saved my life. We sat together and watched our mother die, and you reached for my hand and pressed it! You see? I'm not afraid to remember!" He shook his fist before Fred's pleading eyes. "None of that matters! It is only the Party!"

So completely did anger possess him that he did not first notice the knocking on the apartment door. When he did he was instantly alert. He moved to the door and looked out into the hall and turned back to the bed not a moment too soon. The buckle of the strap that locked Fred's arms had loosened. One final tug and it was loose. He was reaching to tear the gagging cloth from his mouth.

But though he managed to pull it from his lips, he did not speak. His brother Kurt sprang forward, and it was not merely a clenched fist that descended with unerring aim upon the top of Fred Strohm's head. It was a piece of hard metal, and the sound of the blow was an explosion in the quiet room. And then there was no sound at all, except the knocking at the door.

Quickly Kurt turned off the bedroom light. He walked soundlessly down the hall and darkened the single lamp in the living room. Whoever was at the door was still pounding and calling too, now. "Fred!" a man's voice said. "Let me in!"

Kurt leaned forward, his ear at the door. "Who is it? What do you want?"

"It's Paul. I can only stay a minute."

Kurt Strohm frowned. There was no turning back now. In Fred's clothes, in the darkened room, he could see it through. And if not, there was always the slugging way that he knew best. He opened the door and stepped back.

The man who entered closed the door behind him. "You kept me waiting too long," he said sharply. "Sit there by the window. Don't turn on the light. They may have followed me."

Kurt Strohm sat at the edge of the chair. His brass weapon was ready in his hand. "Who may have followed you?" he asked in a whisper.

"Who do you suppose?" the man said angrily. He came closer, and when he spoke his voice broke a little. "Fred, this afternoon they took in Max. From Max, the trail leads directly to me. You know that. There is only you left."

That accent! It was faint, but it came through, because the man was excited. A sick fear was reaching with steel fingers around Kurt Strohm's heart. "Yes?" he whispered. "Yes, Paul?"

"You are beyond suspicion. You are a decent citizen and a hard-working family man. I've kept you under cover for just this sort of thing. You have a memory like the devil himself. You have memorized all the information I have given you these last six months. Now—"

"Wait!" The fingers had Kurt's heart in their grip now. "I must tell you—"

"Stop talking, you fool, and listen! I have no more than a minute. If I am found here, we are both done for. Are you listening, Fred?"

"I'm listening," Kurt said.

"You and not I will keep the rendezvous tomorrow night." The man's voice was crisp. He was an officer giving a command. "You know the spot on the beach. You will recite to the man you meet all the facts, figures and other information I have given you. He will take it to where it will do most good."

The man moved to the door. But Kurt Strohm was not aware of this. His eyes were flooding with bitter tears that burned so he could not see. The clutching pain at his heart left him weak.

The man was speaking again. "You know what's at stake," he said. "It's the work of twelve of our best men up and down the Coast. I can't stay longer. We won't meet again, Fred. But you'll see it through. Good luck."

Kurt Strohm heard the door open and close, but it meant nothing. His mind was numbed. Then he shook his head and sprang to his feet. He stumbled as he made his way down the hall. His fingers fumbled for the light switch and found it, and finally he fell on his knees beside the bed where Fred lay, his eyes wide and staring, and pleading as well, as though they were trying to tell something important. Something he must say before it was too late.

Kurt Strohm seized his brother's cold hand and pressed his thumb over the pulse. He pulled the shirt away from the chest and placed his ear close, listening, biting his lips to keep back his own sobs. Then, in the manner of a man who moves in a dream, he walked from the room, down the hall, and so to the foyer and the street outside. He did not stop for his hat. He swayed back and forth, walking unevenly now. But his mind raced like a man fleeing in panic, stumbling and falling and going on again, where to he does not know, but going on like a hunted animal for whom there is no escape.

He had killed for the Fatherland, as he had been trained to kill, without scruple and without pity. But it was results and not motives that mattered. The memory of the harm he had done the Fatherland would be a part of him until his dying day . . .

"Better take it easy, bud," said a voice beside him. "You live around here?"

Kurt Strohm wheeled. He saw a man in a blue uniform with brass buttons watching him from a doorway. There was no threat in the policeman's voice. It was casual, even friendly. But the meaning of the man's words did not penetrate Kurt's consciousness. He knew only this man was his enemy, his pursuer.

"I've been watching you come down the street, bud. That last one was one too many. You better get home and—"

Kurt Strohm's fist moved forward. All control left him. He sprang, cursing in rapid German. The man in the blue uniform stepped back, warding off the blows and reaching for his nightstick. Only then did Kurt Strohm turn and run. He ran twenty yards, before he tripped and fell. A heavy hand was on his shoulder before he could move.

His mind cleared slowly. There were two of them now, one on each side of him. "You and your two-bit drunks, Clancy," the second one said. "What's wrong with this one?"

"He slugs, this baby. And he swears in German. I think I'll take him in. The sergeant can ask him some questions."

"He's a spy, maybe," said the other, laughing. "Maybe they'll give you a medal, Clancy. Oh, you and your drunks!"

Kurt Strohm walked beside Officer Clancy, his head bowed. He carried his brother's papers, but they would not help now. Not when they started to ask questions. The alarm had been out for hours. The Military Police would be sent for, and they would force their way into his brother's flat and find what there was to find.

There were few people on the street, but such as there were turned to stare and smile. They would not bother to look in their evening papers for news of this arrest. It was just big Tom Clancy, the cop on the beat, taking in somebody unimportant who'd had one too many.

DEAD AS IN BLONDE

D. L. CHAMPION

I

UNDERTAKER'S DELIGHT

THERE WERE TIMES WHEN I PERCEIVED A DISQUIETING SIM-
ilarity between my fiancée, Ruthie, and Rex Sackler.
This specific evening in October, when we had left the neighborhood movie house, was one of them. I had stopped before
the corner café and suggested we partake of a drink and a
sandwich before going home. I added, throwing in a bit of
salesmanship, that it was a crisp evening and a spot of rye
would cause the blood to circulate.

Ruthie wrinkled her attractive nose thoughtfully.

"All right, Joey," she said. "But beer."

"Beer?"

"Beer," she repeated firmly. "Beer is ten cents and rye is
forty. The difference is another thirty cents for our hope
chest."

"My God," I said, "thirty lousy cents won't postpone the
wedding. I—"

"Three-and-a-third thirty cents make a dollar," she said
primly. "That's something you never seem to learn, Joey."

We went into the joint. Glumly, I ordered a Liederkranz

169

sandwich and beer. Between Ruthie's fanaticism on the hope chest fund and Sackler's inherent penury, I felt I was a persecuted man. I ate in silence as Ruthie prattled on about our future. In her vast pocketbook she had, I knew, two bankbooks registering our savings.

"We only need a few more thousand, Joey. Then we can start with really good furniture. Look, I have the whole thing all figured out—"

Other customers glanced over at us and grinned. I felt like a guy with rice on his coat and a "Just Married" sign stuck on the back of his car.

"Look," I said hastily, "why don't we go over to my room and discuss this? It's more private." Ruthie nodded a dubious assent.

We paid the check and walked around the corner to my rooming house. We climbed the two flights of stairs. I unlocked the door, pushed Ruthie in ahead of me and flicked on the light. I heard Ruthie's sudden intake of breath. Then she turned to me with flaming eyes.

"Joseph Graham," she said. "You dirty, carnal beast. You—"

"It must have been the door," I said indignantly. "I never laid a finger on you."

"It's not me," she snapped. "It's that blonde."

"What blonde?"

"*What* blonde? The one in your bed. There!"

My gaze turned in the direction indicated by her pointing finger. Upon my pillow I saw a mop of flaxen hair. The extra blanket, usually folded neatly at the foot of the bed, had been carelessly tossed over her body. I blinked and moved over to the edge of the bed.

"I might have known," I said, "that if there was a good

looking blonde in my bed, there'd be a catch in it somewhere."

Ruthie was still glaring at me. "Well," she snapped, "I'm
waiting and the catch better be good."

"The catch," I told her, "is that she's dead."

"Dead? But how—"

"Look," I said, "I know as little about it as you do. I don't
even know who she is. But I'll have to call the coppers and
you'll save yourself a lot of trouble if you're not here when
they arrive. Good night, baby."

"You're sure you had nothing to do with this?" she asked
suspiciously.

"Look," I said, "there may be several things you might
suspect me of doing to a blonde. Killing them isn't one. Now,
will you get out before I call the coppers?"

She shrugged, walked toward the door, then stopped suddenly and said: "Here, Joey, I forgot!" She handed me a
one-dollar bill and seventeen cents and added: "Your allow-
ance."

I sighed and took it. The seventeen cents was for a pack
of cigarettes. The buck was for lunch, carfare, opium and any
other reasonably-priced flesh pot that I cared to wallow in.

I waited until the front door had closed behind her, then
picked up the phone and called police headquarters. I made
my report, hung up, then went down to the basement to find
the landlady.

I didn't know Mrs. Dunniger very well. Our relations were
strictly professional. Each week I handed her eight bucks.
Each week she took it. Our acquaintance began and ended
there.

She came to the door, gray and dowdy. Her hair-do looked

like something swiped from Medusa. Her arms and stomach were fat and her bosom unavoidable.

I bowed politely and said: "Do you know a blond girl about twenty-four? Blue eyes and—"

She interrupted me. "Why, of course, that's Frieda. Did you see her? What did she want?"

I ignored this and asked: "Who's Frieda?"

"Why, Frieda Schmitt. A Polish refugee. Nice girl. Studying the violin."

"Do you know how she happened to get into my room?"

"Sure. I let her in. She came to me earlier this evening and told me she had heard you were connected with a detective agency. She said she wanted to see you on a matter of importance. I told her you were out. She asked could she wait in your room because she didn't want to miss you. So I said you wouldn't mind and let her in. Why, didn't she tell you all this?"

"She did not," I said. "She's dead."

Mrs. Dunniger's whole frame, bosom, stomach and all, trembled with agitated indignation.

"Dead?" she cried. "In my house?"

"In your house. Dead. Knifed neatly through the heart. The coppers are on the way."

The shriek of a siren outside assured me that they were already here. I turned and made my way up the basement stairs.

I opened the front door and found myself regarded most coldly by the black eyes of Inspector Woolley.

"Ah, Joey," he said blandly, "I understand that murder has been done—in your bedroom."

Woolley wasn't too fond of me. This was not because of any personal reason. It was simply that he hated Rex Sackler. Some of this aversion carried over in my direction.

I led Woolley and his coppers up to my room. I told him what I knew of the affair. When I had finished he frowned and looked annoyed.

"These fools," he said. "If she was worried, if she was scared why didn't she get in touch with us? What the devil did she go to you for? You damned shamus guys get all the reputation, and cause all the trouble, too. Now, we could have stopped a thing like this."

Finally, they left, taking the corpse with them. I was just about to turn in when the phone rang in the hall. It was for me.

A voice, guttural and with an accent, said: "Mr. Graham?"

I admitted my identity.

"This is Rudolph Gerde. I am the uncle of Frieda Schmitt. I have just left the police station. There I learned of my niece's visit to you. I also learned that you are connected with a firm of private detectives. Will you give me the name and address of the firm? Tomorrow I would like to retain you."

I gave him Sackler's name and address, then went to bed. My last thought before I went off to sleep was that I had been instrumental in getting Sackler a new client. I resolved without much hope to try to chisel myself a hunk of the fee.

Rex Sackler was already at his desk when I arrived at the office the following morning. As I came in, he laid the morning paper down on the desk and stared at me, rather hostilely, with his deep black eyes. His thin face seemed even more unfriendly than usual.

"Good morning," I said cheerily, hanging up my hat. "Bright day, isn't it?"

"Robber," he said. "Ingrate. Traitor and betrayer of a friend."

I stared at him in bewilderment. This was the sort of talk he threw about immediately after I had taken him for a nickel. But I recalled no financial deal of late in which I had been the victor.

"What the devil are you talking about?"

"It is nothing to you, Joey, that you ruin the business I have worked so hard to build up. It is nothing to you that you cost me thousands of potential dollars. It would, doubtless, bring glee to your vindictive and malicious heart to see me in tatters on the street, begging for a crust of bread."

That at least was true. Sackler broke, if you could possibly handle the concept, was something which would delight me. But I still didn't understand the rest of it.

"It isn't so much the money," he went on, "it's the treachery, the betrayal."

I unleashed a heavy sigh. "Look," I said, "for years you have claimed that I am not celebrated for my quick mind. So, would you kindly tell me, in simple words, precisely what you are talking about?"

"Last night," he said heavily, "you permitted a dead woman to be found in your room."

"Permitted! What the devil did I have to do with it?"

"You permitted the police to find the woman there. How do you think that looks to the general public? What do you think their reaction will be? A murder committed in the room of Rex Sackler's assistant! That's just *wonderful* for business, isn't it? Do you think anyone will ask us for protection when every paper in town asserts that a woman, who apparently went to you asking for aid, was found dead in your bed?"

"On the contrary," I said, "I'm making money for you. The dead girl's uncle is coming down here this morning.

He's going to retain you. I steered him here. I dare say you'll be liberal enough to see that I get a cut of the fee?"

"Cut of the fee!" He clapped a hand to his head. "After what you have done to me? After wrecking my business, you dare ask for money? God, what gall!"

There was a long pause, then Sackler's natural cupidity got the better of him.

"Besides," he said, "how do we know that the dead girl's uncle has any dough?"

"Now you sound more natural. I don't know whether he has or not. But since he was quite agreeable to hiring a private dick, he apparently has. And granting that he has, do I get a piece of it for steering him this way?"

He shook his head, and said in a hopeless tone: "Joey, you are absolutely money-mad."

Now, I do not claim to be any free-handed philanthropist, but compared to Rex Sackler I am the prodigal, profligate, young son whose life's mission is the dissipation of the family fortune.

For Rex Sackler is as tight as a hangman's noose and as cheap as a dish of rice in prewar Japan. For several years now, he has drawn in vast and many fees. Yet he lives like a coolie who has never seen the reassuring gleam of a ten-cent piece. His two suits are snappy little numbers, patched and rewoven, which he acquired when Roosevelt was still governor of New York State. His lodging is a bare furnished room, the rent of which is so low as to stagger even the Office of Price Administration.

Thus, Sackler's calling me money-mad aroused me to righteous indignation. I made some bitter remarks about the pot smirching the kettle, then lapsed into silence.

II

THE POLISH CENTENARIAN

Some ten minutes later, the door opened and Inspector Woolley came in. Sackler lifted his head and glared at him.

"All right," said Sackler bitterly. "Go ahead and ride me. Let me have it. Gloat, damn you!"

Woolley looked surprised. "What about?"

"The corpse in Joey's room. You know very well that will lose me clients. You know quite well it will cost me a fortune in fees. Probably, I shall finish starving in the gutter. I'm not eligible for Social Security, you know."

Woolley shook his head sadly and sat down. "I regret," he said, "that I disagree with you. I do not believe it will cost you a cent." He paused and sighed. "A most unpleasant task has been wished upon me—namely, to offer you some money."

Sackler blinked. "Money? From you?"

"Indirectly. The commissioner and Tobias Winterly decided you should be retained."

Now the Commissioner of Police sending someone to a private detective is an odd enough circumstance to evoke comment and curiosity. However, Sackler asked only for one item of information when he spoke.

"How much?" he asked. "How much do I get for it?"

"Five hundred dollars," said Woolley miserably, "and it's an outrage."

"What do I have to do?"

"Nothing," said Woolley. "That's the ghastly part of it."

Sackler beamed. "It sounds good," he said. "Tell me the details."

"You know of Tobias Winterly?"

"Naturally. I'd like to own ten per cent of his steel mills—or one per cent of his dough."

"You probably do," said Woolley. "Anyway, you may remember that Winterley's only son was kidnaped some thirty-odd years ago."

"Of course," said Sackler. "Wasn't ever found, either. Now, if I had been on that case. . . ."

Woolley ignored that. "Well, it seems the son has returned."

"After all these years?" I said. "Where has he been?"

"Mexico, apparently. From what I know, everything seems to be in order. You see, the kidnaper got panicky. There was so much police activity at the time, he got scared each time he prepared to collect the ransom. He scrammed to Mexico, taking the kid with him. There, he got a few financial breaks and actually became fond of the kid. Educated him well and brought him up as his own son. From what the commissioner says, the whole yarn appears to check."

"So? How did he finally get back to Old Man Winterly's golden bosom?"

"The kidnaper, whose name is Gomez, finally wound up on the wrong side of the Mexican law. He's doing life for murder. Since he couldn't live with the kid any more, he decided to do the decent thing. He made a deposition telling all."

"It's a hell of a good story," said Sackler. "I haven't seen it in the papers."

"It hasn't been in the papers," said Woolley. "Old Man Winterly's saving that. You see, first, he wants to be absolutely certain that this guy really is his son. The kid's birthday comes up next month. Winterly wants to give a tremendous brawl and then announce officially to the press that his lost son has been found."

Sackler nodded. "I get it. Winterly's been having a lot of labor trouble in his mills. A flood of human interest publicity wouldn't do him any harm. But what about my five hundred bucks?"

"Well," said Woolley, with a sigh, "there's no evidence of any crime. On the contrary, it's all on the up-and-up, so it isn't a job for the police. But both the son and the old man wanted a positive check-up, so the son, Arthur, suggested you. The old man and the commissioner agreed you were about tops in the field. So you get five hundred bucks to check."

"And you say that the commissioner has already looked into it?"

"He has. And he's decided it's quite all right. In short, you merely send Joey out for a routine check and then collect five hundred dollars."

Sackler's grin was broad as he jotted down the address of the Winterlys. Once more dough had fallen into his lap—dough which he would collect and I would earn.

"You're having a nice day," I remarked after Woolley had left. "Five hundred bucks for nothing and whatever you can chisel out of this Gerde."

He opened his mouth to say something insulting but before he could deliver it, the telephone rang. I picked it up and entered into a short conversation. A moment later I said, "Hold the wire," held my hand over the mouthpiece and addressed Sackler.

"This is Gerde now. He's sort of tied up and wants to know if we can go out to his place to see him tonight."

Sackler, doubtlessly thinking of the carfare, looked a little dubious. "He wants us for dinner," I added.

"O.K.," said Sackler. "Sure. Why not?"

I relayed his message into the mouthpiece and hung up. Sackler said: "Go and get some lunch, Joey. Then gallop over to the Winterlys and check up. From what Woolley said it should be simple enough. Pick me up here about five-thirty and we'll go out to Gerde's together. By the way, where does Gerde live?"

"Forest Hills," I said. "It's twenty-six cents on the Long Island Railroad."

"We'll lay it out," said Sackler munificently. "Later, we'll slap it on the expense account."

Going from Rex Sackler's dusty, broken-down, second-hand furniture into Winterly's Sutton Place mansion was like sliding from a foxhole into the drawing room of the Sultan's palace.

A butler escorted me through a paneled hall into a living room which would have made an ideal spot for the Army-Navy game. As I entered, three men rose to greet me.

Old Man Winterly I recognized at once. His photograph had graced the front pages of every paper in the country from time to time. He was a stooped, old man of about seventy. His nose was corvine and his black eyes ruthless and alert.

I shook hands with him. "This," he said, indicating a portly, well-dressed man of about forty, "is Harrison. My right hand. He knows more about my business than I do myself."

Harrison's grip was firm. He was a well-groomed, suave man of affairs, looking and talking like a personified Chamber of Commerce.

The third member of the group was the newly-found Arthur Winterly. Blond, blue eyed, about thirty-five, he came forward and greeted me in friendly fashion.

"Glad you're here," he said. "Both Dad, if I may call him that yet, and I want to be absolutely certain of our relationship. I don't want any cloud on my title, as it were. That's why we're sparing no effort to make sure that all these affidavits are O.K. The Commissioner himself recommended you and Mr. Sackler."

They brought all the affidavits and I studied them over a big mahogany table.

"You'll find them all right," said Harrison, "I'm sure. I know a little of legal matters myself. Here, for instance, is the deposition signed by Gomez, notarized by a Mexican official. Then, here, you will see other statements to the effect that the signers swear that right after the Winterly kidnaping, Gomez and a young child returned to the Gomez home in Guanajuato. Moreover, we have the statement of Gomez' housekeeper in whom he confided years ago when she was looking after Arthur here."

I nodded and thumbed through the papers. The originals were in Spanish with an English transcript attached. They had been notarized, I observed, by Mexican Government officials and also a representative of the United States Embassy.

It looked air-tight and I said so.

"Of course," said Winterly, "it's air-tight. But it's good business to have things like this O.K.'d by a detective and a lawyer just in case there's trouble about the will some day."

"Well," I said standing up, "as far as I can see, it's all quite kosher. I suppose Mr. Sackler will want to drop in himself some time tomorrow just as a matter of form."

"Naturally," said Harrison. Then: "Oh, we're forgetting to tell Mr. Graham of the birthmark."

"It slipped my mind," said Winterly. "If there were the slightest doubt of Arthur's identity, this would dispel it. My son had a small red birthmark just below his right elbow. Had it as a baby. Has it now. Show him, Arthur."

Arthur Winterly rolled up his sleeve and thrust out a

muscular arm. About two inches below his right elbow was a small, red birthmark. I nodded without interest. This obviously was one of Sackler's less interesting cases.

"Very well," I told them. "I'll have Sackler call you tomorrow before he drops in."

"Try to make it before three o'clock," said Harrison, "I'd like to meet Mr. Sackler. But I'd also like to get in my Turkish bath."

"He's a fanatic," said Winterly, smiling. "He has a Turkish bath almost every day. He's talked Arthur into it, too, since my son has returned."

On the way to Forest Hills in the train, I told Sackler what I had seen at Winterly's. He nodded his head sagely as I talked, trying to give me an impression that he was thinking deeply.

Gerde had a small house a mile or so away from the station. It was surrounded by trees and from the porch no other houses were visible. It was hard to believe that we were still in the limits of New York City.

Gerde opened the door himself. He was an incredibly old man. He greeted us in a quavering, halting voice. He shuffled along as he took us into the house and waved us to chairs. His eyes were rheumy, his hands palsied, and his face cratered with wrinkles.

"Sir," he said to Sackler, "I need your help. I distrust the police. And even if they should merit my trust, I would still doubt their competence."

Sackler beamed and nodded a hearty assent. With these sentiments he was in complete accord.

Gerde blinked and looked around the room. "My glasses," he explained. "I—"

His glasses were on the table at the side of his chair. I picked them up and gave them to him. He thanked me. "I am afraid I am almost blind and quite absent-minded. However, let us get to business.

"Mr. Sackler, I am frankly worried. My doctor, my murdered niece and I are all from Poland. Our village was totally destroyed by the Germans and all in it killed. We managed our escape through devious and secret channels. Candidly, I am afraid that my niece was killed by German agents, since they once vowed to slay all who lived in our town. If that is true, my doctor and I will be next."

Sackler nodded. "What you want is someone to find out who murdered your niece and also to protect you and your doctor?"

Gerde nodded. "I only hope the compensation I am able to offer you is adequate."

Sackler's face fell.

"You see, I have very little cash," went on Gerde. "I do, however, have an insurance policy for ten thousand dollars. I am prepared to make you the beneficiary."

Sackler stared at Gerde appraisingly, as if he were trying to figure out how long the old guy had to live. At last he nodded, said: "That arrangement will be quite satisfactory. We can attend to specific details tomorrow, and then I shall be able to undertake my investigation."

"I should warn you," said Gerde, "that my doctor is a man who has made a thorough study of longevity. He attends me and is certain I shall live for many more years."

Sackler donned his righteous robe. "Sir," he said, "does the money matter, when I shall be fighting the enemies of mankind?"

Gerde bowed at him. "Your sentiments do you proud, sir. Dr. Lapslav is coming to dinner. You shall meet him. In the meantime, I shall see if the meal is ready. Excuse me."

A moment later, the outer door opened and a gaunt figure

shuffled into the room. We both blinked at him. If we had thought Gerde ancient, this guy was Methuselah himself. His face was almost gray. His skull was a shining, hairless egg. But his eyes were bright and alert. He bowed to us.

"I am Dr. Lapslav," he announced, and sat down.

Sackler nodded to him and an odd expression came over his face. He seemed worried. He coughed embarrassedly, then cleared his throat.

"Doctor," he said hesitantly, "I trust you will not think me impertinent, but would you mind telling me your age?"

"Not at all," said Lapslav. "I am one hundred and two years old. Hearty, too, thanks to my research into the subject of longevity."

Sackler's face fell. I grinned. I knew what he was thinking. A moment ago he had figured that Old Man Gerde couldn't live more than six or seven years, that any doctor who told him differently was a charlatan. But now he had seen the doctor who, himself, had achieved the very ripe age of a hundred and two. If the doctor could do as much for his patient that meant that Sackler would have to wait at least twenty years for his insurance money.

At this point Gerde returned and we all went in to dinner.

In spite of the high quality of the food, and the fact that it was free, Rex Sackler didn't seem very happy. Toward the end of the meal, he pulled himself together sufficiently to ask a series of questions calculated to cast some light on the murder of Frieda Schmitt. As far as I could tell he got nowhere at all.

Later, as we smoked our cigars, the storm came up. Wind and rain pelted against the house for a solid hour without cease.

"Look here," said Gerde. "It will be impossible for you

gentlemen to get a taxi at this hour. And walking to the station is impossible. Why not stay here overnight?"

Sackler snapped the offer up quickly. Almost any bed was more comfortable than the ancient cot in his cheap room. Moreover, if we stayed we would doubtless partake of a free breakfast in the morning.

We turned in to twin beds in a neat guest room. I rolled over and went to sleep almost immediately.

III

ESSENCE OF VITRIOL

I was awakened by an ear-splitting scream. I opened my eyes just as Sackler switched on the light and sprang out of the bed. As I reached for my trousers, Sackler was already going through the door.

A moment later, I followed. As I pattered on by bare feet through the hall, I heard another shriek of agony, then a series of dull groans. Then Sackler's voice shouted: "Hurry, Doctor. Hurry, for God's sake."

I saw Lapslav enter Gerde's bedroom as I rounded a corner of the passageway. Sackler yelled at me: "Joey! Get on that phone. Call an ambulance. Quick!"

I pattered down the stairs to the telephone in the living room and put in the call. Then I went upstairs again. Gerde's door was closed now and Sackler was pacing up and down outside. I glanced at him inquiringly.

"Acid, Joey."

"Acid?"

"Yes. Thrown in his face. Burning the hell out of him."

"What kind of acid?"

"Probably vitriol."

"But why? Would that kill him?"

"Hardly. But it will probably disfigure him badly."

We went down to the living room where Sackler helped himself to one of Gerde's cigars and smoked it thoughtfully. A little later an ambulance bell clanged and Gerde was carried downstairs. Lapslav went along with him, leaving Sackler and me alone in the house.

"How did the guy get in the house?" I asked.

"The window, I guess. It was open. There's some lattice work outside. It wasn't too hard to climb up to the sill," he replied gloomily.

"You didn't see him?"

Sackler shook his head. "I saw a car drive off on the road a good thirty yards from the window. There was too much rain and darkness for me to see the plates. No point in trying to go after him."

He stood up and shuddered. "It was a close call," he said. "Suppose that guy had wanted to kill him? He could have done it easily enough."

He paused for a moment. Then he added the fact that was closest to his heart. "And he hadn't fixed up that beneficiary business yet, either, Joey!"

He sighed heavily, then resumed his pacing up and down. "I don't get that acid business," he said. "There's something there which probably is the key to the entire case. But I don't get it, that's all. The guy could just as easily have killed him. Why didn't he? I think I'll go up and look over the bedroom once more."

He went back up the stairs. Having nothing better to do, I followed him. In Gerde's room, I observed that there was a single wet footprint beneath the window sill as if the assailant had merely put one foot in the room before hurling the acid.

The pillow was eaten by the vitriol as was the table-top at

the side of the bed. Gerde's glasses, upon the table, were also stained.

Sackler paced up and down for a while, cursed, then said: "Well, we may as well go back to bed. There's no profit in this."

"Then, naturally, you wouldn't be interested," I said and got out of the room before he could answer.

We rolled into bed and stayed there until ten o'clock. The cook prepared our breakfast, after which Sackler phoned the hospital to ask about Gerde.

"Well?" I asked him as he hung up. "Anything?"

"Nothing of importance. The doctor was with him all night. He's in pain and suffering from shock and will probably lose the sight of his right eye."

"That's fine," I said. "Then he's bound to live long enough to make over that insurance to you. I was awfully worried about that."

He was so utterly immersed in his own thoughts that he neglected to call me a nasty name in return for that last crack.

"You know," I suggested, "if we take a train back to town, then a taxi up to Winterly's, we can stick the cab on *that* expense account."

He nodded and grunted glumly. He didn't speak all the way into New York.

At Winterly's, I again met Arthur, Harrison and the old man. They greeted Sackler effusively and offered him refreshment. He refused it—a fact which staggered me.

Perfunctorily, he examined Arthur's Mexican documents. It was easy to see that his mind wasn't on his work.

Finally, he laid the papers aside. "These seem to be in order," he said. "I have no doubt, Mr. Winterly, that Arthur is your son."

Winterly put his arm about the boy's shoulders. "I was

certain of it," he said. "I shall have my secretary send you a check in a few days."

Even this promise didn't banish Sackler's frown. He sighed and leaned back in his chair.

"You know," said Arthur genially, "it must be exciting in your business, Mr. Sackler. Have you solved the murder of that girl yet? The one who was killed in your assistant's room."

Sackler shook his head sadly. "No. Nor the attempted murder on her uncle last night. And while *we* were in the house, too. These things will be very bad for business."

So that was what was troubling him! He had howled loudly enough at me after Frieda had been killed on my bed. Now that Gerde had been assailed with acid in the same building that housed Sackler he was doubly worried about his reputation and the financial results which might ensue from the sullying of it.

The conversation became desultory and boring. Old Man Winterly turned the talk to Mexico. Since Rex and I had been there once, I put my oar in and spoke of the sights in Mexico City. I mentioned the huge bronze statue of a horseman near the Paseo de Reforma.

Arthur smiled at me and said something in Spanish. Since that is a language I know three words of, none of which may be used in a drawing room, I would have forgotten them at once, save that I saw Sackler suddenly snap out of his lethargy and regard Arthur oddly.

I dug into my memory and figured that Arthur had said something that sounded like *"el cabalyo brontha."* But it still didn't make sense to me.

Sackler stood up suddenly and announced he must keep an appointment. Everyone ushered us out, bade us good-by effusively.

We arrived back at the office a little before noon. Sackler made a dive for his swivel chair and sat deep in thought, sighing regularly every fifteen minutes like Old Faithful. I busied myself with the afternoon papers.

A taut silence ensued until I got to page three of the newspaper. "Hey!" I said.

Sackler looked at me wearily.

"There's a story in here about Gerde."

"Naturally. The reporters would get it from the police report."

"Yeah, but right under it is a story about another guy. A guy who also had acid thrown in his face last night. He's lost both eyes."

Sackler's eyes glinted. He sat forward in his chair and his weary air dropped from him. "Who is he? What's his name?"

"His name is Wencel. He's a Pole." I read a little more. "Say, what was the name of that town Gerde and the doctor came from?"

"Slovonia. Why?"

"Well," I said excitedly, "this guy was from Slovonia, too. Now, what the hell do you know about that?"

He got out of his chair, crossed the room and snatched the paper from my hand. He read the item eagerly.

"I get a ray of light," he said. "But only a ray. By God, could it be— No, it couldn't. It couldn't possibly. But then . . ."

"For the love of heaven, stop arguing with yourself," I told him. "What's the ray? What's it all about?"

"I want you to recall everything that was said, everything that was done when you went over to Winterly's yesterday. Now, go ahead and start talking."

I told him what had been said at Winterly's. I made it as

detailed and dull as possible. As I spoke he made notes on a scratch pad. When I had finished he got up and put on his hat.

"Where to?" I asked.

"The hospital. I want to see Gerde. You can go home."

He slammed the door behind him and left me alone. I closed up my desk and went out, wondering what the devil was going on in his head. So far, we had a murder and two acid-throwings. But Sackler seemed to be ignoring them and stressing my conversation with Winterly.

I arrived at the office the next morning before Sackler, which was unusual. I had just finished reading the item about Gerde when he came in.

"Say," I said, "have you seen this? Gerde has lost his sight, too. Both eyes gone."

"I know. I had a hell of a time with Woolley about it, too."

"Woolley? Why should you have a hell of a time with him about it?"

He glared at me without speaking.

"So what's our next move?" I asked.

"*Your* next move is to sit quietly. For the next couple of days I won't need you. I shall be busy with the censor and the War Production Board."

"Why?"

"I need a priority."

"For what?"

"Telephones."

"Are we going to put another phone in here? Why? We've got two. You know there's an extra charge for each phone, Rex. I think—"

"The hell you do!" he snapped, taking some papers from his desk drawer and stalking out of the office.

I hardly saw him at all for the ensuing two days. Then upon my arrival Friday morning, I found Sackler at his desk. He was hanging up the phone as I entered.

"Well," I said brightly, "everything all solved? Tied up, in the bag and the fee collected?"

He stared at me and did a long take. "My God!" he said. "The fee! Imagine me forgetting the fee!"

"Imagination totters," I said. "I simply can't do it."

"Joey," he said in his most reproachful tone, "you do not know the inner Me. I have been so absorbed in working for others lately that I completely forgot myself. Now, however, I am about to arrange a conference between Gerde and Winterly."

"Gerde and Winterly? For what?"

"In order to make the necessary financial arrangements. In the meantime, you will remain by the telephone. When I have concluded my affairs, I shall call, telling you precisely where to meet me."

It wasn't until half-past three that Sackler phoned. He instructed me to come downtown to Winterly's offices near Wall Street at once. I tossed my newspaper in a drawer, went downstairs and took a bus.

IV

THE SEEING EYE

Less than half an hour later, I entered a huge, richly-carpeted office, illuminated by indirect lighting, filled with white leather furniture and cigar smoke.

This last item emanated from the end of a panatella held firmly in the mouth of Inspector Woolley. Woolley did not seem pleased. He leaned against a mantelpiece and glared at

Sackler with eyes which mirrored the distrust in his heart.

Winterly sat in one of the chairs and registered anxiety. A frown furrowed his brow and his fingers beat a nervous tattoo on the desk before him. Across the room, with heavy bandages covering his eyes and most of his face, sat Gerde. Standing at his side in attendance was Dr. Lapslav.

There was an air of melancholy in the office broken only by the somewhat jaunty demeanor of Mr. Rex Sackler. Sackler was perched on the edge of a desk, smoking a tailor-made cigarette he undoubtedly had filched from someone. He looked very pleased with himself.

Woolley regarded him without enthusiasm. He took the cigar from his mouth and glanced at his wrist.

"Well," he said, "it's almost four o'clock, Rex. Aren't the proceedings about to start?"

"What proceedings?" I asked.

Woolley looked at me sourly. "I haven't the slightest idea," he said, aggrieved. "Mr. Sackler the eminent detective, doesn't confide in me."

Sackler slid off the desk, ignored Woolley's crack. He nodded in Lapslav's direction. "O.K., Doctor. Take him in now. Bring him out when I call you."

Lapslav inclined his head. He helped Gerde to his feet and led him from the office, through a door at the rear. Winterly licked his lips nervously. We all sat about in a rather tight silence for several minutes.

Then the office door opened. Harrison and Arthur Winterly came in.

"Hello," said Harrison, a note of surprise in his voice as he noted the assembled company. "What's up? Arthur and I just got back to the house from the Turkish bath and received your message to come down here. What's it all about?"

Winterly didn't answer. Harrison's inquiring gaze moved

in Woolley's direction. Woolley took the cigar from his mouth and grunted.

"The celebrated detective, Mr. Rex Sackler," he said, laying the sarcasm on with a trowel, "has announced that he is about to solve a crime. He has never yet been known to perform this trick without an audience. Hence, the assemblage."

Sackler never batted an eye. "Several crimes," he corrected.

"One is enough for me," said Woolley. "And you'd damned well better solve it. Do you know what the newspapers will do to me? They don't like guys who—"

"Shut up!" said Sackler sharply. "And I'll hand you the case on a salver."

"For heaven's sake!" said Arthur. "Don't tell me there's anything wrong with those papers of mine?"

"If everyone will sit down," said Sackler, "I shall begin at the beginning."

Harrison and Arthur sat down. Woolley remained standing and impatient. Sackler ground out his cigarette in a hammered silver ashtray and cleared his throat.

"It is an odd case," said Sackler reflectively. "Odd because it is all so damned fortuitous. Had it not been for a lucky coincidence, it never would have started at all. However, owing to a simple and, I suppose, common enough habit, we have encountered quite a bit of trouble."

"And a couple of fees," put in Woolley looking more annoyed than ever.

"Case?" said Harrison. "What case? What on earth is the matter?"

"The matter," said Sackler, "is that you have taken your last Turkish bath, Mr. Harrison. It was that habit which started you on this little venture, as you well know."

Woolley unleashed a sigh that sounded like an irritated bellows.

"For the love of heaven, Rex, stop being so damned mysterious. Are you solving a murder or aren't you?"

"The murders come later, Inspector. First, I'm handling a common swindle. Remember, you sent me the case."

I blinked at that. "You mean Arthur Winterly's not on the level? You mean those papers are forgeries?"

"The papers aren't forgeries, Joey. But they're equally valueless."

Arthur stood up. "If there is anything wrong with my claim," he said, "I am innocent of any chicanery. Naturally, I do not know if all those signatures are legitimate. That is why I wanted an investigation."

Sackler grunted sceptically. He fixed his eyes on Arthur and spat out a question.

"Where did you first meet Harrison?"

"Why, at the Winterly home. I was introduced to him by Mr. Winterly."

"That was not the first time you met him."

"Now look here," said Harrison. "I'm quite sure it was. I remember it distinctly. I—"

"And you don't remember first meeting Arthur in the steamroom of a Turkish bath, where neither of you was wearing clothes and you could see the odd birthmark on his arm?"

Harrison didn't answer. I noticed he shifted his gaze to Arthur as if he expected the younger man to answer for him. Arthur stared back at Sackler, showing no alarm.

"Go on," he said slowly. "Tell us what you know."

Sackler opened a box on Winterly's desk and helped himself to a cigar. He lit it with deliberation. Woolley coughed impatiently.

"Very well," he said. "Harrison first saw you in a steam-room. He noticed the mark on your arm which was very much like the birthmark on Winterly's son which had been greatly publicized several years ago. The germ of an idea crawled into his brain at that moment. It was a long shot but it would cost him nothing to try."

"Do you mean," inquired Woolley, "that merely because this guy has a birthmark similar to that on Winterly's boy, the two of them faked this huge swindle?"

"That began it. Harrison, his scheme still nebulous, culti-vated Arthur, checked up on him. He found out that Arthur was a foreigner, not known to many people. He found out that he was in rather poor circumstances financially. Then he made his proposition."

"Which was?" said Arthur, still quite calm. I would not have said the same of Harrison.

"For you to become the long lost Arthur Winterly."

"But what about all those notarized statements from Mexico?" asked Woolley. "They are notarized by responsible people, people who couldn't possibly be a party to a swin-dle."

"They were victimized," said Sackler. "They believed the yarn as much as we all did at first. It was easy enough. Don't forget Arthur is a linguist. He's not an American, but would you know it from his speech? Well, he speaks Spanish equally well. That is—almost equally well. Moreover, Harrison, as manager of the vast Winterly enterprises, has a number of connections in Mexico."

"But what of Gomez' story?" asked Woolley.

"What could be simpler? You search the Mexican prisons for a somewhat intelligent lifer. You offer cash and security to his family if he will confess to the Winterly kidnaping.

What had Gomez to lose? He was serving Mexico's greatest penalty anyway. Of course, he signed."

"And the corroborative witnesses?"

"In Mexico that sort of affidavit can be purchased as easily as War Stamps. The men who notarized the papers firmly believed they were reading true confessions, seeing no motive in these apparently freely-given statements."

"So you mean that Harrison rushed Arthur into Mexico just long enough to collect the papers for which he had arranged, then brought him back as the Winterly heir?"

"Right. Sooner or later Winterly would die. They would split the estate and that was quite a hunk of money to split."

Sackler sighed as if dreaming happily of how he could stash all that money somewhere himself.

Harrison bit his lip. I observed that he carefully avoided Winterly's eye. Arthur still met Sackler's steadily.

"You can prove this?"

"And more. I have been in communication with the Mexican Government, after a hell of a session with the W. P. B. to get priorities on the phone calls. Gomez has been examined and cracked. Your other collaborators are being rounded up now."

"Then," said Arthur, without turning a hair, "it would appear that I have been tricked. Under the circumstances I would not claim a cent of Mr. Winterly's money."

"Under the circumstances," said Woolley, "that's damn nice of you."

"However," went on Arthur, "as I see it, you can prove me guilty of nothing. If you try to hold me on attempt to defraud, you'll have a hell of a time getting witnesses from Mexico. Without admitting anything, I may say that if you speak the truth, Sackler, then Harrison will doubtless be fired. Nothing at all will happen to me."

There was some truth in that. We could hardly extradite the witnesses from Mexico. And granting Sackler was right, we didn't have enough for even a Tom Dewey blue ribbon jury to convict. Woolley, judging from his worried frown, was thinking of that, too.

"Don't give it a thought," said Sackler. "I shall make no attempt to indict either of you for fraud."

"You see?" said Arthur to Harrison. "You get fired. I get nothing."

"I shall indict you both for first degree murder," said Sackler as if he had never been interrupted.

There was a taut silence in the room. Old Man Winterly leaned forward in his chair and stared at Arthur. There was implacable bitterness in his eyes. Harrison's chubby face was pale. Arthur retained his calm, but now for the first time it seemed to cost him some effort.

"Yes," went on Sackler conversationally, "it was that damned acid throwing which baffled me at first. It was such a mad thing to do. The trick of a jealous woman to destroy the beauty of her rival. But not for a killer, a murderer, who had already slain Frieda Schmitt. Two acid throwings in one night—both times the vitriol hurled in the faces of old men with no claim whatever to physical beauty. But, *they both came from Slovonia!*"

Sackler got up from the desk on which he had been sitting and strolled around the room cockily. Woolley and I shrugged at each other.

"You've got a lot of gall, Arthur," said Sackler. "Or should I call you Stanislaus, which is your real name. Gall and nerve. You killed Frieda Schmitt in my assistant's bedroom. Then, before the police commissioner, you boldly suggest that I be retained to check your papers."

"Why would he do that?" asked Woolley, looking like a man lost in a maze.

"Because of his arrogance and conceit. He was quite certain he could outwit a poverty-stricken shamus like myself, sure that one who wrested as little fortune from this civilization as I—"

"For God's sake," shouted Woolley, "do you want us to pass the hat? Stop breaking my heart and get on with it!"

Sackler did his I-am-more-hurt-than-angry pose and went back to the former subject.

"Well, he figured he could out-think me. And if I were retained by Winterly, he could keep an eye on me. If I ever came close to the truth of the murder and acid throwing he could make some move to throw me off the trail again. If I were also working for him, he could keep an eye on me."

"If he committed murder," said Woolley, "if he threw that acid, why? What was his motive?"

"He came from Slovonia," said Sackler. "So did the other three. And only those three. And now one of them is a corpse and two are blind men."

I remembered something and light flooded me.

"It was he, then, who talked Winterly into holding the announcement of his son's return until his supposed birthday. He knew there'd be a tremendous splurge with his picture plastered all over the front pages."

"Right," said Sackler. "Blind men can't see pictures. Neither can a corpse."

"But why did he kill the girl and blind the men?"

"That," said Sackler, "only he can tell you. I suspect that somehow he tipped his hand accidentally to the girl. Perhaps he had tried to kill or blind her once before and failed of his purpose. That was why she went to your room to see you, Joey. He followed her that night and found her. Since she saw him, since she apparently knew the identity of her assailant, he knew he had to kill her. But with the men, blinding them was enough."

"I get it," said Woolley. "Just so these people wouldn't see his picture in the paper and recognize little Arthur from Slovonia and give the entire thing away. I get it."

"If you get it," said Sackler, "I guess everybody does."

Harrison's face was a death mask. Arthur lit a cigarette with steady fingers. Winterly said: "But what brought you to these conclusions, Mr. Sackler? It is incredible."

"The acid first. It couldn't kill. It certainly wasn't meant to disfigure. It must have been calculated to blind. Then later I heard about the Turkish bath habit and saw the birthmark. But the Bronze Horseman was the clincher."

"The Bronze Horseman?"

Sackler nodded. "You'll recall Joey, here, mentioned Mexico City's famed Bronze Horseman the day we were at your house. Arthur smiled and called it by its Spanish name, *el caballo bronce*."

"Well?"

"I told you Arthur was a linguist. But he learned his Spanish in Europe. He learned classical Castilian Spanish, the same as is taught in the schools here. I knew at once he had never learned it in Mexico."

"How?"

"By his pronunciation. First the double 'll's' in *caballo*. The Spaniard pronounces them as an 'lli' in English, as in our word 'million'. The Mexican pronounces them as a simple 'y'. He would say *cabayo*. Not *caballyo*. And the 'c' in the word *bronce*. A Spaniard would aspirate that 'c' making it sound like an English 'th'. He would say *'brontha'*. Anyone who had learned Spanish in Mexico would have said *bronce* pronouncing the 'c' soft as in the English word 'prince'. I knew then that Arthur had never spent the major part of his life in any Latin American country."

Arthur put his cigarette out deliberately. "Once again, Mr. Sackler, you run into the difficulty of legal evidence. You have already stated that neither corpses nor blind men see. Are you going to identify me by the Braille system? How can two blind men swear that I am Stanislaus Ratowski of Slovonia?"

Sackler smiled faintly and lifted his voice. "O.K., Doctor, bring him in."

The rear door opened. Doctor Lapslav slowly led the bandaged Gerde into the room. He sat him down upon the sofa, then, taking up a position behind him, proceeded to remove the gauze which covered the upper half of his face.

His forehead and cheeks were horribly disfigured. His right eye was a mass of swollen flesh. His left pupil was discernible, however, through almost closed lids.

"Do you recognize this man?" said Sackler.

Gerde nodded. "It is Stanislaus Ratowski of Slovonia."

Stanislaus inhaled sharply. "This is a trick," he snapped. "He can't see."

"Test him," said Sackler.

Stanislaus approached Gerde. He held three fingers up before the other's face.

"How many fingers am I holding up?"

"Three," said Gerde.

Stanislaus tried again.

"Four," said Gerde.

Stanislaus' poise slipped slowly from him. "But it's impossible," he cried. "A vial of vitriol landed full in his face. I saw it myself."

"There was something else you didn't see in that gloomy room," said Sackler. "His glasses."

"His glasses?"

"Right. Gerde is an absent-minded man. He went to bed with his glasses on. You hurled the acid into his face from the window sill without bothering to observe him too closely. His glasses saved him the sight of his left eye. And that, my boy, will burn you."

"But the newspapers said—"

"Inspector Woolley reluctantly arranged that."

I sat next to Sackler in the cab on the way back to the office. He was grinning happily like a banker who has just foreclosed a mortgage.

After the identification Stanislaus, or Arthur, cracked completely. He told all and implicated Harrison all the way. Even Sackler's surmise regarding the Schmitt girl had been correct.

He had attempted to get through her window with his tube of acid earlier that evening. Frieda had recognized him and had run from the room before he could get in. Instead of telling the police she tried to tell me. Arthur followed her, entered my rooming house and this time found her.

As far as I was concerned there was but one consolation. I gave voice to it in the taxi on our return to the office.

"Anyway, you'll have to wait a while for your dough. Gerde's good for a few years yet."

"Oh, that, Joey. Don't worry about it. I renegotiated the whole deal."

"Renegotiated it? How?"

"That was why I held the conference with Gerde and Winterly. Winterly agreed that if I was right about Arthur, he would give me five thousand bucks for the policy and let Gerde make it over to him. Moreover, he paid me twenty-five hundred in addition for exposing Arthur. I did pretty well on the deal."

I clapped my hand to my head. *"Pretty* well? You cleaned up again. And what do I get? Nothing! And you collect seventy-five hundred clams. My God, it's a wonder you didn't insist that on top of it he pay you the five hundred for going over Arthur's papers as well."

Sackler gasped and tapped madly on the back window. The driver turned his head.

"Stop at this drugstore," said Sackler. "I have to make a phone call."

"To whom?" I asked.

"Winterly. Damn it, Joey, I'm getting amnesia. I completely forgot that five hundred. I'll just remind the old man to put it on the check. Thanks for reminding me."

The man's gall was colossal. But that was no reason for me not to have kept my gibbering mouth shut.

DEATH IN THE TANK

HUGH SPEER

———

"I HAVE NEVER DENIED THE EXISTENCE OF VAMPIRES," SAID Dr. Gabriel a little crossly. "I never deny nor affirm anything without evidence to go upon. Surely you have seen enough of my methods to understand that!"

I said nothing. The little doctor was unpredictable. He was always touchy when anyone suggested that he was mixed up in any way with psychic matters. He claimed to be purely a scientist, and, while admitting the existence of a whole range of phenomena as yet unclassified, stoutly resisted any attempt to enroll him as a believer in the supernatural.

Now, nearing the end of a tedious train journey, I had attempted to put him in good humor by ridiculing the purpose of our visit to Teppan, only to be snubbed for my pains.

I looked out at the dreary scenery. The single track ran beside the Atlantic shallows, now on a roadbed that looked as if it might at any moment crumble, now over little culverts that trembled crazily beneath the weight of the train. There was but the single coach, in which the doctor and I were seated. The line was, in fact, half-derelict, and maintained in use only for the preservation of a franchise.

Out of the marshes rose the little town of Teppan. A century ago whalers had sailed from the now hopelessly choked up bay. Now Teppan was as nearly a ghost town as any on the Atlantic coast. It was miles from anywhere; its sea trade was abandoned and forgotten; a glance at the unpainted shacks on either side of the tracks showed that Teppan had ceased to be an ordinary American community; and was reverting to a kind of shiftless pioneer existence.

The one-coach train came to a grinding halt about two hundred yards from the station.

"Now what are the fools stopping for?" demanded the doctor irascibly.

I looked out of the window and saw a dilapidated freight truck blocking the line. "I suppose they've got to get it out of the way," I said to the doctor.

"We'll get out of here and walk," he said.

"There's been a flood, or an overflow, or something," I replied. "The water looks knee-deep on either side of the roadbed."

"Damn!" said the doctor.

"But it looks as if there's an engine getting up steam enough to pull that car out of the way."

"Why don't they use our engine to butt her off the line?"

"I don't know," I said. "Teppan looks like a crazy place to me. I suppose they know their own methods. Maybe the couplings would break."

Gabriel's irascibility never lasted very long. Suddenly he smiled. "I believe I'll take one of your cigarettes," he said. "I'm getting to be an impatient old man, and that's the truth of it. I should have paid no attention to that crazy girl's letter, but I was interested in the vampire angle of it. If she'd been a Slav, I'd have disregarded it, but Hilton's not a Slav name, and the revival of the vampire legend in this corner of New England interested me. Besides, I've never seen this part of the country. She's insane, of course, and it looks to me as if all Teppan's insane.

"I must say, I'm interested in the set-up, too," he added. "Exhibit One—this old sea-captain's widow, living among his relics, brooding over his memory, and that of the grand-daughter who killed herself for love and is allegedly a vampire. Exhibit Two—this grand-niece, Judy Hilton, who threatens suicide also, unless I can lay this vampire that threatens the lives of all. Exhibit Three—Cousin Jared, who seems, from the letter, to be the only sane person in the outfit. Exhibit Four, Cousin Jared's son, Enoch, who seems to be the bad boy of the party, and acts as the medium for the vampire.

"It's a pretty set-up, and the physical phenomena appear to be lively, to say the least. Almost worth coming to Teppan for."

The line had been cleared; the train began to move, with infinite slowness, toward the station. On a hillock beside the water a large, square house came into view, surmounted by a belvedere.

"That must be the house," I said. "All those old whalers built belvederes, so that their families could watch for their incoming ships."

"It looks like it. It's a gloomy sort of place," said Gabriel, "rising out of the scrub forest. Well, do you feel like stretching your legs a bit? Or shall we see if they've ever heard of motor-cars in Teppan?"

That question was answered when we got off at the little station, where a dozen loafers were assembled to see what must have been the sensation of the day, the train's arrival. Their was a car drawn up, evidently for hire. It was a T-model Ford, the first I had seen in several years, and the driver looked equally interesting as a survival.

"Can you take us to the Hilton house?" I asked.

"Reckon I cain't," answered the old man, and the loafers closed in about us in evident surprise.

"Why not?"

The old man cackled. "They ain't in good repute around here," he answered. "If you're going to the Hilton house, misters, the only way you'll git there is on shanks' mare."

"That's the house over there, isn't it?" I asked.

"That's her," said the driver, and the crowd began to grin. I turned to Gabriel. "I suppose we'd best walk, then," I said.

"If you was to ask me, you'll be walking out quicker than you walked in," said the old man. "Straight along the road, and through them pines. You can't mistake her."

We started, and the loafers followed us at a little distance, gradually slackening speed, and finally falling away. It was late in the afternoon, the sun was hidden behind rain-clouds; the dead, brown leaves of late Autumn were dropping from the trees.

"It looks like a good setting for a vampire," I said.

Gabriel made no answer. He plodded on beside me, apparently absorbed in his own thoughts. We passed through the strip of pine forest, and saw the house before us.

It stood in an unweeded lot, in which little pines were springing up everywhere, like Christmas trees. In one corner was a garbage pit, filled with smoking refuse.

A girl came out of the back door of the house, and went toward it, carrying something in a parcel. We were quite near her before she seemed to realize our presence. She stopped, hugging the parcel to her, apparently uncertain whether or not to take flight.

"Stay there!" called Gabriel. "You're Judy Hilton, aren't you? My name's Gabriel. What have you got in that parcel?"

"It's nothing," she whimpered. "I—I never thought you'd

come. You've got to go away. I didn't mean what I wrote to you."

"Let me see that parcel," said Gabriel, taking it from her with quiet insistence; and the girl burst into sobs.

There was a dead cat in the parcel. It seemed to have been subjected to some tremendous pressure, for its back was broken, its ribs were crushed in, and the throat had been gouged by some creature that seemed to have drained the blood from the body.

Gabriel wrapped it in the paper again, and deposited it in the smoldering heap. The girl was still sobbing when he came back. She was a pretty, fair-haired girl of perhaps nineteen or twenty. She lifted woebegone eyes to the doctor's.

"Well, you see I did come," he said. "But you've nothing to be afraid of. Where's Jared Hilton?"

"He went away yesterday," she said tremulously. "He—he found out that I'd written to you, and he was angry. He said he had business in Boston, and, if you came, you—you were not to be admitted."

"Ah, well, I expect he *was* just a little annoyed. What did he go to Boston for?"

"It's something to do with granny's money. She wanted him to put it into war bonds, and he said he would—but I don't believe he intended to. And then there was the question of the settlement."

"What settlement is that?"

"Why, Cousin Jared has a claim on a part of the estate. I don't know the details, but he said, since granny is not likely to live long, it all ought to be settled properly."

"I see. And who's this Cousin Enoch? No, never mind," added the doctor hastily, as the girl broke into a fresh exhibition of distress. "We're coming up to the house to make your grandmother's acquaintance. By the way—was it Cousin Enoch who killed your cat?"

"No, sir. Enoch wouldn't do a thing like that. It was"—her voice sank—"it was the vampire."

"Come, now, Judy, you don't seriously believe that your cousin Molly became a vampire after death? Wasn't she a good girl?"

"Indeed she was. But the—the thing says it's Molly, and it's killed my dog too. It strangled him, and sucked his blood, just like my cat. And unless I do what it tells me, it's going to kill me too."

"What have you got to do?"

"M-marry Enoch," whispered Judy.

"He's the medium?"

"She says—Molly says that afterward she'll go away and leave everybody in peace. That's why I wrote to you. I'd heard of you and your wonderful psychic cures."

Dr. Gabriel frowned at that word, but he kept his equanimity. "I'm sure everything will come right," he said. "Run up to the house, Judy, and tell your grandmother that we'll be her guests for supper."

To me, after she was gone: "It looks as if this Cousin Jared is at the bottom of things. I think this is going to be more interesting than I had expected it would be."

Mrs. Hilton must have been nearly ninety, a very old lady, her mind confused, but very proud of her house and of her memories. She apologized for Jared's absence, took us for friends of his, and personally conducted us all over the old rambling structure.

Her mind was quite clear as to the past. She spoke with pride, but some repetition, of the days when her husband brought silks from China, and spices from the Indies, and of her watching for his ship from the belvedere. She showed us nearly a score of rooms, replete with old-fashioned furniture and antiques, and spoke of the runaway slaves that had been secreted in the house during the Civil War, when it had been one of the reception stations on the route to Canada.

"And where they were hid," she said, for the moment thinking herself a girl again, "I'm not going to tell you this cruel Civil War is over, though I know you're loyal to the Union. Those were my husband's last words to me, before he sailed on his last trip."

It was in the large living room, however, that old Mrs. Hilton had placed most of her husband's trophies. Captain Hilton's mind seemed to have had a fantastic turn, for there were numerous quaintly carved ivories from the Orient, there was a collection of ivory elephants; a huge stuffed and moth-eaten shark occupied the whole side of one wall, and facing it were the enormous, gaping jaws of a whale that must, when whole, have been one of the largest that ever existed.

Perhaps the relic that most drew my attention was an enormous glass bowl, some twelve feet by three, which stood in a nook beside the fireplace. In and out amid the vegetation a few goldfish were swimming. And over the bowl, carved in some dark wood, was a complete replica of a temple. There were the steps leading down to the water, and washed by it, there were the miniature figures of the priests outside the building, in which one could see dozens of tiny figures of worshipers. The carving must have taken the artist years of his life.

"It's the Ganges," said old Mrs. Hilton. "My husband is very proud of it. It was given to him by a rajah. When he comes home, that's the first thing he'll ask to see. I give the fish fresh water every week, though he says they don't need it, with those plants growing in it. And Molly don't forget. She loves her grandfather—"

A sudden change came over the old woman's face. "But she's dead!" she cried. "I'd forgot! She's dead, and she's damned because she took her life. She's damned unless Judy releases her from where she's wandering—"

I wasn't surprised to discover that Enoch Hilton was a moron. That fact seemed to complete the picture of horror in the old house. He was a youth in his early twenties, with a shock of dark hair, a drooping lower lip, and a vacuous expression, save when he leered at Judy, across the table, and then he wasn't a pleasant person to have around.

Judy sat down between the doctor and myself, after she had served the dinner. I could feel her trembling, and I knew that she lived in deadly fear. Gabriel adroitly led the talk around to psychic phenomena, and the half-wit took the bait eagerly.

"I'm sorry your father is not here," said the doctor. "My friend and I have come quite a distance to witness the amazing things that happen at your house. Tell me, Mr. Hilton, do you really believe in the supernatural?"

Enoch answered glibly: "I dunno, doctor. I dunno anything that happens after I go into a trance. But there's an evil spirit afoot in this house, and it's going to take the life of every last one of us unless—"

He stopped, and leered at Judy again. I caught the girl's hand in mine, under the table, and pressed it hard.

Old Mrs. Hilton, who was hard of hearing, but seemed to have gauged the tenor of the conversation, broke in:

"It's not her fault, poor girl. She was the sweetest girl that ever lived, but he was a married man, and deceived her. She took her own life, and that's why she's punished the way she

is. It ain't her soul, it's something wicked that's taken possession of her, and she'll never rest in her grave, poor thing,
until Judy does what she tells her to."

I squeezed Judy's hand again. "Keep quiet! Hold up!" I
whispered, and I saw the moron glaring at me across the
table, though he hadn't heard.

"And when may we have the pleasure of seeing an exhibition of your powers, Mr. Hilton?" inquired the doctor
blandly.

"I dunno. The power comes and goes. I don't feel like it's
coming on tonight," responded Enoch. "Maybe tomorrow,
if you care to stay that long."

"I think we could manage it," answered Gabriel. And now
I saw that Enoch quite divined our purpose. He was scowling
alternately at Gabriel and myself. The young man wasn't so
much of a moron as he wanted us to believe.

That was the doctor's opinion too. Judy had shown us to
our rooms, two pleasant ones with a connecting door. The
furniture was Victorian, the sheets were damp with the sea-
fog that seemed to fill the house.

"Of course it's a matter of the old lady's fortune," said
Gabriel. "Many of those old sea-captains left considerable
funds, and I've no doubt Hilton had a nice little amount
tucked away in investments. I don't think we have to look
for motive here, my boy. The question is: what killed that
cat? And here I'm forced to confess myself baffled.

"It's evident that some tremendous force was used. The
pressure of two human hands would be altogether insuffi-
cient to crush and distort the body like that. No mechanical
contrivance would have produced those results, in my opinion.

"I cannot think of anything in nature that has that power of constriction, except—"

"A python, or boa constrictor," I suggested. "But unless there's a captive one in the cellar—"

"We have to rule that out," answered the doctor, "because a python swallows its prey. The thing that killed that cat inflicted a gaping wound in the throat. I almost thought of one of the sheep-killing parrots, or keas, of New Zealand. But naturally a parrot cannot constrict its prey. I'm frankly baffled."

"It might have been a boa constrictor working in cooperation with a kea," I proposed.

Gabriel shook his head. "It might have been a vampire," he returned, "except that I never heard of a vampire killing its prey by constriction."

"I've heard of a man who was strangled by ectoplasm," I said, half-mockingly, because I was agog with curiosity. But Gabriel returned no answer to my sally.

"I'm going to bed," he said. "I see that there's a key in the inside of my door, and I see there's a bolt on yours. I advise you to use that bolt tonight. It's my opinion that Jared and that alleged half-wit son of his are playing for high stakes, and that they won't stop at very much to get us out of the way."

"But Jared's away," I said. "There doesn't seem to be a telephone in this house. Of course, he may have been notified, but—"

The doctor gave me one of his characteristic bland looks, and went into his room.

I had been faintly conscious in my sleep of the barking of a dog somewhere outside the house. Vaguely disturbed, I went on dreaming of an enormous kea, with serpent coils in place of wings . . . Suddenly the barking was changed to a succession of frantic yelps, and then a long howl of agony.

Next to the cry of a child, I don't think there is anything that racks one so much as the distressing cry of a dog. I was on my feet in a moment, and tugging at the bolt on my door. But Gabriel was in the hall before me. He was in his shoes —he'd evidently slept in them—and I was not. He went down the stairs with surprising speed, and I followed him. I had reached the lower hall when the last howl died away in an agonizing whine.

It came from just outside the building. Gabriel was already turning the great key in the front door. He got it open, and I rushed out in his wake. The night was moonless, but there was a fair amount of starlight, and in a few moments I was able to make out the crushed and mangled body of the dog, lying close up against what looked like a cellar door.

It had been a retriever, a beautiful black and white creature with thick, curly hair. Now it was a twisted mass of flesh and broken bone. And in the throat was the same sort of gouged wound that I had seen on the cat, only the monster, whatever it was, seemed to have been frightened away before it had drained the blood, which was still flowing.

I saw Gabriel stooping down, searching the ground, as if for footprints. Suddenly he sprang to his feet.

"The cellar door!" he shouted, and hurled himself against it with surprising force and agility.

It had been a strong door, but it was rotted with the years, and cracked under the impetus of his body. I flung my whole weight against it in turn. This time a great crack opened for half its length. Once more, and the upper part broke from its hinges. Gabriel sprang across it, and I saw that he had a revolver in his hand.

He was inside, calling to me, and I followed him. There

seemed to be nothing there. It was a small cellar, not running under the whole house, but under what must have been an addition—the addition which was represented upstairs by the parlor. There was a furnace, which seemed not to have been used that autumn, there were the usual pipes, three or four empty barrels—nothing more.

Neither boa constrictor nor New Zealand parrot could have survived that search we made. If the thing had got away up the cellar stairs, it had been incredibly quick and silent. And in that case it must be in the house!

"We'll have to search the house," I said to Gabriel.

"I think there will be no need," he answered dryly.

"You don't think it was in the cellar?"

He made no answer, but I heard a noise outside, and there stood Enoch Hilton, leering at us.

"So she got Morrow's dog," he said. "I was afeared that was what was going to happen, if it came running around here. Told Morrow to keep him chained at night."

"Who's 'she'?" I shot at him.

"Molly Hilton," he answered, snarling.

It was Judy's cry of protest that brought me downstairs rather quickly in the morning. I found the girl confronting Enoch, who had evidently been making advances to her. The moron grinned and leered at me as I entered, and then disappeared through the kitchen door as Gabriel followed me into the room.

Judy was preparing breakfast, but her hands were shaking so that the skillet nearly slipped from them. We sat down in the dining-room, and the girl brought us our meal.

"Fried crabs for breakfast," said the doctor, with elevated eyebrows. "Last night it was shrimps. Now why this superfluity of sea food? I must ask Judy."

He did, when the girl came back. "Granny and Enoch are

fond of sea food," answered the girl. "We have it every day. I'm sick of it. I hope you don't mind."

"These crabs are rather tasty," answered the doctor. "And your coffee's so good that I'm going to trouble you for another cup of it." As Judy went out, he said to me:

"Do you derive any particular deduction from this fondness for sea food?"

"I should say that either the old lady or Enoch liked it," I returned, a little mystified.

When we had finished eating, Judy came in, her face tearful, but resolute. "I can't stand it here any longer, even for granny's sake," she said. "They're driving me crazy. She's crazy, and Enoch's crazy, and he makes life impossible for me. And that poor dog of Mr. Morrow's—"

"Who do you think killed it, Judy?" asked Gabriel.

"Why, she did, of course. She was my best friend," said Judy, breaking down. "She was six years older than me, and like a mother to me. And she killed herself, because of that wretched man, and now— Oh, it's too horrible, Dr. Gabriel!"

"You really believe that that could happen to your cousin Molly? Come, my dear, be sensible."

"But everybody knows that's what suicides turn into," wept Judy. "I want to get away. Won't you take me away?"

"Suppose we solve the problem for you—or, at least, lay this thing. Won't that do?"

"No," she whimpered. "There's Enoch. And Cousin Jared. And you can't solve it unless Enoch gets one of his medium spells. He was saying, if you don't go today, you'll be sorry for it for the rest of your lives, and that won't be for long."

"Threats, eh?" smiled Gabriel. "The plot thickens. Tell Enoch we're staying here until one of those spells comes over him. We're your guests, Judy, my dear, for, if I'm correct, you have a share in the ownership of this house."

We explored the neighborhood during the day. I noticed that Enoch hovered near us whenever we were near the house. I believed we had overlooked something in the cellar in the darkness. Still, it was impossible that any monster of ferocious strength was lurking there. Morrow, our nearest neighbor, came over in the course of the afternoon, asked for his dog, and made a fuss when Gabriel told him it had been killed.

"Aye, there's a killer around here," stormed the old man. "I've seen hens killed and crushed into a ball. And I'll tell you who it is. It's that loon, Enoch. He's got the strength of a vise in them big hands of his. And he ought to be put away. By heavens, I'm going to have him put away! A crazy pair, him and the old woman, and Jared ain't no better."

But he made no move to confront Enoch—in fact, he departed rather hurriedly when Enoch hove into sight. I understood now why the taxi man had refused to drive us to the place.

"How long do we stay?" I asked the doctor. "Till Jared comes back?"

Gabriel smiled. "I'm inclined to think that Cousin Jared doesn't mean to return as long as we're here," he answered. "My dear fellow, do you imagine that it's only we who are making plans? We're upsetting Cousin Jared's applecart."

"Then you think that Enoch has somehow got word to his father?"

"I think Cousin Jared is much more concerned about the upshot of this business than we are. And, just as a tip, my boy, keep your eyes peeled in going upstairs, or around dark corners.

"The next move is strictly up to the opposition, and I think they'll make it today—at least, if Judy gave Enoch that message that I sent him."

"I got a feeling maybe the spell will be coming on to-night," Enoch announced in the living-room before supper.

I glanced at the doctor. He had diagnosed the situation correctly: the other side was making the play. And I guessed that he had already come to certain conclusions at which I couldn't grasp.

Old Mrs. Hilton, wrapped in a heavy shawl, was dozing in the recess near the tank, in which the goldfish pursued their never-ending course. On the hearth a little wood fire was burning.

"Dinner's ready," announced Judy from the doorway.

The main dish was curried crayfish. I was a little tired of shellfish by this time, but it certainly tasted good. I tried to extract a glance from the doctor, but he only sat eating with a sardonic look on his face. There was not much conversation during the meal, mainly a few sporadic remarks from the old lady as to the progress of the Civil War.

"I sure have got that feeling," announced Enoch again, leering at us from across the table. "Gran, she wants to talk to Judy again."

He shouted this remark twice before the old lady under-stood. Then she shrilled out, punctuating her remarks with violent nods:

"You get her to talk to us, Enoch. You get her to talk plain to Judy. Judy and you have got to be man and wife, and then maybe she'll be able to rest quiet in her grave, poor soul. She was the sweetest girl that ever lived, and he was a mar-ried man."

Judy's face was the picture of despair. I tried to press her hand again, but it remained limp and cold within mine. After the meal, Enoch said:

"That feeling's coming over me for sure. I think she'll manifest tonight. I guess I'll go and rig up the cabinet."

The so-called cabinet consisted merely of a dark curtain drawn across the mouth of the recess that had contained Mrs. Hilton's armchair and the goldfish tank. The armchair had been placed outside for the old lady, and the medium's chair was beside the tank. The windows had been darkened with black shades. Outside the curtain three chairs were drawn up in alignment with Mrs. Hilton's, so that we all sat staring at the black folds.

I had the doctor on my left, and Judy on my right. On Judy's right was the old lady, sunk into her chair like some mummy. Enoch extinguished the oil lamp, leaving the room in almost total darkness. Standing between the edges of the curtain, he said:

"I'm asking you folks to cooperate with me. When I'm in a trance, I don't know what I'm saying or doing. I don't know nothing, and I ain't responsible for what happens. You asked for this demonstration, and you're going to get it. If anybody don't agree, nobody's hindering him from leaving this house right now."

I imagined the doctor smiling sardonically at this. It was virtually Enoch's last invitation to us to leave, or take the consequences. I was thankful for the revolver that I had seen in Gabriel's hand the night before, and I would have felt more comfortable if I had had one of my own.

I felt Judy, beside me, trembling, and I was trembling myself, although with anticipation rather than fear. I expected that some abominable monster was to be loosed upon us, something chained up during the day, and let out at night to prey. It must be a species of boa, despite the doctor's doubts. And then I thought of the dragon, the symbol of China.

Might it not be possible that, in the course of his journeys, the old captain had obtained a specimen of some creature unknown to the western world, something between a python and a snake, and brought it home with him?

It must have been many years since Captain Hilton had sailed on his last voyage, but wasn't the dragon the symbol of longevity?

Anyway, it seemed unquestionable that Enoch had somehow got into touch with Jared Hilton, and that the pair had resolved to rid themselves of our presence. It was a desperate gamble, and the stakes must be high indeed.

Enoch had begun to moan and writhe behind the curtains. In the all but darkness I could see old Mrs. Hilton leaning forward in her chair. "What's she saying?" she mumbled. "What's my darling Molly saying?"

She had her hand cupped to her ear. Gabriel, on my left, was sitting tense. Judy was whimpering with fear. The moaning went on and on—and then suddenly was supplanted by the high, shrill voice of a woman.

It was a clever piece of trickery, and it was pitched in a tone that must have been calculated to reach Mrs. Hilton's failing hearing:

"I am in torture. I am enslaved in a foul body that is compelled to roam the earth by night, seeking what it can devour, until Judy releases me."

That wasn't so clever. Poor, amateurish stuff, I thought, and just what one might expect of Enoch. But Judy, at my right, was shaking.

"Judy darling, don't you know me? I am going to try to manifest myself to you—"

Judy screamed. She was about to plunge forward, but I caught her in my arms and restrained her.

"Don't try to touch me, or I must go. Later I shall manifest myself more plainly, but you must not touch me now.

Sit still and look at me. But listen first. You must marry Enoch, Judy, and unite the two branches of our family—"

"She says you've got to marry Enoch, Judy!" shrilled old Mrs. Hilton from her chair.

"Only in that way can you release me from bondage, my punishment because I took my own life." A pause. Then, "I am coming, Judy. I am coming, Gran. Watch closely. I am going to show myself to you. . . ."

A longer pause. And then, against the black folds of the curtain, I saw what looked like an arm, terminating in ill-defined fingers. Luminous paint, of course. It was all the cheapest sort of mummery. And yet I felt that there was tragedy behind it. Something was going to break.

That luminous arm passed across the folds of the curtain and seemed suspended in the air. Then I felt it brush my face, cold, clammy, pliant, and horrible. Old Mrs. Hilton must have felt it too, for she screamed: "It's ectoplasm. It's what she uses to build up. Molly! Molly, my darling girl!"

And then I saw the face, and my blood ran cold. A mask, of course, and the most hideous mask that could have been devised. Two great black eyes, and a beak of a shadowy nose, over which the phosphorescent light played and rippled. It resembled nothing human or animal, but Mrs. Hilton screamed again: "My Molly! My darling Molly!"

Judy had slumped down in her chair in a swoon. I half-rose. The tension was unbearable. I felt that luminous arm about my neck. I clutched at it, but it eluded me, and seemed to quiver, diffusing a faint, unearthly radiance. I was leaning over Judy, and I was conscious of the doctor bending toward me. "Get ready now!" he whispered.

The utter silence that followed was the tensest that one could imagine. Out of that silence I knew murder was creeping stealthily toward us. The mask of a face had disappeared, as if whipped back into the cabinet. And then a horrible shriek broke from the lips of the medium.

Enoch was screaming, not in the affected woman's voice now, but in his own. He was threshing and flopping, and throwing himself about the floor behind the curtain.

"Save me! Save me!" he howled—and then that howl was cut off in a strangled moan.

"Light the lamp!" Dr. Gabriel shouted.

I leaped from my chair, passing the doctor's silhouette as he sat crouched beside me. I knocked into the table, found the lamp, struck a match, and applied the flame to the wick with trembling fingers. All the while those moans went on and on, and then suddenly there ensued a frightful silence, broken only by the mumblings of the old woman.

Before the wick had fairly caught, I heard the roar of Gabriel's revolver. Another shot—another—and still once more. A hideous flopping on the floor. I turned. The curtains were down. The body of Enoch lay, still writhing, and horribly mangled; in the throat was a gaping wound from which the blood was streaming.

For a moment or two longer, until the room was lit, I could discern nothing more. Then I saw that Enoch's body was enmeshed in what looked like black and writhing cords. And close beside his face was a parrot-beak, and two black eyes.

Then I recognized the dying octopus.

Gabriel, who was stooping over the body of Enoch, suddenly raised himself. With a heave of his shoulder he overturned the goldfish tank. The model of the temple went crashing to the floor in pieces, the water slopped all over us. And now I saw two things: that the tank had a false bottom, large enough to have just contained the monstrous devil that had occupied it. And that there was a trap-door beneath the tank, with an iron ring in it.

The doctor stooped, and pulled up the trap-door. "Come up out of there, Jared Hilton!" he shouted. "And come running!"

I realized then that this was the secret chamber, used to house runaway slaves, of which old Mrs. Hilton had spoken to me. It had been built so cunningly into the structure that nobody could have suspected its existence.

I saw a shadowy mass detach itself from the blackness at the foot of the wooden stairs. The roar of a revolver resounded through the vault three times. And then Jared came charging up at Gabriel.

He had reached the top stair before the doctor shot him through the heart, and his impetus carried him forward. Then the revolver fell clattering from his hand, and his body pitched forward upon that of Enoch, into the pool of water in which the goldfish were flopping helplessly.

Jared was a man of great bulk and stature, almost a giant, in contrast to his son's puny form. His hair was red, instead of black, his jowls hung down his throat. So great was his vitality that even now his fingers were going through the motion of discharging a revolver.

A tentacle from the dying octopus moved across Jared's face, and clutched at him. I saw the suckers, and the tiny spots of phosphorescence that had made the tentacle appear an arm. I glanced back. Old Mrs. Hilton was slumped down in her chair, and breathing stertorously, as if in the throes of an apoplectic fit. Judy was, mercifully, still unconscious.

Suddenly there came a hammering at the front door. I crossed the hall and opened it. Two police officers were standing there, and they had drawn pistols in their hands.

"State Police," one of them announced crisply. "What's all the shooting going on in here?"

"I'll show you," I said, and led the way inside. They looked at the doctor, at the two dead men, and at the octopus.

"This is Dr. Gabriel, the well-known alienist," I told them. "He killed that man in self-defense. Let's carry the old lady to her room, and get this mess cleared up, and then we'll talk."

"My God," said the sergeant, "and we came here to see about Mr. Morrow's dog!"

Old Mrs. Hilton died next morning. The doctor and I were detained pending the coroner's hearing. The incident of the octopus was left out, by mutual consent. As the prosecutor said, he didn't want that sort of thing attached to his name, when he was a candidate for re-election, or he'd be known as "Octopus" Johnson for the rest of his days. Besides it was immaterial.

What eased things for us considerably was the fact that Jared Hilton had been under observation for a long time as the leader of a band of narcotic smugglers, and considerable quantities of heroin and cocaine were discovered in the secret room beneath the tank.

Gabriel was considerably irked by the delay, and more so by the title of "psychic" that attached itself to him. In the end, however, we left the court-room as popular heroes. We had broken up a dangerous narcotics ring, and risked our lives to rescue a young girl who was being held captive in the gloomy old house by the sea.

"Do you suppose that the old lady knew of the existence of the octopus?" I asked the doctor. "It must have lived in that tank for years. Her husband must have brought it home with him from one of his voyages."

"I should say 'yes,'" answered Gabriel. "But as to the part it was meant to play, I should say 'no.' Before her mind and memory went, she probably looked on it as a kind of pet. Its growth was probably hastened by appropriate feeding. I've no doubt that, if Judy had insisted on her refusal to marry Enoch, she would have been dispatched by means of it. Apparently they were in the process of trying it out on dogs and cats when we appeared on the scene.

"Jared Hilton's extensive defalcations, and embezzlements of the considerable Hilton property had driven him to the point where he was ready to murder us, rather than face discovery.

"I've no doubt that I was marked for death that night, and you'd probably have been shot. Evidently Enoch had learned how to guide the monster toward its prospective victim, but he slipped up, and it turned upon him instead."

"How much of this did you guess, doctor?" I asked. "And I'd like to know just how."

"You didn't notice that there were two levels of water in that tank? If you'd trained yourself to observation, you wouldn't have missed that. I guessed there was something underneath those goldfish. Then, when they kept serving us with crustaceans, I came pretty close to knowing. Crabs are the main food of the octopus, and all the cephalopoda.

"I'm glad that taxi driver has consented to call for us. It's about time he was here." He shifted the suitcase in the hall. "Judy, are you ready, my dear?" he called up the stairs.

DEATH LIES WAITING

ROLAND PHILLIPS

I

THE DRIZZLE OF THE EARLY EVENING HAD TURNED INTO A steady, cold rain now. Under the scattered lights, the deserted walks and streets were puddled with gold. Water ran ankle-deep in the gutters. Detective McGuire, wrapped in a disreputable slicker that flapped about his long legs, hat pulled well down over his bleak face, splashed along toward the warehouse garage. He had forgotten to put on his rubbers. His feet were wet and he knew his wife would fuss. A man his age ought to take better care of himself. Sort of foolish to be heading this way at this time of night and in such weather, but he had promised to meet Eddie Harper, ride part way home with the patrolman after he had pulled his last call box.

McGuire had been doing this on and off for some time now, whenever he was out late and in the neighborhood, joining Harper at the garage for a mug of hot coffee which old Nick Foster, the watchman, always had brewing around midnight. These meetings would soon be ended, for Eddie Harper was to lay aside his blues for khaki within a week. McGuire was going to miss the young man, but he knew Eddie was eager to tackle his new job and would, undoubtedly, do himself proud. Already, an older brother was with the Marines overseas, and every time he had a letter from him, it was read and reread at the midnight sessions. McGuire got as much of a kick out of the scribbled reports as Eddie himself.

The two big covered trucks that roared out from a dark side street and skidded perilously into the avenue sloshed a sea of dirty water against McGuire's legs. He bellowed and jumped aside, almost lost his footing on the slippery pavement. Army trucks they were, he decided, watching the twin red tail lights wink out in the murk. Plenty of them in the area now, rolling day and night toward the long piers where gray ships were always loading. The husky lads at the wheels certainly knew how to handle the brutes, but they were sometimes indifferent to traffic regulations.

The detective pushed on. The wind was freshening, and when he turned the last corner, the rain whipped into his face and drove the breath from him. Because his head was lowered against the wet blast, McGuire did not notice that the big double doors of the garage were standing open until he was within a dozen feet of them. The unexpected sight brought him up short. The heavy doors were always closed and locked at this hour. The only entrance to the premises was a small door at one side that led into a cubbyhole of an office where the watchman stayed. The door had a foot-square glassed opening cut into the top panel through which prospective visitors were scrutinized before being admitted.

Now that door was closed as usual, but the garage doors were wide open to the driving rain, which was unusual. Moreover, the garage was empty. Suddenly remembering the trucks that had rumbled past him a few minutes before, McGuire began to swear and put himself into motion. He slipped a hand under his raincoat and curled his fingers around the butt of his service revolver as he pounded into the garage. A single light burned overhead, and he saw that the door leading into the watchman's office was ajar.

"Hey, Nick!" he shouted. "You in there?"

The watchman lay face down on the floor, a sack over his head, his arms roped behind him, his legs bound. He began squirming and mumbling through the cloth. McGuire stripped off the sack, slashed the cords and helped the man to his feet.

"Thought that was you yellin', Mac," Foster began. "Wasn't stirrin' none till I was sure. Them dirty apes—"

"Got away with two trucks, did they?" McGuire broke in, reaching for the phone on the desk. "How long ago?"

"They ain't been gone more'n five minutes," the watchman declared, and glanced at the clock. "It was twelve exactly when I opened the door."

McGuire dropped the instrument when he saw the snipped wires.

"Another phone just inside the door at the top of them stairs," Foster told him. He fished a bunch of keys from his pocket, selected one and thrust it at the detective. McGuire bounded up the short flight of stairs, unlocked the door and groped for the light switch beside it. A moment later, he was talking to the sergeant at the neighborhood precinct station.

When he came down into the garage again, Foster was rubbing his head and swearing at the top of his voice, "The dirty apes! They fooled me plenty. I should have been more careful. But seein' the time, I figured it must be Eddie at the door."

McGuire suddenly stiffened. "Where is he? Where's Harper?"

"Ain't showed up yet. I thought it would be him at the

door, the way he always knocked. Three taps and then two with his stick. You know."

"That's the way the mugs got inside, was it? Using Eddie's signal?"

Foster nodded. "That's how it was. I had the coffee boilin'. I opened the door without lookin' or turnin' on the outside light. First thing I knew, I got a clout across the head and a bag over my face. Didn't see who it was. Wasn't hurt much, but I didn't put up no scrap. Just lay quiet where they dumped me, thinkin' you or Eddie would be along and grab the bunch."

Apprehension touched McGuire now. If the culprits had used Harper's signal to get inside the garage, they must have checked up on his regular movements. The watchman saw the look on the detective's face and scowled.

"Say, you don't think maybe—" he began.

McGuire turned and stumbled out into the rain. Presently, he began to shout, but realized that was foolish, and splashed along the dim street beside the warehouse. It was too dark to see much, but he knew the location of the nearest call box and headed toward it. The thieves must have been smart enough to let Harper make his last report, so that no prowl car would be warned and show up to investigate. The job had been carefully planned ahead of time.

The box was a block beyond at the corner of a small park. There was a hooded light on the post, and even before he reached it, McGuire saw the figure sprawled below in the gutter.

"Eddie! Eddie!" he called, and knelt down in the running water to touch the white, upturned face.

He picked the young man up in his arms and started back toward the garage. Before he had crossed the street, a car swept up and skidded to a stop beside him. He was dimly aware of the two officers in slickers who piled out, flashed a light in his face and spoke his name.

"Who you got there, Mac?"

"It's Eddie Harper," McGuire explained. "I . . . I'm afraid he's bad hurt. Get him to the hospital right quick, will you? I'll go along. We better hurry."

The men relieved him of the burden, and one of them turned the light on the patrolman's face, held it there a moment.

"No use hurrying, now," he said.

The garage was filled with men, bright with lights. McGuire, still dazed and unbelieving, sat on a bench in Foster's office. He had let the tears come and wasn't ashamed. It was Inspector Ramsey who came in presently and sat down beside him.

"A lousy, rotten break, Mac," he acknowledged. "God knows we can't afford to lose men like Harper these days."

McGuire knotted his fists. "It wouldn't have been so bad if he'd gone down fighting," he choked. "He might have died for a cause worth while and been proud of it. But to go out like this with a slug in him from some cheap punk, and just for a cargo of liquor."

"Sure, I know," Ramsey agreed. "But we'll round up the bunch. There were three of them, Foster tells me. And their leader was addressed as Skeet."

"Skeet?" McGuire repeated sharply. "Skeet Spofford? Sure of that, Nick?"

"That I am," the watchman assured him. "The Skeet part, I mean. I kept my ears wide open every minute. They done a lot of gabbin', thinkin' I was out cold."

"This would be his dish, all right," McGuire declared bitterly.

"You gct him last time, Mac. He went up for three years and was sprung only last month."

"I'll root him out again. I should have killed him that time when I had a chance."

Ramsey nodded. "You'll get another chance. This is the third job of its kind in the last thirty days. That's just as long as Skeet's been out, too. He's lined up a new racket, grabbing off liquor shipments, likely supplying black markets. Big money and quick. We haven't been able to get a lead on the outfit until tonight. Now maybe we can go to town. Remember who Skeet used to play around with?"

McGuire's mind swung back. "There was Baldy Egan and a louse by the name of Terry. And a girl friend—"

"Egan's doing time," the inspector broke in. "Terry's still around, I hear, but girl friends were a dime a dozen with Skeet."

"One girl in particular," the detective said. "A hoofer with a voice and looks. She changed her name after Skeet went up, appeared in a Broadway show and made a hit. I can't remember how she was billed."

"It'll come to you. Better get along home and turn in," Ramsey advised. "You're soaking wet. We can't do anything until morning, and by that time your mind will be sparking."

McGuire protested, but finally gave in, and a prowl car dropped him off uptown.

He remained awake a long time after crawling into bed. It was still cold and drizzling the next morning, but the detective was up early and was among the first to appear at Headquarters. There he learned that one of the stolen trucks had been found wrecked several miles north of the warehouse, its driver a casualty. The dead man was Terry, one of Skeet Spofford's former companions.

"Too bad he had to croak," Ramsey grumbled. "We might have sweated something out of him. He was packing an automatic, but it hadn't been discharged. The boys from ballistics report that a small gun, a .25, fired the slug into Eddie Harper. That's a thought to keep in mind. Not many crooks tote a rod of that caliber."

The newspapers hadn't devoted much space to the night's affair. After all, the theft of a whisky shipment and the murder of an obscure patrolman were items of a minor importance in a world at war. Spofford's name had failed to appear in print, an omission that Inspector Ramsey thought advisable.

Leo Craig breezed into the office presently, and greeted the occupants. A former private investigator for an indemnity company, Craig had relinquished that arduous post to become part owner of a bar and grill in the theatrical district. A tall, husky blond man, always well-groomed and affable, he had made his establishment popular as well as profitable. Ramsey didn't exactly refer to him as a stool, but McGuire was aware that the man passed along valuable bits of information when occasion required. Whether the inspector had anything on Craig the detective did not know, and cared less.

Craig nodded to McGuire, who was reading the sports section of the morning paper, and turned to Ramsey. "You wanted to see me?"

The inspector said he did and mentioned Spofford's name. Craig shook his head. The name didn't ring a bell with him.

"Ralph Spofford's his full moniker, but he was always known as Skeet," Ramsey added. "Hasn't been in town this time for more than a month. Used to pal around with Terry. Maybe still does."

"Yeah? Well, I saw Terry a couple nights ago. Had a tall, good-looking chap with him. A stranger to me."

The inspector thumbed over a batch of prints on his desk and tossed one across to his visitor. "This the man?"

"That's the bird," Craig declared, scanning the photograph. "Looks more like a movie hero than a punk. The next time Terry blows in I'll—"

"He won't," Ramsey broke in. "Terry seems to have been with an accident early this morning. A fatal one."

"That so?" Craig cocked an eye at the inspector and grinned. "An accident, eh? Well, that's too bad. I had him on the cuff for ten bucks which he promised to pay today."

"Something must have happened," Ramsey commented wryly. "What I want is Spofford's address. See what you can do, will you?"

"I'll try to dig it up," Craig promised. "And in case he should drop around to my place, what?"

"Keep him there and give me a ring. And you can get rough about it if he doesn't want to linger."

"I used to be pretty good at that," the other remarked. "Well, you'll be hearing from me." He waved a hand and departed.

When Craig had gone, McGuire tossed aside his newspaper and reached for the telephone directory. "Jordan!" he exclaimed. "That's the dame. Vera Jordan."

Ramsey stared at him. "What you mumbling about?"

"It just came to me. That girl of Skeet's."

"You sure? Vera Jordan's big time, Mac. She was featured in that big revue."

"She's come up fast," McGuire said. "Here's her address. It might be Skeet's, too," he added grimly, and picked up his hat. "That would be a break, wouldn't it?"

"Hold on!" Ramsey cried. "You can't start any rough stuff with that number. It's liable to get us in trouble."

"Get us out of it, you mean. I've a hunch she can put a

finger on Skeet. He was nuts about that hoofer, and she was on fire, too."

"If the flame still burns she isn't going to hand out any information," the inspector returned. "We've got to watch our step, Mac. I think it would be better if you asked her to come around and see me today, and be nice about it, understand?"

"Sure," McGuire said. "I'll be flawless in my approach. I'll be the very pink of politeness, however painful it may be."

The street itself wasn't one of the best in the Riverview section, but the apartment house was new and ornate, with a preponderance of tile and chromium. The detective passed through the hushed lobby, ignoring the girl at the switchboard who eyed him sharply, murmured Miss Jordan's name to the brown-skinned elevator attendant who let him off on the fourth floor.

McGuire jabbed the button under the engraved card beside one of the doors, and almost at once the door swung open to reveal a startled young woman in a flowing housecoat. He recognized her at once. She was far better-looking than when he last had seen her—shining black hair parted in the middle and combed flat against her head, big gray-blue eyes with long curling lashes.

"The name's McGuire," he announced, and smiled. "Detective McGuire."

"Yes?" she returned faintly, and moved back a few steps.

McGuire walked into the room, closing the door behind him. "Sorry to intrude at this unseemly hour, Miss Jordan," he said, "but Inspector Ramsey would appreciate it if you would call on him sometime this morning."

"I don't believe I know a Mr. Ramsey."

"I'll wait until you get dressed. Ramsey is an inspector, detective bureau. It's about a friend of yours. A one-time friend at any rate. Ralph Spofford. Better known as Skeet. Remember him?"

The woman continued to retreat across the room, her frightened eyes upon her visitor. McGuire wondered why she kept one hand concealed behind her back. He didn't imagine she would have a gun.

"I . . . I remember him," she admitted. "It was a long time ago."

"Three years," McGuire said mildly. "Maybe you remember me. You were with Skeet that night at the Como Club when I picked him up, after knocking him down. You put on quite a battle yourself, called me a lot of hard names. Seems like I had to slap you a couple of times. It was a big night."

Vera Jordan had backed away now until she was standing against the table at the front window. She hadn't removed her hand from behind her back. The table held a tall vase of roses, some books and a potted flowering plant.

"I haven't seen the man since that night," she stated quietly. "I never expect to. I didn't know he was a . . . a criminal. I heard afterward that he had been sentenced to a long term in jail."

"It wasn't long enough. He's out now and back in town."

"And you want him again?"

McGuire nodded. "We like to keep in touch with the fraternity. It's an old police custom."

The woman straightened. She used both hands now to smooth back her hair. She seemed more composed. "I don't know why you should come to me for information. You can go back and tell your inspector—"

"I'm sure he'd rather you told him yourself," McGuire put in patiently. "Those were my orders."

"This is an outrage!" she broke out. "Do you think because this man's back in town that I'd be seeing him? What do you take me for? I'm not being dragged down to police headquarters now or any other time, Mr. Detective, and you can tell your big shot just that."

McGuire swore under his breath and tried to keep his temper in check.

"I'll tell Ramsey how you feel about the matter," he said, surprised that he could speak so calmly. "Maybe I'll be able to persuade him to come up here. The only thing against that is—well, he'd have to be cagey about the visit and shake off the flock of newspaper boys."

"What have they to do with it?" she demanded.

"They've been hanging around headquarters all morning, smelling a story, I guess. You know how they are. That's why the inspector asked me to see you. If you'll let me use your phone—"

"Never mind." The woman's tone and manner changed abruptly, and she started across the room. "I just remembered I've a rehearsal at noon. I can stop off on my way. I'll get into some clothes. It won't take long."

"I don't mind waiting," McGuire told her, and sat down in a chair near the hall door.

When the door closed behind the woman, he grinned. He had called her bluff, scared her. She might not have objected so much to Ramsey calling, but it was evident she didn't want reporters nosing around, possibly trailing her. Sometimes they were worse than detectives.

He got up and surveyed the comfortable room and its furnishings. There were a number of framed photographs on the wall and piano, but none of them aroused his interest. He eyed the door through which the woman had vanished and wondered if she were alone on the premises, considered inventing some excuse to prowl the rooms beyond, but decided against the idea. If he should stumble upon Skeet Spofford, well and good. If he did not, there might be the devil to pay.

Suddenly recalling Vera's singular behavior when he first confronted her, and her actions afterward, he stepped over to the table. Between the books and the potted plant lay a pair of opera glasses. He stared at them and frowned. Apparently, these were what the woman had held behind her all the time and finally managed to drop here. But there didn't seem to be much sense in doing that, he reflected, and scanned the table closely to see if it held anything more significant, but he saw nothing except the half dozen books.

A queer piece of business, McGuire reasoned, hiding the glasses and doing it clumsily at that. What had the woman been afraid of? He glanced out the window that overlooked the roofs of the houses and small shops across the street. The view certainly wasn't inspiring, particularly on a day like this. The tallest of the buildings was almost directly opposite —a three-story brownstone front with its conventional iron railing, areaway and high stoop.

He picked up the glasses, leveled and adjusted them to his eyes. The lenses were powerful. The few pedestrians on the walks and the passing cars fairly jumped up at him. When he shifted the glasses higher, he could look into the rooms opposite where the shades were not drawn, see almost as clearly as if he had had his nose pressed against the windows.

Perhaps Vera got a kick out of spying on her neighbors, he thought. Some women were like that. Maybe that was what she had been doing when he knocked.

McGuire held the glasses on one of the windows for some time and finally let out a grunt. He was still intent upon what he saw when a sound reached him from somewhere in the apartment. He dropped the glasses back on the table and moved away quickly from the window. Vera Jordan, dressed for the street, found him sitting in the same chair when she swept into the room.

"I'm having my car brought around," she announced.

McGuire got up and put on his wet hat. "It'll save waiting for a taxi," he said.

They descended to the lobby with no more words between them, and stood under the sidewalk awning until a sleek, gray town car drew up at the curb. The driver, a short, unsmiling man with a flat nose and wide through the shoulders, jumped out and helped the woman into the rear seat. He wore a cap and belted raincoat. McGuire eyed him speculatively, surprised that so smart a car did not rate a liveried chauffeur.

The man held open the tonneau door and glanced inquiringly at the detective who remained on the sidewalk.

"Aren't you coming with me?" Vera asked.

McGuire shook his head. "You know the address, don't you? Ramsey will be expecting you. I just remembered I've got an appointment."

The woman frowned and shrugged. The driver shut the door and got into the front seat. McGuire turned and walked away briskly. He did not look up when the car rolled past him, and it was not until it had swung around the corner that he cut across the street and headed toward the brownstone front.

A faded sign on the stoop read "Furnished Rooms." About to ring the bell, the detective noticed that the front door was slightly ajar, pushed into the dimly lighted entry and mounted the stairs.

Except for a radio playing somewhere below, the house was quiet. He met no one in his ascent. Reaching the top floor, he moved along the hall to the door of the middle front room. There he listened a moment, his hand on the knob. Hearing no sound, he turned the knob and stepped into the room.

The overhead lights were burning, although the shades were not drawn, and they shone down upon the pallid, upturned face of the man lying full length on the floor. His eyes were wide open, glassy, his coat unbuttoned, the front of his shirt soggy red. He had been dead for some time.

After a quick glance about the room, McGuire went out into the hall again, careful to close the door behind him, dropped a coin into the pay phone at the head of the stairs and waited to get through to the inspector's desk.

"Hello, Ramsey," he greeted softly. "Vera Jordan show up yet?"

"Haven't seen her. I thought you—"

"Stall off the quiz program until later," McGuire broke in. "And if you should see her, don't give out you've talked with me."

"What's the idea? Where are you?"

"I don't know the number, but it's the brownstone front opposite the Jordan apartment on Riverview. Get up here in a hurry."

"Why'd I do that?" the inspector demanded.

"Because I've found a very dead man in the third-floor front who happens to be Skeet Spofford," McGuire replied, and hung up.

II

Grinning a little at the shock he had handed his chief, McGuire went back to the room. This time he leisurely explored the shallow closet, the contents of a suitcase, and opened some of the dresser drawers. Later, he knelt and went through the dead man's coat pockets. They gave up a pack of cigarettes, matches, some keys and a little silver, and the stub of a reserved seat ticket for a prize fight. He examined the latter speculatively before returning all the articles.

When Ramsey's car drove up below, McGuire met the inspector in the hall and led him into the room.

"It's Skeet, all right!" Ramsey exclaimed jubilantly. "No mistaking that handsome mug. How in thunder did you find him?"

McGuire explained in detail what had taken place in the Jordan apartment and afterward. The inspector stared at him incredulously.

"Well, I'm damned! Suppose she could have been holding the glasses on Skeet when you walked in on her?"

"Don't know what else there was to see," the detective replied. "I wouldn't have thought much about it if she hadn't tried so hard to conceal the things."

"Think she suspects you might have found and used them?"

McGuire doubted it. "I waited until the car got out of sight before coming over here," he added.

"Vera rolled up just as I left the office," the inspector said. "I made my apologies, told her I'd try to see her later on today. She seemed agreeable enough. Where'd that flat-nosed chauffeur appear from?"

"He brought around the car, that's all I know. I wasn't introduced."

Ramsey contemplated the dead man. "How've you doped out this afterpiece?"

"From where I'm standing," McGuire observed, "it would look as if Skeet and his partner, who might have been on the truck we haven't found yet, drifted back here last night and got into an argument. They could have collected for the job and the partner wasn't satisfied with his split, so he pots his chief and departs with the bank roll."

"Sounds O.K. to me," Ramsey approved. "You stumble across any lead yet that—"

"We've been discussing her, haven't we?"

"Meaning Vera Jordan knows who's responsible? Could be, but how're we going to prove it? If the woman sticks to her story we'll have to swallow it. We can't put on the pressure simply because she knew Skeet three years ago and you caught her juggling a pair of opera glasses. No, she's out, Mac. Safest thing to do is let it ride for the present.

"After all," Ramsey went on, "this little episode isn't anything to get excited about. One two-bit lug smokes his playmate. So what? Nobody cares. Hell, the thing won't rate a dozen lines in any paper. It's murder, of course, and we'll try to find the killer, but we can't drag Vera into the affair. I'll phone Carson and his homicide squad to take over. Maybe they'll dig up something that isn't too hot to handle. If they don't—"

A knock brought both men alert. McGuire being nearest the door, opened it slightly. The tall, angular woman with dangling jet earrings who stood in the hall, addressed him sharply:

"I'm Mrs. Huss, the landlady. I want to speak with Mr. Spofford. He's in, isn't he? I've come about the rent."

"If you're in charge here," Ramsey spoke up and gave McGuire the nod, "you better come inside. Your roomer seems to have met with an accident. We're from the police."

The woman glanced into the room and fell back with a cry. Ramsey took her arm, led her to a chair. "Sit down, please. I'll have to ask some questions."

Mrs. Huss controlled herself with an effort, her eyes upon

the dead man. "Mr. Spofford killed himself?" she gasped.

"What can you tell us about him?" Ramsey parried.

The landlady knew very little. Spofford had engaged the room a month before, remained in it much of the time during the day. No, she hadn't heard any disturbance on this floor, and evidently none of the other tenants had, since they failed to mention it.

"He owed a week's rent and promised to have the money for me this morning," she declared. "He told me that when he went out last night."

"Do you know what time he returned?" McGuire asked. "Was he alone?"

Mrs. Huss shook her head. "I don't know. He always stayed out late. I don't know what his business was either, but he didn't seem to have much money. I tried to get him to move to a back room, which was cheaper, but he wouldn't. He didn't say why, but I knew the reason. Wanted to keep an eye on that place across the street."

"The apartment house, you mean?" Ramsey asked. "He was interested in it?"

"Interested in a woman living there," the landlady snapped. "He thought I didn't know, but I soon caught on."

"Ever see them together?"

"No, but I've seen her often enough, going in and out. Her name's Vera Jordan. She's an actress of sorts. I've seen her picture in the magazines."

"She's pretty well known," McGuire acknowledged.

"It's dreadful," Mrs. Huss broke out, wringing her hands. "A suicide in my house. I hope it won't be written up in the newspapers. Bad enough to lose a week's rent and have the police romping over the premises. I'll have to have the rug cleaned, too. And all these lights burning this hour of the day!" she added indignantly, and jumped up to switch them off. "Times like this—"

"That'll be all for the present," Ramsey interrupted, opening the door. "Thanks for your information. We may have to call on you later. Until then, please don't discuss this matter."

The woman turned and marched stiffly from the room. Ramsey watched until she had descended the stairs before closing the door.

"Well, well," he murmured. "So Skeet apparently takes these quarters just to get an eyeful of Vera Jordan. It must have been love. And Mrs. Huss persists in calling this a suicide. The old girl's due for a relapse when she learns it's a slight case of murder with the victim an ex-con who pulled off a neat job himself."

"Does it occur to you that all we've got to go on there is what the garage watchman told us?" McGuire ventured.

"You think Nick Foster lied?"

"No, but some things happened last night that—"

"Listen, Mac!" Ramsey broke in. "Use your head. We know Terry was driving one of the stolen trucks. He's been palling around with Skeet. Both men were broke, both owed money which they promised to pay today. Evidently, they expected to grab off some ready cash last night, and it isn't hard to figure what they had in mind. Besides, these whisky raids, three in a row now, didn't commence until Skeet showed up around here a month ago. All that's something to back up Nick Foster's statements, isn't it?"

The detective admitted as much. "I was just thinking aloud, that's all," he said. "Just wanted to be damned sure we get all the punks who were in on Eddie Harper's murder."

"We got a pair of them," Ramsey came back. "We'll round up the third before long."

McGuire decided not to argue the matter and walked glumly to the window, looked down into the street. "Vera Jordan must be home again," he observed. "That's her car out in front."

"Forget it!" Ramsey snapped. "That dame may be wise to a few things, but we're not sticking our necks out. Not right now. We're not tossing charges her way until we've got something to back them up."

The inspector buttoned his coat, started toward the door and turned. "You stay here until Carson takes over," he said. "Then report back to the office, straight back. If I catch you talking to Vera again, I'll plaster you with a three-month suspension. Understand that?"

"Just as you say," McGuire responded.

He heard Ramsey at the phone in the hall, heard him tramp downstairs, saw him cross the walk below, climb into his car and drive off. With a resigned sigh, the detective turned from the window. He supposed he should have mentioned finding that bit of pasteboard in Skeet's pocket, but Carson would eventually do that. Perhaps the inspector would make something of it and not be so cocksure of himself, so quick to jump to conclusions.

Looking down at the dead man, McGuire suddenly recollected that the murder victim wasn't armed. There was no gun in his coat, and he wore no shoulder holster. Might be something on his hip, though, he reflected, and knelt beside the body to investigate. No luck rewarded him. He was getting to his feet again when a glint of something under Spofford's arm caught his attention.

He thrust a finger into the crevice and, with a grunt of surprise, extracted a ring—a wide, plain gold band. He stepped to the window where the light was better and inspected his find critically. Pondering over the discovery, Mc-

Guire finally concluded that the wearer of the ring must have placed his hands under Spofford's arms and, for some reason, dragged him into the middle of the room before leaving the premises. The ring must have been loose on the man's finger, had slipped off when he removed his hand. There seemed to be no other way to account for its presence in that singular spot.

Undoubtedly, the wearer was Spofford's murderer, or had been a participant in the killing. But the evidence the man had left behind wasn't much to crow about just now. There was nothing distinctive about the ring, no engraving inside the gold band. McGuire realized that he hadn't a single suspect in mind, and it would be several days before the police could round up a few likely prospects. Carson's men would probably turn in a batch of fingerprints, and some of them might provide a lead. But all this would take time, and McGuire chafed at delay, the slow, cut-and-dried routine. He saw no excuse for it at all, except Ramsey's confounded stubbornness.

McGuire felt pretty certain that Vera Jordan could identify the ring and name its owner, but there wasn't a remote chance of that coming to pass now since the inspector had warned him to steer clear of the woman. Even with this new bit of evidence, it was doubtful if the overcautious Ramsey would relent.

The detective swore to himself. His hands were tied. Given the opportunity, he might find a way to wring some information from the woman without getting himself or the department in hot water. All he wanted was a chance, and that had been denied him. The idea of treating Vera like a sacred cow was absurd, and for a moment he was tempted to disregard Ramsey's orders, confront the woman. The inspector wouldn't learn of it, and with any kind of luck—

He scowled down at the car parked across the street and instinctively raised his eyes to the fourth floor. Vera Jordan and probably the man who had driven the car were somewhere back of those windows, and not too far back, he wagered. They must be interested in what was taking place in this room. As that thought registered, McGuire's scowl gradually vanished, and he brightened as a plan began to shape itself in his mind.

Smiling now, he inspected the ring again, turning it over slowly in his fingers. Then, tucking the ring into a vest pocket, and with a final glance about the room, he closed the door on Spofford, walked briskly downstairs and stepped out upon the stoop where a frayed awning offered some protection against the rain. If Mrs. Huss had seen or heard him, she gave no sign of it, since she did not make an appearance.

Lieutenant Carson and his squad arrived presently. The detective told them where to find the evidence they were looking for, but without the particulars leading to its discovery.

"So it's our old chum Skeet Spofford, eh?" Carson said, after his men had disappeared into the house. "A lovely surprise for a wet day. How in thunder did you stumble onto him in these remote diggings?"

"Well, I wouldn't want it to leak out," McGuire confided, "but I'm just naturally psychic. I happened to stroll past here and—"

"Yeah?" The lieutenant chortled. "Got a crystal ball stowed under your belt, have you? I always figured it was your stomach that made the bulge— Hold on!" he exclaimed, as the detective turned up his coat collar and started down the steps. "Aren't you sticking around?"

"Not with your bunch of ghouls. You tell Ramsey when

you see him that I might be a little late reporting back to the office as he requested." From the tail of his eye, McGuire saw a figure appear in the street doorway of the apartment house, thought he recognized the thick-shouldered man in the belted raincoat who had played chauffeur to Vera Jordan that morning.

"And if I don't get in touch with him by dark," the detective added, "the inspector better hold that postponed quiz session with a certain female party in this area who might know the reason."

"That's very clear indeed," Carson grunted. "I'll relay the message. I suppose the chief can dope it out."

"It shouldn't be hard to do," McGuire returned, and started away.

He plodded along the walk for some distance, not looking back, before crossing the street. When he reached the opposite sidewalk and glanced guardedly over his shoulder, it was just in time to see someone dart out of the apartment house and climb into the parked car. The activity did not surprise him, nor was he surprised when, a moment later, the gray car rolled alongside him at the curb and the flat-nosed driver leaned from the window.

"Going downtown?" he called out. "Hop in. I'll give you a lift."

"Much obliged," McGuire said, and promptly squeezed himself into the front seat beside the unsmiling driver.

"Seen you before, ain't I?" the man remarked, as the car moved swiftly away. "You was with Miss Jordan this mornin'. From the police, she was tellin' me. You a detective, huh?"

McGuire admitted he was, and covertly eyed his husky companion. The man certainly didn't look the part of a hired chauffeur, and the detective wondered just how he rated among Vera's associates.

"You been around here all the time since we left, huh?" the driver asked. "Seein' about business, eh? Have any luck?"

"Considerable," McGuire admitted.

The man turned his head slightly. "Must be somethin' stirrin' in the neighborhood," he ventured. "I thought I seen a bunch of coppers pilin' into that brownstone front just now."

"They get around." McGuire glanced speculatively at the man's gloved hands on the steering wheel. It was possible that the ring he had found might have encircled one of the driver's fingers.

The car swerved presently from the avenue and turned into the park. "Not so much traffic here," the driver explained. "We can make better time."

Although the rain-blurred windows were difficult to see through, McGuire realized they were following one of the more secluded, winding roads.

"I'm in no hurry," he said. "You can drop me off somewhere near police headquarters if you're headed in that direction."

"Goin' right past the place," the other declared. "Get that pack of smokes out of the side door pocket, will you?" he added.

McGuire leaned over to unbutton the flap and the gloved fist caught him on the jaw, slammed his head against the door. The blow was hurried and poorly timed and the detective did not immediately lose consciousness. He kept his eyes closed, his body limp. He heard the brakes applied, and almost before the car stopped, he felt the man pressing close to him, probing his pockets, cursing as he did so. It was not until the car had started up again that he slipped contentedly into oblivion.

III

McGuire opened his eyes and blinked up at the dim ceiling. He was flat on his back and not uncomfortable, except that his jaw thumped a little and one arm, cramped under him, felt numb. Moving a hand across his chest, he was abruptly aware that he was in shirt sleeves, that his coat and vest and shoulder holster were missing. His shoes were off too. It was almost like being at home, stretched out on the sofa and waiting to be called to supper.

When he tilted his head slightly, he could make out the confines of the room where several floor lamps were burning —a spacious, well-furnished room, its walls covered with pictures, the window shades down. A mumbling voice reached him faintly from some quarter beyond. He started to sit up, but changed his mind when the voice lifted angrily, and he lay back, ears alert.

"I told you what happened, didn't I? Stop yellin', will you. I couldn't dump him off in the park. . . . Sure, nobody seen us. I come around back and Tony helped me. . . . Yeah, the car's there. You better get over here."

The voice sank again and McGuire cautiously lifted his head, looked through a doorway into an alcove that adjoined the living room. The flat-nosed man, still in cap and raincoat, was hunched there over the phone, his back toward the detective. Only a few words of the ensuing one-sided conversation were audible now, but what McGuire had overheard and readily interpreted, brought a smile.

He lay back and closed his eyes when he heard the receiver slam, opened his eyes again as if for the first time when footsteps approached and he felt a prod in the ribs.

"Come out of it, McGuire!" the man snapped. "You been snoozin' long enough. Set up and get your tongue oiled."

The detective blinked, propped himself to an elbow and, as if with an effort, swung his legs off the divan.

"You don't pull your punches, Shorty," he remarked with a grimace.

"Didn't intend to." The man shed his raincoat and pulled up a chair. He had a gun in his hand and McGuire recognized it as his own. "You and me are goin' to have a talk. I want that ring. I seen you put it in your pocket and—"

"Good strong glasses you were using, weren't they?"

The man shrugged. "You ought to know. I drove around the block and seen you duck into the brownstone front."

"Knew what I'd find, didn't you?"

"I want that ring," the other repeated.

"You know I haven't got it," McGuire said, and looked down at his coat and vest on the floor, and at his shoes beside the divan. "You frisked me in the car, and you must have done a more thorough job up here."

"You know where it is."

"Sometimes I mislay things."

"You better start rememberin'."

McGuire calmly raked one of his shoes toward him and slipped it on. "Put up the artillery and skip the threats, Shorty. I don't scare easy. You're not getting too rough until you find your property."

"Maybe I don't have to find it. I could play safe by puttin' you out of the way."

"A little late for that. You've got yourself nicely hooked." McGuire did not look up as he fumbled for his other shoe, stamped his foot into it and tied the laces. "I'm just marking time until the man you phoned to walks in."

The divan under him acted as a springboard. He launched himself swiftly, accurately. The top of his lowered head rammed the man's chin, and at the same time he struck aside the gun, sent it across the room. The man and the chair crashed backward, and when they hit the floor, the detective was uppermost. He scrambled to his feet. The man, tangled in the wreckage of the chair, groaned and stirred a little, finally lay quiet.

McGuire rubbed the top of his head and grimaced. Commando tactics brought results, but they were somewhat wearing on a man's skull. Still unhurried, he donned his coat and vest, scooped up the service revolver, saw that it was in working order and thrust the heavy weapon into his shoulder holster which he rescued from behind the divan.

That done, he stepped over to where his victim's raincoat lay across a chair, reached into a side pocket and came up with the ring, having prudently transferred it there shortly after getting into the car that afternoon. Even before he bent down and tried the gold band on the man's fingers, he realized it was much too small. But the discovery failed to distress him. Better luck later on, he reflected, and put the ring back into his own pocket.

McGuire now gave his attention to the apartment, prowled through the other rooms, returned and lugged his victim into an adjoining bedroom. Working swiftly, making use of the sheets, he trussed the man securely, and after dumping him upon the bed, proceeded to rummage the desk and dresser, seeking some clew that might identify the occupant of the premises.

In the top dresser drawer he came upon a small, stub-nosed revolver, fully loaded and apparently new, with an ornate, imitation tortoise-shell butt. He looked over the weapon speculatively, but did not remove it.

Out in the living room again, ears cocked toward the door, he continued his explorations. Among the framed photographs on the walls, he suddenly spied one of Vera Jordan.

It was larger than the others. Across the lower half, and above the signature, was written, "To Tommy with all my love." The detective saw that all the photographs bore inscriptions of similar nature. Obviously, Tommy, who must be the owner of the apartment, was popular with the ladies, and Vera Jordan seemed to stand high among them.

When further search brought no more definite information, McGuire moved to a front window and raised the blind, curious to learn just where he had been made prisoner. It was already dusk outside and still raining, and what he could see told him little. Opening the window and leaning out, he judged he was five or six floors above the street, but what street it was McGuire was unable to determine.

There was not much traffic. Some distance beyond, and on the opposite side of the street, he saw the projecting marquee of a theater. After a prolonged scrutiny of the dim sign, he finally spelled out what appeared to be the title of the picture showing there. Repeating it, the detective grinned. The three words were rather ominous and perhaps appropriate, considering the present situation.

McGuire closed the window and turned back into the room, no wiser than he had been before. The sight of the wrecked chair and the garments of his victim lying nearby, reminded him he should put the room in order. But as he started to remove the evidence, the ringing of a bell halted him. Deciding that it announced a visitor, and was not the telephone, he eased the gun from under his arm, stepped to the door, opened it.

Vera Jordan stood in the outer hall, stood transfixed, wordless, staring at him. For an instant neither moved nor spoke. Then the woman turned as if to run away, and the detective caught her arm, drew her into the room and closed the door.

"It's all right," he assured her, and put his gun out of sight. "Needn't be alarmed. I was expecting somebody else. Evidently you were, too."

The woman shrank against the wall, her face stricken. "What . . . what are you doing here?" she faltered.

"Just hanging around," he said. "Waiting for Tommy. He ought to be along any minute now. You know him, don't you? I didn't get his last name. Perhaps you'll tell me."

Vera Jordan did not answer, did not seem to have heard. Her frightened eyes darted past him to the damaged chair, swept on to the cap and raincoat that lay on the floor.

"Your chauffeur and I—" McGuire began, and sprang forward to catch the woman as she went down.

He carried his burden to the divan. A poor time for a thing like this to happen, he grumbled. His experience with fainting females was limited. Just let them alone, he decided, and trust they wouldn't go into hysterics upon awakening.

What had brought Vera Jordan here puzzled him. No doubt she had witnessed the pickup this afternoon, knew where the car would be headed afterward, but why she wanted to appear on the scene had McGuire mystified. That she had realized what must have taken place in the apartment was obvious, and the detective promptly carted the broken chair and the garments into the bedroom, regretting that he hadn't done so before. The man on the bed, wrapped like a mummy, still slumbered.

Returning to the living room, McGuire suddenly recalled the instructions he had given Carson. By this time, the lieutenant must have finished his routine job at the brownstone front, reported back to headquarters and delivered the message. Ramsey would suspect what had happened, would be worried.

That thought carried McGuire to the phone. He dialed the number, waited expectantly, and after the connection had been made, heard the inspector's impatient bark.

"McGuire reporting," he announced, and braced himself for the anticipated eruption. The explosion fairly deafened him.

"Hold everything!" he protested, when the roar momentarily subsided. "Don't blow a fuse, chief. The situation's well in hand. . . . Sure, I'm all right. . . . Yeah, that's what happened. Carson saw the pickup, eh? Well, I asked for it. If you'll pipe down, I'll try to explain. I'm liable to be interrupted any minute, so I'll make the talk short and snappy."

McGuire told of his discovery in Spofford's room, of the ruse that had brought about his ride and the events that followed. He was on the point of mentioning Vera Jordan's unexpected arrival, but checked himself. The inspector would probably collapse if he knew the woman was on the scene.

"So now," the detective concluded, "I'm standing by waiting for Tommy Something-or-other to make his entrance. Is everything clear?"

Although somewhat pacified, Ramsey did not get enthused over the setup. "I figured out what had happened after talking with Carson, but I didn't know why, and I wasn't messing with Vera Jordan unless it was necessary."

"Something tells me that's on the program," McGuire said. "The way things look from here—"

"I don't see where this Tommy person fits in," Ramsey grumbled. "We've got Terry and Spofford. If the bird you've nabbed turns out to be the third member of the trio, that's all there were, according to Nick Foster."

"Well, whoever is missing seemed to be mighty upset because I was parked on his premises," McGuire replied. "Besides, the ring I found doesn't fit my present victim's fingers. So I'll have to try my luck elsewhere. Like the prince and Cinderella," he added. "Only it doesn't happen to be a slipper."

"Where'd you say you were?"

"I didn't say. Can't see much from my window. It's a nice layout on the fifth or sixth floor. There's a flicker house on the opposite side of the street that's featuring 'Death Lies Waiting.' You could check on where it's showing and—"

"Your phone's got a number, hasn't it?" the inspector cut in. "Or can't you read?"

"Yeah, that's right. I'd forgot," McGuire said. "But listen," he pleaded, "don't gum up things. Keep your eager beavers in the background until you hear from me. I'll handle the situation. The phone's Belgrade 2666. Got it?"

The inspector did not respond, but McGuire abruptly hung up and turned when a sound reached his ears. Vera Jordan was on her feet now, clinging to the edge of the table, watching him intently.

"You passed out on me in a hurry," he remarked, walking toward her. "But now that you're awake, and before we're interrupted, we ought to compare notes. You're in a tough spot, lady. It's too late to stall. You see that, don't you?"

"I'm listening," she said quietly.

"You knew where Skeet Spofford was this morning, didn't you? You saw him lying on the floor in that room across the street, just as I did later. You were scared, tried to keep me from seeing the glasses you'd been using. Right?"

"I saw him," the woman confessed.

"Knew he was dead?"

"No, no! Not that. I didn't know what to think. I was frightened and—"

"Why were you holding the glasses on him?" McGuire demanded.

"I wanted to see if he was in his room before I phoned."

"Oh, you've been doing that, have you? Giving his place the once-over? Phoning him? Seeing him, too? You're still in love with him then?"

"You should have guessed that much," she replied. "He was going straight this time. He promised."

"Sure, they all say that. So his three years in the jug didn't extinguish the old flame, eh?" McGuire shook his head. "I should have guessed it. You didn't know he and a couple of playmates were suspected of pulling off a robbery and murder last night. But you got jittery when you heard the police were looking for him. Maybe you had a hunch he hadn't kept that promise. Just the same you intended to protect him. All right. You tried to. Then, suddenly, you decided to take my advice and see Ramsey. You phoned for your car. Who's the driver?"

"Fred Keenan, a friend of Skeet's. It was his car. I told him what had happened, what I'd seen and about you being at the apartment."

"That brought him around in a hurry, didn't it? I suppose he didn't tell you anything, even when he saw me heading for Skeet's house later."

"He seemed angry, but he wouldn't tell me why or answer my questions. I . . . I didn't know Skeet was . . . was dead until we came back."

McGuire eyed her skeptically. "No? What did you think after you'd returned, watched me from the window and saw what I'd found?"

"Keenan used the glasses. I didn't know what you'd found and wasn't told. All I know is that he suddenly became excited and hurried downstairs. I saw him get into the car and drive off."

"And it meant nothing to you when you saw him pick me up?"

She met his gaze steadily. "I didn't see that."

"I'd like to believe it. You must have known something, knew where to find Keenan, or you wouldn't have shown up at this place."

"I came to see Mr. Barnes. Mr. Tommy Barnes, my manager. This is his apartment."

"Barnes? The theatrical producer?" McGuire exclaimed. "Why would Keenan bring me here?"

"I don't know," she said. "I didn't know why you met me at the door with a gun. But when I saw the cap and raincoat on the floor, recognized them—"

"You realized you'd stepped into trouble," McGuire broke in. "I don't wonder you blacked out. Keenan talked with somebody over the phone," he went on. "I judged it must have been the owner of this apartment. Maybe I'm wrong. It's hard to believe that Barnes would—"

He broke off. The woman didn't seem to be listening. She was staring past him. He spun around to see Leo Craig standing in the doorway that led into the rear of the apartment, his hands thrust into the pockets of his topcoat.

McGuire gaped at the newcomer, too confounded to speak or act. It wasn't until the man stepped into the room that the detective's mind began functioning and he reached toward his shoulder.

"Don't do that!" Craig warned sharply. The hand that came from his pocket held a gun. "No fireworks! Just relax!"

McGuire slowly let his arm drop, cursing at his stupidity. Craig's eyes shifted to the woman.

"What are you doing here, Vera?" he asked. "Is this a pinch?"

"Not yet it isn't," McGuire spoke up.

"The old bloodhound," Craig murmured, surveying him. "I had an idea I'd find you on the premises. I let myself in the back way, intending to surprise you."

"You did," McGuire admitted. "I was expecting somebody else. Apparently, you weren't just sure how you'd find things here. You couldn't depend much on Keenan."

"Perhaps he's learned a lesson," Craig said. "I unrolled him, packed him off. He made himself a lot of trouble, jumping at conclusions."

"He seems to have put the finger on you, Leo. The inspector's going to feel hurt the way his pet stool has turned rat."

Craig shrugged. "Ramsey won't hear of it." He turned to Vera Jordan. "Get his gun. It's under his left arm. Don't be afraid."

The woman hesitated a moment, then came up to the detective, tugged the revolver from its holster and stepped back. Craig took the weapon from her hand, dropped it into his pocket.

"You haven't told me why you're here," he reminded her.

"I came to see Tommy Barnes."

"Oh, that's it. And ran into McGuire instead." Craig seemed relieved. "I forgot to tell you, Barnes went out to Hollywood for a month and I've taken over his place. Sorry. You better run along now."

"I'm not going yet," she returned calmly.

"I want to keep you out of trouble, Vera. Go home and stay there. If Ramsey shows up and asks questions—"

"I've told McGuire all I know," the woman broke in. "I'll tell Ramsey the same. Why shouldn't I?"

McGuire looked on, surprised and not a little pleased. Vera Jordan wasn't frightened now. She was angry and defiant, and Craig seemed disturbed.

"Don't let McGuire upset you," he protested, his face darkening. "What he thinks he knows won't be repeated. He and I are having a talk presently and reaching an understanding."

"Might as well start now," the detective spoke up. "Miss Jordan ought to be interested. I'm beginning to think she's been kept pretty much in the dark about Spofford. We found him this morning, you know. Murdered."

Craig's face remained expressionless.

"Keenan makes a dumb play by taking me for a ride through the park and bringing me here, after seeing me pocket the ring I'd found under Skeet's arm," McGuire continued. "I discovered it wasn't his property. He wanted to do you a good turn by recovering the evidence, because I've a hunch the ring fits one of your fingers, Leo."

"Got it all doped out, have you?" Craig charged placidly.

"Just about. You and Keenan walked in on Skeet and one of you knocked him off. It wasn't originally planned that way. You intended to pin a job on him he didn't do and later, when you were afraid he might have an alibi and queer the setup, you killed him just to be on the safe side."

Craig remained as indifferent as before, idly juggling the gun in his hand. Vera Jordan was staring at him, wide-eyed, incredulous. McGuire smiled. He had let himself talk, not only to enlighten the woman, but to give Ramsey time enough to check on the phone number and reach the scene. A lucky break, the detective reflected, that he had talked with the inspector before Craig's surprising appearance.

McGuire had no doubt but that his captor proposed to take desperate measures, shut his mouth permanently. There was no other way out for the man now. But he was far too smart to go that far here, wasn't leaving any evidence behind him, any trail for the police to pick up. He would be forced to escort his intended victim off the premises, and that couldn't be done once Ramsey's men were posted at every exit.

Almost as if he had read what was passing through the detective's mind, Craig spoke.

"You can wipe that grin off your face, McGuire," he said quietly. "Ramsey isn't going to show up. The line you talked to him over is an extension. I was listening in on the phone in the bedroom. When you started to spill the number I hung up, which cut short your conversation."

McGuire suddenly recalled that the inspector hadn't responded to his last query, remembered now that, hearing a sound in the room, he had hung up and turned to find Vera Jordan awake and watching him. The situation wasn't so cheerful, but he did not become panicky, did not betray alarm.

"We won't be interrupted," Craig went on, smiling. "You run along, Vera," he said. "I'll get in touch with you later, tomorrow."

Vera Jordan's reaction was swift, impulsive and wholly unanticipated. The bulky handbag launched from her fingers caught Craig across the mouth, rocked him back on his heels. As it struck, McGuire sprang. His attack carried the man off his feet, slammed him against the wall. The gun in his hand sailed from his up-flung hand. McGuire's knee rammed him hard in the stomach and the man went down, the detective sprawling beside him.

Cursing, Craig rolled over. His foot lashed out and the heel of his shoe ground into McGuire's cheek. Stunned for an instant, the detective groped blindly for the gun on the floor, found it. Rearing to his knees he heard the woman's shrill, warning cry, saw that Craig was on his feet again and tugging to free a gun from his pocket. McGuire abruptly remembered that it was his own revolver.

He fired twice. The gun in his fist jumped against his palm and the explosions sounded loud in the closed room. Craig lurched and slipped sidewise, staggered toward the rear hall, doubled over as he reached it and pitched to the floor. The detective was up then and standing beside the fallen man. Craig was quiet. The two slugs had ripped through his chest and the sight wasn't pleasant.

McGuire put his gun away and walked back into the room. Vera Jordan was huddled against the table. He reached down, picked up the handbag and extended it.

"Quick, wasn't it?" he said. "I'm much obliged."

The woman's voice was a whisper. "I . . . I knew what Leo meant to do. I couldn't let it happen."

"It didn't." McGuire eyed her a moment, fingering his bruised cheek. "I guess I've got the answer to one thing that's puzzled me," he said. "The motive back of this whole affair. I hadn't suspected you and Leo Craig were acquainted. He was in love with you, of course."

"But . ... but I never thought he'd do the terrible thing—" she faltered.

McGuire shook his head. "Leo wouldn't stand for competition, and Skeet made himself an easy fall guy."

Vera Jordan began crying, and he waited patiently until she had quieted.

"You want to be more careful who you pal around with from now on, lady," he advised. "You might not get out of a jam so easy next time." McGuire stepped to the door and opened it. "Get along now. I'll try to do what explaining is necessary."

The sound that reached him seemed to come from the rear of the apartment. He stiffened, wondering if perhaps Keenan had risked coming back. Vera Jordan looked up and started to speak, but McGuire took her arm, thrust her into the outer hall, closed the door and leaned against it, gun in hand.

The faint scuffling of feet reached him now. He moved cautiously across the floor, halted with an exclamation as Ramsey emerged from the bedroom and Carson loomed up behind him.

"Here you are!" the inspector cried, and stopped short, staring down at the dead man on the floor.

"Don't go busting a blood vessel!" McGuire protested. "It's Leo Craig, all right, and I potted him. I'll give you the whole story with sound effects, but it'll take time and I'd like to know first how you found this place."

"By using my head, that's how," Ramsey came back tartly. "When you cut short your chatter I decided somebody must have busted in here. But what you'd mentioned about the picture gave us a lead. We learned where it was showing, and this happened to be the only six-story apartment house across the street. Carson and I prowled around back, discovered the gray car parked there, and when we stumbled over that flat-nosed chauffeur in the areaway—"

"Keenan?" McGuire exclaimed.

"Dead as he ever will be," the inspector said. "From the shape he was in, we concluded he'd fallen from the fire escape while trying to make a getaway. So we climbed up until we found an open window, decided it marked his point of exit and that you would be somewhere inside, crawled through, and here we are."

"Craig turned Keenan loose," McGuire explained. "Maybe he did fall as you say, or maybe he was pitched out the window. I wouldn't put that past Leo. He knew we were look-ing for the man, and if caught, might be induced to talk."

"Then Craig walked in on you, not the Tommy person you expected?" Carson asked.

"He let himself in through the service entrance and caught me napping. Seems he was occupying these premises while the owner, Tommy Barnes, was away, and of course had keys to the place. He lifted my gun and blamed near succeeded in using it on me. But before that happened, I'd got hold of his gun and beat him to the fireworks. It was quick and unexpected," the detective added, but he did not go into details on that point.

"It must have been," Ramsey agreed. "Just how—"

"Here's the trinket I found," McGuire hurried on, and tossed the ring to Carson. "Seems to be a mark around the middle finger of Craig's right hand that shows a ring has been worn there a long time."

Carson knelt beside the body. "The thing fits all right," he declared a moment later, and got to his feet. "How the devil did you—"

"And here's his gun," the detective interrupted, passing it to Ramsey, "He lifted it from a dresser drawer in the bed-room. I saw it there after I'd tied up Keenan. It happens to be a .25, too, which ought to remind you of something."

The inspector took the weapon, examined it closely. "Might be the one used on Eddie Harper. We'll soon know." He looked up. "Ballistics just reported that a bullet fired from the same gun was dug out of Skeet. That means one gun did both killings. Be nice if we find this is the rod and that it's sunk a couple slugs into Craig."

"There's a word for it," McGuire said.

Ramsey nodded. "Yeah. Retribution. But look here, Mac!" he grumbled. "I can't hook things together. We know Skeet and Terry were in on last night's job, and more than likely, this bird Keenan. That accounts for the trio which Nick Foster claims took part in the raid. Where's Craig fit in? You want to make it out a foursome?"

"I don't think Spofford was there."

"No? Seems to me you intimated something like that before."

"I started to, but you weren't in a mood to listen, so I laid off," McGuire returned. "Maybe you will now. For instance, didn't it seem queer to you that these mugs should make short shrift of Eddie Harper, but handle the watchman with gloves, barely tap him on the jaw and tie him up? And that afterward they'd do so much gabbing? Crooks don't usually toss a name around on a job where outsiders might get an earful. Not unless they want the name repeated."

"Come to think of it—" the inspector began.

"You find a seat check stub in Skeet's coat pocket?" McGuire asked, turning to Carson. "A green stub torn off a prize-fight ticket?"

"Among other things, yes," the lieutenant admitted. "I didn't pay it any mind. Why?"

"The fight was pulled off last night at the Eastend Arena, a good ten miles from the warehouse. The main bout didn't wind up until midnight, according to the newspaper I read. And you may recall that Eddie Harper was shot down a few minutes before twelve o'clock. Does that mean anything?"

"You want to believe Skeet was framed?" Ramsey demanded.

"I'm pretty sure he was."

"Maybe Skeet didn't stay for the finish," put in Carson. "Or he might have got hold of the stub somehow to flash on us in case we picked him up."

"What's the odds?" Ramsey contended. "Why argue? It doesn't make any difference one way or another now."

"Perhaps not, but it started me thinking we might be following a blind trail," the detective said. "I wasn't particularly worried over Skeet's passing. I just wanted to be damned sure we'd get all the punks concerned in Eddie Harper's murder. That was the important thing. We might have learned something from Vera Jordan," he added, "but you couldn't see it that way, so I had to dope out other means to confirm my suspicions. After I'd found the ring, stood looking at it in the front window and realized that probably certain interested folks across the street would be training the glasses on me, the idea popped into my head."

"You get good ones once in a while," conceded Ramsey. "A bit risky, though. You got a lucky break this time."

"More ways than one," McGuire admitted, grinning. "Of course, the ring itself wouldn't have been much help. We'd have had a job trying to locate the owner. I saw that and had to count on somebody being dumb enough to fall into my trap. Keenan was, and did. He was foolish enough to try to retrieve the ring and convict himself, and blundered still more by carting me here."

Ramsey nodded. "Looks like Craig's been the leader in these whisky raids. And all the time I'm banking on him for information. I hope my face isn't too red."

"It's a trifle on the pink side," McGuire asserted.

"The one thing I'm thankful for is that we didn't crack down on Vera Jordan. I was afraid you'd go off half cocked and get us in trouble. Sometimes you don't know when to let well enough alone, Mac."

"You warned me to steer clear of her apartment, and I did," McGuire said. "I usually obey orders."

"I'll pin a medal on you this time." The inspector stared off across the room, frowning a little. "You know," he mused, "it would be interesting to learn just how Vera figured in this affair, wouldn't it? Why she was using the glasses on Skeet's room, why Craig framed Skeet, if he did, and why it had to end up with a killing?"

"Well," McGuire ventured. "I've got sort of a theory. Vera was still in love with Skeet and had been seeing him all the time. She might have been taking a squint through the glasses, just before I showed up, intending to phone if he was in his room. Craig was in love with the lady himself, didn't like competition, and decided to eliminate it. It seemed easy enough to pin a job on a man who'd already served time for robbery. He might have succeeded, and without resorting to violence, except afterward he learns Skeet attended the fight last night and could probably establish an alibi. So Craig thinks he'll play safe by blasting him, only he forgets to lift the green stub out of his victim's pocket. That's the way it looks to me."

"Sounds pretty far-fetched," Ramsey grunted, "but we'll let it go at that."

"Yeah," chortled Carson, "the old swami himself speaks! You must have been looking into that crystal ball of yours again."

McGuire nodded and smiled. "The second time today."

NEED A BODY CRY

H. WOLFF SALZ

ETECTIVE O'FLAHERTY'S LOOSE-FITTING BLUE GABARDINE suit hung like an awkward drape over his large-boned powerful figure and emphasized his elephantine bigness. Though I'm considered tall, I felt frustratingly dwarfed by contrast. And Louise, walking between us, actually appeared tiny.

The detective's easy strides were those of a born athlete as he cleared a path for us through the crowd of curious neighbors at our apartment door. Already my pulse was racing in apprehension. The surreptitious glances of our former neighbors merely added to my mounting sense of foreboding. This was increased as we pushed into the living room of our old apartment.

If I hadn't recognized the disordered furniture I would have been sure we were in the wrong place. Of course, everything had been upset the day before, when we'd had all our worldly goods packed and ready for the storage people. You know the unholy sort of mess a small apartment can be during moving time. Books stacked in wooden crates, bric-a-brac and dishes wrapped in newspapers and stored in barrels, rugs rolled to one side, naked spots on the walls where pictures had hung.

Now, adding to the general disorder, strange men crowded

the living room. Cops in uniform, a photographer shooting pictures from various angles, several young men who looked as if they might be reporters.

Talking to several of my fourth-floor neighbors in a corner was a wizened sparrow of a man in a tight-fitting gray suit. It was to him that O'Flaherty guided Louise and me.

"Well, here they are, Lieutenant Wesley."

Wesley stared first at me, then at Louise. I've often seen men stare at Louise—they couldn't help it—and I'd seen the way their eyes usually brightened in interest as they observed the startling depth of her china blue eyes, the loveliness of her ivory complexion, the heap of fine-spun yellow hair that framed her perfectly oval face.

However, Wesley's wasn't that sort of look. His pinched features reflected no emotion whatever. His was a long soul-probing stare, as if he were slowly and deliberately stripping us of all the defensive barricades that humans learn to erect about themselves. A slight chill ran down my back, and that had the effect of stirring embers of anger within me.

"Suppose you tell us what this is all about, lieutenant?" I demanded. "We were having breakfast at our hotel, bothering no one, when your Detective O'Flaherty barged in and insisted that we come here, without a word of explanation. I think we've got a right to know."

"Of course," Wesley nodded amiably. "You're George Raeburn, I take it?"

"That's right."

He glanced at Louise. "And you're Mrs. Raeburn?"

Louise nodded.

"Now suppose, Raeburn, you tell me something about yourself," Wesley murmured.

"What do you want to know?"

"Why are you storing your furniture?"

"I won't need it where I'm going—the army."

"You're being inducted?"

"I've been inducted. Two days ago. I'm on two weeks induction furlough."

"And you decided to live at a hotel during that time?"

I nodded. "We packed everything yesterday, got it ready for the storage people. This place was in a mess, as you can see, so we went to the hotel last night."

"What time did you leave this apartment yesterday?"

"About three."

"In the afternoon?"

I nodded.

"You had everything packed and ready for the storage men then?"

"Yes."

"When were they to come for your furniture?"

"This morning, nine o'clock."

"What line of work have you been in, Raeburn?"

"Chemist—with the Sedgwick Laboratories."

Wesley was silent for a moment, then glanced at Louise. "What are your plans while your husband is in the army, Mrs. Raeburn?"

"I'm going on with my work as usual, of course," Louise answered. "I'm a laboratory technician at the Sedgwick Laboratories. That's where George and I first met, three years ago."

"And you're going to live where?"

"With my sister."

"Then you are not leaving the city?"

"No."

I was growing impatient. "Why all the questions, lieutenant? What is this all about?"

"Are you sure you don't already know?" Wesley asked softly.

"What do you mean?" I demanded.

"Well, off hand," the lieutenant said in a mild voice, "I'd say it looks pretty bad for you."

"What looks bad?" Louise cried. Her cheeks were flushed, a sure sign of mounting anger.

"The fact that along with your furniture, you were planning to store a body. The body of a dead man."

I heard Louise's startled gasp. For a moment I stared at Wesley uncomprehendingly. Then as the full significance of his statement penetrated my dazed mind, I felt my knees grow watery.

"Whose body?" I heard myself rasp in a dry voice.

"That's what I want you to tell me," the lieutenant answered. "Come in here with me, Raeburn."

He moved to our closed bedroom door. I followed him numbly. At one side of the other room, a short stocky man in rolled shirt sleeves was bowed over the open cedar chest like an impassive Buddha figure. As we entered, he straightened, took off his steel-rimmed glasses and began polishing them diligently with a handkerchief.

"Well, doctor?" Wesley asked.

The short man pursed his lips. "Without committing myself officially just yet, I'd say he's been dead, say, between eighteen to twenty-four hours."

"Anywhere between ten o'clock yesterday morning to about four o'clock?"

The doctor nodded. "You can have your complete report as soon as I can remove the body to the morgue."

"In a few minutes," Wesley said, as the medical examiner went out of the room and closed the door.

When we were alone, the lieutenant gestured towards the cedar chest. "Suppose you tell me who he is."

I moved towards the open chest numbly, as if I were walking in my sleep. Indeed, I felt sure I was dreaming.

As I stared down at the completely naked, awkwardly curled up body in the chest, I fought down the sudden sickening nausea that welled up in me. My breath lumped in my throat. I dug my fingernails into my palms to keep from turning suddenly to dash out of the room.

I backed away slowly, shook my head. The dead man was a complete stranger to me. I not only didn't know him. I had never seen him before.

"How—how did he—get here?" I mumbled. "We packed some blankets in that chest yesterday. The chest was locked, ready to go into storage."

"It was ready to go into storage, all right," Wesley nodded. "But not with blankets."

"But—I've never seen that man before!"

"Which is easy to say."

I stared at the detective in growing horror. "Don't you believe me?"

Wesley shrugged. "My job isn't to believe or disbelieve. My job is to gather evidence that can be turned over to the district attorney's office. The evidence is right in front of your own eyes, Raeburn. There's the body. Locked in a cedar chest that's being sent to a storage warehouse. If one of the moving men hadn't noticed a smear of blood that seeped through a crack on one side and gotten suspicious, the body might not have been discovered for months."

"Meaning that I would have been far from here by then," I finished for him. "But that's crazy. No matter where I'd be with the army the law could still reach me."

"Right," Wesley agreed. "But I didn't say you intended

to leave that chest in storage. In a few weeks or maybe days you or your wife could have taken the chest out of the warehouse and gotten rid of the body at your leisure."

"Then why would I have put the body in the chest to begin with?"

"Because a body isn't easy to get rid of in a large apartment building. You might have been observed taking it out of this apartment. But this way, well—"

His gesture made all the implications clear, indeed. So clear, in fact, that I could see far beyond the immediate situation. I could see the road that Wesley seemed to have mapped out for me or Louise, a smooth road leading straight to a courtroom. And from there—

Dazedly, I watched Wesley move to the door, open it and beckon to someone in the living room. A moment later a broad-shouldered man in a tweed sport jacket appeared in the doorway. Jack Tilden, who lived in apartment 4B. He was a young man of about thirty, with a pleasant face and easy manner. He had but recently moved into the apartment and I knew him only casually, from chance meetings in the automatic elevator. I knew only that he was a bookie and small-time gambler.

"I understand you were in your apartment most of the day yesterday, Tilden," Wesley remarked.

"That's correct." Tilden smiled easily, self-assured.

"Did you hear any shots any time at all while you were at home?"

"No."

The lieutenant gestured towards the open cedar chest. "Know who that is?"

Tilden moved a few steps across the room, took one glance into the chest and turned away quickly. His self-assurance seemed to have evaporated suddenly.

He swallowed and answered in a dry voice, "No."

"Ever see him before?"

"No."

Wesley waved him away. "That's all for the present."

The detective walked to the door with Tilden, called to someone in the other room.

A moment later another neighbor, tall, dignified-looking Mr. Gordon Hickey entered the room. I knew Hickey well, as I had often talked with him about old books. He was one of the better known rare book dealers in the midwest. His old curio shop downtown was a mecca for those strange fanatics who would sell their souls for a rare first edition of Boswell's *Life of Johnson* or a Shelley letter.

Despite his physical bigness he was a gentle sort of man, and now he avoided my eyes, as if he wished to spare me the pain of seeing in his look what I might construe as accusation.

"Mr. Hickey, would you step over to that cedar chest and see if you can identify the body?" Lieutenant Wesley murmured.

As Hickey glanced down at the gruesome thing in the chest, his face seemed to grow white and apple green by turns. He retreated quickly, an expression of horror on his face.

"Did you know him?" Wesley asked.

"No." Hickey's voice was a muffled croak.

"Ever see him before?"

"Never!"

"Were you at home any time yesterday between ten in the morning and four in the afternoon?"

Hickey looked vague for a moment as he searched his mind, then he said, "I returned from my curio shop at about three o'clock."

"Did you hear any shots while you were in your apartment?"

"Why, no. I heard nothing like that."

"All right, you may go now, but I'll want to talk to you later."

Hickey walked out without a glance at me.

I turned to Lieutenant Wesley, struggled to repress my mounting anger. "Look, lieutenant, is this some kind of an ordeal? Are you trying to impress me with the fact that only I—or my wife—could have murdered that man?"

Wesley shrugged indifferently. "I'm not trying to impress you with anything. The facts are there for you—and me—to see. If you don't want to stand by while I question your neighbors, good enough. You can rejoin your wife."

I strode out of the bedroom without another word. I knew words would be a futile defense. As I rejoined Louise I observed Wesley beckon to another neighbor, Mrs. Thelma Brinker, of apartment 4D. She sniffed haughtily as she passed me. In her eyes I was as good as pronounced guilty by a jury.

And yet it was all so stupid! A man had been discovered murdered in my apartment. That was true. But that man was a total stranger to me. I had never seen him before today. Then what was the body doing in my apartment? And who was he?

Louise's troubled expression told me that same question was foremost in her mind, too. I told her what I knew she was most anxious to hear. "It's no one we know."

"And still they think we—we did it!"

I took her cold hand in mine, squeezed it with a reassurance I did not feel. "It'll work out okay, dear. The police aren't stupid. They'll find the murderer."

But events didn't work out that smoothly. When Lieutenant Wesley had concluded questioning the neighbors, he announced briefly, "I'll have to ask you to come down to headquarters, Raeburn. You, too, Mrs. Raeburn."

"Are we under arrest?" I demanded.

"We won't call it that, for the present," he answered coldly. "There are a few more questions I'd like to put to both of you."

At police headquarters downtown Wesley's few questions developed into a seemingly endless all-day barrage. Deftly, deliberately, he and his assistants probed into every remote corner of our lives. In the end we were back where we had started. Wesley was frank enough. He was half convinced that either I or Louise was guilty of the murder. The fact that the body had been found in our apartment, in the circumstances of our sending the furniture into storage, weighed heavily against us. But he was honest enough to admit that the body could have been hidden in our apartment by a neighbor. The strongest point in our favor, he admitted, was the fact that so far he had been unable to unearth a motive for the murder.

"But that," he said softly, "may clarify itself as soon as the body can be identified. And let me tell you, that's only a matter of time. A body may appear to be absolutely unidentifiable. No clothes. No scars or birthmarks. But modern criminal investigation has ways of getting to the bottom of such problems."

"You have no right to accuse us!" Louise cried angrily. "We've told you we know nothing about the murder!"

Wesley sighed wearily and waved us to the door. "We're letting you both go now. But don't think you've heard the last of us. We're only beginning our investigation. Until you hear from me, don't try to leave town. I'll inform your induction center."

It was after five by the time we left police headquarters.

We had been there the better part of the day. My head was reeling and I was too exhausted to realize that neither of us had had a bite to eat since breakfast.

At the corner we found a cab. I instructed the driver to take us back to the Claridge Hotel. For a few minutes, as the cab rolled through the darkening streets, we remained silent. I was thinking bitterly that this was a hell of a beginning for the gay fling we had planned on for my two weeks' furlough.

Louise seemed to read my thoughts. She said, half to herself, "We won't have a moment's peace of mind until the murderer is found."

"What do we do, turn Sherlocks?"

"We know," she answered, "that neither of us is the criminal. That's a good place to start."

"Fine, now all we've got to do is find the murderer among the other eight-hundred thousand people in this city."

"Not at all," retorted Louise. "We can eliminate everyone except our neighbors at the apartment house. The man must have been killed by someone in a fourth-floor apartment. No one would have taken a chance bringing the body up or down the elevator. That leaves only three neighbors."

That sounded logical. "In other words," I nodded, "the guilty party is either Jack Tilden, Mrs. Brinker or Gordon Hickey."

"It has to be someone who could have carried the dead body into our apartment and placed it in the cedar chest," Louise added. "I don't think Mrs. Brinker is strong enough to have done it. That leaves either Tilden or Mr. Hickey."

"Unless Mrs. Brinker had an accomplice."

The cab stopped in front of the Claridge. After I paid the driver, I paused at the hotel entrance to buy an *Evening Journal*. In the lobby we stopped to read the complete front-page story of the murder, and I felt my face grow red as I read the words describing Louise and me as principal suspects.

We ascended in the elevator to the fifth floor in silence. I was engrossed in my own depressing thoughts as I opened the door and stepped aside to let Louise enter. I followed her into the room, closed the door, then I heard her sudden intake of breath and bumped against her as she stopped abruptly.

"What is it, Louise!"

As I stepped around her, I saw for myself what was wrong. The room was in semi-darkness and the figure at the other end of the room was a blurred shadow that merged with other darker shadows.

As the figure moved, I saw that it was a woman. She was standing in a corner and remained silent as we faced her.

"Who are you?" I demanded.

The woman's first words, spoken in a grief-choked voice, sent a spine-tingling wave down my back. "I'm going to kill you."

"You must be crazy!" Louise cried. "Why should you kill us?"

"Because you killed him!"

"Whom?"

"You know whom you killed!" the strange woman cried. She moved slowly in our direction. As my eyes became accustomed to the gloom, I saw that she was a strikingly beautiful girl of about twenty-five.

"He told me he was going to see you," she sobbed. "He said we would be rich if everything turned out right. But you killed him. And I'm going to kill you."

I could see her well enough now to observe the small revolver she was pointing in our direction.

"You'll never get away with it," I said softly. "The police—"

"What if I die!" the girl cried out in a voice choked with emotion. "Why should I want to live now. I waited two years for Michael to come back. We were to have been married next week. Now he's dead. . . ."

I listened to her in growing bewilderment. "He told you he was coming to see us! Why? Who is Michael?"

"Don't pretend you don't know!"

I had been moving slowly towards her and to one side, drawing her attention away from Louise. Now I was less than two yards from her. I thought I could see her long, red-nailed finger tightening around the trigger of her small revolver. I knew she was too distraught to listen to reason. Her black eyes glowed with the intensity of single-minded purpose. Her whole slim body seemed shaken by the power of her emotions. I realized that this girl, overwhelmed by grief, and evidently on the verge of a breakdown, could not be controlled by words. One abrupt movement on my part might snap her last thread of restraint. Equally, to stand helplessly waiting for her to press the trigger would mean death for Louise and me.

I was left with but one slim choice. I took it. Cautiously I inched closer to her, talking soothingly as I moved.

"Look, you're not being fair to yourself, to us, or to the man you say we killed. You want revenge, but suppose it turns out that we're innocent. Would you ever—"

I was close enough to act then. My right arm swooped out suddenly, and my fingers closed around her gun wrist. I jerked her arm upward and backward. The entire movement took but a few seconds. I had caught her completely by surprise. She cried out sharply once, then as I twisted her wrist, her fingers went limp and the gun dropped to the floor.

Releasing her arm, I bent forward and swept up the gun.

As I straightened, I heard Louise's cry behind me, "Catch her, George! She's fainted!"

As the girl started to sag, I circled an arm about her waist, holding her up. Louise ran to my side, took the gun from my hand, leaving me free to carry the limp girl to the bed. Behind me, Louise turned on the room light.

The girl was unconscious for only a few seconds. When she opened her eyes there was a stunned look in them, then she turned her back suddenly to us and began to cry. Her whole body was shaken by sobs.

It was only after Louise had folded an arm around her and talked soothingly to her for a few minutes that the girl stopped crying and consented to listen. It was Louise who persuaded her that neither of us had murdered the man she called Michael and that we knew nothing about the murder.

The girl, whose name was Mona Bonney, explained that the dead man was Michael Dudley, her fiancé, an engineer who had been working in northern Canada for the past two years. Last week he had returned from the north and they were to have been married in a few days.

Dudley had told Mona that in a short time they might come into a fortune, if everything worked out right. He hadn't revealed how he would acquire the fortune, explaining that he didn't want Mona to know the details, as there was a possibility nothing would come of his plans.

"And Michael told you he was going to see me or my wife?" I asked the girl.

"He didn't mention your names, but he said the place he was going to was on Rutgers Avenue and that's where your apartment is. Then when I read about the police finding the body in your apartment, I became frightened. I went to the morgue to see—"

"And when you learned that it was Michael," I finished for her quickly, "you were convinced that we had murdered him."

Mona nodded, buried her face on her arms. "The papers said the police wouldn't hold you because there wasn't enough evidence, so I came up here to wait. I made up my mind you would pay for Michael's death."

"Michael didn't mention any names?" I asked. "Anyone in particular that he intended seeing?"

Mona shook her head.

I leaned forward and said urgently, "Think back, Mona. Didn't he talk about anything unusual—anything that even remotely might have some bearing on the case?"

She seemed to have no need of thinking back. She was certain Michael hadn't mentioned anything that might possibly be worth a fortune.

"Did he seem to have any particular interests that he hadn't had before he went to Canada?"

She started to answer negatively, then changed her mind. "Well, he did talk about books—and he'd never been interested in them particularly."

I turned away disappointedly. I couldn't see how books could have any bearing on Dudley's death. Then I frowned, turned back to face Mona.

"What kind of books? Did he mention titles?"

"He mentioned some books by Thackeray and Dickens—literary works." She spoke slowly, as she probed her memory. "He'd been telling me about some of his experiences in Canada and he talked about the old trappers sent into remote places by the Hudson Bay Company more than a hundred years ago."

"What connection did that have with books?" Louise asked.

"Well, he said that some of those old trappers really became well educated men. They had nothing to do on long, cold winter nights and most of them were isolated from the rest of the world for months at a time. The Hudson Bay Company sent trunks full of books to the trappers to help them pass the months of loneliness."

I was staring fixedly at Mona, no longer listening to her words. A sudden startling train of thoughts was spinning through my head.

Louise saw my expression and something of my inner excitement must have transmitted itself to her.

"What is it, George?" she cried. "Have you got an idea?"

"I'm not sure." I spoke to Mona, "Where does—did Michael live?"

"His room is here at the Claridge."

"We've got to see his things!"

"I have his key," Mona offered quickly, observing my eager expression.

Dudley's room was on the seventh floor. We used the stairs to go up there, avoiding possible snooping by a suspicious elevator operator.

After we had closed the door, Louise asked impatiently, "What are we looking for?"

"I'm not sure."

I was already busy pulling open drawers of the dresser, scanning through the usual assortment of shirts and underclothes. In a few minutes I found what I'd been seeking. It was a Custom's Bureau receipt, showing that Michael Dudley had paid duty on twenty books that he had brought from Canada on his return to this country. The significant thing about the list of books was the titles. My excitement mounted as I quickly scanned the list.

"What is it, George?"

I showed Louise the list.

She read some of the titles, her voice puzzled. "Boswell's *Life of Johnson,* Scott's *Waverly,* Dickens' *Old Curiosity Shop.*" She lifted her eyes questioningly. "I don't understand, George."

"That list," I answered, "may be the key to Michael Dudley's murder."

"All right, I'm dense, dear. Now tell me."

"Dudley must have found those books in an old forgotten trapper's cabin in the Canadian wilderness. He brought them back with him and probably planned to sell them to a dealer."

"You mean that was the fortune Michael had in mind?" Mona asked doubtfully.

I nodded emphatically. "Some of those books were probably rare first editions. At the time they were shipped to the trappers by the Hudson Bay Company more than a hundred years ago the books were new."

"But how could a few books be worth a fortune?" Mona asked.

"Not a few books," I explained. "Even one rare old volume may be worth thousands of dollars. You may remember reading the newspaper story a couple of months ago about a barber who found an old volume of *Pilgrim's Progress* in his attic. That one book brought $40,000 when it was sold at an auction."

"Forty thousand dollars for one book!" Mona exclaimed incredulously.

"That's right," I repeated. "Some collectors are like religious fanatics. They give up their business, their family life, their homes—devote all their time and energy wandering around the world trying to find rare old books."

Louise grabbed my arms, guided me toward the door. "What are we waiting for!" she exclaimed.

I knew what she had in mind. Gordon Hickey, our neighbor at the Rutgers Avenue apartment, was a dealer in rare books. Hickey was just the type of book fanatic that I had mentioned, with the exception that he didn't have the money to buy books for himself. He merely served as agent for wealthy men who could afford the expensive hobby of book collecting.

Louise had evidently followed the same trend of thought as I had. Suppose Michael Dudley had sought out Hickey and asked him to act as his agent in the sale of the books. Hickey, knowing that Dudley's books were recent discoveries and uncatalogued by collectors and other dealers, had murdered Dudley and stolen the books, knowing they could not be traced to their source. Selling them later, he'd realize a fortune on the deal.

All this, however, was mere speculation. If we went to the police now with our unsubstantiated suspicions they'd laugh us out of the place. What's more, they'd have probably believed that I was trying—not very subtly—to shift suspicions from myself. What we needed was proof that Hickey did steal Dudley's books.

I said to Louise, "You go back to our room with Mona. I'll get better results if I handle this alone."

"What are your plans?"

I really had no definite plan. I know only that I wanted to talk to Hickey, see if I couldn't somehow trap him into revealing that he knew Dudley. When Lieutenant Wesley had questioned him, he claimed he'd never seen Dudley.

Louise didn't care for the idea of my going to Hickey alone, but agreed that if we both went it would put him on his guard immediately.

We went down to the Claridge restaurant, had a hasty meal. Then Louise and Mona returned to our room and I proceeded to the street, located a cab and gave the driver the Rutgers Avenue address. As the cab pulled away from the hotel, I touched my suit coat pocket, nodded in satisfaction as I felt the reassuring pressure of the small Colt revolver I had taken from Mona. Just in case events got out of hand, I told myself.

In front of my old apartment building I paid the cab driver, proceeded up to the fourth floor and knocked on Hickey's door. There was no answer. I knocked again. After waiting a few minutes I decided Hickey was out. I tried the knob, but the door was locked.

I left the building in a hurry. The dark street was deserted. The cab was no longer there. There was nothing for me to do but take a street car, though that would mean the loss of valuable time.

Hickey's curio shop was on a quiet street in what years ago had been an exclusive residential neighborhood. As the city had spread westward many of the old homes had been converted into better class rooming houses, antique shops, photographers' studios and pretentious service stations.

Hickey's shop occupied an old two-story yellow limestone house fronted by a small well-kept lawn and enclosed by an iron fence. An hour after I had left Louise and Mona at the hotel, I stood on the sidewalk in front of the curio shop. The place was dark and appeared deserted.

My right hand firmly gripped the revolver in my pocket as I slipped across the lawn to the deep shadows of the building. Soundlessly I moved along a narrow cement walk bordering the building's left side. As I groped around the corner to the rear of the house, I felt my heart suddenly execute a somersault.

There was a faint patch of light at one of the rear windows, embossed in the darkness like a beacon. It didn't matter that the window shade was drawn to the sill. It was enough satisfaction discovering that someone—Gordon Hickey, I assumed, was there in the curio shop.

I slipped noiselessly towards the rear door, leaned against it to listen. There were no sounds within.

What made me whirl suddenly in the dark I don't know. Whether it was a sixth sense warning of lurking menace or a faint sound behind me isn't important. What is important is that when I did finally pivot about I was too late.

Not a yard behind me stood Hickey, tall and motionless as a specter. My right hand in my coat pocket still clutched Mona's revolver, but I knew it would be fatal to try drawing it out for a proper aim. The cold glint of metal in Hickey's hand warned me that the gun he was pointing at my midriff would speak first.

"I've been waiting for you, Mr. Raeburn," he said calmly.

"You've been waiting!" I gasped incredulously.

"Your wife is waiting, too," he added.

"Louise!"

I was stunned by Hickey's statement. His words had no meaning, no significance, yet they seared my brain like a flame.

"You're lying!" I said what I wanted to believe. "Louise is waiting for me at the hotel."

Hickey ignored my exclamation. "Take your hand out of your pocket—slowly."

I could do nothing but obey, at least until I understood the full meaning of his statement about Louise. He stepped forward cautiously, prodded his gun against my chest, while his left hand reached into my pocket, withdrew the small Colt, and transferred it to one of his own pockets.

From another pocket he drew out a key ring. He inched past me, unlocked the door and moved back again, all the while keeping his gun steadily pointed at me.

"You first, Mr. Raeburn."

My pulse throbbed at my throat as I entered the gloomy back room. My eyes hardly noticed the old relics and stacks of dusty books that cluttered the room. I saw only Louise, sitting in a swivel chair behind a scarred mahogany desk. I noticed only the distress in her blue eyes as she stared at me. That her mouth was gagged and her arms securely bound to the chair penetrated my dazed mind only after a crushing interval that seemed like years.

In rage I whirled upon Hickey, who had stepped into the room immediately behind me. I froze as he waved his gun menacingly.

"How did Louise get here?" I demanded. "Why have you got her tied?"

"How she got here, I wouldn't know, as she was already here when I arrived," Hickey answered. He seemed as calm, dignified and detached as always. "As to why she is bound, that was a necessary measure, while I went out to invite you in."

"That still doesn't explain the need for the bonds—nor your gun."

"Let's not be coy, Mr. Raeburn. When I arrived a short while ago, I found your wife had broken into the place, evidently by way of a side window. She was very diligently examining a few books which I had only recently acquired."

"Michael Dudley's books," I guessed.

Hickey nodded gravely. "There is no need for dissemblance now. It's quite evident that you and your wife have somehow discovered the truth about my transaction with Dudley. When I found your wife here, I knew that you must be somewhere in the vicinity. As a matter of fact, from a front window I observed you out on the sidewalk before you made your way to the rear of this building."

"And now?" I questioned, though I half-guessed what his answer would be—what his subsequent steps must be. Just as I realized now how Louise happened to be here. The answer to that was like the answer to many other questions. A man and his wife, after three years of marriage, so frequently think alike. It had happened often before. Thinking along the same lines as I had, Louise must have decided that the best possible place to look for Dudley's books was here at Hickey's shop. Impetuous as always and too impatient to wait for my return, she had come along to search the place.

"And now," Hickey said calmly, "there is but one thing left to do. I must kill both of you. Then somehow—I confess I haven't solved the problem yet—I shall have to dispose of your bodies where they'll never be found. After that, you see, the police consider that you were actually guilty of Dudley's murder, as they had suspected, and that you had taken flight."

"Unless," I said, "the police happen to know that you killed Dudley and stole his books."

Hickey laughed shortly, as if my remarks weren't worth answering.

I ganced beyond Hickey towards the door and smiled. "Well, come in, O'Flaherty. Mr. Hickey won't believe you're here unless you announce yourself."

Again Hickey laughed. "That, my friend, is the corniest gag in the book. If you expect me to whirl about so you can jump on me, you're a good deal more stupid than I thought."

It was then that Detective O'Flaherty, who had appeared silently behind Hickey a few minutes ago as he explained his plan to murder us, spoke up:

"No," O'Flaherty said, "Raeburn doesn't expect you to

turn around so he can jump you. But I expect you to drop that gun."

Hickey gasped as if he were suddenly choking. His face grew white and he turned slowly. When he saw the gun in O'Flaherty's fist, only inches from his face, his body seemed to sag. The gun dropped from his lax fingers. His shoulders drooped and he sighed in weary resignation.

"Well," he murmured brokenly, "the stakes were high. I would have been rich if my plan had worked."

"That," retorted O'Flaherty coldly, "is something men with crooked minds never seem to learn. Their plans never work." Then the detective glanced at me, where I was freeing Louise's bonds, and winked slyly. "Though maybe it would have worked this time if Lieutenant Wesley hadn't suspected you and given me orders to shadow you wherever you went."

It didn't take long, once Lieutenant Wesley arrived on the scene, to clear up the entire matter. It was shortly before midnight when Louise and I walked out of police head-quarters, completely cleared of all suspicion.

"Midnight," I said to Louise, "is as good as any time to start our fling."

Louise, as often before, appeared to have been thinking the same thing. We had enough gaiety the next two weeks to last us a lifetime, and were both ready to get down to more serious jobs.

Before I took the train for camp, Louise handed me a small brown paper-wrapped package.

"If things get dull," she remarked with a mischievous gleam in her eyes.

I tore the wrapper open right there. It contained a nice new book. I glanced at the title. Boswell's *Life of Johnson*. Nice sense of humor Louise has.

SUICIDE

FRANK KANE

———

JOHNNY LIDDELL BIT OFF THE END OF THE CIGAR, SPAT IT IN
the general direction of the spitoon. He scraped a wooden
match on the sole of his shoe, lit the end of the cigar and
inhaled deeply.

"Nobody's convincing me that Johnny Carroll killed himself," he said flatly. He blew a cascade of dirty white smoke
ceilingward. "You might as well ask me to believe that Hit-
ler has underwritten a Jewish asylum."

Detective Sergeant Terence Grady grunted. His cold, gray
eyes studied the private dick's face. "I've got to believe the
evidence of my own eyes, Johnny," he said. "He was still
warm when we got there. He did the job himself; no question about that."

Johnny Liddell growled. "He wouldn't give the world a
break like that, Terry. He was mean enough to live forever."
He tapped a thin film of ash to the floor. "A guy that has so
many birds out gunning for him just naturally doesn't knock
himself off."

The detective sergeant fumbled through his jacket pockets,
came up with a paper pack of cigarettes. "This one did,
Johnny." He hung a cigarette in the corner of his mouth
where it waggled as he talked. "Ever hear of a guy like
Johnny Carroll letting anybody stick a rod in his mouth and

blowing out his brains?" He lit the cigarette, flipped the burnt match on the table. "There wasn't any sign of a struggle; even his clothes weren't mussed or wrinkled."

"How about the gun?"

"It was his," Terry Grady nodded. "Kept it in the drawer of his table in the library."

Johnny Liddell digested that bit of information. "That's where he was found, isn't it?"

The homicide dick nodded.

"Fingerprints on the gun?" Johnny Liddell asked.

"Just his own," Grady grinned. "That makes your hunch bat 1,000, doesn't it, Johnny? Shot through the mouth; no struggle; his own gun and nobody else's prints on the gun. That sure makes it out a good case of murder."

Johnny Liddell grunted. "Sure, sure. It sounds screwy, but not as screwy as the idea of Johnny Carroll knocking himself off!" He inhaled deeply, frowned fiercely at an imaginary spot on the ceiling. "Bullet match the gun?"

Detective Terence Grady plucked at a minute crumb of tobacco on his lower lip. "Haven't got the bullet yet," he admitted. "Not that it's important—"

The frown left Johnny Liddell's face. "Who says it's not important?" He scraped his chair back, pulled himself to his feet. "Your whole suicide theory falls to pieces unless you can match up the slug and the rod. Even a homicide dick ought to know that."

Grady motioned him back into his chair. "Relax, Sherlock. It came from the same gun all right. His doc says—"

"What do you mean his doc? Didn't the M. E. see him?"

The homicide dick nodded patiently. "Sure, sure. Only his doc, Matthews I think his name is, was there when we got there. Emmy Wilson, Carroll's secretary, found him and called Matthews right off. His office is in the same building."

Johnny Liddell applied his tongue to a loose piece of tobacco on the cigar, pressed it back into place. "I didn't know Carroll was doctoring."

"There's a lot of things you don't know, Sherlock," Terence Grady chided. "It seems that Johnny Carroll was doctoring for a cancer of the throat. The doc came in to see him three times a week."

"How bad was the throat?"

The homicide dick shook his head. "It's a funny thing about that. Doc Matthews says it was mostly in Carroll's head. He kept imagining his throat was bad and insisted that the doc keep coming in." He shrugged expressively. "After all, his dough was as good at the doc's bank as any other patient's."

Johnny Liddell screwed his eyes up into a thoughtful scowl. "Then we only have the doc's word for it that Johnny Carroll thought he had cancer?"

"Well, I guess Carroll's secretary would back him up on that." He studied the private dick's face. "What's buzzing around in that skull of yours, Johnny?" he asked.

"I don't know," Johnny Liddell admitted. "How's for looking Carroll's apartment over?"

Terence Grady squeezed out his cigarette on the corner of the wooden-topped table. He had had enough experience with Johnny Liddell's hunches in the past not to run counter to them.

The uniformed man on duty outside Johnny Carroll's apartment saluted smartly as Terence Grady and Johnny Liddell entered. He did not succeed entirely in wiping the boredom out of his eyes.

"Through here in the study," Grady led the way. He stopped in the doorway. "There's where he was, right next to the desk."

Johnny Liddell stared at the chalked outline left by the coroner's men. He transferred his eyes to the ceiling. There was no evidence of a bullet scar in the plaster.

"You said the slug tore through the top of Carroll's head?" he asked. The homicide man nodded. "Then how come no bullet in the ceiling?" Johnny Liddell wanted to know.

Detective Sergeant Terence Grady pushed his fedora back on his head. "Just a freak probably. Maybe by the time it tore through his skull it was spent. We'll find it on the floor someplace."

Johnny Liddell grinned. "Spent? Just going through the top of his head? Not unless he had it reenforced with bullet-proof steel." He walked over to the chalk-outlined space, stood looking around. "Which way was the body lying?"

Grady stared at him a moment, then shrugged. "Facing the door, I think. Why?"

Johnny Liddell scowled, stood inside the chalk outline, and faced the door. Then he turned around and looked behind him. "A glass door, eh?" He walked toward the door, examined the glass. "No sign of a hole. It didn't go through the door, so he must have been facing the bookcase." He stared for a moment, then nodded his head. "Sure, that would be right. The desk would be at his back—"

The homicide man stared. "I don't like to be picky, Sherlock, but how about letting a poor working man in on your brainstorm?"

Johnny Liddell ignored him, walked to the desk. "That would mean that wall—the one with the tapestry."

"What about it?" Grady growled.

"That's where your bullet probably is. In the wall underneath the tapestry."

Grady made the tapestry-covered wall in five steps. He

pulled aside the tapestry, peered a moment, then grunted. "Right on the head, Sherlock. How'd you guess?"

Johnny Liddell grinned. "Elementary, my dear Watson. Elementary." He hoisted a thick thigh onto the corner of the desk and watched patiently as the homicide dick pried the misshapen hunk of lead out of the wall with a penknife.

"This still doesn't change the fact that he knocked himself off." Grady's voice wasn't quite so final. He carried the lead pellet in his palm as though it were something priceless.

Johnny Liddell ignored the statement. "How much money did you find around the place?" he asked.

"Just a couple of hundred bucks he had in his pocket. Why?"

Johnny Liddell shrugged. "Just curious." He fingered the desk furnishings. "How's chances of seeing this doc you spoke about?"

Terence Grady nodded. "Raftery?" he called. The door opened and the bored-looking cop stuck his head in. "Run downstairs and see if Doc Matthews is in. Tell him we want to see him."

The cop saluted, withdrew his head.

Johnny Liddell wandered aimlessly about the room, picking up small objects d'art and replacing them. "How about Carroll's secretary, Emmy Wilson? Any chance of seeing her for a few minutes?"

"What's going 'round in that skull of yours, Johnny?" the homicide dick growled. "If you've got any ideas, spill 'em, but don't horse me around. This case is closed as suicide and for my part I'm willing to let it stay like that, unless—"

"Unless I deliver a killer all wrapped up in cellophane and with a pink bow on his hair? Well, maybe I can do that, too."

Terence Grady stared at the private dick, then shrugged. "I can call Emmy. She'd be here in a few minutes—"

Johnny Liddell nodded. He dropped into a large over-stuffed leather chair while the homicide dick dialed. While Grady was talking to the girl, the door opened and a tall, thin man entered.

"I'm Dr. Matthews," he said. "Did you gentlemen want to see me?" His eyes had a disturbing habit of twitching as he spoke.

Johnny Liddell nodded, indicated a chair with a toss of his head. The doctor sat on the edge of a chair and waited patiently for Grady to get off the phone. Finally, the homicide dick hung up.

"Emmy'll be right over," he told Liddell. Then, turning to the doctor, "Sorry to bother you, Doc. Mr. Liddell here thought you might be able to help us out. He wanted to ask a couple of questions."

The doctor nodded jerkily, turned his eyes to Liddell.

"Know Johnny Carroll very well, Doc?" Liddell asked.

The tall, thin man shrugged. "He's been a patient of mine for some time now. I've known him in that capacity."

"Know what his business was, Doc?" Liddell's voice was soft. He was apparently interested in a spot inches over the doctor's head.

The doctor's eyes twitched. "A gambler, wasn't he? I mean, I've read quite a bit about him."

Johnny Liddell nodded. "Yeah, a gambler. Ever play the horses, Doc? Or roulette?"

The doctor's eyes roved from Liddell's face to the homicide dick's and back. He pulled himself erect. "I don't see what this has to do with—"

Johnny Liddell pulled a pack of cigarettes from his pocket, stuck one in his mouth, lit it. "Take it easy, Doc. It'd be easy enough to find out if you owed Carroll any dough—"

The thin man seemed to shrink. He sat down heavily. "Oh,

I see. You wanted to know if I owed him any money?" His eyes twitched maddeningly. "Well, matter of fact I did. A couple of hundred dollars—"

Terence Grady got to his feet. "What's going on, Johnny?" He permitted himself to be waved to silence by the private dick.

"What's with this cancer of the throat gag?" Liddell asked.

The doctor raised a shaking hand to his mouth. "Somehow he got the idea he had a cancer. Insisted on being treated. I prescribed an antiseptic spray and tried to talk him out of it. I—I never realized he would—"

Johnny Liddell blew a thin stream of smoke through his nostrils. "Can the act, Doc. You know Carroll never bumped himself."

The doctor's face was ashen as he jumped to his feet. "I don't know what you mean. I examined the body. He'd killed himself. His gun was there beside him!"

Johnny Liddell's voice was lazy. "How do you know it was his gun, Doc?"

"I've seen it before. He always had it near him."

Terence Grady's eyes went from the shaking figure of the physician to the indolent figure of the private dick in the chair. He started to say something, then changed his mind, clamped his lips.

Johnny Liddell solemnly regarded the glowing end of his cigarette. "When was the last time you saw the gun?" he asked.

The doctor rubbed the back of his hand across his lips. "This afternoon. I had been examining his throat. He opened the drawer to get the money to pay me. It was laying there. I commented on it—"

"What then?" Terence Grady's voice was harsh. He was leaning forward with interest. "What then, Matthews?"

The twitching eyes darted from face to face. "I—I picked it up. Firearms have always had a fascination for me—"

"Then you killed him," Grady accused.

"No, no. I gave the gun to him. He gave me the money, dropped the gun into the drawer and closed it—"

The door opened to admit the head of the bored cop. "The secretary's here, Sergeant. Says you wanted to see her."

Terence Grady growled under his breath. "Okay, send her in," he told the cop.

Emmy Wilson reeked of Broadway from her blondined head to the nyloned leg her dress generously exposed. She looked from face to face, nodded at the doctor.

"What goes?" she asked.

"We're just about to decide who murdered your boss," Johnny Liddell informed her. His eyes took bold inventory of her obvious assets.

Her eyes became round. "Murdered? You're kidding. He killed himself. The cops said so." She turned to Terence Grady. "Is this a gag, Lieutenant?"

"Sergeant," Grady corrected her sadly.

"But how?" the girl asked.

Johnny Liddell struggled to his feet. "The thing that led everybody to believe that he knocked himself off is the fact that he got shot through the mouth." He looked at Detective Sergeant Grady. "Sure, Johnny Carroll never would let anybody stick a rod in his mouth. But suppose he didn't know it was a rod?"

Terence Grady stood up, slid his hand into his jacket pocket. The doctor straightened up in his chair, stared ahead of him.

"If Carroll had stuck the rod into his mouth and had pulled the trigger, then the bullet would have gone through and into the ceiling," Johnny Liddell continued. "But it didn't. It went into the wall." He paused to let that sink in. "Know why? Because Johnny Carroll had his head thrown back when the gun was shoved into his mouth. Thrown back the way it would be if somebody was treating his throat—"

Emmy Wilson jumped from her chair. Her mouth was a round "O" of horror. She looked at Doc Matthews with loathing. "That must have been the way it happened. I knew you hated him—"

The thin form of the doctor seemed to shrink even further in his clothes. He wiped his mouth with his hand, his eyes twitched painfully. "I didn't. I didn't, I tell you."

"Arrest him, Sergeant," Emmy Wilson ordered. Her eyes were hot beds of fire. "He killed Johnny Carroll."

Detective Sergeant Terence Grady grabbed the thin man by the shoulder. "Let's go, bud," he said.

Johnny Liddell's voice was calm, unhurried. "Why not listen to the end of the story?" He settled one hip on the corner of the desk. Grady let go the doctor's shoulder, but stood behind his chair. "There was the case of the gun. The doc admits having handled it—"

"But I told you how that happened," Doc Matthews wailed.

"Sure, Doc. And that's maybe going to save you from the chair." He ground out his cigarette in the glass ashtray on the desk. "After all, Doc, we wouldn't want you to burn for a killing that Emmy Wilson did, would we?"

Detective Sergeant Terence Grady's jaw dropped. New life seemed to come into the doctor's face.

"Is this a rib?" Emmy Wilson's white little teeth showed in a snarl. "If it is, I ain't amused." She started to get up.

"It won't work, Emmy," Johnny Liddell sighed. "It had to be either the doc or you. It ain't the doc, so it's got to be you."

The girl moved like lightning. She was out of her chair and halfway across the room before Grady could yell. When he did, the door opened and the bored-looking copper stuck his head in. The bored look disappeared as he caught two armfuls of fighting curves. It took him almost a minute to subdue her.

"O.K., Johnny," Grady grunted when Emmy had been returned to her chair. "Why?"

Johnny Liddell grinned, offered a cigarette to the doctor who accepted it gratefully. "Like I said, it was either the doc or Emmy. Johnny Carroll would never let anybody else get close enough to shove a rod or anything else in his kisser." He lit his cigarette, held the match for the doc. "When I found the slug in the wall, I was sure of two things. Johnny had been bumped, and he had been bumped by someone who he thought was taking care of his throat."

Grady grunted. "Sounds like the doc."

"That's what I kept thinking," Johnny Liddell admitted. "Yet, there are so many better ways a doc can bump a guy off, particularly if he's going to write the death certificate. Besides, Emmy as Carroll's secretary would probably do all his throat spraying. And a gun barrel isn't too different from a spray nozzle."

Doc Matthews leaned forward. "But what decided you?"

"Well, when you admitted that you'd handled the gun, I began to see how it shaped up."

Detective Grady scratched his head. "I don't see where that fits. So what if he handled the gun?"

Johnny Liddell tapped a thin film of ash into the glass ash tray. "Because there were no prints on the gun except Carroll's." He looked up. "When the killer wiped his own prints off, he wiped everybody else's off, including the doc's. The doc had no reason to do that. He's already admitted handling the gun—and he wouldn't have done that except that he probably thought we'd found his prints on it. Therefore, it must have been Emmy."

The girl struggled to her feet. "He had it coming to him," she screamed. "He'd had it coming from away back."

Johnny Liddell took a last drag from his cigarette. "Then there was the matter of the money in the drawer—"

"That's where you're off the beam, Sherlock," Grady grunted. "There was no money in the drawer."

"That's just what I mean, Watson," Johnny Liddell countered. "There should have been. A big-time gambler like Johnny Carroll always carried enough cash on hand to take care of an eventuality like when the wrong horse won, and besides the doc saw the money in the drawer. That's where Carroll paid off from." He looked at the girl. "When you opened the drawer for the spray, I guess the temptation was too much, eh, Blondie?"

"I don't know what you're talking about," Emmy snarled.

"Johnny Carroll standing there with his head thrown back; all you had to do was take the gun instead of the spray, and the money was yours," he persisted.

The girl got to her feet. She held her arm out to Detective Grady. "We're wasting our time here, Sergeant," she said. "Let's get on down to the jailhouse where I can see my lawyer. I can't wait to find out whether it was in a fit of temporary insanity or whether I was defending my honor."

MIDNIGHT RENDEZVOUS

MARGARET MANNERS

THE MOON WAS JUST RISING AS LESTER RUNGATE WALKED UP
the flagged walk to his house and let himself in with his
key. All his movements were quiet and deliberate. He passed
the living room and the library without a glance, and ignored
the broad invitation of the carpeted staircase. He knew his
wife would not be on the upper floor. Stairs were a strain
on Ellen's heart. So they had turned the light pleasant room
in the rear into a ground-floor bedroom for her. It was on
the other side of the house, well away from kitchen and
dining room. Dressing room and bath were attached.

He walked swiftly to the back wing. She would be there,
he knew, sitting in front of the mirror doing things to her
already too beautiful face. That a woman could be too beautiful was irony unheard, but everything about Ellen was
heavily accented. Full red lips, large melting eyes, and soft
black waving hair that framed her face and emphasized the
creaminess of her complexion. She was life and warmth, she
symbolized all the good rich things of earth, lavishly given.
No one would think to look at her that her heart was such a
weak, treacherous thing. He himself, thin, gaunt, overworked,
looked sicker than she did. He had actually been amazed
when a few months before the insurance doctor had given
him a clean bill of health.

He had explained to her that the law firm wasn't doing as well as it might. He thought it best to be heavily insured. In case anything should happen to him she would be sure of protection. She hadn't liked the topic, he remembered. She never liked to be reminded of death. Perhaps that was because of her heart.

He reached her door, knocked lightly, and opened it. Her eyes met his in the mirror and she turned pale. Yes, he'd been right. There she was fussing with her face!

She turned slowly, staring at him.

"What's the matter?" he said. "You look as if I were a ghost or something!"

She gave a sharp gasp and put her hand to her heart.

Instantly he was solicitous. "What is it? Can I get you something? Medicine?"

She shook her head. He watched the spot where the white expanse of bosom and throat rose out of crimson folds. God, she knew how to dress!

Her color returned and she smiled. "I just wasn't expecting you, Lester! You said you'd stay in town, remember?"

He nodded absently. "What a stunning negligée, Ellen! But what vanity! Putting on make-up before you go to bed!"

She flushed. He felt her eyes follow him as he put his brief-case on the spinet desk, turned on the lamp and sat down.

"You aren't going to work in here, surely?"

"No, I'd much rather talk to you. I certainly intended to stay in town. It's no pleasure commuting with this exhausting trial on. But through some silly mix-up the damn hotel hadn't made the reservation. After I'd called six other hotels I decided it would be simpler to spend an hour and a half on the train and be sure of a comfortable bed at home. Sorry I frightened you."

She turned back to the mirror, and the hand applying the

lipstick trembled. With an exclamation of annoyance she wiped her lips and drew the full arc again.

"What elaborate preparations for bed!" he teased gaily.

"As a matter of fact, Lester, I thought I'd go for a walk."

"All that artistry for the dark Long Island night?"

She laughed. "Habit! You know what women are!"

"Yes," he said. "I know. All right, since you want a breath of air, I'll go with you."

"Why, I shouldn't dream of it! You're tired."

"Nonsense, good to stretch my legs after that ride."

He saw her hesitate. "Well, thanks very much. I'll slip on a dress . . ." She vanished into her dressing room.

He waited a short time and then opened the door into the rear hall. There was no sound, and the hall door leading into the dressing room was closed. He went swiftly to the front of the house and opened the library door. His wife was dialing a number on the phone there.

"I beg your pardon," he said. "I thought I'd make a call to the office while you were changing. Sorry. . . . No, go on. I can wait."

"Just Minna," she said awkwardly. "But the number is busy, and anyway, it's a bit late for me to be calling them."

"If you heard the busy signal they must be up. Try again."

"Make your call," she said, pushing the telephone toward him. "Mine can wait till tomorrow."

Watching her rising color, he dialed his office. There was no reply. "Too bad!" he said. "My secretary said she'd work late, but I seem to have missed her. You haven't put on your dress, my dear. Hurry up!"

"There's no hurry, Lester. Maybe I ought not to go out, after all. I haven't been feeling very . . ."

"That's what I've been thinking," he said quickly. "Your heart bothered you a little when I came in. Shall we go and

sit in your room? I can entertain you with some little anecdotes about the trial. And talking of anecdotes, I had rather
a narrow escape today!"

She walked ahead of him into the bedroom. "What was
that?"

"Got into a jam at the corner of the hotel, traffic mixup.
Almost got pushed under a truck. It actually felt as if someone were deliberately shoving me. Funny thing, somebody
did get run over. Someone we know. Do you remember that
chap who was my secretary for a while? Had to fire him for
impertinence to you. Blake—George Blake. Most amazing
thing ever happened to me! First he was behind me, and I
was almost killed, and then the crowd swerved or something.
Saw him crushed to a pulp before my eyes. I was close enough
to touch him.

"You're cold," he said. "I'll get you something to wrap
around your shoulders. That thing is very pretty, but much
too revealing."

Indeed she looked cold, he thought, blue and pinched. He
reached down a crocheted wool square from her closet shelf
and threw it around her shoulders. It was a bright shade of
orange that made her crimson negligée hideous, but she
didn't notice.

"If my reflexes had been better I might have saved him,"
he went on, "though, Heaven knows, I had little reason to
like the chap."

She shuddered and pulled the wool around her. He watched,
fascinated, as a little edge of pallor crept under the rouge.

"Poor devil!" he added. "That accident probably cuts into
his love life."

"Why do you say that?"

"Well, you see, I'd come down in the hotel elevator from
my room—I—I mean, the room of a friend I'd been visiting—

and was getting some cigarettes at the stand behind the palms when I saw him. He'd evidently just come in. I was behind him and couldn't help overhearing when he used one of those open wall-bracket phones. I heard him make an appointment to meet someone, a lady, after eleven. He asked her to leave the window open. Obviously a sub-rosa rendezvous! I went out just as he was hanging up. He must have come right behind me. Then I had that close shave with the truck, which somehow ended with him going under the wheels. I had to have a drink. It shook me up horribly.

"If it's so cold in here," he said suddenly, "it seems silly not to shut that window. Shall I?"

"Yes, thank you."

"I believe you *are* feeling badly, Ellen. You were certainly wise not to go for a walk."

"Yes."

"Wonderful night! Look, one could almost read by the moon out there. Shall we turn out the lights and sit in the moonlight?"

"Oh, please!" She seemed almost grateful. "The light hurts my eyes, and feeling this way I'm afraid I don't look very . . ."

"Not at all," he said gallantly. He turned off the lights. "You always look beautiful. . . . About poor Blake—or rather about sudden death in general— reminds me of the pilot who showed up for a date in town three hours after his plane was shot down."

"What in God's name do you mean?"

"Not a thing. I don't take such stuff seriously. You were the one that used to read about the spirit world. I gather there's a theory that if a person is violently cut off in the process of planning or doing something he very much wants to, the spirit fails to realize it is dead and goes on acting just as it would have if it had lived. You know, accomplishing the desired thing. Complete nonsense. Still, in wartime one hears stories . . . I guess it would depend on how much you wanted to do something."

They sat silent for a while watching the moonlight steal across the rug. At last she spoke. "Did you hear everything he said over the telephone?"

"Who?"

"George . . . George Blake."

"Blake? No, not *everything*. He was very discreet. Said something about removing the last obstacle to happiness and freedom. He liked to fancy himself a gentleman. That's what made him so repulsive. It didn't quite cover his coarseness, did it?"

"No." She choked a little. "He was as coarse as the earth."

"And just as primitive, I imagine. No moral restraint would keep him from getting what he wanted. I've often wondered why he didn't try some dirty trick to get back at me for firing him. Just the type!"

"Yes," she said. "I think he had the courage for wickedness."

"My dear, you almost make it sound like a virtue! Of course, he didn't know what happened to him. It would be funny if he still didn't. If he were going on about his business not realizing he was dead!"

"Stop! You're horrible, Lester!"

"Sorry, dear, I didn't think you were so sensitive."

"It's hardly a topic for . . ." She stood up suddenly, breathless. "Listen! Did you hear something?"

"Only tree toads and—"

"There! What was that?"

"Nothing!"

Her eyes were wide and shining with terror. The moonlight made her cheeks and lips unpleasantly green.

"What in the world is the matter, Ellen? Do you hear something?"

"That whistle! Listen!"

"You're imagining things. I'll open the window. See? Quiet as the grave!"

"I can hear it coming closer. Oh, God! Let me see!"

She rushed to the window and stared wide-eyed at the lawn that lay illuminated in silver light. The shawl slipped to the floor. "Look, he's there!"

Despite himself he was thrilled by the horror in her voice. "Who?"

She turned to him, her eyes feverishly bright. "Look, Lester! Standing right in the center of the lawn!"

He stepped closer to the window and looked out. "My dear," he said compassionately, "there's nothing there but the light of the moon."

She took his shoulders, pleading. "A man on the lawn! Don't you see him?"

"No, Ellen, there's nothing to see. There's *nobody* there!"

"Ah-h-h!" The full weight of her body slumped in his arms. He heard her hoarsely fighting for breath, but by the time he had dragged her to the center of the room she was quite still. He laid her gently on the floor and ran through the hall to the library phone.

"You'll have to send someone quickly," he cried when he got the number. "I'll do what I can. Yes, in my wife's bedroom."

He opened the drawer in the library table and lifted out the weapon that lay there. Then he moved swiftly and quietly back to the bedroom. He thought he heard the faintest rustling whisper through the door. "Where are you?" But it might have been the breeze.

He opened the door and turned on the light switch. "A

prowler!" he shouted in a loud, angry voice. "Put your hands up!"

The man in his wife's bedroom blinked at him stupidly.

"Good God!" Lester cried. "My wife! You've frightened her! She fainted! Her heart! No, stay where you are or I'll shoot! Why, it's Blake! So you wanted to rob me . . ." He waved the man back with the pointed muzzle and knelt beside Ellen. "She's dead," he said quietly. "What did you do to her?"

"Nothing!" The intruder was badly frightened. "I just climbed in the window. She wouldn't have been frightened like that. Why, she expected . . ."

"Shhh!" Lester said. "Here they come!" He stepped back to the open door and called, "In here! He's in here!"

Policemen seemed to fill the room. "Well," the sergeant said heartily, "looks like you did all right without us, Mr. Rungate." Then he saw the woman lying on the floor. His face changed and he dropped on one knee to examine her.

"My wife died of fright. She had a very weak heart. Must have seen him climbing in the window and the shock was too much for her."

"Do you know this man?" the sergeant asked.

"Unfortunately, yes. He was once my secretary. George Blake. Had to fire him for impertinence and a tendency to dishonesty. He swore he'd get even, but I never took it seriously. He must have been after my wife's jewelry. I was working late in the library. For some reason I happened to go into the darkened living room and saw him from the window, crossing the lawn. I went back and called you. This pistol was in the library. It's unloaded, but the bluff worked."

"Well, we'll lock him up," the sergeant said. And then, awkwardly: "I'm sorry about your wife, Mr. Rungate. One of the men has called for the doctor."

Lester's voice was tight and strained. "I know the man had no wish to harm her, but she died because he broke into my house illegally. There's a law, you remember, Sergeant, which states that if you cause someone's death while committing a felony the charge is *murder in the first degree!*"

The man standing between the policemen went wild. "You damned swine! I should have killed *you!*"

"Oh, you wouldn't have frightened me to death," Lester said. "My heart isn't weak. You'd have had to think of something more ingenious, like pushing me under a truck or something. But I don't doubt," he went on bitterly, "that you'd have liked to."

I'LL SLAY YOU IN MY DREAMS

BRUNO FISCHER

There's no logic in a nightmare. Clare Cobb was dead—mur-
dered—and I was the fall-guy. I could have laughed in grim
appreciation of the way the evidence had been built up
against me, bit by bit, except you can't when there's a gag
blocking your mouth. I could only be sure of two things: I
hadn't killed Clare, nor were these ropes now binding me a
figment of my imagination—ropes with soft padding provided
by a killer with a strange concern for my comfort . . .

I

THE LETTER

THE MAN ACTED QUEER FROM THE FIRST, BUT EVERYTHING
he did and said made sense. That's what I want to get
straight—it could have happened to anybody. I'm no dumber
than the next fellow. It's only that I had the tough luck to
be hitching in that direction at that time.

At twilight I had only twenty miles to go to reach Coast
City, and I was worried about getting a lift before dark.
Then this swanky coupe came along. When it slowed as it
approached me, I thought I was set.

The car didn't quite stop. As I moved toward it, it abruptly
picked up speed. The mudguard missed me by a hair.

I figured that it was my fault. My good suit was in my bag. For hitching I wore unpressed army pants and a faded windbreaker, and I hadn't had a chance to shave since the day before. Probably I hadn't looked prepossessing enough to be given a lift, with darkness coming on. But as I stood there looking after the car, it began to roll slowly, as if the driver were trying to make up his mind about me. Apparently he did, for the coupe soon came to a complete stop.

I broke into a run. The driver was waiting for me. He had the right door open, but his arm barred me from entering. He was a heavy-set, middle-aged man, with a florid face in which the skin sagged loosely. Through shell-rimmed glasses, he peered suspiciously at me in the gloom.

"I don't make a habit of picking up strangers," he said fussily. His eyes dropped to my battered straw bag. "I assume you don't live in Coast City."

"No, sir. I've just been discharged from the Army. I heard there were good jobs in Coast City shipyards."

His arm still blocked me. "Why were you discharged?"

It was none of his business. All I wanted was a lift, and he was acting as if he were interviewing me. I explained: "I'd had rheumatic fever as a kid, and it came back."

At last he seemed satisfied. "You look like a clean-cut boy," he conceded and removed his arm from the door.

It wasn't until I was sitting beside him in the car that I got a whiff of his breath. He smelled pretty drunk, but he didn't look it or act it. Seemed to hold his liquor like a real gentleman as they used to say in books.

For a while, we drove in silence. Then he mumbled: "She can't mean it. If she'd only let me explain."

"What's that, sir?" I asked.

He glanced sideways at me, somewhat vacantly, so I realized that he hadn't been speaking to me. He said: "What's your name, son?"

"Elliot Tucker."

"Have you come far?"

"From Trevan," I said.

"That's pretty far."

"Only four hundred miles," I told him. "It's a small place with no industry and little work, so yesterday morning I left to hitch to Coast City."

"Relatives?" he asked.

"Just my mother. If I get a good job, I'll send for her and—"

I stopped. Men who gave you lifts generally did so because they wanted company and conversation. They often asked personal questions, and that was all right, but this guy was different. I had a feeling that he was intensely concerned with my answers.

"I'm Howard Cobb," he said suddenly.

He said it as if I should be impressed. I wasn't. I just sat there.

Howard Cobb laughed. "I suppose you've never heard of the Coast City Cobbs?"

"No, sir."

"Naturally not," he said. "You're a stranger."

It seemed to me that he was leading up to something, but suddenly he became silent again. In a little while he turned the car off the highway.

It was dark now, but I could distinguish empty stretches of sand on either side of me. The road wasn't much, hardly wide enough for two cars to pass each other. There were no houses.

"Is this a short cut?" I asked.

"I have to stop off at my cabin for a minute," he said. "You don't mind, do you?"

"Not if I get to Coast City tonight."

He laughed again, a dry, thin sound. "You'll get there."

Now I could smell the wet, salt smell of the ocean, and I heard the dull rumble of breakers. Tall pines grew here, and amid them stood a rambling log cabin. Howard Cobb stopped the car.

"How about a drink?" he invited.

I'd have preferred supper, but a drink was welcome. He unlocked the door and put a light on in the hall and then in the living room.

The place might have been a cabin to Howard Cobb, but it was a palace to me. The living room in which I found myself wasn't much smaller than a barn and furnished in a way I'd seen only in the movies. Howard Cobb was money, all right.

He opened a liquor cabinet and poured two Scotch and sodas. With the glass in his hand, he crossed the room and brooded at the photo of a woman in a silver frame on top of the grand piano.

"She will," he said thickly. "If she'll listen."

I felt embarrassed.

Cobb turned to me. The folds of his fleshy face seemed to hang more loosely, and his wide shoulders drooped. "That's Clare, my wife."

"She's attractive," I muttered politely, though she wasn't, particularly.

Glumly, he nodded. "She kicked me out of the house."

I wished he'd stop it and drive me on to the city. I drained my drink and put it down with a thud to let him know I wanted to go. Through his glasses his pale eyes appraised me intently.

"How would you like to earn a thousand dollars, son?" he asked.

"A thousand dollars a year or a month or what?" I said.

"For a few hours' work tonight."

I stared at him. Anybody who made that sort of offer couldn't be honest—not even a rich man—or couldn't be sober.

"Oh, it's nothing shady," he said quickly. "It's like this. My wife and I quarreled and now she refuses to see me. When I enter the house, she locks herself in her room. When I phone, she hangs up before I can say a word. It's all a silly misunderstanding. I'm sure I can patch it up if I have five minutes with her. I want you to bring her here."

"Me?" I said.

Eagerly, he came forward and placed his untouched drink next to mine. "We have to be subtle, of course. Clare loves me, that I'm sure of. If she heard that I was here, injured, she'd come at once. And that would give me my chance to explain."

He didn't sound drunk or crazy now. A man in love would do something like that.

"You think I won't pay you the money?" he said. "Here." He took out a roll of bills which dazzled me. I saw a hundred-dollar bill on top, but what he peeled off were five twenties. "Here's a hundred dollars in advance. You'll get the rest when you bring Clare here."

I took the money from his outstretched hand. Why not? He could afford it and what I had to do to earn it wasn't in any way crooked. Even if he didn't shell out the rest of the money, this hundred dollars would be the easiest I had ever made.

"Will she believe me?" I asked.

Cobb thought that over and scowled. "She might suspect

a trick." His fingers snapped. "I have it. Sit down at that desk and write a letter to her. Say that I fell outside of my cabin and injured my spine. Sign the letter 'Dr. H. L. Davidson.' He's my physician."

I went to the oak desk and found paper and a pen. With the pen in my hand, I hesitated. "This will be forgery, sir."

"Nonsense. You're not imitating Dr. Davidson's handwriting."

No, but I would be signing the doctor's name. I didn't like it. Then I looked at the money still clenched in my left hand and that decided me. After all, she was his wife.

I said: "Do I write 'Dear Clare,' or 'Dear Mrs. Cobb'?"

" 'My dear Mrs. Cobb.' " I wrote as he dictated the letter. Then he told me the address which I wrote down on the back of the letter.

"You'll have to use my car, of course," he said. "It's the only way you can get to the city."

Nodding, I stuck the letter into my pocket and walked over to the piano. The woman whose photo stood on the piano was a brunette who might have been thirty, but no more. Her husband was a good twenty years older. She wasn't bad looking, except that her face was too plump for my taste.

Howard Cobb came up behind me. "Don't you trust me?" he said softly.

"I want to make sure I'll give the note to the right person."

"That's what I mean," he said. His mouth smiled, but his eyes didn't. They kept studying me. "Do you think my scheme is far-fetched?"

I shrugged. "It's your money, sir. I hand her the letter, and either she comes or she doesn't."

"You understand that you are to drive her back?"

"Of course," I said. "I'd have to return your car anyway." Suddenly I frowned. "Talking about trust, aren't you trusting me too far with your expensive car? You don't know me. I might never come back with it."

"I think you will. Nine hundred dollars in cash is more than you can get for a stolen car. And you look honest." He made an impatient gesture toward the door. "You'd better go. It's getting late."

When I was in the hall, I glanced back. Howard Cobb was avidly gulping down the drink he hadn't touched before.

All the way to Coast City I was uneasy. One thousand dollars was too much for the job. Even if I didn't get more than the one hundred I had already received, it was too much. I would have considered myself overpaid for twenty bucks.

After a traffic cop gave me directions, I had no trouble finding the Cobb house. It occupied an entire block in the swellest section of town—final proof that the Cobbs were very rich. You could expect anything from the wealthy. They didn't know the value of money. A thousand dollars meant nothing to them. Besides, Howard Cobb was probably drunker than he seemed, and he was in love with his wife. Add that up and the whole thing was reasonable.

For the first time in my life I came face to face with a butler at a door. He looked at my clothes in haughty astonishment, making me feel socially unclean.

"I have a message for Mrs. Cobb," I said quickly. "Mr. Cobb is hurt."

Gingerly he took the letter from me and was about to close the door in my face. When I told him I was to receive an answer, he reluctantly permitted me to wait in the foyer and somberly walked up a curving staircase.

In a matter of seconds a woman came flying down those stairs. Though at the moment she was wildly distraught, there was no doubt that she was the woman whose photo stood on the piano in the cabin.

"What happened to Howard?" Mrs. Cobb cried. "Did you see him?"

"No, ma'am," I said. "I was passing the cabin when a man came out and said that Mr. Cobb was injured and asked me to drive to town and take you there. He said he didn't want to leave Mr. Cobb and he couldn't move him."

"Was that Dr. Davidson?"

"That's what he said his name was."

My letter was a crumpled ball in her hand. She was taking the news very hard, and I felt like a heel. It was a dirty trick.

The butler appeared with her coat. "Shall I call the car, madam?"

She glanced at the paper ball in her hand and shook her head. "Dr. Davidson said this young man would drive me. It will take less time."

"Yes, madam." The butler looked narrowly at me. "Do you think, madam, you ought to go alone with—a stranger?"

I suppose what bothered him mostly was the stubble on my chin, though my clothes didn't help any.

"Nonsense, Willow." Mrs. Cobb's eyes were on me and at the same time had a worried, faraway look. "You can see he's a nice young man. My coat."

She dropped the paper ball on a table, got into the coat the butler held for her and went out to the coupe with me.

II

THE NIGHTMARE

For a while Mrs. Cobb didn't say anything as we drove. She sat forward in the seat, her hands working convulsively on her knees. There was no doubt she loved her husband.

They'd be reconciled in the cabin, and Howard Cobb would be so grateful that he wouldn't hesitate to fork over the remaining nine hundred dollars. This was my lucky night.

She spoke for the first time when we were almost there. "Why didn't Dr. Davidson telephone me instead of sending you?"

"What?" I said. "Oh, the telephone." I hadn't known there was a telephone in the cabin. Why hadn't Cobb thought of that question? "Dr. Davidson said it was out of order."

She gave me a sharp, sidelong glance. "Then how did my husband call Dr. Davidson?"

"I don't know, ma'm. Maybe the doctor was there when it happened. He didn't tell me anything except to deliver this letter and drive you back."

She didn't press the matter. I suppose she was too worried over her husband to think about details. Anyway, we were practically there by then.

She slammed out of the car the moment I brought it to a stop. As she ran, I tagged after her a little distance behind. She left the front door open. I was in the hall when it struck me that it would be better if I waited outside. Howard Cobb wouldn't want an audience.

Then I saw that the living room was empty. Mrs. Cobb had already crossed to a door on the other side. Apparently Howard Cobb was waiting in one of the other rooms. I sat down to wait for my money at the desk where I had written the letter.

Doors slammed in other parts of the house. I heard feet out in the hall. Then Mrs. Cobb was back in the living room, standing just inside the doorway with her hands tightly clasped.

"There's nobody here," she said.

"Are you sure?" I asked. "Did you look everywhere?"

"He's injured. Where would he be but in one of the bedrooms?"

I thought I had the answer to that. The idiot had got himself cockeyed drunk while waiting and had wandered out of the house. He'd be back, though. I was sure of that.

Her eyes were frightened as she waited for an answer. With a shock, I realized that she was afraid of me.

"Perhaps Dr. Davidson managed to get him to a hospital after all," I said.

She relaxed at that. "Then Dr. Davidson must have left a message at my house. I'll phone—"

"The phone's dead," I reminded her. "Dr. Davidson knew I was driving you here. He'll come back for you or send somebody to tell you where your husband is. I think we'd be better off waiting a little while."

"He would have left a note," she argued distractedly.

I was anxious to keep her here until Cobb returned. That was my only chance to collect all of the thousand dollars. I said: "Anyway, there's no harm waiting a couple of minutes."

"No harm?" she muttered and kept looking at me through wide, scared eyes.

To show her that I was harmless, I took up the pen, drew a sheet of paper to me and casually started to make a sketch.

When I looked up again, Mrs. Cobb was pouring herself a stiff drink. She drank the stuff straight and the glass shook in her hand. Silently, I cursed Cobb. I wouldn't be able to keep her here much longer.

After a minute I felt her standing beside the desk. "Oh, you're an artist," she said indifferently. Her eyes remained distant and preoccupied.

On the paper was a rapid ink sketch of her face. "I'm not very good," I said with a dry laugh and stuck the sketch into my pocket. "It's just a hobby."

I doubt if she heard me. She had turned to a window and stood tense, listening to the voice of the ocean. There was nothing else to hear. Abruptly, with quick, agitated strides, she went out to the hall. Then I heard the thin whirring of a phone being dialed.

I felt like a criminal being caught red-handed. What was I to do now?

The hell with Howard Cobb, I thought, and went out to the hall. Mrs. Cobb was bent over the phone, whispering: "Dr. Davidson? Did you—"

"I can explain, Mrs. Cobb," I said.

Her dark eyes tilted up at me in terror. The hand-set fell from her fingers. She cowered back. It wasn't a nice feeling to have a woman mortally afraid of you.

"The phone isn't out of order," she said, in a voice so hoarse that I could hardly distinguish the words. "Dr. Davidson is home. You tricked me into coming here."

"Don't be afraid of me, please. Your husband—"

She never let me finish. In panic she darted toward the door. Weakly, I put out a hand. It was so important that she let me explain. My fingers brushed her arm. She screamed and plunged past me.

"Damn Cobb!" I said aloud. It wasn't worth a hundred dollars, or a thousand, to have any woman look at me the way she had. At the least, she would drive off in the car and leave me stranded here.

I didn't hear the car motor spring to life. I waited, and there was nothing but the relentless rumbling of the waves breaking on the shore. In her terror, she must have run wildly into the darkness, forgetting about the car. Or maybe she was crouching somewhere out there, waiting for me to leave.

I went outside. The night was black except for the area around the lighted windows.

"Mrs. Cobb," I called. "If you'll only listen to me—"

A step sounded behind me. *She's come back*, I thought, puzzled, and started to turn.

I felt nothing. The night closed in on me and entered my brain, and then I knew nothing.

Slowly I pulled myself up into consciousness. I had been drifting in a state between sleeping and waking, and now I thought I lay in my bed at home trying to remember the bad dream I had had. It was something obscurely absurd about earning a thousand dollars in a couple of hours by luring a woman to meet her husband.

I opened my eyes, but the darkness remained. It was still night. My stomach was queasy, my limbs were stiff, and my head throbbed. I decided to get out of bed and go to the bathroom for a drink of water. That was when I learned that I couldn't move.

My limbs were weirdly rigid and numb, and there was something wrong with my tongue. My mouth was distended in a kind of frozen, silent scream, my tongue was fixed against my palate and tasted vile. And I heard the ocean.

Then I was fully awake, and truth came with a sickening rush. I wasn't at home. I was lying on a hard wooden floor, and I was bound and gagged.

It hadn't been a dream. All that business with Mr. and Mrs. Cobb had happened. Tentatively, I lifted my throbbing head. Fire stabbed the back of my skull and I sank back. That last instant of awareness outside the cabin . . . I must have been knocked out. Then I'd been dragged back into the cabin and my arms and legs had been tied and a gag shoved into my mouth and the lights turned out.

But by whom? Howard Cobb? Why would he do that to me? And what had happened to Mrs. Cobb? I hadn't heard a sound out of her after she had fled from me. Maybe she was the one who had socked me. That was as reasonable as anything else.

In frenzied revolt against the unfairness of what had been done to me, I started to struggle. That only made my head hurt more. I subsided. Whoever had tied me had done the job very well, though strangely, I couldn't feel the ropes.

My fingers were free. I stretched them, groping, and felt the material of a Turkish towel around my arms, under the ropes. Was somebody stark, raving mad? The only explanation I could find for the towel was to prevent the tight ropes from digging into my flesh.

I laughed at that notion, or tried to. One can't laugh against a gag. Why would the person who had knocked me out be so solicitous of my comfort as to see to it that the ropes didn't hurt me?

Maybe I was still dreaming. Maybe I was really home in bed at this very moment and deep in a nightmare.

It wasn't many hours before grayness appeared in front of my eyes. Dawn was breaking. I'd lost consciousness around ten o'clock last night. Unless my sense of time had become completely cockeyed, that meant I'd been out cold for several hours, at least.

In bewilderment I stared up at the ceiling. The cabin ceiling, I was sure, had been beamed and paneled. What I saw above me was the underside of a tin shed roof.

Risking the pain of movement, I lifted my head. I wasn't in the cabin. This was a small shack, completely unfurnished. Inches of grime covered the plank floors. There were two doors, one leading outside and the second to another room or perhaps a closet. The two windows were both tightly shuttered. What light and air trickled in came through cracks in the siding.

Was this an outhouse of the cabin? One thing was plain— I was still very close to the ocean. The breaking of waves on the beach made an endless rumble in my ears.

Hours later I decided that I had been left here to die. There was no reason for it. I was nobody, I had nothing valuable, I was nobody's enemy. There were no answers to questions, only facts like this. Enough air came through the cracks to keep me from suffocating, but death would come even harder than that. I would die of thirst. Already my tongue seemed to swell against the gag. And my stomach twisted with hunger. My last meal had been lunch the day before.

From then on nothing mattered but thirst and hunger. The pain of the blow subsided, but that didn't atone for lack of drink and food. Nobody would find me here. Probably nobody had looked into this shack in years.

How long before I would die? How great the agony? Please God, make it come quickly.

It never grew lighter in the shack than that dismal grayness. Eventually it deepened and gave way to blackness, and it was again night. I thought that if I could sleep it would make it easier for me. I shut my eyes.

A cool breeze swept over me. Instantly I was alert. The door was open. Somebody was in the shack with me.

I could see nothing. I could hear no more than the creaking of a plank. Then somebody was breathing close to me. A hand fumbled on my body. I was pushed on my side and something hard and cold touched the back of my hand. It was the flat side of a knife. Whoever had knocked me out and tied me up had returned to kill me.

Now that I would die quickly and cleanly, I wanted desperately to live. I tried to plead with him against the gag. I squirmed away from the cold steel.

The knife moved up along my windbreaker sleeve and then down, over the towel and through the ropes which bound my wrists. I was free, except for my legs.

I didn't dare move. My arms were too stiff, and besides, he had the knife and probably another weapon. Now he was going away from me. A plank creaked again. Softly the door closed, and the silence that was louder than the clamor of breakers was back.

Slowly, I sat up, removed the gag from my mouth and rubbed the agonizing numbness from my arms. Somebody had made me a prisoner here and somebody else had freed me. Maybe the same person. But why slug me and tie me up in the first place? And why hadn't my rescuer wanted me to see him—or perhaps her? There was no logic in a nightmare.

The rope around my ankles wasn't easy to untie. Another Turkish towel was around my legs and the knots had become imbedded in it. When at last I rose to my feet, I tottered like an infant learning to stand. I stumbled in the direction of the door.

Light glowed dully outside the shack. It couldn't have been on when my rescuer had entered because I would have seen it through the open door. Blinking, I rubbed my eyes, though the light was far from blinding. It came from the dimmed headlights of a car parked only a few feet away.

"Who are you?" I asked. "What do you want?"

Nobody answered. Now that I was outside, I could smell the ocean as well as hear it. I had a sense of being terribly alone, though my rescuer had to be nearby.

I walked around the hood of the car. The dashboard light showed me that nobody was in the coupe.

Coupe! I stepped back, sweeping my eyes over the graceful length of the car. This was Howard Cobb's coupe. I had driven it for at least twenty miles to Coast City and back. So Cobb was the one who had freed me—or maybe Mrs. Cobb. Then why all this mumbo-jumbo about not letting me see who my rescuer was?

I got behind the wheel. The key was in the ignition lock. The motor turned over sweetly, everything was in order. It struck me that it was as if the car had been placed here at my disposal, with the lights on to show me where it was. That was absurd, of course. Cobb, or whoever it was, had parked the car here and gone to the cabin.

I switched on the brights and weaved the car back and forth across the narrow road, so that the headlights covered the area beyond the shack. Then I turned the car and searched the other side of the road. There was no structure of any kind visible. Nothing but a stretch of endless desolation. I headed the coupe away from the ocean.

This was not the firm concrete road which led to the cabin. It was crumbling tar, broken by murderous ruts. Where was I? At the moment, though, I couldn't really care about anything but food and water.

Soon, I was sure, this outrageous caricature of a road would get me to the Coast City highway. It didn't. I reached a better road, but one that seemed fiendishly to avoid stores, houses, any sign of life. My thirst became a kind of madness, and I was back in the nightmare on a road that had no end.

Presently, I came to a tiny village with only one street, and a lunchwagon. I stumbled in. The smell of frying food made me fight nausea, and I spilled half the contents of that first glass of water over my shirt as I gulped it down. Thirty minutes later, having eaten and drunk my fill, I felt as if I had just recovered from a long illness.

Over a cigarette, I asked the counterman how I could get to Coast City. His directions puzzled me.

"Look," I said, "I'm north of the city and you're telling me to drive north."

"Brother, you're really lost," he said. "You're a good thirty miles south of Coast City."

The cigarette turned to straw in my mouth. While unconscious, I'd been transported forty miles from the cabin where I'd been knocked out, then left in the shack for twenty-four hours, then released and provided with transportation to get back. Who was stark, raving mad?

I took out my wallet to pay my check. Before closing it, I counted my money. One hundred and sixty-three dollars—what remained of the money I had left home with, and the five twenties Howard Cobb had given me. Whatever else had been done to me, my wallet certainly hadn't been lifted. Somebody hadn't been interested in money.

But something else of mine was gone. My valise hadn't been in the shack and it wasn't in the car. When I left the lunchwagon, I tried the ignition key in the coupe trunk. It worked. No valise. I didn't think that anybody who had transported me forty miles to get me away from the shack would have carelessly left my valise behind. On the other hand, why steal it? All it contained was some clothes and a few personal belongings.

III

THE AWAKENING

It was close to midnight when I reached Coast City. I not only had a car to return and a bag to get back, I was, by God, going to get an explanation. I had no taste for being pushed around, especially by rich people who thought they could buy anything for a hundred bucks.

Lights were on in the Cobb house and the butler was up. He wasn't surprised to see me. "Mr. Cobb is expecting you," he said stiffly.

Just like that. I'd been plenty sore before. Now I felt myself tremble with rage. With my hands clenched, I followed the butler into a sitting room.

Two men were in there. One was tall and slender and somewhere in his thirties. He would have been smooth-looking if not for the lines of strain around his eyes and mouth. The second was a bear of a man, looking as angry as I felt. I had never seen either of them before.

"So you came?" the younger man said tightly.

"You're damn right I came," I said. "Where's Mr. Cobb?"

"I'm Howard Cobb," he told me.

I wasn't interested in any of Howard Cobb's relatives who had the same name. I said: "I mean Clare Cobb's husband."

The younger man opened and closed his hands convulsively. His eyes were bloodshot. "Don't be wise. I'm Clare's husband. I'm the only Howard Cobb there is."

I couldn't seem to extricate myself from the nightmare.

"You can't be," I protested. "Howard Cobb is a short, thick-set man who wears glasses. And he's older."

"Cut it out," the younger man said testily. "You spoke to me twice over the phone today. The second time I told you I'd have the twenty-five thousand dollars waiting for you. You offered to come here. You were pretty cocky. The butler had seen you last night, so we knew what you looked like, but you thought your threat to kill my wife would keep me from going to the police. Well, now that you're here—"

"Just a moment," I broke in. "I don't know what you're

talking about, except that I couldn't possibly have phoned you."

The bear-like man spoke for the first time. "This is getting us nowhere. You admit you have Mrs. Cobb?"

"I what?" I stared from one to the other. "Didn't Mrs. Cobb come home last night?"

"Do you mean to say you released her?" the younger man asked· eagerly.

I thought I had it then. These men were impostors. They had taken possession of this house and the butler was in on the hoax with them.

I asked the older man: "Who are you supposed to be?"

"You should know," he replied. "You sign my name to letters. I'm Dr. Davidson."

I didn't believe him. If the younger man wasn't Howard Cobb, then this one wasn't Dr. Davidson. I turned to the door.

"Wait," the younger man called. "I've the money ready. Tell me where my wife is and it's yours."

I kept going. I'd been played for a sucker once by an offer of money. This was a matter for the police.

"All right, Lieutenant Kearny," the younger man said wearily.

Two strange men plunged into the room. One grabbed my arm and the other leveled an automatic pistol at me.

"It didn't work," the man who called himself Howard Cobb said bitterly. "Something made him suspicious."

I stared at the sour, rugged features of the man with the gun. "Lieutenant?" I said. "Are you a cop?"

"What do you think?" The lieutenant stuck out his jaw at me. "You sure played this dumb."

There could be two impostors—but four? And that wasn't counting the butler. The two detectives looked genuine.

I said tightly: "Was Mrs. Cobb really kidnaped?"

"You answer that."

"But I don't know," I said.

"Where's that butler?" Lieutenant Kearny turned his head and the butler stepped into the room. "Is this the man who drove away with Mrs. Cobb last night?"

"It certainly is." The butler's eyes flashed hatred. "I warned Mrs. Cobb, but she was considerably upset by the note and would not listen to me."

"That's true," I admitted, "but—"

The lieutenant stuck a sheet of crumpled paper in front of my face. "Did you write this?"

It was the letter I had written in the cabin, to which I had signed Dr. Davidson's name. Dully, I nodded.

"And did you phone Mr. Cobb twice this afternoon, each time demanding twenty-five thousand dollars' ransom for Mrs. Cobb?"

"No, sir," I said firmly. "Even if I had wanted to do such a thing, I couldn't. I—"

The lieutenant cut me short. "Mr. Cobb, was it his voice you heard on the phone?"

Cobb scowled at me. "I'm sorry, Lieutenant. The voice sounded distant, as if disguised. He was perfectly willing to come here for the money. He said his accomplice would kill Clare if anything happened to him. He said he would be here between eleven and twelve tonight. What more do you want?" His voice went shrill. "Make him tell! Torture him! You've got to get Clare back alive!"

The fingers of the detective who held my arm tightened. On a wall there was a mirror, and for a moment I didn't recognize myself in it. The stubble on my cheeks, the wild look in my eyes, made me appear like what they thought I was—the worst kind of criminal, a kidnaper.

"Listen!" I said urgently. "The guy who said he was Howard Cobb used me as a dupe to kidnap Mrs. Cobb. Give me a chance to tell what happened."

"Go on," Lieutenant Kearny said quietly.

They listened to me in silence. I left nothing out. When I finished, their faces remained hard, merciless. They didn't believe me. I had trouble believing myself.

Dr. Davidson yanked up my right arm and pushed up the sleeve of my windbreaker and then of my shirt. His mouth went crooked as his thick fingers ran over my smooth skin. "So you say your wrists were tightly bound for many hours?"

"I forgot to tell you about the towels," I said. "There were two heavy Turkish towels, one wrapped about my arms and one about my legs, so that the ropes would leave no marks."

With a snort of disgust, Dr. Davidson threw my arm from him.

"Why not leave marks?" Lieutenant Kearny asked, as if he didn't care what I answered.

"So I could be framed, of course, by the guy who claimed to be Howard Cobb," I replied hotly. "Isn't it plain that he used me to kidnap Mrs. Cobb and then fixed it so I couldn't prove that I hadn't done it? Besides, how did I get hold of Mr. Cobb's car? It's outside now."

"What's this about my car?" Cobb said. "Both my cars are in the garage."

Of course, I thought. It wouldn't have been one of Cobb's cars. The nightmare had dissolved. Looking back, everything the man with glasses had done fitted into a pattern.

The lieutenant moved away from me and consulted in whispers with Cobb and Dr. Davidson. Even the detective who held my arm seemed to be ignoring me. I had a sense of having reached an end, of my fate having been decided. If they'd only believe me enough to look for that other man! My description wasn't enough. If I could show them—

"Listen!" I cried excitedly. "I'm pretty good at sketching. Give me paper and pencil and I'll make a drawing of the man who said he was Howard Cobb. Maybe he's a well-known criminal and you'll recognize him."

The lieutenant wasn't impressed, but he asked the butler to fetch pencil and paper. I sat down at the table. I'm not much of an artist and ordinarily it would have been difficult for me to sketch somebody from memory, but I would never forget that face. When I was finished, I thought it was a rather good likeness.

The four men stood around the table and stared down at my sketch. Hopefully, I looked from face to face. There was no recognition anywhere.

"He's sparring for time, Lieutenant," Dr. Davidson growled. "It's obvious this man never existed."

"He did!" I felt trapped. Walls were closing in on me. "Why don't you come to the shack where I was held prisoner? You'll see the ropes that tied me. Maybe there'll be other clues."

"That's what I've been thinking," Lieutenant Kearny said quietly. "Let's go."

A third detective was behind the wheel of a black sedan. The lieutenant sat in front with him while I was in the back seat with the detective who had held my arm in the house. Now he had handcuffs linked to his wrist and mine.

His name, I learned, was Sergeant Donlin. He had a round face and pleasant, round eyes. Unlike the lieutenant, he was capable of smiling.

"Why don't you get wise, son?" he told me confidentially. "They hang kidnapers these days. Tell us where Mrs. Cobb is and you'll get off easy."

"I told you what happened."

Sergeant Donlin shook his head. "It doesn't fit. To begin with, why all that hipper-dipper to kidnap a woman? It's not so hard to snatch somebody. And why frame somebody else for it before the whole purpose of the thing—collecting the ransom—has been completed? Cobb has to be convinced that a certain person kidnaped his wife before he'll pay out money. If Cobb thinks it was you, why should he fork up to anybody else?"

He was right. All that had happened didn't add up to kidnaping—except for one thing.

"But somebody did phone Mr. Cobb and demand ransom for Mrs. Cobb's return," I pointed out.

"That's what I mean. Your story is screwy. Now why don't you confess, son?"

The car stopped. We had reached the village where I had eaten and the driver turned to me for further instructions. I leaned forward in the seat, trying to work it out. Twice we took the wrong road and had to go back when the ocean stopped us. The cops got fidgety. They seemed to suspect a trick. I knew the third road was the right one as soon as we got on it. No other could be quite that bad.

The shack appeared in our headlights. Howard Cobb and Dr. Davidson had been following us in another car and they pulled up behind. The door of the shack was still open, the way I had left it. I started forward, but the handcuffs which attached me to Sergeant Donlin jerked me back. All three cops had flashlights. Lieutenant Kearny and the driver entered first.

The first thing I saw when I followed with Donlin was my straw bag near one wall. And there was nothing else in the shack. The ropes and towels had been removed.

My legs turned watery. Nothing had been overlooked. The walls closing in on me were all set to crush me.

"Well?" Lieutenant Kearny snapped fiercely.

Weakly, I said: "He came back. He removed the ropes and the towels. And he brought my bag. It wasn't here when I left. He—he . . ." I fought for air. "Don't you see how he's framed me?"

Nobody answered me. The lieutenant meandered across the room to that second door. He turned the knob, but the door stuck. He pulled his weight back and the door flew open.

"Here she is!" he yelled.

They all pushed forward. I tried to, also, but Sergeant Donlin held me back. I saw that it was the door to a small closet, and the converging beams of the flashlight showed me the oddly contorted body of a woman.

"Clare!" Howard Cobb cried and flung himself toward the closet.

Roughly, Dr. Davidson blocked his way. "Give me a hand with her, Lieutenant. I'm afraid we'll have to work quickly."

She wasn't wearing her coat, though I saw it in a crumpled pile in the closet. Her face was completely covered with a Turkish towel, and what I could see of her body seemed to consist of rolls of flesh, like tires of varying sizes placed together so as to form the shape of a woman.

"God!" Dr. Davidson said hoarsely. "She's been tied with wires. Wires all over her body tightened into her flesh. And she's—"

His strong fingers worked frantically to remove the towel from her face. That, too, was secured with wires. It seemed to take him forever. Then the towel was off and her face—

"No!" Howard Cobb shrieked. "Clare!"

Awkwardly, Dr. Davidson pushed his big body upright. I felt myself cringe under the look he gave me. "She's been dead for some time," he said tonelessly. "I should say, off-hand, that she suffocated—the towel, the wires, the lack of air in the closet."

That was when Howard Cobb hurled himself at me. His hands were on my throat when the cops pulled him off. They pulled him off me reluctantly.

IV

THE DEAD ACCOMPLICE

All the rest of that night and most of the next day they shouted at me and nagged me and bullied me. In the late afternoon I was permitted some rest, and at once I fell into a sleep of utter exhaustion. After a few hours I was yanked out of my cell and deposited in an office where Lieutenant Kearny and the district attorney were waiting.

The D.A. was a kindly-looking man. He offered me a comfortable leather chair and held a light for a cigarette he had given me. New tactics, I thought dully, to make me confess. On the desk I saw my Army discharge paper which had been in my bag and the sketch I had made of Mrs. Cobb and the letter I had written in the cabin.

"We all make mistakes, Tucker," the D.A. said amiably. "This seems to be your first one. I have ascertained that you had an excellent record in the Army. I had a number of your home-town authorities on the phone. Some of them know you and think highly of you. If you were the criminal type, I'd slap a murder indictment on you and see that you hang. But in your case, if you meet me halfway—"

"Whoever murdered Mrs. Cobb," I broke in, "deserves to hang."

Lieutenant Kearny started angrily to his feet. The D.A. waved him silent.

"I'll tell you precisely what happened," the D.A. said to me. "You must have planned this job right after you left the Army hospital. You said you'd never been in Coast City before. I doubt that—you knew too much. You knew that the Mintons were the richest family in Coast City, and you knew of the Cobbs' summer cabin and that nobody would be using it at this time of the year."

"Minton?" I said. "Are they the ones who own the shipyards in Coast City? Everybody's heard of them. But what have they got to do with Mrs. Cobb?"

"Come now, Tucker. I'm sure you were aware that Mrs. Cobb's maiden name was Clare Minton. You planned carefully. After your discharge from the Army, you returned to Coast City, ostensibly to look for a job. On the way you stole a car. We've traced the owner, a highly respected citizen living on the route you must have taken from Trevan."

"The man with the glasses stole it," I maintained. "Then he drove along looking for a sucker. He studied me before picking me up and asked personal questions before he decided that I had the makings of a fall-guy."

The D.A. went on, as if I hadn't said anything: "The Cobb ocean-front cabin is easy to break into. You thought you were clever. You wrote the letter with paper and pen you found there, and made a sketch of Mrs. Cobb from the photo on the piano to be sure you abducted the right woman."

"And took her to the cabin where the butler knew we were going," I said dryly.

"For a short while, yes. She would have become suspicious if you had driven her anywhere else, and you couldn't afford a row on the highway or any road on which cars passed. The cabin was isolated. There you could render her helpless without fear of interruption. You took your time when you reached the cabin, but when Mrs. Cobb saw that nobody else was there, she started to phone Dr. Davidson to check up on the letter. You pulled her away from the phone, tied her with the wire, gagged her with the towel, and transported her to the shack."

I opened my mouth to interrupt again, but I was too tired, too overwhelmed with a sense of futility.

"I doubt if you intended to kill Mrs. Cobb," the D.A.'s voice purred on. "There would have been easier and less brutal ways. She died because you're not a criminal. Everything you did smacks of the amateur. A professional would have known that she could not survive the towel and the wires and the airless closet. A professional wouldn't have been so confident that he had Howard Cobb so scared into helplessness that the ransom could be boldly collected at the house."

Bitterly, I laughed. "Everything that doesn't make sense you explain by saying that I'm young and stupid and an amateur. Why would I take the police to the shack to show them the body of Mrs. Cobb?"

The D.A. frowned, but Lieutenant Kearny had the answer to that one. "You figured the jig was up when Mr. Cobb handed you over to the police. You tried to get out from under. You had a cock-and-bull story prepared. You figured if you showed us Mrs. Cobb, we'd believe you."

"In that case Mrs. Cobb would have accused me of having kidnaped her," I pointed out.

"Only she wasn't in a position to accuse anybody." The lieutenant turned his sour face to the D.A. "That's one thing I disagree with you about. He deliberately murdered Mrs. Cobb."

It was plain that the D.A. thought so, too, but he was trying to give me enough rope to hang myself—literally. "Let's assume it was an accident," he purred. "This is your one chance, Tucker." His manner was urgently ingratiating. "It was an accident, wasn't it?"

I leaned against the back of the chair and closed my eyes. All of me, including my throat, was so tired that I had to push my voice out. "It was murder," I said. "I know enough law to know that however she died the kidnaper is legally guilty of murder."

Lieutenant Kearny pounced. "And you admit you kidnaped her. You wrote that letter. You called for her."

That was it. Whichever way you looked at it, I had tricked her into coming to the cabin, I had brought her to her death. I hadn't known what I was doing, but I had done it.

The door opened. A voice said excitedly: "I think I located the accomplice."

I opened my eyes and there was Sergeant Donlin with my sketch of the guilty man in his hand.

"Ah!" The D.A. rocked gently in his chair. "I considered the probability that there was somebody in this with Tucker. The sketch Tucker voluntarily made for us bears the stamp of the amateur criminal, the attempt to immediately shunt off the guilt on his accomplice."

"I've been showing this drawing around," Donlin said. "There's a bartender on the east side who says the guy comes to his joint for drinks. Then a stoolie knew him. The guy's name is Augie Brill. He's new in Coast City, but the stoolie knew him in Chicago where Augie Brill was an all-around bad guy. My idea is Brill is hiding out from the Chicago cops. We'll check."

The sergeant's words were like a cold shower reviving me.

I sat up. "Let me get my hands on him. I'll make him tell me the truth. Where is he?"

"We located his place," Donlin said, speaking to the lieutenant. "Brill lives over a grocery store on the east side. His door was locked when we got there. I've got men posted. They'll pick him up when he comes home."

"*If* he comes home," the lieutenant growled. "Maybe he took a powder. Maybe he's up there asleep. Why didn't you go in?"

"Well, I figured—"

"I'll do the figuring." Lieutenant Kearny strode to the door and turned. "Bring Tucker along. I like confronting criminals with each other. Sometimes it produces interesting results."

Donlin snapped handcuffs on my wrist and on his. The D.A. stood up and wished the detectives good luck. By good luck he wasn't thinking of the same thing I was. He was after a closed case—I was after my life.

We drove to a shabby part of the city near the shipyards. The moldering, wooden building consisted of a small grocery store and a single story above it. From the car I could see a dim light in one of the two windows over the store.

A man in overalls and cap came over to our car. He was obviously a detective.

"So he came home?" Lieutenant Kearny said, gesturing toward the lighted window.

"That's a funny thing. Nobody came or went. That light's been on all day, but it's so far back that I didn't see it till it got dark. Guess he left last night and forgot to put the light out."

"Maybe," the lieutenant snapped. "We'll see."

I don't know where the other detectives came from, but

there were five, including Kearny and Donlin, when we went up the rickety stairs. The door was locked. The lieutenant barked an order, and a beefy detective hurled himself against the door and snapped the lock.

Augie Brill was inside. His stocky body lay face down under the light of a floor lamp. His shell-rimmed glasses had fallen off and were just beyond reach of the fingers of one outstretched hand. The hilt of a carving knife protruded from his back.

"That's why the light's still on," Lieutenant Kearny muttered. "He was murdered last night." He swung toward me in cold rage. "Smart lad, aren't you? You drew that picture of Brill last night because you knew he was already dead."

I sat crushed and silent in that room while the homicide squad moved about its job. Sergeant Donlin remained linked to me by the handcuffs. He was a good guy. He kept feeding me cigarettes and didn't nag me the way Lieutenant Kearny or almost any other cop would have done.

The body of Augie Brill had been removed to the bedroom. Before that, through the open door, I had seen a suitcase sitting on the bed. It was open and half-full, as if somebody had been interrupted while packing.

After a while, the medical examiner came out wiping his hands. He told the lieutenant that Augie Brill had been dead for approximately twenty-four hours.

"That would make it ten o'clock last night," Lieutenant Kearny commented happily. He practically beamed down at me. "That's the time you claim Brill released you in the shack."

"I didn't say it was Brill. I didn't see who it was." I roused myself. This was terribly important. I looked at the medical examiner. "Can you be sure of the exact time of death, sir? I mean, it was many hours ago, and I understand that the longer the interval since death the harder it is to tell."

"I said *approximately* twenty-four hours," the M.E. pointed out.

"Could it be less?" I persisted. "Could Brill have been murdered, say, twenty hours ago?"

The lieutenant watched me narrowly, but he didn't try to stop my questions. At my side, Sergeant Donlin smiled.

"Certainly," the M.E. said. "Twenty hours ago or twenty-eight hours ago. The window was open and the room temperature varied. Even after the post-mortem, I doubt if I'll be able to be more definite."

"Good enough, Doc," Lieutenant Kearny snapped. "Still trying to be wise, Tucker? If it could be shown that Augie Brill was murdered after midnight, that would let you out because that was when we nabbed you. It can't be shown. Anyway, it didn't happen that way. Before going to the Cobb house for the ransom, you stopped off here to stick a knife in Brill. He was packing his bag as if he intended to leave as soon as he got his share. But you wanted the whole twenty-five grand for yourself, so you liquidated him."

Angry, desperate words poured from my mouth, but Lieutenant Kearny wasn't interested. He had his case. "Take him away, Donlin," he ordered, and turned from me. I felt the steel cuff tug gently at my wrist as the sergeant rose to his feet.

Our shoulders touching, Sergeant Donlin and I walked down those dim, narrow stairs. They wouldn't listen to me, wouldn't believe me. I was being taken to my death. Rage completely possessed me. I swung my free fist at Donlin's jaw.

V

THE TRAP

e sergeant bounced back from the banister and put the heel of his hand hard against my chest. I tried to hit him again, but he jerked the handcuffs and got me off balance. I tottered on the edge of a step.

"Don't be a sap," he said harshly. "I can bring a dozen cops here in no time by yelling. Or I can get out my gun."

I sagged against the wall. "I'm sorry," I murmured. I had nothing against him personally. He was the best of the lot.

"That's better," Donlin said.

We continued down the stairs. A police sedan waited at the curb. The driver leaned against the mudguard. "Take a walk around the block, Shapiro," Donlin told him, and then we got into the back seat.

Dully, I wondered what the sergeant was up to now. More fatherly advice, probably, aimed to get me to confess so that the road would be cleared to the gallows. The hell with him! They'd hang me, but not with my help.

Donlin rubbed his jaw and looked sideways at me in the dimness of the parked car. "You're mighty sore, son, aren't you?"

"I said I was sorry," I replied testily. "If I had to hit somebody, why wasn't it Kearny?"

He grinned at that and handed me another smoke. After we both had lit our cigarettes, he said musingly: "You know, Tucker, I have a boy just about your age. He's in the Navy. Petty officer. He's a good boy. Clean-cut, like you. Eyes like yours—decent, honest."

"Stop the oil," I said bitterly. "You think I'm a kidnaper and a murderer."

"Do I?" He flicked ash from his cigarette. "Get something straight, son. Mrs. Cobb came from important people in this town. The D.A. has to wrap up her killer quick. Good politics. Lieutenant Kearny is in line for a captaincy. It won't hurt him any if he closes this case successfully. Me, I've been on the force nineteen years. I'll never be more than a sergeant. My eyes aren't clouded by ambition."

I stared at him. "You mean you don't think I did it?"

He didn't answer that directly. "I saw the reports the D.A. got on you by phone. You have a fine record in the Army and in civilian life. Criminals don't just happen over-night—not the kind that plan a hellish crime like this in advance. I think I can judge character. And you're not stupid —you're a bright lad. If you were kidnaping Mrs. Cobb, you wouldn't show your face to the butler. Not even a halfwit would come openly to the house to collect the ransom. Too many other things besides, such as the way Mrs. Cobb was tied."

"That was deliberate murder," I said.

"Uh-huh. Not kidnaping—murder! Which makes sense in only one way."

"Don't you think I know that?" I said. Through the car window I saw the driver returning to the car. "If Mrs. Cobb was a Minton, she must have been pretty rich in her own right. So what? Everything you police have points my way and nothing any other way."

"Not if it wasn't kidnaping," Donlin said.

The driver poked his head in the window. "O.K. now, Sarge?"

"O.K., Shapiro."

As we drove, Sergeant Donlin had no more to say. Actually, he hadn't committed himself to anything. Maybe he would be able to do something, but I couldn't see what. The thing had been too carefully planned, and I was on my way back to jail.

Suddenly I sat up. The neighborhood was familiar. I had been here twice before. The car swung up the Cobb driveway.

"We'll be quite a while," Donlin told the driver as we got out.

We went up the flagstone walk to the house. At the foot of the porch-steps Donlin stopped and unlocked the handcuffs.

"What will happen to you if I escape?" I said.

Shrugging, he dropped the handcuffs into his pocket. "I'll be broken, maybe. But you won't try, son. Not if I put you on your honor."

"No," I said, "I won't."

We went up to the door. As he rang the bell, he looked at me with a kindly smile. "It's a long chance, son. I can't promise anything."

"I don't understand," I said. "What—"

The door opened. The butler looked surprised to see me there. He said that Mr. Cobb was in the library.

Howard Cobb and Dr. Davidson were drinking highballs and listening to the radio. They jumped up to their feet and stared at me.

"What's this?" Dr. Davidson demanded. "I thought this young man was in prison."

Sergeant Donlin moved into the room with his hat in his hands. "Have you heard the latest developments?"

Cobb nodded, not taking his eyes off me. "We heard it on the radio. It seems that Tucker actually had an accomplice, a man named Brill. He was found murdered, and Tucker murdered him."

"Did the radio say that Tucker murdered Augie Brill?" Donlin asked, in a puzzled tone.

"Definitely. Besides, isn't it obvious?"

"No," Donlin said. "It's only obvious that we were intended to see it that way. The fact is, Augie Brill was seen going up to his apartment at one o'clock this morning."

I couldn't follow the sergeant. What he said wasn't true. If there had been such a witness, Lieutenant Kearny would not have assumed my guilt.

"I see," Dr. Davidson said slowly. "Tucker was in the hands of the police since midnight last night, so he couldn't have—"

"But that's impossible!" Cobb exclaimed. He glanced away and then back. "I mean, it doesn't change anything, does it? Tucker still murdered my wife."

Donlin smiled without mirth. "Do you think, Mr. Cobb, we would let Tucker walk around free like this if we thought he did?"

Cobb walked stiffly around the big library desk and dropped into the leather chair. "Stop talking in riddles, Sergeant," he said.

"There's no riddle, Mr. Cobb." Donlin turned to me. "Tell him how it was, son."

I was completely bewildered. Where would this get me? Cobb would merely say I was lying, and that would be the end of it. But Donlin's gentle smile urged me on. Maybe he knew what he was doing.

"All along it was a crazy kidnaping," I said. "The only way the district attorney and Lieutenant Kearny could explain it as a kidnaping was by saying that I was a stupid amateur. I knew better because I was on the inside. I knew that I was the fall-guy for Mrs. Cobb's murder. But why murder her like that? It was much too complicated. I didn't really get it until a little while ago when I learned that Augie Brill had been murdered last night—it seemed likely a few hours after midnight. In a way I was responsible for his murder because I had drawn a sketch of him."

I paused for breath. "You're doing fine," Donlin encouraged me.

"I think Brill's job was over when he tricked me into bringing Mrs. Cobb to the cabin," I continued. "Murder itself could be handled by the man who had hired him. I might describe him, but descriptions at best are vague. Brill was about to leave town, not hurrying much because he believed himself safe. Then the man who had hired Brill saw me make a sketch of Brill, a rather accurate one, if I do say so, and Brill became a menace to him. Since Brill was a criminal, his photo would be on record. He'd be identified, captured. And to save his own neck, Brill would accuse the real murderer."

Dr. Davidson scowled at me. "Only Cobb and I, besides the policemen, saw you make that sketch."

"That's right, sir," I said. "You or Mr. Cobb. I learned something else—that Mrs. Cobb was the one who had the money in the family. I'm pretty sure Mr. Cobb hadn't a cent of his own."

Donlin said: "You're dead right, son. Not a red cent."

At the desk, Howard Cobb cupped his chin in his hands. He said nothing, but the corners of his mouth twitched.

"Probably Mr. Cobb is quite a man with the ladies," I went on. "He's quite handsome. Isn't that right, Dr. Davidson?"

The doctor stood with his hands clasped behind his back and looked at the floor. His silence was answer enough.

"That's it, then," I said. "It couldn't be any other way. If it wasn't kidnaping, it had to be murder—and who but Mr. Cobb would murder her in that way and get a sucker like me to take the rap? If Mrs. Cobb were found murdered, he'd at once be suspected. Don't you see, nobody but Mr. Cobb would murder his wife that way, and Mr. Cobb couldn't murder his wife any other way and hope to get away with it."

I had finished, but what had I accomplished? Cobb sat back in his chair and laughed.

"Sergeant, I'm surprised that you should annoy me with such nonsense," he said. "I shall certainly make a vigorous complaint to your superiors."

Donlin shifted his hat over one hand. "Would I come here if I didn't have evidence? A man was seen going up to Brill's place after Brill went up. You're pretty well known in Coast City, Mr. Cobb. You were recognized."

Though Cobb didn't move, he gave an impression of jumping inside his skin. That was another of the sergeant's lies, but it was so close to the truth that Cobb couldn't know it wasn't true.

"I was with you and the other policemen most of last night," Cobb protested.

"Till two o'clock. It was after two when you were seen going up to Brill's place. Then there are the fingerprints."

The third lie, but again it could have happened. I saw now what Donlin was doing. It was an old police trick. A murderer's nerves start to fray the instant he begins to contemplate the crime.

A wild look came into Cobb's eyes. "But I—" he started, and caught himself.

"You mean you were careful?" Donlin said. "But you can't be careful enough when you murder somebody. Take the wire you used to tie up your wife. Thin stuff, you thought, but it's thick for wire. Police science does wonderful things, Mr. Cobb. A wire will hold fingerprints—tiny bits of prints, but lots of them and they can be put together. Remember last year when we got everybody in town to file their finger-prints as identification in case Coast City was bombed? Yours, too, Mr. Cobb, and they match the prints on the wire."

Police third-degree consists chiefly of bluff combined with what is known, and Donlin was giving it to Cobb right here in his own home. Cobb seemed to shrivel behind his desk.

"But I—I was right there when we found Clare. I touched the wire."

"Dr. Davidson pushed you away before you could reach the body and you were never near it again," Donlin pointed out. "Right, Doc?"

Dr. Davidson nodded heavily. "Lieutenant Kearny undid those wires. There's only one way Cobb's prints could have got on them, and that was before we arrived." He turned to Cobb. "If ever a man deserved to hang, it's you."

I think it was that last sentence that did it. Cobb pulled open a desk drawer, and leaped to his feet with a small re-volver in his hand.

"I'm getting out of here!" he croaked. Sweat glistened on his brow, his tongue flicked over his lips. "I'll shoot if any-body moves." And he started to back toward a window.

There was no sound then. I looked at Donlin. His hat dropped from his right hand, and his fist held an automatic. Calmly, expertly, he put a bullet into Cobb's gun hand.

Cobb slumped to the floor and sat there, whimpering like a hurt kitten.

Donlin swept up the revolver and stepped back. "Better fix him up, Doc, so we can get him to jail. Sorry I had to do it this way, but I knew he had a gun permit and I hoped he'd pull the gun. That's as good as a confession."

I stepped to Donlin's side and touched his arm. "Thanks, Sergeant."

He grinned at me. "That's what we cops get paid for," he said.

MURDER IS STUPID

KERRY O'NEIL

I

THE THOUSAND EYES OF THE ETRURIA TOWER WERE, ONE BY one, winking out that evening; and Mickey Sayre, secretary to Jerry Mooney, was making ready to close the office when the door suddenly opened, a girl slipped in, closed it behind her and put on the catch.

Mickey, who had been employed with Mooney for quite some time, and was accustomed to all sorts of happenings, looked quietly at the girl who stood white-faced and shaking, and seeming unable to speak.

"Stand away from the door," Mickey advised her. "Whoever it is you're hiding from will see your shadow on the glass."

Obediently, the girl shrank to one side. She was someone who belonged in the building; Mickey remembered having often seen her in the elevators as they went up or down.

"There's a man!" gasped the girl. "He's been following me. I'm afraid of him."

"You belong in the building, don't you?" asked Mickey.

"Yes; in the office of Darrow & Company, on the top floor."

Mickey knew of Darrow & Company. They did Government work; there were military and naval people going up and down on business there at all hours of the day. And so when she saw the figure of a man, a burly figure, showing

346

blackly on the frosted glass of the door, and then heard the knob of the fastened door turn, she motioned to the girl to go into Mooney's office. The girl did so. Mickey then silently took the catch from the door and stepped back to her desk. She had taken up the telephone and stood waiting when there came a knock on the door.

"Come in," she called.

Again the knob turned, and this time the door opened. An immensely fat man entered; he had a great round face, smooth and boylike; he stood looking at Mickey with a placid smile.

She spoke into the telephone.

"Police, please," she said. The man closed the door and stood with his wide back against it, still smiling. Mickey added: "This is 1708 Etruria Tower. Please send police here at once." She put down the telephone and said to the man, "If you'll sit down, they'll be here in a few minutes; then you can tell them what you want."

The placid smile had not left the round face; indeed, it had grown still wider.

"It is Mr. Mooney I have wished to see," he said. "The police I do not know."

"Mr. Mooney can be seen in the morning. From ten to eleven is always a good time."

"So smart a girl!" the man said admiringly. "You should not waste your time." He opened the door and made a good-humored little bow. "Tomorrow, in the morning, I shall be here."

He went out, closing the door softly behind him. Mickey waited for a space and then went into the side office.

"He's gone," she told the girl. "But if I were you, I'd not leave just yet. He might be outside somewhere."

"I'll be scared to death," said the girl. "I'll expect to see him every place."

She was a pretty girl, and very smartly dressed; but there was something in her large eyes and rather heavy face that gave her that expression covered by the word *dumb*.

"I've been a terrible fool," she said. "I thought I knew, and was being smart. I even told Freddy he was crazy, and I know he had a lot more sense than I had."

"That man who was just here didn't look like a pick-up guy," suggested Mickey, a questioning note in her voice.

"Oh, he wasn't," said the girl. "If it was only that, I wouldn't have been afraid of him. I know how to get rid of that kind."

Just then the door of the outer office opened and closed. Instantly Mickey took up Mooney's desk phone, contriving to rattle it as she did so.

"I'm obliged to you, Captain Pash. When will the policemen be here? Oh, they are on their way! Well, that's fine!"

"What's that about policemen?" asked the voice of Jerry. He appeared in the doorway as he spoke. Mickey laughed and put down the telephone.

"It's all right," she said. "Only a bluff. We had a visitor a few minutes ago, and I thought he'd come back."

She told Jerry what had happened; and he looked appraisingly at the girl.

"You work for Darrow's?" he said.

"Yes," the girl replied. "I've been with them for a year."

He asked her some questions, and she told him something of what she'd said to Mickey.

"If you didn't think this party wasn't trying to pick you up," Jerry said, "what did you think?"

"Well, that's the thing that makes me believe I'm a fool. It all started with Freddy Locke, who is also in Darrow's.

He's a terribly nice boy, but he does like to go around a little, and when you go around, you meet people. Well, he met some that maybe he shouldn't have met—though he didn't know what they were until they started to hint about things."

"What kind of things?" asked Jerry.

"Well, I guess he'd got a few drinks in him, and he talked too much—about Government things; and afterward he was scared almost into fits when they began to hint what a fix he'd got himself into, and what would happen to him if they went to the FBI and told about it."

Jerry sat down, facing the girl; he was beginning to be interested. "They said that to Freddy, did they?" he inquired.

"Well, I didn't think much of it when Freddy told me about it." She said this with a sort of toss of the head; but nervousness was evident in the little break in her voice. "I said they were kidding him. But then he told me they'd been asking him about the office. They mentioned a drawing he'd been talking about one night in a bar. They said they wanted it."

"How long ago was this?" asked Jerry.

"About two days. Freddy was scared. He told me about it. He said he was sure he would be fired; and then we couldn't get married, like we are planning to. Well, that got me kind of worked up too, and I said why didn't he give them the drawing."

"You did!" cried Mickey, horrified. "Don't you know all Government things like that must be kept secret?"

"Well, I was excited," said the girl. "I'd been wanting to be married to Freddy, and right then it looked as if it wasn't ever going to happen. When I said for him to give them the drawing, he was scared worse than ever, and I saw he wouldn't do it."

"And then what did *you* do?" asked Jerry.

The girl hesitated. The look on her face was one of fright.

"He'd told me who these people were; and so I met one of them without Freddy's knowing it, and I said if they'd not mention anything about him, I'd get them the drawing."

There was a pause. Then Mooney asked:

"And did you?"

"I took it out of the safe. About an hour ago." Here the girl began to sob. "I telephoned the parties; but on my way there I had to pass the *Globe* office, where they have the radio outside one of the windows, and I heard a man telling about spies and traitors. And right then it came into my mind that that's just what I was meaning to be. And I got scared and hurried back here to the Etruria Tower to put the drawing where I'd got it from."

She wiped her eyes with a handkerchief.

"I saw what a fool I was; and I saw what Freddy'd think of me, too. But then I noticed that fat man following me," she said to Mickey, "and I got in kind of a panic. I remembered there was a detective office on this floor, and I got out of the elevator and ran in here. I didn't mean any wrong," she said. "I just didn't want anything to stop Freddy and me being married, that's all."

"You still have the drawing?" asked Jerry.

"Oh, yes. It's here in my bag."

Jerry reached for the telephone. "I'll have to report this to the FBI," he said.

But she got up, much agitated.

"Oh, don't do that! Freddy'll be got into it. I don't care for myself. I deserve it, I guess. But he was so grand about it. He wouldn't do a wrong thing like that, no matter what happened."

Jerry valued this, and it impressed him. No matter how

stanch Freddy was, the FBI, if they got the case, would put him through the wringer.

"Would anybody be in Darrow's office now?" he asked the girl.

"Freddy should be there. He works some nights. But I wouldn't want him to know about this, not for anything," said the girl.

"Would the safe still be open at this hour?"

"Oh, no."

"If Freddy is in the office, could he open it?"

"No, sir. No one knows the combination but Mr. James Darrow, and Mr. Gross, the manager."

Jerry considered the situation. Finally he said:

"Do you think you'd have enough confidence to turn it over to me? I might be able to find a way to get it back into the office before it's missed."

The girl hesitated; then she opened her handbag and searched in it. They saw a gradual renewal of her fright. At last she cried out:

"It's not here! What could have happened? The bag has never been out of my hands since I put it there!"

Mickey took the bag from the girl's shaking hands and emptied its contents on the desk. There was a quantity of all sorts of things, but the drawing was not among them. Mickey searched all the pockets inside the bag. But the looked-for thing was still unfound.

The girl covered her face with her hands; she wept and cried out; and they were some time quieting her. When she was in a state permitting her to listen and understand, Mooney said to her:

"It's up to you, now. You've got to think back and remember. Were you still in the Darrow office when you put the drawing in your bag?"

"Yes. I was."

"Who else was there?"

"No one but Freddy Locke."

Jerry's fingers pattered on the arms of his chair; he studied her attentively.

"You weren't talking with him about anything, were you?"

"Yes—about our wedding. He said if he was fired, it'd have to be postponed. And I told him it wouldn't be postponed."

"You said that to him?"

"I said no matter what else happened, our marriage was going through."

"What'd *he* say?"

"I don't think he said anything."

"Well, how did he look?"

"I didn't notice how—" Then she paused and said: "He watched me. He was thinking about something."

"Keep on as you're going," said Jerry. "Get your mind on the bag. Are you sure you never laid it down after you put the drawing into it? Am I to understand that you held it in your hands all through the time afterward?"

"Yes, I did."

"You didn't put it down anywhere at any time—on a desk, or on a chair? While you went, maybe, from one office to another? Maybe only for a minute?"

The girl stared at Mooney; then she cried out and ran toward the office door. But Jerry stopped her.

"Freddy!" she said. "Freddy's got it! He took it. Let me go! Please let me go!"

"You're going up to Darrow's?"

"I must. I must see if it's so."

"Well, we'll both see," said Jerry. He nodded to Mickey.

"You can shut up the shop. I'll let myself in when I'm through."

He went down the corridor with the girl, rang for an elevator, and they ascended to the top floor.

II

Darrow & Company occupied a good deal of space. They did certain sorts of photography, made blueprints, did fine engraving, all of a scientific kind, and maps for highly specialized use.

The place was dark now, and the elevator operator said:

"I think everyone's gone for the night—though I did see a light there a while ago."

They knocked, but there was no reply. The girl, sobbing, said she had no key. Jerry looked at the elevator man.

"When you go down, pass the word to the night superintendent. There's a little something happened, and we want to get in." After the car had gone down, he said to the girl: "What's Freddy's home telephone?"

She gave him the number, and he called it at an open telephone in the corridor.

"He's not here," a voice said. "He's at the office tonight. He telephoned awhile ago he'd be there for a couple of hours."

"He must have changed his mind afterward," said the girl when Jerry had told her this.

In a few minutes a man advanced along the corridor. He was tall and thin, with a nervous manner; he looked at them searchingly and asked what they wanted. When told, he said:

"Any person with common sense would understand that unknown people are not permitted to enter the offices in the building after hours."

"This girl is employed by the Darrow Company," said Jerry.

"My name is Elsie Homer," said the girl. "I'm a stenographer here."

"That may be," said the man, "but it doesn't change the rule."

"I can see what you mean," Jerry told him, "and as far as it goes it's all right. But there was a young man here tonight that we want to see. And as far as we know, he should be here now."

But the man remained cold. Jerry had been studying him and didn't like him. There was a sidelong furtiveness about him that might mean a number of things, and none of them favorable.

"Before the office can be opened," said the man, "I must have the permission of Mr. Gross, Darrow's manager."

"This," said Jerry, "may turn out to be a vital matter. It might really be one for the police." The man looked at him with a sudden intentness. "As a matter of fact," went on Jerry, "I think calling them would be the easiest way to go about it."

"What," asked the man, the gray of sudden fear gathering about him, "would the police have to do with it?"

"When a person is not sure of what's behind a thing," Jerry told him, "they are handy people to whistle for."

"This building," said the man, and he seemed to bite his words viciously, "is a high-class place. We do not need the police, and we will not have them."

"Fellah," said Jerry, and eyed the man coldly, "I'm not so sure about not needing them as you are. If you don't unlock this door, you're going to have them here whether you like it or not."

For a moment it seemed that the man would leap at him;

perhaps it was the big, athletic, fast-looking shape of Mooney that warned him not to. He stood perfectly still for a moment or two; then he took a key from his pocket and unlocked the door.

"This," he said, "is against all our regulations. And I do it only because it is the best of two undesired things."

He led the way into the office, and turned on the light. Elsie Homer looked about timorously.

"Freddy can't be here," she said. "He wouldn't stay in a dark office. There wouldn't be any reason for it."

"What part of the place did he work in?" asked Jerry.

"In one of the back rooms. He's an engraver, and they gave him most of the particular work to do. He has been working hard of late; he may have fallen asleep."

"That wouldn't account for the lights being shut off," said Jerry. He turned to speak to the man who'd let them in, but he was not in sight. There were quick soft steps in the corridor; Jerry went to an open doorway and looked out. There was a stairway opening downward, about a dozen yards away, and he caught a hurried *pat-pat-pat* of hastening feet.

Mooney reached the head of the stairs in two or three leaps. Two floors down he saw a hand sliding along the slanted rail; the rapid beat of the hurrying feet was plainer than before. There was something about this sudden flight that aroused Mooney to the pitch of pursuit, and in an instant he was down the stairs and after the man. But he'd taken no more than a dozen steps when he heard a sudden and piercing scream from the girl in Darrow & Company's office. Jerry turned about and hurried back. The door leading to the rear offices was now open; the light had been turned on. And Mooney, as he entered, saw the girl crouched on the floor beside the silent body of a young man.

"They've killed him!" she cried frantically. "They've killed him, and it's all my fault!"

"Take it easy," Jerry said. "You've got to hold yourself together. Maybe he's not dead."

"He is," she said. "He's dead! His poor head is all bleeding. He's dead!"

Jerry got her to her feet and put her in a chair, where she collapsed in a sobbing heap. But she was right. Freddy Locke was dead. His head had been crushed in by a single blow. The weapon with which this blow had been struck—a hammer—lay on the floor beside him. Jerry, after an effort, silenced the girl, and told her:

"This is a police job, and I'll have to call them. When they get here, they'll ask a lot of questions. I think it will be as well for you to say nothing just now about the drawing. That'll come up sometime later; but just now we'll not have the cops fumbling with it. Freddy had got into some kind of trouble. That'll be your story. You don't know what it was. You came to me to see if I could do anything. We came up here to speak with him. And we found him like this."

Within fifteen minutes the police were there—two uniformed men and Engle, Captain Pash's favorite forerunner. Engle looked at the body.

"Dead," he admitted. "And likely by way of the hammer. Who found him?"

Mooney motioned toward the girl.

"She works here. So did he."

Engle looked attentively at the girl, who sat huddled in her chair.

"What are the chances?" Engle asked.

"Not any. She was down in my office when the thing must have been done."

"In your office, eh?" Engle grinned. "Kind of funny, you having a homicide thrown into your lap, so to say."

"I'm thinking that, right along with you," said Jerry.

In a few moments Pash arrived. So did the photographers, and later the police medico. While they were going through their motions, Pash talked.

"How do you come to be in this, Mooney?" he asked.

"There's some of it FBI business," said Jerry. "And I think they ought to be called in."

"If you don't mind," said Pash in his usual biting fashion, "I'll be the judge of that. So let's hear your story. And you might as well tell about this girl as you go along."

Jerry always found Pash rather a heavy person to handle; the scornful beak of a nose, the big, prying lenses astride it, the bitter tongue, the constant suspicion and disbelief made him a trying person.

"As I've seen it, the thing begins with the girl," said Jerry. "And so the story is hers, not mine." He knew the homicide captain very well; the man's animosity toward him was deep and eager. Jerry believed Pash would go to any length to get him in a position in which the Department would have a free hand with him. But it was necessary to say something, and he gave a sharply abridged version of what he'd heard, and a sketchy account of what he'd seen.

"What's your name?" asked Pash of the girl.

"Elsie Homer," she said with an effort.

"What became of this night superintendent?" the man asked Jerry.

"I wouldn't know. The last I saw of him, he was what is known as hastening downstairs."

"Huh! It's queer he'd run out on you like that."

"That's what I thought," said Jerry. "Maybe it'd be a good idea to put a man or two on him."

Pash gave him a nasty look.

"Why didn't you call the police when the girl first came to you?"

"Up to the time we got to this office, it looked like a private case. I called you as soon as I knew it was something else."

"It takes a murder to get you started, does it?"

"All right," replied Jerry. "It's still a murder; let's see how nice and quick you'll get going."

Pash's look was thick with disbelief.

"You've always got a trick up your sleeve," he said. "How much are you holding back?"

"Only my own ideas of the thing, that's all. I know how you treat anything I think of, so I never bother to hand you any unfinished business."

"I'm going to run you through in the morning," said Pash, glowering. "You be at Headquarters, no later than ten."

"It'll all depend on how fast the FBI works," said Jerry cheerfully. "They sometimes take quite a while listening. I might be delayed."

"You always have some kind of a twist, don't you?" said Pash with a sardonic grin.

"It's wartime; and some things come before others."

"Murder's pretty important," the Captain suggested.

"Yeah, but you have them every other day," replied Jerry. "They fit into the routine."

The police medico had been examining the girl.

"This might be a hospital case," he said. "And she's going there right away."

An ambulance was called for; it arrived and the girl was taken away. Pash then had the man who ran the night elevator up for questioning.

"You saw a light in this office earlier tonight, I hear?"

"Yes, I did."

"How long ago?"

"About an hour or so."

"Is that usual?"

"Lately it is. Darrow's have a lot of hurry-up Government work, I hear. Besides that, they are having some repair work done. Workmen are in there some nights."

"Did you, at any time past the usual closing-time tonight, bring up anyone you didn't know to this floor?"

"No, sir. The only people I brought up since that time were Miss Homer, the girl who has just been sent to the hospital, and Mr. Mooney. I know them both."

"You didn't bring up anyone after that?"

"No, sir."

"Are you forgetting you brought up the night superintendent?"

"I didn't bring him up. Mr. Mooney asked me to, but he wasn't in the building. I was told that he'd sent in word in the afternoon that he wasn't well. I was asking around for someone who might be acting in his place when the police came in."

Pash looked at Jerry, his mouth drawn to one side in a crooked smile.

"What about that, Mooney?"

Jerry spoke to the elevator operator.

"You didn't bring the night superintendent up?"

"No, sir. Like I was just saying, he wasn't in the building."

"What kind of a looking man is he?"

"Well, he's about medium size; and he's pretty bald. And he's a little lame in his left foot."

Jerry looked at Pash.

"Not the same party. The one I talked with was tall—he

was thin and nervous looking. And he had a full head of hair. I'd say he was less than forty years old."

"Mr. Hooker, the night boss, is more than sixty," said the elevator operator.

Pash laughed, and it had an ugly sound of gratification in it.

"So the party that opened the office door and afterward ran out on you was not the night man of the building but a stranger." He looked at Engle. "Begins to be interesting, doesn't it?"

"It's surely countin' up," agreed the assistant. "You missed one there, Mooney."

"I think," said Pash to Jerry with enjoyment, "I'm going to do something special on you tomorrow. So get in early. It looks like there'll be a thing or two going on."

III

Mooney had a cocktail at a neighboring bar, also a sandwich and a glass of ale. Then he went back to his office. He called Mickey on the telephone.

"About that girl who came in awhile ago," he said. "You might have the police on your telephone about her; if so, say as little as possible."

"Something has happened?" asked Mickey, noting sharpness in his voice.

"That young fellah, Freddy Locke, that she talked about. When we got to Darrow's office, he was dead."

Mickey drew in her breath sharply.

"Oh, no!" she cried.

"I've called you to ask you not to mention anything the girl said about the drawing. I'm going to talk with the FBI in a few minutes. It's a case for them, and they don't like the police mixing in."

"I understand," said Mickey.

"If Pash or any of his people call you, tell how the girl came in, frightened. But you don't know anything else—because you went home a little while afterward."

A few minutes later Jerry had the local FBI headquarters on the wire and talked with Dave Shugrue, one of the operators whom he knew.

"There's been a killing done in this building," he told Shugrue. "The police are on it, but it has Federal angles that might interest your department. How'd you like to step around to my office and listen awhile?"

"All right, Jerry. I'll be there in a half-hour."

Mooney put the telephone down, pulled his chair up close to his desk, got out a block of paper and a pencil and began drawing circles—large circles. Then some that were smaller; later some that were smaller still. This continued until he was making some so small that they were hardly more than dots. He ruminated for a while over what he'd done; then he drew quite a wide circle; he drew another inside this, and still another inside that. He continued to draw circles one inside the other until the original was a solid mass, its former emptiness clogged with reductions.

Then he began a row of circles, each succeeding one growing smaller. They stood sharp and round in a long line, a big one at the left, a very small one at the right. Into this uninfluenced space created by repeated zeros his thin store of information was slowly trickling:

A girl. A young man. Engaged to be married. They work in the same place. Closely kept Federal work.

The young man talks where and when he shouldn't. A

proposition is made to him, and he's scared. Then he is threatened.

The boy had nerve and said no. But the girl was short-sighted. She picked the matter up and carried it midway. Then she too grew scared, and tried to run out of it.

"That's how it stood when I first heard about it," Jerry summed up. "From then on, I'm not sure. But there are a few things I'm looking at.

"When the girl discovered the drawing wasn't in her hand-bag she at once suspected Freddy had it.

"My guess is that she *did* go out of the room where she'd been talking to Freddy. Also that she'd been saying so much that he'd begun to suspect something; and while she was gone, he opened the bag she'd left behind her, and found the drawing.

"She left the office, thinking she still had it, and with the intention of trading it in for enough silence to marry on. But while she didn't know Freddy had taken the drawing, some-one else did—someone who wanted it badly enough to snap the boy's life out to get it," decided Jerry. "Someone who was in the office at the time, saw him take it from the girl's hand-bag and knew what it was."

Jerry continued the rounding of zeros on the block of pa-per. He made a complete circle of them, and in that circle he saw the tall, thin man whom he'd thought to be the night superintendent. Also he again heard his clipped, rather vicious habit of speech.

"What," said Jerry, "if he'd been in the office? Hidden in that room? When the girl left, he could have finished Freddy, taken the drawing and slipped away."

But he'd returned! If he'd finished with the job, why did he do that? Jerry got up and walked the floor. After the girl had fainted, he had searched the body of the dead young man for the drawing—but he had not found it, and had thought the murderer had taken it. But when the chips were down, this sort of snap reasoning was never found in Mooney's cold, unemotional circle of zeros. Freddy might not have put the drawing in his pocket. He might have put it somewhere else. The murderer might not have found it. He might have gone away beaten. And he might have, in a sort of desperation, returned for another try.

Jerry had reached this point when there came a tap on the door; then it opened, and a man appeared.

"Good evening," the man said. "I am Jano. Baritz Jano. It is with Mr. Mooney I desire to speak."

The man was enormously fat; his face was round and boy-like, and he regarded Mooney with an engaging smile.

"I'm Mooney," said Jerry, looking at him with interest. The words the man used were well formed, but he put them together oddly. These things, together with his size, seemed to stir faintly in Mooney's mind.

"It is nice that I am seeing you," said Jano. "It is, I know, after the time for business, but possible not too much after. Once before, tonight, I am here, but you are not present."

Jerry now realized who the man was. Mickey had spoken of him. He was the man the Homer girl said had followed her.

"Often I'm out," Jerry said. "But there are times I'm in. Sit down; and tell me what the trouble is."

Jano sat down.

"You are a private policeman," he said. "And there is business we may have together." There was a pause, then he added: "Myself, I am an agent of the Swiss Government. And I am written down so in the American records, as the law asks."

"If you've come here on Government business," Jerry said, "I'm telling you I'm not the party to speak to."

"It is not Government; the wish I have is to speak of murder," said Jano pleasantly. "It is of the murder that has taken place in this building tonight."

"You're also wrong in coming to me about a thing like that. The regular police attend to murders," Jerry informed him.

But Jano disregarded this.

"Murder is a stupid proceeding," he said. "A man kills; in a few hours"—and he smiled in a shy sort of way—"he himself is killed! It is not intelligent." As Jerry did not reply to this, the man took up his subject from another angle. "The girl," he said, "would not speak to me. She was afraid." He looked at Jerry attentively. "The murder: did it happen before she came to this office, or afterward?"

"I don't know when it happened," Mooney said. "The police surgeon is always the judge of that."

Jano nodded. And he looked mildly at Jerry.

"There was a thing stolen?" he asked. "A drawing?"

"Things stolen are also the business of the police," Jerry told him.

"The girl is maybe your client? She may have mentioned something," suggested the fat man.

Jerry grinned. Jano was unusual.

"The principal thing she said was that you had been following her."

"It is true." Baritz Jano agreed to this willingly. "There were warnings I wished to speak to her. This drawing: she meant to give it to some people who are dangerous."

"How do you know that?"

Jano shrugged his great shoulders.

"A knowledge of things is my profession," he said, beaming at Jerry. "In Europe I am said to be clever." He seemed to expect an answer to this: but Jerry crossed one knee over the other, dandled his foot and was silent. "It is my thought," Jano then continued, "that the death of the young man may have something to do with the theft."

"The police are very careful in things like that," said Jerry. "Maybe if you went to them, they'd tell you something."

Jano smiled.

"I am acquainted very well with the police," he said. "And the way between us I make very wide." He studied Mooney for a few moments. "You are, I think, in business for the profit; it is also my thought that I can speak to you in a way you might understand."

"As I've said, I don't touch Government work," said Jerry. "A party who operates with a private license likes to work quietly. Government cases go off too loudly, especially at a time like this."

Jano rubbed his hands together.

"You are careful," he said. "I have always admiration for carefully done things." He arose. "It may be there will some time be something. A person, when things swiftly happen, does not know." He paused for a moment and then added: "There are large sums of money often placed where an intelligent man might reach for them." He nodded his head. "Often it is that a change of mind means much intelligence."

It was almost an hour after the departure of Jano that Shugrue arrived. He was a compact young man with a quick eye and an active mind.

"I'm sorry I've kept you waiting," he said. "But there were some things came over the wire that had to be gone into."

He sat down at the end of Jerry's desk and listened to the matters that were told. As Jerry went on, the agent's interest picked up constantly, and at the finish, he leaned back in his chair and said:

"This man Jano, I know. And as he told you, he is a foreign agent and is recorded as such. But the Swiss interest may not be all of it. Sometimes these people serve a number of governments; and we've thought that of Jano for some time."

Shugrue went into the matter of Darrow & Company. They were skillful people and had always deserved trust. They were careful; their employees had been shown on many occasions also to be trustworthy. But as Shugrue said, vigilance is not capable of forever guarding against dishonesty or treachery.

"A love-affair is likely to branch off in any direction," said Jerry. "This girl is nice looking, but none too keen; the young man knew more, but was weak. As I see it, someone's had the eye on him for some time, nursing him along for a chance at something. When he began to talk about the drawing, the spies felt they could settle for that."

"Threats, robbery, then murder," said Shugrue. "They usually follow in that order."

"I keep thinking," said Jerry, "that the thing could have been worked from the inside."

"In the Darrow office?"

"Maybe not. But inside the Tower. The things that have happened seem to work closely together. I got that impression right at the beginning. Jano's coming here increased it."

After some further talk, Shugrue left, Jerry saying he'd keep in touch with him. A little later Mooney closed his office door after him for the night and rang for the elevator. It was operated by the same man who'd taken him up with the girl just before the discovery of the murder.

"A lot of things keep happening, don't they?" the man said.

"Sometimes they do," Jerry returned as the car descended.

"That Christie was always a funny kind of bird," said the operator. "But I never expected to hear a thing like this about him."

"Christie?" said Jerry.

The car was now at the street level, but the man didn't open the door.

"Ain't you heard about it?" he asked. "Christie, one of the men in the building maintenance department, was found dead in a side-street about a half hour ago. Somebody'd shot him. Word's come in that they've got him in the morgue."

Outside, Jerry called a cab, and he told the driver, who knew him:

"Take me to the morgue."

The driver grinned and said:

"Private cops certainly do some funny visiting."

When they'd pulled up at the city dead-house, Jerry told the man to wait. Then he went inside.

"Hello, Jerry," said an attendant. "Glad to see you. Is it business or pleasure?"

"There's a body I want to see. Must have been just brought in. A man. And shot."

"Oh! You interested in him? Yes, we've got him. Right in there, at the end of the row."

The attendant led Jerry deep into the place. At the end of a long line of shrouded shapes he paused. Drawing back the covering, he said:

"Here he is."

Jerry gazed into the face, gray with death, the thin-lipped, bitter-looking mouth twisted into a sort of grin. And as he stood there, the words of Jano, spoken only a short time before, came into his mind.

"A man kills. An hour later, he is himself killed."

Mooney motioned the man that he'd seen enough, and turned away. In the office he took up the telephone, called FBI headquarters and asked for Shugrue.

"Mooney again," he said. "I'm calling from the morgue. I've been looking at a man brought in awhile ago. It's the party I told you about—who opened the door of the office for the Homer girl and myself. He's been shot in the chest—and is very dead."

IV

It was about nine o'clock next morning when Jerry awoke. While he went through his calisthenics, took a shower, and dressed, his mind worked with the problem of the night before. He telephoned police headquarters and was put through to Pash.

"I saw the FBI people last night," he said, "and I'll be on hand this morning as soon as you like."

"Well, I'd like it right away," said Pash, in no good humor.

"In ten-fifteen minutes," said Jerry. "And while I'm on the way, there's another thing I ran into last night that you might start thinking about. Have you heard about a fellah named Christie: one of the workmen at the Etruria Tower—"

But Pash interrupted him.

"Yeah, I know. He's in the morgue."

"Well, here's something maybe you don't know: I went out there to look at him last night, and I found he was the party I told you about—the one I thought was the night superintendent at the Etruria Tower."

"The one you let slip away on you!"

Jerry grinned.

"Well, if you want to put it that way—yeah," he said.

There was a silence; finally Pash said:

"All right. You get down here. And I'll see what I'm going to do."

At police headquarters, a little later, Jerry talked with Berg, the desk sergeant.

"The skipper is pretty sore," Berg said. "The FBI are moving in on this case, and he don't like it. There was some sharp talk between him and them awhile ago."

Shugrue came into the room a little later, and he drew Jerry aside.

"Pash is beginning to get difficult," he said. "And I want to ask you to tell as little as possible when he questions you."

"Do you know," said Jerry good-humoredly, "I had that very thought in mind. I have a fixed plan with him. When a thing's almost finished, he can be called in; but it's a mistake to tell him much as it goes along. He knows the formula for a kind of police hash, and he tries to cook everything accordingly."

"They've got the girl here; but I saw her at the hospital awhile ago," said Shugrue. "And I told her to refuse to say anything about the drawing or the attempt of these people to get hold of it. I suggested that it was Federal business, and she need not make a statement to the police at this time. She asked if the FBI would back her up, and I said it would."

"That makes it easier for me," said Jerry. "Pash'll not like any of it, but we'll not worry about that."

"And by the way," said the Federal man, "this morning I had a talk with one of our agents—one whose interest lately has been keeping an eye on Jano. And he happened to drop a bit of information that may have some meaning. Jano has an office in the Etruria Tower."

"No!" said Jerry, in surprise.

"Under the name of Sallust Frères. It's supposed to be a firm of French importers."

"That," said Mooney, "is something to keep in mind."

Pash, a little later, sent out word for Jerry to come in. When he did, the homicide captain sat huddled behind his desk and eyed him with evident disbelief.

"Mooney, I want to hear what you know," he said. "And all of it."

Jerry cheerfully repeated what he'd said the night before. But Pash wasn't satisfied. He shook a bony finger at him and yelled:

"I want what that girl told you last night: and I want all you said to her. This is murder, Mooney; you're not going to get away with a story like that."

"The girl came into my place because she knew I was a private cop," said Jerry. "She was frightened. Someone was following her. She wanted to get back to the office she worked in, on the top floor. And because she was scared, I went up with her. The rest of it followed just as I told you."

Shugrue was standing near by, and the angry eyes of Pash went to him venomously.

"This department has been suffering from an undercurrent of influence for some time," he said. "Serious harm is being done. Now, it seems, murder can be committed and the matter can be taken out of the hands of the proper authorities and nothing must be said or done about it."

A dapper young man with an entirely self-possessed manner, who stood at one end of the Captain's desk, now spoke.

"This matter, for the moment, has been taken out of the hands of the local police by agreement with the county attorney. Good and sufficient reasons for this transfer have been shown," said the young man, "and it is quite possible that the case will be returned to the State and county after certain ends have been served."

Jerry, when he had the opportunity, talked with Miss Horner for a few moments.

"This man who unlocked Darrow's office door for us last night—had you ever seen him before?"

"Yes, I had—in the office, talking with our Mr. Gross. I knew he was employed in the building, but nothing more than that."

Pash was outspoken in his desire to hold the girl, but the Federal attorney claimed custody.

"There is a possibility that her evidence will be necessary to the Government," said this nattily dressed young person. "If there is shown to be a reason for returning her later, it shall be done."

Jerry, leaving Headquarters, went at once to the Etruria Tower. After a glance at his mail and a few words with Mickey, he ascended to the top floor and engaged in a conversation with Mr. Gross, manager for Darrow & Company.

Gross was heavy-set, had an affable manner and talked with the readiness of an experienced man of affairs. He already had the police version of the happening in the Darrow office, and now Jerry gave him the remainder of it.

"The whole thing has not only been shocking, but puzzling," Gross said. "But now I begin to understand."

"This man Christie," said Jerry, "what can you tell me about him?"

"As far as I know, he was employed by the Tower Company. He was a skilled workman, and bossed many of the small jobs that are so often needed to be done in a big building. My only experience with him has been in the last three or four days; we'd had some difficulty with the ventilators, and he came in to look things over. The idea was that the work was to be done after our office hours."

"Was Christie acquainted with Freddy Locke?"

"I've seen him talking with him, but thought it had something to do with the repairs. Young Locke was usually interested in what was going on around the place."

"I've looked at the hammer used in the murder," said Jerry. "It has the Etruria Tower brand on the handle."

"There were a number of tools belonging to the building in the back room. I've been told they intended finishing the work tonight."

Gross took Jerry into the room where the murder had been done. There was a policeman there, sitting in an office chair and smoking a cigar.

"Hello, Mooney," he said. "I hear the old man's mad at you."

"He always is," replied Jerry cheerfully. "But that ought to make it easy for you people. The more he swings at me, the less time he'll have to work on you."

"He seems to have lost his interest in the case," said the policeman. "I've just had word that my shift here will be the last."

"The police called off?"

"That's the idea."

Jerry saw some evidence in the room of things having been torn out and of replacements having been made. He looked at these while they talked—casually, but several times a certain thing seemed to catch his attention. Gross noted this and said:

"Some of the work is experimental. We talked about different ways of getting the result we wanted, and tried some of them out."

"Is there a way of getting out of these rooms from this rear section?" Jerry asked.

"Yes; there is a door in the room next to this that opens

into a side corridor. That in turn opens into the main one."

Jerry mentioned the matter of the drawing. But Gross shook his head.

"The office has been asked not to discuss that. Of course, I suppose you know about it, and because of that I'll say this to you: If it is not recovered, there are other copies accessible. The troublesome point is that if the drawing has fallen into the hands of the enemy, a very clever and useful invention will have lost most of its value."

"That is what the persons behind the thing must have had in mind," said Jerry. "But who took it? Who has it? Where is it? If Christie killed Freddy Locke to get the drawing from him, then the man who killed Christie now has it."

"But," said Gross, shaking his head, "where is that man?"

"The trick will be to find him," said Jerry. "And maybe someone'll be able to do it."

Jerry went to the office of the Etruria Tower Company after leaving Gross and got the address of the night elevator operator. The house was a narrow-fronted one on a side street; and the man had to be awakened to greet his visitor. He sat up in bed and blinked.

"I gotta do my sleeping in the daytime," he said. And then: "What's the matter? I hope nothing else has happened, Mr. Mooney."

"No; Christie was the last."

"I've heard he was in this business in Darrow's office. I'd never thought it. He was a guy that never said much."

"The real dangerous ones never do," Jerry told him. And then he said: "I came out here to ask you a couple of questions. You know it was a hammer that the job on Freddy Locke was done with?"

"Yeah; I seen it. All gummed up with blood."

"Well, what I want you to do is think back to last night.

You told me you saw the Darrow office lighted up about an hour before the killing, and that you remembered it because there was the sound of hammering inside."

"Yes, there was."

"I've been told there was repair work going on there."

"Yeah; but none of the men working on that job had come up at that time. It was kind of early. I know they hadn't come up, because my car was the only one that was running. It would have been me that'd carry them."

"Have you ever had any talks with Christie?" asked Jerry.

"No. As I say, he wasn't much for conversations."

"From what I hear he was friendly with Freddy Locke."

"Well, maybe, but I don't know about that. The only ones in the Tower I could say he was sociable with was these people on the ninth floor—Sallust Frères."

"He was chatty with them?"

"Anyway, he went in there once in a while."

Mooney talked with the man for a space and then left. When he reached his office, Mickey was out getting lunch, and the place was in charge of Ates Haley, the office boy.

"What's happened?" Jerry asked.

"You had Headquarters on the telephone twice," Ates told him. "Captain Pash is a-honin' to see you. And if you know anybody by the name of Jano, *he* wants you too. He said to call him. The telephone is Middle City 0098."

"Call that number and say I'm now in the office," said Jerry. "Then take fifteen minutes—no more—for a sandwich and a glass of milk. When you are through, hang around where you can see this door and not call any attention to yourself. When you see a fat man leave here, follow him. As soon as you make up your mind he's not coming back soon, telephone me from wherever you are, and let me know." Jerry looked at Ates inquiringly. "Have you got all that?"

The boy ran over all the items in these orders to Jerry's satisfaction. Then he took up the telephone and called Middle City 0098.

"This is Mr. Mooney's office," he said. "Mr. Mooney is now here and will be pleased to see Mr. Jano."

Ates put down the telephone and departed for a neighboring lunch-counter. Then Mooney called police headquarters. When he got Pash, that official began to speak in his most strident tones:

"I didn't have a chance to speak to you before you left," he said. "And what I want to say is that I'm not letting the FBI or any other outfit crowd me off this case. I'm still on it. Also I'm telling you if you get anything, I want to hear about it, and I want you and everybody else to know that the Government side of the thing isn't the only one. I insist on having the right to judge what belongs to the police and what does not."

"Have you passed that word on to the Federals?" asked Jerry.

"Never you mind about the Federals," said Pash heatedly. "The one thing you've got to remember is that you operate on a license, and that license wasn't given to you by the Federals. Keep that in your mind, or you'll get yourself in trouble."

"What I've got in mind just now," said Jerry, "is more along the line of who killed Freddy Locke, and this party Christie. And the only thing I ask of you is to be a little bit co-operative."

Pash gave a sort of yelp at this.

"Don't forget, this is the established police you're dealing with," he said. "And we are expecting co-operation from *you*."

"All right," said Jerry, "I don't care which way you head

it; the idea is to get it done. If you want to start doing that, give a listen to what I'm going to ask you."

"What is it?"

Jerry then spoke no more than two dozen words; but they were in a tone which Pash had heard on more than one important occasion and to which he always gave attention.

"What am I to expect will come of this?" he asked when Mooney had finished.

"Just now," returned Jerry, "I can tell you nothing. But when I'm ready to step in for the killing, you'll be there to do your stuff."

"All right," said Pash. "Only, I don't like stepping into anything blindfolded."

"You'll not be blind when you begin to go," said Jerry. "Do what I ask, and then wait until I call you. From that moment, you'll begin to know."

"When will you call?"

"I can't say. It may be in ten minutes—maybe not until tomorrow. Only, have patience and don't grump; I've got to wait myself until the thing begins to open."

After he'd put down the telephone, Jerry smoked a cigarette.

Then there was a hand on the door of the outer office, and he heard the voice of Baritz Jano. He called to the man to come in, which he did, softly and easily for all his bulk.

"It is a thing most satisfying to see you once more," he said. "I have called you several times on the telephone, but you were not here."

"Business," said Jerry. "As I've said, it keeps me moving in and out."

"Energy is a pleasing thing! And you have much of it." Jano nodded his big head. "That is why I wish to so employ your services." He was silent for a moment, and then said:

"In the newspapers this morning it is told of another man who was found dead."

"Shot," said Jerry. "Through the body."

"It is unfortunate," said Jano. "I tried to have it not happen."

Jerry lifted his brows.

"You knew murder was going to be done?"

"Things come to me out of nowhere. But at that time I did not think of Christie. It was the girl I feared would be killed. I tried to warn her, as you know."

"But why should they want to kill her? For the drawing? She was intending to give it to them."

Jano smiled.

"Maybe not to them?"

"I get from that," Jerry said, "that there might be two groups. And it might account for Christie being counted off."

"Of Christie I have small knowledge," said Jano. "The sudden deaths of such men are often strange. He may have been a traitor. Someone may have paid him sums of money to get the drawing for them. And underneath he may have planned to get it for himself."

"But he didn't get it," said Jerry. "As you know, the girl never reached him—if it was Christie she was to meet. More than that, I happen to know that when she left this building last night, she didn't have the drawing with her."

Jano sat smiling at him. And Jerry, as he smoked a cigarette, fancied that for all the beaming quality of this it had a quality that told of sudden interest.

"I do not understand," said the man. "It was an engagement that was made. She went to keep it. If she had not the drawing—why?"

Jerry shook the ash from his cigarette.

"Well," he said, "she thought she had it. After she'd told

me her story last night, here in this room, she still thought
so. But when she opened her handbag to get it, the drawing
was not there." Jano sat upright in his chair, his big body
motionless. "She was frightened when she found the thing
was missing," continued Jerry. "And she thought Freddy
Locke, her boy friend, might have suspected she had it in her
bag, and had taken it, not telling her he'd done so.

"I went with her to the Darrow office," said Jerry. "Freddy
sometimes worked there after hours. But we found the place
dark. Then we saw Christie in the corridor."

"Christie!" said Jano. "Ah, yes."

"We'd asked for the night superintendent; I thought
Christie was the man and asked him to open the door."

"Why?"

"There was a thought in my mind," said Jerry. "Anyway,
he refused to do it. But I spoke of having the police in; then
he unlocked the door. The girl found the body of Freddy in
the rear room. Christie knew it was there; he knew it would
be found. That's why he didn't want to open the door; that's
also why he ran out on us when he did open it."

"I remember reading," Jano said thoughtfully, "that this
young man Locke was killed by a blow of a hammer."

"He was; and the hammer was right there. You see," explained Jerry, "there had been some workmen doing repairs;
they hadn't finished, and their tools were still there." He
pondered for a space. "A funny part of it was a thing said by
the elevator operator," he told Jano. "It seems to me it means
something, but I don't know what."

"A funny thing? You mean a strange one?"

"Yes. It was after business hours at Darrow's—last night.
The lights were on, showing that someone was still there.
The workmen who had been doing the repairs had not yet ap-

peared; and yet, so the elevator operator said, there was the sound of hammering."

There was a short silence after this. Jano sat with his head sunken on his bulging chest; his body was shaking.

"Anything wrong?" asked Jerry solicitously.

The man roused himself.

"No; I am well. Do not fear. But these things which you tell me are disturbing." As he got to his feet, he covered his face with his hands, and again his huge body shook. In a little while, however, he grew more composed. "The air," he said, "will do me good. I shall go out." He beamed suddenly at Jerry. "I am pleased and grateful," he said. "I shall see you perhaps tomorrow; we will talk once more of these things. There may be then some solution."

Jerry waited for a few minutes after the man had gone; then called Shugrue.

After that, Ates came bustling in.

"I didn't have to move a step away from the building," he said, elated. "I saw the fat man come out, and went down in the elevator with him. When he got outside he called a cab and I heard him tell the driver he wanted to go to the Spencer House. And he went."

"Fair enough," said Jerry. He called Pash once more.

"The thing's moving fast," he said. "Just when we'll close in, I don't know. It depends on a couple of matters I must take a chance on. But there's a thing I want you to do right away. I've heard you are going to take the police guard out of the Darrow office, and—"

"Why should we keep a man there?" interrupted Pash sourly. "With the FBI taking over everything else, let them take that job, too."

"I'm asking you as a favor," said Jerry, "to call the newspapers and tell them the police are now out of the office of Darrow & Company. And to make no mention of the Federals. Also to call right away so the news'll have time to get into the evening editions." Pash was inclined to protest, but Jerry talked him down. "This thing will keep," Jerry said. "And all the more if there's no delay. We've got it going, and now's the time to start riding it." . . .

The office force at Darrow & Company had left some time before, and the night shadows were gradually filling the rooms when Jerry Mooney unlocked the door to the main office and went in. He turned on a light, closed the door behind him and made sure the catch had shot into place. Then he went in to the rear office of Gross, the manager. Here he left the door partly open. There was another door to the office; this gave access to the rear room where the body of Freddy Locke had been found. This he set partly open, the same as the other. He made sure where the light-switches were in each room, and then he went to the main office and sat down.

The shadows gradually thickened into a deep dark. There was no moon that night, and the rays of the street lamps did not reach as far as the top floor of the Etruria Tower. The hum of night traffic lifted with a steady monotony; the horns of motorcars sounded their never-ending announcements. An hour passed—two hours.

Jerry every now and then shifted in his chair to make the wait easier. He sat up straight so that he'd have no support for his back. Experience had shown him that comfort must be avoided in a vigil of this kind if the senses were to be kept sharp and drowsiness kept away. A few times he got to his feet and stretched himself this way and that. Then he quietly sat down again.

V

For a time the elevator could be heard, but its trips up and down gradually grew less frequent; in the third hour there were long intervals of silence. It was during one of these that Jerry heard a sound in the corridor. He listened intently. Someone was standing at the door of the main office; he could hear breathing—deep, labored breathing, as though the person had been toiling up long flights of stairs. Jerry arose like a shadow, and slipped behind the door leading into the main office. He put one eye to the opening between the door and the frame and watched. There was a pause; then a ray, thin as a pencil, shot across the floor and began to creep around the room. This finally lighted up the doorway at the rear, the door through which Jerry had passed the night before when he'd come upon the sobbing girl kneeling beside the body of the murdered young man.

The holder of the light began slowly moving toward this door. The light pointed downward at his feet for a moment; as it did so, the rays struck upward from the floor and Jerry saw a bulky shape that could belong to but one person: Jano!

The man, moving with that soft tread so often noted in people of great weight, disappeared into the rear room. And then Jerry noiselessly shifted his own ground to a place behind the other door of the office in which he'd stationed himself. Again, in the same way, he had a view of the traveling pencil of light. It went waveringly here and there in the rear room. Finally it touched the litter of workmen's tools which Jerry had noticed that morning at one side of the office. It held there for a few moments, and again began to travel. It picked up the spots in the wall and around the windows where the repair work had been going on. Places were shown where old work had been taken out, and others where new work had been put in. Backward and forward the slender rod of light went, and again it came to a halt; after a few moments there came a whispering of satisfaction from Jano.

The man's shape, bulking hugely in the dim light, stooped over the heap of tools. Jerry saw him select a claw-ended steel bar. He put the hand torch carefully down so that its rays would fall on a piece of planking which seemed to have been nailed to a part of the work for some purpose. He put the end of the bar under this and began to pry it loose. The nails were drawn loose; the bit of timber was caught as it fell, and the watching eyes of Jerry saw a sheet of drawing-paper fall to the floor.

Instantly Jerry switched on the light. With an exclamation, Jano twisted his great body around; he seemed to be groping in the breast of his coat for a weapon; but just then there was the sound of an opening door and Shugrue and Pash appeared.

"On the floor, there," said Jerry to the Federal agent, and pointed to the sheet of paper. "That's the thing you want."

Jano's hands dropped to his sides; he watched Shugrue pick up the paper, his great face blank. He stood motionless while Pash snapped the handcuffs on his wrists. Then he turned his eyes on Jerry. Gradually the blank expression faded out; the boyish eyes beamed.

"For one, two hours I had lost the confidence. I thought my judgment of people was no longer good. I had looked at you and thought you shrewd. Then you talked like a fool; you told me everything, and I thought you did not know you were doing it. But it was a trap—a trap so excellent that I, Baritz Jano, walked into it." He laughed, his great body shook. "I am pleased. My judgment is still good. You are what I thought you were when I first saw you."

"Why," said Mickey Sayre, when Jerry told her about this the next day, "he seems to think it better to have good judgment than his liberty."

"It's not only his liberty he's going to lose. It's his life. Shugrue made a visit to the office of Sallust Frères yesterday when I reported to him that Jano had gone out. He found a revolver. The Federal laboratory test showed it was the one Christie had been killed with. And Jano's fingerprints were all over it."

"Oh!" said Mickey, awed. "It's really dreadful, isn't it?"

"Jano has admitted he did it. You see, Christie was a kind of stooge for him, and he'd been planted in the Etruria Tower, knowing that sooner or later they'd get a chance at something valuable in the Darrow office. Christie got acquainted with Freddy; they'd gone out together often.

"But when the man finally got hold of the drawing, after killing Freddy, he made up his mind he wouldn't turn it over to Jano; he'd hold it for a big price from someone higher up. Evidently he was afraid to take it with him when he'd done the murder; if he was caught with it on him, it was sure evidence against him. So he nailed up the section of planking in the office, with the drawing under it—meaning to get it at a later time.

"But Jano suspected him. He'd found out, somehow, that the man was double-crossing him. So he finished him off, as we've seen. He was still in Darrow's office when I got there with the girl. He'd appeared by way of that side corridor."

"I think it was awfully clever of you to guess where the drawing was hidden," said Mickey, admiringly.

"It wasn't a guess," said Mooney. "I noticed the way the piece of board was nailed to the rest of the stuff. It didn't mean anything that I could see; it wasn't supporting or holding anything together. So why was it there? I was talking to

Gross at the time. And as I looked at it, I remembered what the elevator operator had said about hearing hammering in Darrow's office at a time when he knew none of the workmen were there. And that gave me the idea."

"But," said Mickey, "why didn't you look and make sure?"

"At first I was going to," replied Jerry, "but then I began to see what I might use it for, and I let it ride for a while, just as it was. I played dumb with Jano, telling things that led up to it, saying it must mean something. He laughed," said Jerry. "I could see his whole body shake. Me being such a simp, as he thought, gave him a lot of amusement." Jerry grinned and nodded his head. "He didn't know it, but I wanted to laugh too."

THE CAT'S-EYE

JOHN VAN DRUTEN

THE TROUBLE WAS THAT HE COULD NO LONGER DISENTANGLE what he remembered from what he had been told and what he had read. For he had, quite naturally, read every word that he could find on the subject, ever since they first told him about it when he was fourteen. And there had been a good deal published on it; not only books on famous crimes, which almost always had a chapter on the Cawthra case, but there had been a play and two novels based on it, and a movie based on one of the novels. Jim had read or seen them all.

It was only natural, then, that after all this time his memory and his reading should have become fused, and that he should no longer know which details came from which. The cat's-eye brooch; he knew that he remembered that, because of his childhood fear of it; but Mrs. Pamphlett, and Auntie Lilian's lace bedspread—did he really remember them? He thought he did, but he had read about them so often now, that he could not longer really be sure. It was twenty-seven years ago, and on the other side of the world, and he had been only seven at the time.

But at least Mrs. Pamphlett and the bedspread had existed, whereas there were other things that he thought he remembered, which he could not find in the accounts. Albert, for instance. There was no mention of him anywhere; yet he was sure that he remembered him. How did he fit into the story?

There was nobody to tell him, nobody he could ask. Everyone who could have known was dead, or else four thousand miles away. Except her, Auntie Vi-Vi, and nobody knew where she was. She had disappeared entirely after the trial; he had read in some book that she had gone to America; he supposed she would have changed her name. In any case, she was lost, and it was she alone who could have told him about these things for certain.

There had been an afternoon, for example, when he was on his way home from school, and he had run into her with Albert in the street, and she had walked back with him to the house, and asked him not to say anything about it, not to mention seeing Albert, not to anyone, especially his father. She had given him sixpence as a reward for his silence, and he had had quite a time deciding what to spend it on, for he had never had so much money in one lump before. That must have happened, surely? He couldn't have imagined a thing like that.

Here in Chicago in 1939, it was hard to believe that any of it had happened. Kilburn, the drab northwestern suburb of London, in 1912, seemed an improbable place in itself. Had he really lived in it, and gone to school in Salisbury Road, and bought Liquorice Allsorts at the sweetshop at the corner? What connection was there between that small boy and the married young insurance broker with thinning hair at thirty-four, who lived in a small house in Evanston? None that he could see, except continuity, and that was the odd part of it.

He had been born in the United States, and his mother died in giving birth to him. When he was three, his father took him to England. He thought that he remembered the trip, but he was not sure. Perhaps it was the journey back that he was thinking of. In London, Auntie Lilian became his step-mother. He remembered her, or thought he did, as a tall, languid woman, with huge dreary eyes and untidy masses of black hair that seemed too heavy for her. She was given to invalidism and to lying on sofas, dressed in a tea gown, making lace; there seemed to be yards and yards of it, in his memory.

They lived in a semi-detached house, with dark, sooty evergreens in the front garden, in a long road of exactly similar dwellings. The house, in the photographs he had since seen of it in reports of the case, looked smaller than he remembered it. On the gate was his father's brass plate, announcing: FREDERICK C. CAWTHRA, TEACHER OF MUSIC.

At the back of the house was an oblong piece of garden of which Mr. Cawthra was very fond. Jim used to potter with him on summer evenings when he did his gardening; digging plantains out of the patch of grass they called the lawn; fetching the trowel and the watering pot from the tool shed, trying to make himself useful.

Apart from those evenings, he seemed to spend most of his time in the kitchen, getting in the way of Annie, the general servant, or being regaled by her with stories of crime or illness; she had a large family which included a consumptive sister and an epileptic brother, and she loved to talk about them. The kitchen was in the basement, and there was always strong, sweet tea and cold bread-pudding.

Upstairs, the house was dark, summer and winter, for Auntie Lilian could not bear the sunlight and kept the shades drawn; from the back room came the sound of the piano, and the pupils practicing *The Maiden's Prayer* and *The Dance of the Little Silver Bells*. Sometimes a girl's voice would float out, singing *The Garden of Sleep*, or *The Blue Alsatian Mountains*. While these went on, Auntie

Lilian would lie on her sofa with her eyes closed, dabbing Eau de Cologne on her temples, and say that it was all killing her. Sometimes when he was in bed at night, he would hear their raised voices below, quarreling.

Mr. Cawthra was a little man with a pointed beard and twinkling eyes. He was mild and jolly, and when he took Jim for walks they always had fun together. At first they used to go alone; later, Auntie Vi-Vi joined them. That was Jim's own name for her. Her real name was Violet Delcey. According to the books, his father met her in 1911, and she came to live with them the next year. She was a cashier in the local department store, called the Bon Marché, and came to Mr. Cawthra for music lessons. She had a sweet mezzo-soprano voice, and Jim though her singing of the Flower Song from *Faust* the most beautiful thing he had ever heard.

Here again, he was not sure what he remembered and what he had read. The books described her as a quiet, modest, gentle-spoken girl, with titian hair; one of them, more flowery than the rest, said that she had the pale, grave face of a Madonna. Jim thought that he remembered a tip-tilted nose, which gave her face a saucy look. According to the story, she became his father's mistress, and Auntie Lilian made scenes of violent jealousy, weeping and threatening to kill herself. Jim could almost swear now that he had heard her do so. According to the story, too, Violet Delcey felt her position very keenly and tried to break off the relationship and leave the house. Mr. Cawthra's evidence was that they ceased to be lovers, but that he begged her to stay on because she was so good with the child.

Good with him? Had she been, Jim wondered? It seemed, as he looked back, that they were always having secrets—secrets from his father and Auntie Lilian; that they used to call at houses when they went for walks alone, and have tea with servants in the kitchen, and that sometimes there were young men present, and a lot of giggling went on; and then on the way home, Auntie Vi-Vi would take him to a tea-shop for a threepenny ice, and tell him not to say anything at home about where they had been. And there was Albert, too. Albert was a sailor.

But on the other hand he could remember her reading aloud to him from the storybooks, sitting in the big armchair while he balanced on her lap, her arm around his waist, her red hair tickling his face; and when he had earache she used to come and sit on his bed, and bring him salt-bags and sing to him until the pain left him and he went to sleep.

She wore a brooch, which she told him was a cat's-eye, and this frightened him because he thought of the stone as being a real eye, extracted from a cat's head and in some way petrified. Even her reassurances, when he confessed to this after a nightmare, failed to remove his fear of the brooch completely; it remained a sinister thing in his memory, even now. He could not recall her wearing any other ornament, and saw her always in his mind as very neatly dressed, in a white blouse and plain gray skirt, and a patent-leather belt at her waist. This was the Violet Delcey of recorded fact; how did the Auntie Vi-Vi of his memory square with her?

In the summer of 1912 Auntie Lilian was taken ill—ill enough to have to stay in bed, this time. It was a hot summer, and Aunt Bet and Uncle Harvey were visiting them from America. They were relatives of Jim's own mother, childless, and they took to him at once. They stayed in a boarding-house just down the road, because the only spare room at home was the one in which Violet Delcey slept, and she was needed there to nurse and look after Auntie Lilian. Jim spent his days with them, and presently moved over to the boardinghouse altogether, because the house was upset with illness and he was in the way. After Jim had been with them a little while, Aunt Bet asked him how he would like to go back to America with them.

"We planned to adopt you almost as soon as we saw you," she told him, when she was giving him the whole history some years afterwards. "You were so like poor Gertrude, and such an unhappy-looking little boy. It wasn't any fit household for a child to be brought up in. We could see that, the minute we arrived, even though your Aunt Lilian was sick in bed, and Violet Delcey was taking care of her and keeping out of everybody's way. But I caught a couple of looks between her and your father that told me all I needed to know, so we spoke to him about it—about taking you back with us, I mean—and he didn't make any objection. Of course, at that time, we hadn't the least idea what was going to happen."

After a couple of weeks in London, his uncle and aunt went on a trip to Scotland, where Uncle Harvey's family had come from, two generations back. Jim went with them, and it was while they were away that Auntie Lilian died. They hurried back to London. Jim thought he could remember the funeral, and being given seedcake to eat, and Auntie Vi-Vi wearing black, with a large black hat that had a big pearl hatpin in it.

At any rate, it was two weeks later, so Aunt Bet told him, that they sailed for America, and after that there was the house in Rockford, Illinois, and school, and new playfellows; a new life and new interests. Everything was different. He missed his father sometimes, and when he asked for him, Aunt Bet said, "You're our boy now," and took him into the kitchen, where she gave him something to eat. One day she told him that his father was dead. He was surprised, and worked himself up into crying a little in bed that night. Then he forgot him.

It was when he was fourteen that Aunt Bet told him the whole story. Uncle Harvey had died two years before, and she herself was ill at the time. She must have known or guessed that she had not long to live. She sent for him to come to her room, on a sweltering summer afternoon and, sitting up in the double bed, pushing the streaks of her gray hair off her damp, red forehead, she told him as kindly as she could the facts of the Cawthra case.

"It's a dreadful thing I've got to tell you, Jim, and I've dreaded having to do it, ever since you came to live with us. But if I don't tell you, somebody else will, and not in a nice way, either."

He sat on his chair by her bedside, and fidgeted. He wanted to be out with the other boys, and not in here listening to her.

"Come up on the bed, Jim," she said, "and give me your hand."

He seated himself on the high bed, and put his hand unwillingly into hers, which was moist and work-scarred.

"It's about your father," she said, "and I don't know how to tell you now any better than I'd have done in the beginning, even though I've had seven years to think about it. Your father was hanged, Jim; he was hanged for murdering your Aunt Lilian; and that's all there is to it. And you'd better know it from me than from gossiping busybodies later on."

Father; Auntie Lilian; it was so long now since he had thought of them. Their names brought back another life: the dark house with the drawn shades, and the sound of the piano from the back room.

"It all happened that summer we were over there and brought you back with us. It's all dead and forgotten, and I hope you'll never think about it, any more than you can help or will have to. Uncle Harvey and I made you our own son from that time on, and gave you our name, for your poor mother's sake, and it hasn't anything to do with you, except that it did happen, and he was your father, God forgive him."

She was sparing with the details, telling him only that it was poison—some kind of weed-killer, she said. Jim, with a memory of the summer evenings when they used to spray the stunted rosebushes to destroy the green-fly, could not escape a childish picture of his father turning the syringe on Auntie Lilian, or forcing her to drink from the bucket into which the syringe was dipped.

"Why did he do it?" he asked. "Why did he want to kill her?"

"It was on account of that girl. Violet Delcey. He wanted to marry her."

Jim, who was by then beginning to be acquainted with the facts of sex, wondered whether his aunt was using a euphemism out of regard for his supposed innocence. He blushed; this part of the story affected him more than any other.

After that, Aunt Bet refused to talk about it. He knew enough, she said. When she went to the hospital to have her operation the next year, she told Jim that if anything happened to her he would find the press clippings about his father in an envelope in a secret drawer in the bureau.

"You can read them or not, as you want," she said. "Your uncle and I kept them for when you were old enough to know about it all."

Nothing did happen to her then except to return from the hospital and linger another year in pain. But Jim read the clippings, all the same. She had hardly left the house before he did so, kneeling on one of the green plush chairs in the living room, with the faded sheets of newspaper spread on the table cover before him. He read them greedily and guilt-ily, as though they were a dirty book.

For weeks he was terrified—terrified at the memory of the little house, and of his picture of his father stealing out to the tool shed that he so clearly remembered, getting the weed-killer from the shelf, and mixing it with Auntie Lilian's medicine, carrying it up the narrow stairs to her room. Worse were the descriptions of Auntie Lilian's symptoms, the ex-humation, and the post-mortem examination. They were appalling, but they fascinated him, and he gloated over the details in his room at night.

Now, it was all a tale so old and so familiar that it was like a book that he had read too many times. The story of the murder was simple enough. Auntie Lilian was taken ill in July, 1912. The doctor attended her, and diagnosed gastritis. He prescribed medicine, and within a couple of weeks she was better. It was during those weeks that Violet Delcey nursed her. When she was out of danger, Violet went on a holiday.

This, Jim figured, must have been about the time that he himself was in Scotland with his aunt and uncle. Mr. Caw-thra and his wife were alone in the house with Annie. Auntie Lilian was up again, and spending her time on the sofa, tak-ing a tonic that the doctor had ordered her three times a day. Mr. Cawthra used to pour it out for her. Suddenly, she had a relapse; the former symptoms returned, and in three days she was dead. The doctor gave a death certificate, and the funeral took place at Kensal Green, Violet Delcey return-ing from her holiday specially for it. It was clear she had nothing to do with the murder.

Two weeks after the funeral (which must, Jim reckoned, have been just after he himself left for America), she re-turned to the house to live, chaperoned now only by Annie.

Auntie Lilian's friends were scandalized, and one of them, a Mrs. Pamphlett, paid a visit to the house to question Annie about what was going on. Finding Violet Delcey absent, she went on a tour of inspection and discovered that the girl had moved into the best bedroom, and that Mr. Cawthra was sleeping in the little room that she had occupied.

This, thought Mrs. Pamphlett, was outrageous, but what was worse was that across the bed, the marriage bed in which her poor friend had breathed her last, and in which her supplanter was now sleeping, was a lace bedspread that Auntie Lilian had finished making just before she died and had promised to Mrs. Pamphlett. She had a further conference with Annie, who had taken a dislike to Violet Delcey since she became mistress of the house. Encouraged, Annie now voiced dark suspicions; other friends joined in, and an exhumation order was applied for. Arsenic was found in large quantities in the body, and the police paid a visit to the house. They found the weed-killer in the tool shed, but they did not find Mr. Cawthra and Violet Delcey. They had fled.

They were discovered ten days later in Boulogne, living as father and daughter in a tiny *pension,* where they might have remained completely unsuspected, had not Violet Delcey had occasion to visit a dentist and objected to going to a French one. There was one English dentist in the town, and it happened that he had that day seen the police description in the London papers. It was the cat's-eye brooch which gave her away; the dentist recognized it and communicated with the police. Faced with them, Mr. Cawthra confessed his guilt immediately, but stated passionately that Violet Delcey knew nothing about it. After some trouble, they were extradited and brought home to stand their trials.

These were brief in the extreme. Mr. Cawthra persisted in his plea of guilty, all hope and interest seeming to have deserted him. "I did it," he said in his statement to the police, "and even if I hadn't, now that she knows I've been accused of it, there couldn't be any possibility of happiness for us. She's all I care about in life." The rest of the statement was concerned with establishing her innocence. It was the only thought he had left. Her trial as an accessory followed his by a couple of days, and she was acquitted without witnesses being called. Three weeks later he was hanged at Pentonville.

It was Mr. Cawthra's single-mindedness and his solicitude for her that appealed to the public imagination, turning him almost into a hero and a martyr, and giving to what would otherwise have been a sordid and commonplace story of wife-poisoning an enduring quality of tragedy and romance. It was this angle, too, that attracted the dramatist and the novelists who fictionized it; all three told the same essential story, with the same central characters: the nagging, fretful, or shrewish wife; the mild, agreeable little husband who murdered her from motives of respectability, so that he could marry the other woman whom he loved with a tenderness and an intensity that flooded the drab suburban background like a radiance; and the girl herself, meek, shrinking, and refined, inspiring by her gentleness and her devotion a depth of passion that she could never have dreamed of, dragged by it into the tragic whirlpool of the flight and the trial.

The story and its interpretation were so familiar to Jim now that, like the public at large, he accepted them without question. All that bothered him was the puzzle of how to resolve the inconsistency of the two figures—the Violet Delcey of fact and fiction, and the gay, mysterious Auntie Vi-Vi of his recollections. He would have liked to be able to assure himself that those recollections were untrustworthy; in his heart, he knew that they were not.

But in any case, it was all so long ago. So much had happened since then, to him as well as to the world. He was married to a wife who knew nothing of the case or his connection with it; he had a house, and a job, and the future to worry about; what did the dead remote past matter? It mattered only to the playwrights and the novelists, and to the compilers of books on criminology; to himself, it was hardly more, now, than would have been a mystery story he had read in his childhood and left without reaching the solution, in a volume long since lost and out of print.

And then one afternoon he saw her. It was in a department store in St. Louis, which he was visiting on business. She was standing at a counter a few feet away from him, and at the first glance he was certain that it was she. She had aged, changed, and filled out, and her titian hair had faded to a pale ginger, but the tilt of her nose, the discontented, down-drawn line of her mouth, and the flat, level setting of her eyes in her face took him back suddenly across the years to his little room in the house in Kilburn, where she used to come and sit on his narrow bed and sing to him.

The next moment, doubt assailed him. Was it really she? How could he be sure? He could not possibly remember, after all this time. He stared at her, and his doubt grew. He was crazy to think of it; it was ridiculous to suppose that he would know her any more. And then, as he was about to abandon the idea, she turned towards him, and he saw that she was wearing a cat's-eye brooch, the brooch that used to frighten him in childhood.

Jim felt as though his heart had stopped for a moment; then it began to beat violently, choking him in his throat.

She had passed him by, now, and was making for the street. In a moment she would be lost to him. He hurried after her, leaving his order uncompleted at the counter. As he went, he tried to think how he should greet her. If he said: "Aren't you Violet Delcey?" she would be certain to deny it.

He came abreast with her at the entrance to the store, and, as she was about to pass him, he said casually—as casually as he could for the excitement that was throttling him: "Hello, Auntie Vi-Vi!"

She started violently, and looked around to see who had spoken. He was smiling at her, with a nerve twitching uncontrollably at the corner of his mouth.

"Were you speaking to me?" she asked.

The moment she spoke, he knew her voice, English, and pseudo-refined, with impure vowel sounds. He had not heard a voice like that for years.

"Yes. Don't you remember me?" he said.

She looked at him for a moment and then dropped her eyes, assuming the indignation of a woman who is being accosted.

"No, I don't," she answered, and started to move on.

He caught at her arm.

"It's Jim—Jim Cawthra," he said, speaking the name he had not borne for nearly thirty years.

And now she turned to him again, her eyes widening, and her mouth falling open in surprise.

"Jim!" she breathed in amazement. "Not little Jim?"

"That's me," he said.

He could see that she was trembling as she tried to laugh and to treat the situation as a social coincidence.

"Well!" she said, but her voice was shaking, too.

"Can't we go somewhere and talk?" he asked, urgently. "I want to talk to you."

They went to a place near the store, choosing it because it was dark and empty, and seated themselves in a far corner. Violet Delcey ordered a banana split. She had put on a good deal of weight in the years; she was plump now, and matronly, and her face had lost the delicate contours that he remembered. It was the face of a resentful, self-indulgent woman.

"How did you recognize me?" she asked. "You were only a little boy when I last saw you. I've changed, too. How did you know me?"

"By that." He pointed to the brooch.

She squinted down at it.

"Oh, that!" she said. "Well, fancy your remembering that!"

"It used to scare me, don't you remember? I used to think it was a real cat's eye."

"Did you?" she said. "How silly! I don't know why I still wear it. It isn't very pretty. Habit, I suppose. It's sort of silly, too, seeing it was that that really gave the show away before."

She gave a little laugh, and he stared at her. This could not be Violet Delcey speaking. But it could be Auntie Vi-Vi; he remembered that laugh: it recalled to him the afternoons in other people's kitchens, and the giggling conversations with the servants.

"Do you live here in St. Louis?" he asked.

She shook her head. "I'm not telling," she said. "I'm not telling you anything about me now."

"I wouldn't give you away."

"Well, that's as may be," she said, and the phrase struck him as odd and old-fashioned. "But I'm not taking any chances. What I was, or used to be, is all over, and no one knows about it. I wouldn't have come here with you now, except that—well, you're different. You were only a kid, and it's nice to get a chance to talk about old times, just for once."

"Do you think about it—much?" he asked. It was something he had long wondered about.

Again she shook her head.

"Not really," she said. "No. Now and then, of course, I suppose you can't help it, but it doesn't do you any good."

She took a spoonful of whipped cream. He could not think of what to ask her, what to say next. What did he want to know? "Was it awful?" That was really what he wanted to say, but it sounded such a silly question. Besides, what could she answer? Yes or no—neither would take him any further. He wanted to know what it had meant to her—what it felt like to have lived through all that she had lived through and to have come out on the other side, as she had done; but he could think of no way of putting the question so that she would understand it.

"Will you tell me about it?" he asked, at length. It was the best he could do.

"What? What do you want to know?"

He could not say. He thrust for a question of fact, rather than of point of view.

"Did you ever suspect what he had done? He never *told* you, did he?"

"No, of course he didn't. He didn't want me to know. That was the whole point. He knew I wouldn't have anything to do with him if I did."

"But when you were looking after her—the first time she was sick? He'd already started then, hadn't he?"

"Oh, that was only to make her ill enough to have the doctor in. For the sake of the death certificate the next time, you know. At least, that's how I figured it out afterwards. I suppose there was weed-killer in the medicine he used to pour out and give me to take up to her. But he always used to pour it out himself, and never let me do it. Just so that I couldn't be mixed up in it, I expect. He was always very thoughtful of me."

"Did you love him?" The questions were beginning to come of their own accord now.

Violet Delcey stared at him.

"Love him?" she repeated, incredulously. "How could I have loved him? He was old enough to be my father. But he was always respectful to me. And kind. You wouldn't believe how kind he was. Of course, he was crazy about me."

"But you *were* his mistress, weren't you?"

She looked offended. "Mistress? I don't know what you mean," she said.

There was no point in pursuing that.

"When you went away together—when you ran away—what did you think?" he asked. "He didn't tell you then what was wrong?"

"No. Of course, I knew there was trouble. I caught that Mrs. What's-her-name in the kitchen one day, talking to the skivvy. That girl had always hated me, and taken Mrs. Cawthra's side against me, and I guessed that she'd been saying things, so it wasn't any surprise to me when Freddie came and said there was a lot of gossip going on, and that it would be a good idea if we were to go away for a while till it had blown over. He said we could get married on the Continent. We were *going* to get married, you know," she went on. "I wouldn't have had anything to do with him in the first place if we hadn't been. Right from the beginning, he said he wanted to marry me, and that he would, as soon as *she* died. She was always being ill, you know, and I think he sort of hoped from the beginning that she wouldn't last. I suppose he got tired of waiting, same as I did."

"What—what do you mean?" Jim stammered.

"Well, wouldn't *you* have? I told him that I wasn't going

to put up with it any longer. I mean, I wasn't getting any younger, and I wasn't going to spend the rest of my life just waiting for her to die."

"And what did *he* say?"

"Oh, he cried," she said, lightly. "Said he couldn't live without me, and if I'd only give him a little time, he'd see if he couldn't do something about a divorce, or something. So I said I'd give him three months, and after that I'd have to give Mr. Joplin his answer."

"Mr. Joplin?"

"Yes, don't you remember Joplin's, the paper shop? Old Joplin had been after me for ages."

A forgotten cupboard opened in Jim's memory. He saw a tall, stooping figure with thin streaks of hair plastered on a shiny scalp, steel-rimmed spectacles, and a prominent Adam's apple, giving him the pink paper "Books for the Bairns" in exchange for his weekly penny. Old Joplin; he hadn't thought of him for years.

"Were you going to marry *him?*" he asked.

"Well, I might have. He had a nice little business, and he was crazy about me, and I wasn't getting any younger. That's what I told Freddie, and he saw my point."

"When was that?"

"Oh, about a month before she was taken queer."

It was odd to hear the old expressions again.

"It wasn't till we were in France that I really began to put two and two together, but by that time there wasn't anything I could do. Of course, I knew there was nothing against me, but it did look bad. I was scared to death of the trial, because you never know how they can twist things, those lawyers, but *he* saw to it that it was all right. I knew he would, of course. I knew that I could trust him. He was always the gentleman, your father was."

She looked at her watch.

"Here, I've got to go," she said.

"Not yet," Jim pleaded.

"I must." She began gathering up her things.

"Tell me just one thing more," he asked.

"What?"

"Who was Albert?" That memory had to be cleared up. She looked at him blankly.

"Albert?" she repeated. "I don't remember any Albert."

"He was a sailor."

Recognition came into her face.

"Oh, Albert," she said, laughing. "Fancy you remembering him. Yes. Albert—what *was* his other name? I've forgotten."

"Who was he?"

"He was a friend of mine. He treated me very badly, Albert did. That was the time I first started going to Freddie for singing lessons. I was having trouble with Albert, and I remember one day when I had a headache, it all sort of got too much for me, and I began crying, and Freddie tried to comfort me. That's how it all started, really. I mean, he sort of asked me questions, and I told him all about it, and that's what really started him getting keen on me, I think. Funny, I'd forgotten all about Albert."

"But you went on seeing him. I remember meeting you with him, and your telling me not to say anything about it at home."

"Well, I didn't want to upset Freddie, when he was being so kind to me," she said. "I was supposed to have been all through with Albert, and I didn't want to worry Freddie, knowing that I wasn't. I remember wondering whether I'd hear from Albert when the trouble came, but of course I didn't. He was a bad lot, really, but he was very good-looking, and he had a way with him. I wonder what's become of him."

A thought seemed to strike her suddenly, and she smiled, looking down at the cat's-eye brooch.

"What is it?" Jim asked. "Have you thought of something?"

"I've just remembered," she said. "It was Albert gave me this brooch. Funny, my forgetting that!"

She fingered the brooch, and then unpinned it, taking it out and looking at it as though she had not seen it for a long time. It was a meager little thing, Jim thought; queer that it should have seemed sinister to him all these years.

"Yes," she said, as she replaced it. "He said it was good luck, or something. Well, I dare say it has been. I've been lucky. Did I tell you I was married, by the way?"

"No," said Jim.

"Oh, yes, I've been married nearly twenty years," she said. "He really does very well. We're getting one of the new Plymouths next month. I haven't done badly for myself. There is just one drawback, though, to no one knowing who I am."

"What's that?" Jim Cawthra asked.

"Well," she said, a smug and almost coy look coming into her face. "You see, they don't know, and looking at me now, no one would believe that I was once good enough for a man to commit a murder and get himself hung for me. But," she sighed philosophically, "I suppose you can't have everything."